The Wooden Man

R. A. Britton

Barcheston

First published in 2007 by
Barcheston

CIP catalogue records for this book are available from
the British Library.

ISBN 978-0-9557284-0-2

Printed and bound in Great Britain by
Cox & Wyman Ltd, Reading, Berkshire

About the Author

R. A. Britton was born in Oxford, England. A scholar in Archaeology & Anthropology at Cambridge University, he first encountered the Maya of Central America while mapping ancient ruins in the Belizean rainforest. He lives in Hackney, East London, where he wrote his first novel, *The Wooden Man*.

To Mum and Dad

And as the words are spoken, it is done.
The doll-people are made with faces carved from wood.
But they have no blood, no sweat.
They have nothing in their minds.
They have no respect for Heart-of-Sky.
They are just walking about, but they accomplish nothing.
'This is not what I had in mind,' says Heart-of-Sky.
And so it is decided to destroy these wooden people.

Extract from the Mayan Indian creation story, as told in the Popol Vuh, *a sixteenth-century sacred book.*

One

19 August 1997, Chiapas, Mexico

Lines of Tzotziles, people of the bat, stood before a bonfire of wood, palm and mud-brick. Sparks of burning thatch launched into the dawn sky and palm ash parachuted down amongst solemn spectators. Lucio pushed his way to the front of the crowd. His hands and arms shielding his bloodshot eyes from the heat, the shaman inspected what was left of his home. He turned his back on nothing but smouldering timber and, his skin burning and his heart beating faster, scanned the weeping faces for his wife and two sons.

Someone's hand tugged at the black woollen mantle draped over his shoulders. It was, he recognized from the spiky hair, cuts and bruises masking the teenage boy's face, his eldest.

'Father!' Horatio raised his voice above the roar of fire and the wails of people. 'The Cardenistas . . . they . . .' He pointed at a bundle of blankets and bodies on the ground. Another crowd surrounded the slumped figure of Maria Gomez.

An unearthly vapour descended upon the mountainous lair of the ancestral gods. On what was supposed to be the brightest of equatorial nights, clouds masked the full moon, while a sea of mist flooded valleys of sweeping pine forest. Like drowning sailors gasping for breath, the trees raised their spiny heads above the dank air. The moon of First Mother, who had made her ascent from the bowels of Xibalba, the subterranean other-world of the Maya, cast a halo of light over this primordial setting. Conditions were perfect for righting a wronged and ancient world.

At the bottom of the highest and bluest of the mountains, a man stopped to rest in the foggy forest. Lucio Mendez Gomez took a swig of posh, the potent drink of a Mayan shaman bottled in a squash gourd, and spat out a little for the earth before he gulped

1

the rest. The posh burnt the back of his throat and seasoned his already giddy head. Coughing, he plugged the gourd with a cork and returned it to his knitted backpack, a black sack with a pattern of white zigzags woven into it. A chilly gust hit him unguarded and he shivered. Goose pimples pricked up on his bare arms. He blew into his hands, drew himself under the wraps of his black woollen mantle and thanked the gods for his wife.

Maria Gomez had been as meticulous as her husband in the preparation for First-True-Mountain. Where he tended to the spiritual, she saw to the practical. The mantle that she had woven, spun from the finest and hardiest highland wool, a fact that the great shaman's wife made clear to the rest of San Felipé's women, proved to be a godsend against the elements of the spiteful Earth Lord. Notwithstanding the morning's argument over the quantity of tortillas for a hungry hero, which resulted in Lucio packing his own meal for the mountains, Maria and Lucio were a team. Lucio might have been able to commune with the gods, bring order back to the world and stop the paramilitary attacks on their community, but it definitely didn't progress to back-strap weaving or the kitchen stove. It was in their small orchard, outside their mud-brick and palm-thatched home, where she handed down her orders.

'Now don't you go straying from the path,' she said, as she hung his cleaned crimson trousers on a rope tied between two banana trees, a basket of wooden pegs tucked under her muscular arm. 'And watch out for that sheep muck: it's a devil to get out and we're low on detergent. Which reminds me – when you're back, you have to go to Pantelhó for a shop. Your son is out of hair wax, and you might as well pick up some more washing powder while you're there.'

'Yes,' Lucio replied, sitting up on his stool and stuffing maize husks with crystals of copal incense. Maria shook her head, her platted ponytail flicking over a red and white collar of embroidered monkeys and bats. She sighed at the weathered face under a combed-forward fringe. But for his wrinkles, her husband, on his small stool and with a pudding-bowl haircut, looked like more of a shy schoolboy than a god-taming shaman.

'Is that all you've got to say?' she asked, as she turned her back on him and pegged a WWF – World Wrestling Federation – T-shirt next to the trousers. 'Sometimes I wish that you'd behave like any normal hero: stand up for yourself, answer back, *fight* back.'

'Yes,' he replied, concentrating more on his job than what his wife was saying. He deposited the shaman's ammunition, husks stuffed with copal, into a plastic freezer bag by his bare feet.

'And I want you to take that new mantle that I made for you.' She turned round again, her face softer. 'It can be chilly up there, and I know what you're like with even a little drizzle. I don't want you getting ill. San Felipé needs you healthy.' A gentle frown set above her dark brown eyes. 'I need my shaman, my husband, healthy.'

'Yes.' Finished with his incense packing, Lucio stowed the bag of copal husks in his backpack. He stood up from his stool and, half the size of his wife, in stature if not in height, helped her hang up the rest of the laundry. 'I do fight back,' he eventually said, examining a wooden peg in his hand, before facing his surprised looking wife, 'but as an Abejas, my love, and a shaman, I fight back without violence. The Cardenistas don't scare me. There are powers far greater than those mortals. It is those who I must control.' A yellow butterfly landed on the back of his head.

'I hope you're right, Lucio. You have the whole village counting on you.' A white shirt fell off the line and landed in a muddy puddle. Gathering up her long and woolly black skirt, Maria held in her tummy, bent down and picked it up. 'Sometimes I feel that the gods have left us, that the rest of the world has left us behind. After last week, I think that we would be better off as Zapatistas, not as Abejas.' She cuffed the butterfly off her husband's hair and put the shirt in an old maize sack.

'Maria.' He touched the back of his head. 'We have gone through this before and so has the village council. We survived the Spanish and we'll see off the bad government. We are Abejas. We are bees.' He watched the butterfly soar into the sky. 'Unlike butterflies, we sting.'

Peeking out from behind the clouds and streaming through gaps in branches, the moon caught the embroidered lightning streaks on Lucio's shins and the dew beneath the trees. He followed the flickering runway of terrestrial stars to navigate his own orbit. Through worn-out sandals, holes in leather soles, he felt damp layers of pine debris squelch underfoot. Each step that he took emitted an ensemble of squeaks and snaps. Crickets and other six-legged insects screeched in his ears, as if they believed the noise of trampled-on wood to be a massacre of their brethren, and with them, real or imagined, danced reptilian shadows and predatory illusions. He wrapped the mantle closer to his shivering body and recalled his late mother's stories of the Lokin, a race of cannibals who were descended from the 'wooden people,' the unfeeling race that the creator gods washed away in a flood. These antecedents of the first men of maize, the forefathers of the Maya civilization, now resided in far-off lands with pale skin and secular customs, or hid in the depths of the forest as scurrilous monkeys and child-snatching Lokin. The latter, Sasquatch-like and with backward-facing feet, were said, by Maya mothers to their children, to pounce upon lost travellers in the mountains and jungle.

Yet on that night of First Mother, a full moon in the sky, crickets at their loudest and storm clouds on the horizon, it was not the feeble-minded Lokin who perturbed Lucio. His danger was far greater: it germinated from the bad seeds of the men of maize, those who had strayed from the fields from which they were culti-vated. They were the loathsome Indians and Mestizos who had forsaken their Mayan blood, men corrupted by the bribes of nameless officials, their greed leading to treachery and murder. They were the black uniformed devils who, in a cloud of dust, rode four-wheeled stallions into San Felipé, beat men with iron rods until they signed up to fight their brothers, the masked Zapatistas. They were the paramilitaries that worked for the 'bad government,' the one-party state of the PRI.

It was only last week that a group of eight paramilitaries, the bad government's Cardenistas, drove their trucks into San Felipé. The men of the village, including Lucio, fled to the surrounding forest: the alternative was to be arrested or, for someone as highly prized as a shaman, torched alive. Through the cover of low branches Lucio observed the Cardenista leader, Commandant Hernandez, or 'Fat Tapir' to Maya victims, the obese Latino resembling a waddling mountain elephant, sit his bulk down on a crate of Pepsi-Cola. To a congregation of frightened women and children, Commandant Hernandez offered his stool of soft drink. Waiting for a response, he took a bottle for himself and popped it open with his machete. The soda dribbled out of his grin, trickled down his jowls and splashed his propped-up semi-automatic rifle.

While others cowered and cried, Maria Gomez pushed her way forward. Her husband covered his eyes from afar. Looking the bully in the eye and announcing her preference for potent posh and not Pepsi-Cola, Maria spat at Commandant Hernandez's polished boots and the crated insult. She then glanced at the forest, beyond the maize fields, in the direction of the men in the trees. Lucio watched her every move. His nails dug into a tree's soft bark.

The crowd applauded the rebel in their ranks. Commandant Hernandez stood up to face the incompliant Indian, his move opening up the goal to the crate of Pepsi, and Maria gave his sickly sweet gift the penalty kick. When the Abejas had smashed all of the bottles, Maria's battalion of arm-linked women, who piggybacked infants in woollen slings, forced the Cardenistas back into their 4x4s. They cheered as the paramilitaries sped out of the village. The queen bee had won a sweet victory.

An owl hooted and Lucio jumped. The bird swooped low over his head, its copper feathers catching the moonlight and Lucio's hair catching a twig, and he watched it glide through the trees. He freed his hair and took a deep breath. His hand on the handle of his sheathed machete, its red tassels flowing down his legs, he resumed his walk under the trees. Although the branches and mist prevented a clear view of the sky, he could see the clouds growing thicker. If the ritual was to coincide with the storm, lightning was to charge his pulse on the slopes of First-True-Mountain, he knew that he had to speed up. It was certainly not the time to be scared of owls passing off as fat paramilitaries or child-scaring Lokin.

'Lokin,' he said to himself, smiling and patting down his hair. The owl hooted back and he jumped again. He wished that he had allowed his son and apprentice to join him. 'Lokin don't scare Urbano,' he whispered, smiling.

The Gomez family lived in San Felipé, a small village of Tzotzil Maya in the municipality of Chenalho, a community hidden away in the mountains of the state of Chiapas. Unlike the majority of

Tzotzil families, which comprised ten members each, Lucio and Maria had only their two sons to house in their one bedroom, dirt-floored hut. Their youngest, Urbano, a wistful thirteen-year-old, was closest to his father. As his father's apprentice, Urbano renounced the machismo of the playground, the school of the machete, preferring instead the ways of the shaman and the mythology of the ancients. When working the fields, slashing maize or picking coffee beans, he took his lunch breaks, a Tupperware of tortillas, away from the rest of the boys and transported himself to a different age. In the shade of tall maize stalks, he would eat with his father and learn the knowledge of the shaman.

'For me?' Urbano asked his father, who had handed him a newly carved blowpipe. Lucio smiled at his son and nodded.

'After the gods destroyed the wooden people,' Lucio said, slicing a knife through an unripe mango, 'turned them into monkeys and scary Lokin, they sent two twins to deal with a vain old parrot.' He brushed an ant off a chunk of mango.

'You mean the Hero Twins?' Urbano passed a pot of powdered chilli to his father.

'Yes.' Lucio paused to sprinkle chilli over the mango. 'Hunahpu and Xbalanque were their names, and with their blowpipes it was they who destroyed the parrot and his evil sons. It was because of them that the Lords of Death were banished from the world and sent back to Xibalba, the other-world. It was they who brought order to the earth and made the way for the gods to create man out of maize.' He bit into the mango. 'Do you like it?' he asked, pointing at the blowpipe and with his mouth full.

'I love it,' Urbano exclaimed, hugging his father and standing up, 'The weapon of the Hero Twins.' He held up the blowpipe to the sun. 'Wow.'

Days later, on the eve of the full moon and after the village's emergency council meeting, Lucio broke the news to Urbano.

'*Please* can I go with you to First-True-Mountain,' Urbano begged his father. Tucked up in bed, a gold-painted cross on the mud-brick wall above him, he poked his head out of a blanket of red and black zigzags. The blowpipe lay beside him.

Lucio put down his rucksack, sat down on his stool and pulled up next to the bed.

'I'm afraid not,' Lucio said, stroking a parting in his son's silky black hair. 'Tomorrow I must go alone. It's the way it should be.'

Urbano pushed his father's hand away and dropped his fists on the blanket. The blowpipe fell off the bed.

'Your time will come,' Lucio continued, picking up the blowpipe and returning it to his son's side, 'One day you'll have to enter the cave of the White-Bone-Snake and speak to the gods by yourself. When I'm gone from this world and the gods have paddled me to Xibalba, it will be up to you to save San Felipé from the chaos of the Earth Lord.'

'But if you defeat him tomorrow,' Urbano frowned, 'then what will you leave me to fight? You must take me with you. I'm ready to face the Earth Lord.'

'No!' Lucio's rarely raised voice startled his son. 'You're not ready. This is not a fight with the Earth Lord. It is about bringing peace and order to our land through prayer and sacrifice. People are being killed. And your duty is to stay at home and look after your mother.'

'But mamá can look after herself,' Urbano mumbled, 'and Horatio won't let anything happen to her. Please can I go with you?'

'This has nothing to do with your older brother.' Lucio stood up from the stool and looked up at the palm-thatched ceiling. 'Horatio and his gun-carrying Zapatista friends don't give me any confidence.' He lowered his head and faced his son. 'I want you to make sure that he doesn't do anything stupid. Yes?'

'But . . .'

'You must be patient, Urbano. First-True-Mountain is not for apprentices. Now get some sleep.' He kissed his son on the forehead and took the gold-painted cross off its nail on the wall. Placing the final piece of the shaman's equipment in his backpack, he picked up a candle and walked outside.

'You missed quite a game today,' a voice called out at Lucio as he stepped out of the hut. Emerging from the shadow of a banana tree, moonlight highlighting short and spiky hair, was Horatio, Lucio and Maria's eldest son. The seventeen-year-old wore a black WWF T-shirt, his favourite, and he spun a basketball on one finger. A red bandana was knotted loosely round his neck. 'We beat the team from Polho pretty bad.' He scratched his waxed black hair with his free hand. 'At least Mum watched it.'

'I'm sorry I wasn't there,' Lucio said, the light of the candle accentuating the wrinkles on his face. 'I had to prepare for tomorrow. I don't know if your mother told you, but the council has . . .'

7

The thud of a basketball hitting hard ground interrupted him.

'Mum told me.' Horatio caught the basketball in his puffed-up chest. 'We were speaking to some Zapatistas at the game. They said they could help if the gods don't.'

In January 1994, when Subcommandante Marcos of the Zapatista National Liberation Army declared war on the Mexican state with the cry of 'enough is enough,' the young Horatio was spellbound. In secret from his parents, more particularly from his father, he planned to run away and join the pipe-smoking Subcommandante and his legion of modern Maya warriors, who wore fashionable ski masks and carried guns. He carved a rifle out of beech wood, sharpened his machete, packed five unripe bananas for the journey, and turned his WWF T-shirt inside out to create a plain black uniform. It was in stealing his father's paisley bandana, and a ski mask hard to come by in San Felipé, that his plan for a seat next to Che, Zapata and Marcos was thwarted. Horatio found himself shovelling shit as opposed to shooting it.

'Goodnight Horatio,' Lucio said, retreating towards his hammock under the palm trees.

'Sleep well father.' Horatio shook his head as he watched his father's candle disappear into the night.

One hand on a root and the other on an outcrop of rock, Lucio looked down the mountain's slope. Below him and on a plateau of boulders and dead trees, which dotted a marsh of mud, reeds and long grasses, a stream glinted in the moonlight. The water dropped off the plateau in a puff of mist, while beyond it and beneath it, the river wound its way through the dark forest. Apart from the moon on the water, the valleys and hillsides emitted no other light; man was second to nature there. He looked up at the formidable slope above him, where First-True-Mountain's peak speared the Milky Way, and breathed in the moist air, continuing his ascent.

Darkness enveloped the mountains and valleys. A large black cloud filled up the night sky and bright constellations were covered up, one by one. First, went the Milky Way, the Maya 'Place of Awe,' then Gemini and the belt of Orion, the three-stoned hearth of Maya Creation. Lastly, the cloud bit at the edges of the moon, First Mother, and the battle was quick: the moon was banished and the earth was starved of light. But it was only a taster of what was to come. Lucio, who could read the skies as well as the scriptures, knew that there was a formidable arsenal of thunder, lightning and rain within the black mass. Moving back from the steep drop and gripping a safety-line of roots and rocks, the wind whipping up the mantle over his shoulders, he peered into the abyss of a cave. He had arrived at his temple, the navel of First-True-Mountain and the mouth of the White-Bone-Snake. Blinking his hair out of his eyes, he bowed his head and placed his palms on his pounding chest. A small smile appeared under his long wet fringe.

The village knew that the Cardenistas would return. The next time round, they feared, Commandant Hernandez would arrive with something stronger than a crate of warm soda. They also knew that it would take more than Maria's cockiness, her verbal bombs and a blockade of women and toddlers, to defend the village from semi-automatic rifles. Increasing the sense of anxiety, news had come two days before of the Cardenistas killing four men in the neighbouring town of Colonia Puebla. The men's crime, like that of the men of San Felipé, was to refuse to fight the Zapatistas: limbs were snapped at the joints and then, in front of screaming wives and children, the men were doused in fuel and put to the torch.

For the Abejas, who unanimously rejected the demands, refusing to bear arms against anyone, let alone the Zapatistas, their allies, there were few options. The police, who were perceived to be complicit to paramilitary violence, were immediately ruled out. As for calling on Zapatista assistance, armed resistance, a motion favoured by Maria and Horatio Gomez, it was rejected by Abejas principles. After a full day of discussion and debate, plenty of posh and tortillas, the council concluded that there was only one solution. On the eve of the full moon and inside the concrete and corrugated iron community centre, they sanctioned the shaman's pilgrimage to First-True-Mountain.

At dawn, the hour of Maya Creation, Lucio bade farewell to his wife and two sons, hugging each of them outside the family's hut. Slinging his backpack over his shoulder, the keys to the ancestral portal digging into his back, he waved goodbye to a crowd of well-wishers and set off for the blue-green mountains, the forested peaks that stretched out across the horizon. He had walked not more than thirty yards along a dusty track, a potholed street that fanned out of San Felipé, when he turned his gaze homeward. With just an hour of sun, baked mud and limestone chips blurred his vision, and he saw Maria dissolve in the doorway of their collapsing hut. The image of her haunted him for the rest of the day and then the night, but the next full moon was not until 16 September. After the murders in Colonia Puebla, the shaman's sting could not wait that long.

Once past the fields of maize and coffee, he picked up a highway of hoof prints, a path favoured by black mountain sheep, and searched for familiar trees within a forest of fir, beech and oak. Although he knew the route well, having followed it since he was a five-year-old apprentice, last using it less than three months ago for another job, the seasonal changes in plant growth confused him. He frequently had to retrace his steps to stay on track.

The heat grew stronger as the day progressed. Drops of sweat stung Lucio's eyes and blisters surfaced on his heels, his sandals slipping on mud and then a moving carpet of fallen pine needles. Three hours later and his clothes drenched in sweat, he reached the Pool of the Paddler Gods, a confluence of chilled water that bled from First-True-Mountain.

The river lugged its depths along a meandering course, its dark green surface reflecting the arboreal upper-world of the banks. Like a cogitating constrictor, its sluggish manner disguised malignance. For beneath the bubbles and ripples lay hydraulics, vertical slipstreams that could suck a man down and send him to Xibalba. The other-world of the Death Lords had claimed many fishermen and heat-exhausted bathers. Upstream, at the bottom of a forty-foot waterfall, was the noisier violence of water smashing on water. About halfway up the falls, a volcanic boulder protruded out of the curtain of water. Eroded into a humanoid form, its hooked nose and soulful eyes sculpted by the elements, the stone face kept watch over the sacred pool.

Lucio took no time to sit on a fallen tree trunk. He removed his sandals and dipped his raw feet into the bubbling water. The loud sigh that he released disturbed a flock of parrots in a nearby bush. He smiled at them as they soared into the sky, their departing squawks drowned out by the thunderous falls. While his blood adjusted to the chill and his toes tensed, he absorbed the presence

10

of the godly spittoon and the stone guardian. He plunged his palms into the pool and, devout to the scenery before him, flung up his arms and showered in the sacred waters. The heat and discomfort removed, he opened his backpack and towelled his wet hair with the mantle that Maria had woven for him. With hair almost as spiky as his eldest son's, he inspected the white zigzags that she had embroidered

'Great lightning streaks Maria,' he said to himself, a drop of water trickling round the wrinkles under his eyes. He wished that one day she would join him, come along on one of those jobs in which a shaman is allowed to bring helpers: a ritual which wasn't a matter of life or death. 'Perhaps one day,' he said to the stone guardian. He carefully folded the mantle and returned it to his backpack.

Three months had passed since he had last visited the falls. Then he had to ask the gods for permission to harvest the fields, and he brought with him Sebastián – an elder – Urbano and three other boys: Emir, Alonso and René. Young and old constructed an altar on the riverbank, arching saplings into an arbour over a table of trimmed tree trunks and crisscrossing the arbour with four vines. Finally, they planted shoots of maize, the symbols of human flesh, at the bases of the arches, the four points of the cosmos.

From his seat on the trunk and toeing a pebble underwater, he observed what was left of the altar. The table strained under the weight of the collapsed arbour, dead saplings and vines littering its surface, the structure's greenness bleached by time. Weeds twisted around the table legs, the cardinal points, and the ground had swallowed up the shoots of maize. It reminded him of his mission, the very reason for him being there. Yet this job required somewhere even more sacred than the Pool of the Paddler Gods. Before he moved on and returned to the path of the black mountain sheep, to ascend the blue-green mountain past the falls, he retrieved five smooth pebbles from the shallows of the river, dropping them into his backpack, and slipped on his sandals. He crossed himself before the stony-faced guardian and, under the flight path of a gliding harpy eagle, began the final stretch of his journey.

'Wish me luck,' he said to the stone face.

A thicket of fang-like thorns guarded the cave's entrance. Lucio drew his machete from its scabbard and, despite his exhaustion, hacked his way in with vigour. The thorns cut into his hands and arms as he lashed out with the machete. A few minutes later, the last of the thicket kicked away, he returned the machete to its scabbard and picked the splinters out of his veiny hands.

Blackness now confronted him.

'You've got to try harder than that, Huitz-Hok,' he shouted to the mountain-valley god.

Only the high octaves of a gusting wind, which piped on the fluted and fanged entrance, responded to the shaman's taunts. Lucio shrugged, pulled a candle out of his backpack and struck a match. In the dim light he looked upwards and saw tiny bats crawling through a labyrinth of stalactites. To his sides, walls perspired through a layer of soot, years of incense smoke leaving a treacle coat on the calcified rock. Slowly moving forward, the candle leading the way and maize husks crunching under his sandals, he walked to the rear of the chamber. He stopped at a large granite slab and put down the candle and the backpack. The gourd of posh rolled out of his backpack. He raised an eyebrow.

When he had finished the last of the posh and laid out his equipment, the gold-painted cross sparkling by the candle on the slab, he collected twigs and dried grass from the cave's shadows, building a small pyre. As the flames died down, he picked up the freezer bag of husks stuffed with incense and scattered them over the embers. He fanned the black and redolent smoke as it spiralled upwards. The smoke flavoured the stuffy air and, murmuring prayers in Tzotzil, he filled a rusty bucket with milky maize gruel and stirred in the pebbles from the river. When the pebbles had been soaked for a few minutes, he pulled them out of the bucket and arranged them on the altar in the positions of the cosmogram: the sunrise and sunset positions of the summer and winter solstices. In the centre of the square and completing the quincunx pattern of the universe, he placed the fifth and final stone. Still reciting his prayers, he held the gold-painted cross to his chest and closed his red and rheumy eyes. His head bowed, he entered the other-world to confront the Earth Lord and banish the evil that threatened San Felipé.

Outside, the waiting was over. On cue and as though it was instigated by the shaman in the cave, rain pounded mountains and valleys, crag and pine, and lightning lit up the sky from horizon to horizon. The crack of struck wood echoed in the forests below, thunder synchronized to each fork of lightning, and gentle streams turned into raging rivers.

It was an onslaught that greeted Lucio as he stumbled out of the cave. Using the mantle to shield his face from the blinding flashes and the whipping rain, Maria's embroidered lightning streaks facing the gods' lightning, he fell to his knees. The meeting with the Earth Lord had used up the last of his energy. He pressed his finger on his wrist and traced his pulse as it gushed forth with each flash. Shivering, water streaming through his woollen umbrella and welling up in the lines of his weathered face, he managed a small smile; with the Earth Lord put in his place, the gods were free to protect San Felipé from the paramilitaries. On the slopes of First-True-Mountain and under his zigzag-patterned cloak, Lucio waited for the storm to end and for the gods to finish their cleansing of the land.

The storm lasted for almost two hours. At long last, the rain petered out until there was just the percussive patter of drips, the gurgle of replenished streams and the distant rumble of thunder. Crickets came out of hiding and, chirping in courtship, were the first to herald a new order. The cloud evaporated and the moon was soon restored to her rightful position; First Mother glowing one final encore before she stepped aside for the sun, First Father, and a new dawn. Lucio dabbed his face with a soggy bandana and looked down at the forested valleys, moonlight captured in the mist off the trees.

Carrying his backpack and plenty of pride, he descended First-True-Mountain. Halfway down, he rested against a tree and imagined the hero's welcome that awaited him. He could see men toast him with gourds of the strongest posh, and even the hardened Catholics, those who were forever cynical of him, admitting that there was still life in the shaman. He then thought of Maria who, when cooking at the outside stove and washing laundry in the river, would narrate the exploits of her storm-controlling and god-facing husband, instilling green-eyed envy into the other women. She would hold him close, like she did when he was a young apprentice, the honour of their coupling being as much hers as it was his.

He especially longed to see Urbano, to describe to him what

13

had happened: the stone guardian, the images of the gods in the black smoke, the voice of the Earth Lord and the lightning in his veins. The next time, Urbano would join him and, in the fields and on the basketball court, he envisaged his youngest encouraging other children to exchange Zapatista ski masks for blowpipes, the beliefs of the ancients. He even thought that Horatio might come to respect him.

Aided by an upbeat gait and downhill momentum, pine needles squelching under his sandals again, he soon reached the Pool of the Paddler Gods. The water was louder, murkier and more aggressive than before, and the excess of the storm, a slurry which slalomed the falls, was about to burst the banks. A transient light, the emergence of dawn, shimmered on the beak-nosed boulder. Partly submerged, the stern face of the guardian was transformed into the haunted expression of a drowning man.

'See you soon, friend.' Lucio shouted out, grinning at the stone face and saluting him like a soldier.

Leaving the river a few miles back, he saw a flamed beacon through the trees. A mix of mist and smoke reflected the fire, the glow hanging low over San Felipé. He stood on his toes, to see over the field of tall maize stalks, and assumed that the celebrations must have already begun. Alternatively, smiling, he imagined his wife and two sons standing next to a 'welcome home' fire, his family guiding him in after his nightshift in the mountain, a stack of tortillas kept warm for him.

A gunshot introduced a third alternative. Branches shook as the forest birds took flight. Under the beating wings of black carrion, Lucio saw the image of his wife melt in the doorway of their collapsing home. Like a moth to light, he ran towards the fire.

An exhaust of mud and sheep dung chased him through the forest, the dirt sullying the embroidered zigzags, the lightning, on his shins. His face and arms scratched by stalks of maize, he dived out of the field and fell head first into a ditch. Picking himself up, ditch-water dripping off his clothes and hair, he saw a silhouette of mud-brick huts and palm-tree orchards. He scrambled out of the ditch and tasted the rancid smoke.

Lucio dropped his backpack and rushed towards his wife. The crowd went silent as they allowed him through. In the flashing light of the fire and past lines of bare feet, he saw her face streaked by blood, tears and soot. On her lap and wrapped up in a blanket of red and black zigzags was the body of Urbano. He crashed to his knees and extended a shaking hand towards his son. Maria took his hand, slowly meeting her husband's eyes with her blood-shot, pain-stricken ones.

'It's too late,' Maria whispered. She looked down at their son. 'He is with the Hero Twins now.'

They sat together for a long time, holding the body of their youngest son as their house burnt behind them, united in a grief more powerful than any shamanistic powers. Eventually, as Urbano's body grew cold, the other villagers came to help them find somewhere to go. Maria refused to let go of her son's limp hand and, looking up towards the sky, the full moon, she fell to the ground and begged someone to make this stop. Flames reflected on her husband's swimming eyes.

Two

'Yes!' Dan whooped, jumping up and down on a hydraulic chair. 'What a bloody result. Have you seen this, Justin? Those pikey bastards have only just got us a half-day.' Dropping a half-eaten bacon roll onto his keyboard, his hangover cure smearing his stationery and spreadsheets, he smudged the screen of his monitor with a greasy finger.

Justin, whose green, white and slightly red eyes reflected on his own screen, pushed his Discman out of the way and stirred his mouse into action. He rubbed his forehead, closed a web page on *An Anatomy of Depression*, a book written a few years ago by an eminent psychiatrist, and clicked open the email.

```
Date: Friday, 22 August 1997 12.23
From: Human Resources
To: All
Subject: Riots in Liverpool Street


The Metropolitan Police have informed us that the bank
may be a target for militant elements of this
afternoon's protest.

In order to ensure the safety of its personnel, the
bank has reluctantly decided to close for the
afternoon. Please leave the building in an orderly
manner and evacuate the vicinity of the Square Mile
immediately. Suit jackets and ties should not be worn,
and we advise everyone to remain vigilant once outside.


Kate Harding
Head of Human Resources
```

Justin studied the authenticity of the email. It looked legitimate, although Dan was a dab hand at writing fakes. Once, having nothing better to do with his time, Dan sent Justin an amorous email from Caroline, a French analyst seconded to London from the Paris office. Justin spent an entire morning drafting a reply. The halitosis of Dan, who was crippled with laughter behind his back, stopped his flow and left a cliff-hanger on: '*It's very sweet of you, but I barely know you and* . . .' He needed a little more proof to be persuaded.

'I'm impressed, Dan,' Justin said, deleting the email, 'So what favours did you pull for your mate in IT this time? A weekend of surfing smut *chez toi*?'

'Piss off, gay boy. Get your shit together and let's get out of this fucking place.' His paisley tie off, top button undone and shirt-tails out, Dan stuffed his suit jacket into a mouldy gym bag and roughed up the few strands of his balding blond hair.

Justin walked over to the window of the open-plan office. Sneaking a look out through metal blinds and a fringe of static black hair, he searched Bishopsgate, the street below, for revolutionary goings-on. Ten police vans were parked outside a boarded-up McDonalds, and Robocop-look-alikes stalked their prey through misted-up portholes of reinforced glass. The familiar flow of sports cars, delivery vans and couriers in leather and lycra were replaced by bobbing dreadlocks, rainbow hats, red flags and placards of the Socialist Workers Party. The mob was probably not more than sixty strong and, from his sixth-floor vista, they looked pitiful: as if the unkempt barbarians were about to meet the might of the Imperial Robocops, their vanquishers transported into battle in souped-up white vans. He released the blinds, walked back to his desk and ran a hand through his dishevelled hair.

'I don't know if I can face it.' He rubbed his sore eyes. 'Where shall we go? Somewhere quiet, please, away from the crowds.'

'How about the Sky Bar?' Dan said, bouncing on his feet. 'It has the best views for this sort of thing – I know that we won't miss any action up there. And, you've got to agree with me on this, mate, it's not every day that we get to see the City turn into the bloody Coliseum. This should be cool.'

'How about you, Beth?' Justin ignored him and addressed a monitor that backed on to his desk. He stacked his papers on developing world labour markets next to printouts from mental illness websites, making sure not to mix them up, and hid the latter under a report on 'European Textile Manufacturing'. 'I'm not sure I can handle Dan's blood sports by myself.' A tuft of blond hair bobbed above the monitor.

Beth was the third component of the team: the female signatory of the French and Spanish analysts. At twenty-four, she was also the youngest – the others were in their late twenties – and yet her maturity and intelligence outranked the men. Justin admired her the most. In contrast to the only other female analyst in the bank, a tarty harpy in the German team, she attained respect, from both colleagues and clients, not by the length of her skirt but by her genuineness. Not that Beth was denied the looks; she could have played and preyed if she so desired. For lurking beneath a puritanical suit, thick Moschino glasses and a trussed-up, blond bob, was, in Dan's words, 'quite a babe.' Justin knew it only too well. In the evenings, when there was no one to call and having sifted through his vast collection of CDs, never quite managing to match music to mood, he regretted breaking up from her. But he knew that she deserved better than a screw-up like him. He had, he admitted, allowed a friend, of sorts, to be an antidote to his ex. After an initial awkwardness in the office, a few sorties to Starbucks and pubs later, he could at least now talk to her.

'You two go ahead,' she replied, a face without make-up appearing over her monitor, 'I'm having too much fun digging a knife into this drug company's P&L. It shouldn't take too long. Not with you guys gone.'

'You and your drugs,' Dan guffawed.

'OK,' Justin said, putting on his black overcoat, 'but I don't like the idea of you going out there by yourself. Give me a call if you want me to come back for you. Yes?'

'I'll be fine.' Beth smiled at him. 'As a matter of fact, I was thinking of joining their cause. Capitalism on a Friday afternoon sucks.' She undid her bob and shook out her locks. 'How do I look? Do you think they'll accept me?'

He smiled back.

'Are you coming or what, Callaghan?' Dan shouted, 'We're missing the show and wasting valuable drinking time.'

'Yeah. All right.' He took off his tie, draping it over the back of his chair, put both sets of research into his tanned leather bag and turned up the collar of his overcoat. 'See you in the Sky, Beth.'

'That's a bit profound,' she said, smiling again. 'I'm sure us scum will survive the lynch mob. Even without you around.' Waving them goodbye with a raised pen, as though that was her defence against the mob, she watched her colleagues join a dressed-down exodus at the doors to the lifts. 'Mine's a double vodka tonic,' she shouted after them.

The bankers made their evacuation through a maze of steps and passageways, a labyrinth of steel and glass, their leather soles clicking on a concrete staircase. The snake of people wound its way down to a ground-level fire door. It was, according to a barking woman in a florescent yellow bib, an 'inconspicuous exit to a side street off Bishopsgate.' To Justin, who had never forgiven the 'Human Resources Executive Assistant' for obstructing his request for compassionate leave, it not being in his contract to be allowed to go on suicide watch, it felt like herding a flock of sheep to the slaughter.

'Shame on you,' a female protester snarled, 'Shame on you!' Wearing red ribbons in strawberry blond dreadlocks, she pointed at the figures sneaking out of the fire escape, faces hidden behind elbows, briefcases and gym bags. Unbalanced by a surge within the crowd, tripping up over a discarded pole and placard on the pavement, the woman fell forward. Justin caught her in his arms.

'Thanks,' she said, gripping on to his overcoat's lapels, speaking over his shoulder and at his leather bag.

'No problem,' he replied into her dreadlocks. Her hand pushed him away.

'Now get your fucking hands off me, capitalist shit . . .'

A Robocop's truncheon struck her on the back of the head. This time, with Justin out of reach, she fell to the ground. Face down on the placard, an extra red ribbon trickled down her freckled back. The blood bypassed a circled 'A', an anarchy sign in lipstick, which was written between her spotty shoulder blades.

'That shut her up.' Dan poked his head over the crowd and looked at the anarchist in the gutter.

'Wanker,' Justin said, pulling his colleague back. He scrummed down, pushing back police and protesters, and crouched down by the injured woman. 'Get back!' He waved his arms over a filthy grey top and torn tracksuit bottoms. The crowd backed off. 'You OK?' He touched her bare shoulder.

'What?' She raised her head off the sign that called for a 'FREE PALESTINE' and 'NEO-COLONIALISM TO FUCK OFF'.

Disentangling her from the broken placard, saving her pale and freckly face from splintered edges of hardboard, he pulled the pole away from her neck.

'What the fuck?' Another woman screamed out from behind him. He dropped the pole and confronted a red-headed Medusa, her dreadlocks twisting as if they were snakes and her red ribbons flickering like tongues.

'She was . . .'

'Get away from her!'

'But I . . .'

'What the fuck did you do?' The woman looked down at her friend, who was sitting up and no longer rolling her eyes. 'You OK Tammy?'

The injured woman nodded. She touched the wetness on her neck and examined her scarlet-tipped fingers.

'You fucker!' The other woman screamed at Justin.

'But I didn't do anything,' he pleaded, the noise of the riot forcing him to raise his voice. 'It was . . .'

Before she could lash out at him with the pole, a Robocop grabbed him by his collar and threw him back to his rightful place, beside Dan and the other bankers. The fight was on and, he commentated to himself, crushed by suits and skinheads, the going was firm. In the blue corner were the starched shirts from Jermyn Street: raised on power lunches, watered by champagne, trained by Adonic Australians in luxurious fitness clubs. In the red corner were the bare-backs from Hackney and Tower Hamlets: raised on soya, pickled by extra-strength lager, trained by Her Majesty's Constabulary on London's streets. The bare-backs released a hail of stones, half-empty lager cans, street signs, traffic cones, cardboard slogans, kebabs with extra chilli sauce, and anything else that could be harvested from the capital's soiled streets. In response, the starched shirts shielded themselves with a wall of Samsonite briefcases – 'unparalleled durability, security and dependability . . . Worldproof solutions', '*Pikeyproof solutions*', he had once managed the brand's account. The anti-globalization walkover was eventually broken up by a ruck of Robocops, who swung their batons above their helmets like psychopathic cheer-leaders. The bare-backs retreated and the starched shirts, dismissed by their yellow-bibbed general with a clipboard, advanced to their watering holes.

Justin hurried out of the crush. He pushed Dan down an alley-way, stopping his red-faced colleague from a confrontation with both the protesters and then the police, and they separated from the other bankers. In a typical Friday night trap, Dan press-ganging

21

him into an after-work session, he had no desire to have to deal with anyone else. They walked down the streets of Shoreditch, newly gentrified and currently abandoned, Dan kicking an empty can of Special Brew against the curb, and he thought of the protester and his weekend's plans. His eyes fixed forward, he skidded on a pool of vomit and only just maintained his balance. He scraped his shoes on the pavement and, looking up, read 'SCUM' spray-painted on a polished granite wall.

The cast iron door of the members only club was set between the neon signed 'Exotic Couch' massage parlour, *Thai and very soothing*', and the 'Shoreditch Hair Removal Company'; 'A cosy arrangement between businesses to churn clientele from one to another,' Dan had once remarked to deaf ears. Justin buzzed the Sky Bar's intercom and, speaking into a microphone while looking at his gaunt reflection on the lens of a mini camera, he gave his name to a husky-voiced female. The door opened and they took a lift to the top floor of the converted warehouse. Leaving their riot-stained apparel with a cloakroom attendant, who turned her nose up at Justin's sticky jacket, they headed for a table with Dan's 'bloody great view.'

'Oh well,' Justin said, as he shrugged at a steamed-up window, a crane and scaffolding blocking the view of Bishopsgate. 'I'd forgotten about that new high rise.' He sat on a squashy leather stool and picked up a menu off a shiny glass table. 'Can't they leave this place alone? It's not like the City is exactly low on banker aquariums.'

'It's called improvement,' Dan said, also moving back from the window. He sat on a bright red armchair, part of the 'chic and sumptuous décor' that Justin read in the foreword of the menu, and lit a cigarette. 'Don't know why you're not protesting with those hippies. In fact, I'm surprised you didn't get that skanky wench's number. You were all over her. Desperate are we now?'

'What?'

'The bitch that the cops decorated, stupid.' Dan blew smoke rings over his head. 'Damn good shot it was, right above the anarchy sign on her back. Bet she is from LSE, studying some poxy social science. Today she protests, tomorrow she'll be doing the milk round and applying for a plum job in the City. They all turn in the end, stupid, lefty students.'

'Dan?'

'Yeah?'

'You're an arsehole.'

Dan shrugged his shoulders.

'Did you also know that most of those wasters went to public school?' Dan continued in a cloud of exhaled smoke. 'I read it in the *Standard*. Some kid from Eton and Oxford mobilizes them. They use mobile phones and the Internet, have some special code to fox the police. Then they demand, while we pay our taxes and fund their waster's lifestyle, a classless fucking society.'

'Afternoon boys,' a waitress said as she approached their table, 'How are you gentleman doing today?'

'Hi Steph,' Justin addressed the reek of perfume over his shoulder. 'Apart from having shit thrown at me by the Bolsheviks, listening to *Mein Kampf* from the Führer opposite me, the day's been lovely. Thanks for asking.'

'So what can I get you thirsty soldiers?'

'A Stella for me,' Dan said, sulking at a candle in a paper lampshade on the table. 'I can't believe that we're missing it.'

'A Dos Equis for me. Thanks Steph.'

'Good choice of beer, Mexican,' the waitress said.

The waitress smiled again, only more directly this time, but her target was too busy reading the sales blurb on the menu, the bit about the Sky Bar being the 'place for sophisticated and sexy urbanites to meet likeminded people'. She turned on her high heels and returned to the bar.

'Look,' Dan paused to look at the waitress's bottom in a black miniskirt, 'I've worked my balls off to get where I am. Why should I let snotty-nosed, half-wit students tell me what I can and can't do? I bet half of them don't even know what globalization is – they probably think it's a club-night at the Ministry of Sound. What the fuck do they know about what's good for the world?'

'And what, exactly, do we know?' Justin's raised voice silenced a neighbouring table's conversation. Dan slouched further into his designer armchair, to hide from the circle of silent and inquisitive faces. Oblivious to them all, Justin continued. 'Do you really think that we're qualified to know what's good and what's bad? There we are in our glass boxes, jerking off on spreadsheets for at least twelve hours a day, screwing over companies and individuals for a fast buck. We work for tossers that hardly know our names; nooses round our necks, ready to be hung out for the vultures, recruitment consultants, when profits dictate. Perhaps you should have saved your precious balls for something else. Something a bit more worthwhile.'

'Unlike you, gay boy, I do use my balls for something else. And it sure beats listening to your liberal crap.' Dan sat up and grinned. 'So have you heard anything from what's-her-name? Tania wasn't it?'

Three years ago, Justin met Tania at a Christmas party. The party was fancy dress and a large crowd was expected. He had thought of excuses and only agreed to go when Martin, a well-fed advertising executive, who had a reliable supply of weed, promised him an eighth for his company. It had been two years since Justin's father had died and his mother was showing no sign of improvement. The weed helped him to help his mother, it at least numbed his pain, and so he bought a cheap Zorro mask to blend in.

'Don't go there, Dan,' Justin said, ripping holes into a paper napkin.

Not long after Justin had made his entrance, Batman, a solicitor by day and a caped bore by night, accosted him by the coats in the hallway. Batman went on to describe his riveting job in commercial law, his Dutch model girlfriend with a taste for the outdoors, his flying lessons and his Porsche 911. It was hell and, Martin on the pull and nowhere in sight, he longed to go home, pour himself a whisky, turn on the TV, roll a joint and watch some programme that could wash over him. It had also been a few hours since he called his mother.

'She was a babe,' Dan said, nodding in agreement with himself.

Justin ignored him and stared at the steamed-up window.

Dressed up as Catwoman, Tania essentially rescued Justin from Batman. They talked until they were the only ones there, the host of the party actually having to pull them apart before he kicked them out. Outside in the rain and in a dark street, ignoring the jeers of passing drunks, catcalls to Catwoman, they removed their masks. They exchanged numbers on the backs of cigarette packets and he hailed her a black cab. After a year, they moved in together. After two years, they planned to marry and, as an added bonus, his mother's condition improved. His mother loved Tania.

'Got to be careful with that sort, though,' Dan continued, trying to attract Justin's attention. 'Can't trust them.'

It was Martin, the blubbery matchmaker himself, who delivered the killer blow: 'Just an office fling is what I heard, that's all.'

24

Justin simply couldn't face telling the truth to his mother.

'Two beers,' the waitress said, placing their drinks and a bowl of roasted cashew nuts on the table. 'Would you like to order some food?' She addressed Justin and not Dan.

'No thanks,' Justin replied. He put the shredded napkin down on the table.

The waitress turned her back on his apologetic smile, picked up the remains of his napkin and returned to the bar.

'So what happened to you and Beth?' Dan said, spying the waitress's bottom again as he swigged his Stella.

'Don't you ever let go?' He picked up his beer. 'Can we please change the subject?' He looked down at the menu again, reread the foreword and wished that he were in The Green Man pub, reading a newspaper in his local, alone.

The Sky Bar filled up with refugees from the riot. Credit cards and wads of notes were waved about at the bar, while the exposed-brickwork interior reeked of a cocktail of cigarette smoke, alcohol and sweat. Past the squeals of a pretty blonde, who laughed at her monosyllabic companion as he moaned about the squatters on his Notting Hill street, Justin tuned into the jazz-funk fusion in the background. Through a communion of Cosmopolitans and foreign beers, the blood pressure of the trading floor dropped under the steel girders and industrial light fittings. To Justin, who checked his mobile for his mother's missed calls, it was an all too familiar religion.

'Where's my vodka tonic?' Beth appeared. She sat on another squashy stool beside Justin. The waitress spotted the new addition from her bar-side perch, rushed to the table and took Beth's order.

'What the hell are you wearing?' Dan waved his bottle at Beth's low-cut pink top, black skirt and fishnet stockings.

'Drastic circumstances sometimes require drastic measures. I'm going on a date. Remember them, Mr Married?' she said to Dan.

'Your vodka tonic,' the waitress said, returning in super quick time.

Justin sipped his beer and imagined an invisible umbilical cord, a bungee lifeline, attaching the waitress to victims of inebriated bullies. *'Hi, I'm Stephanie. I'm your waitress and saving grace for the evening. Just give me a shout if this creep is bothering you. Have a nice day!'*

'I think you look great,' Justin said, rolling a foil Dos Equis label

25

between his fingers and squinting at Beth through the haze. 'It's Jeremy, right? The architect? He seems like a nice guy.'

'Thanks,' she replied, 'and yes, I decided to dress like a whore for the architect. I mean, he's a bloody architect and so I had to at least try to look arty and cool. It's all from Portobello market, you know.'

'You're Beth. You don't have to try to be anyone else.'

'Very sweet of you, Justin, but you're not like me. I'm sick of being single and by myself. I really want something to happen with this guy.'

'Is he taking you anywhere nice?' Dan said, checking out his colleague's fishnet stockings under the glass table.

'Somewhere out of the paparazzi's reach.' She crossed her legs.

'Don't worry about me, darling, I'm having a quiet night in with the missis. But I'm sure that the good man here will chaperone you to the lucky fella.'

'What are you doing tonight?' she asked Justin, who was destroying another paper napkin.

'Sorry?'

'Your plans for tonight – what are they?'

'Oh, I, umm, invited Martin to meet me back at my place.' He glanced at his mobile again. 'Nothing definite, though. Which way are you headed for?'

'Upper Street. But don't feel that you have to . . .'

'It's on the way home. It's no big deal. When do you want to go?'

'Half an hour or so. Are you sure? I don't want to interrupt any of your plans.'

He looked at the label-free bottle on the table and the shredded napkin on his lap.

'I'm sure.'

Stumbling down a street of empty warehouses, Afro-Caribbean grocery stores, halal butchers and a gang of Eastern Europeans playing cards under a railway line, a young woman clutched the back of her head. Her fingers passed under strawberry blonde dreadlocks and red ribbons, nails scratching off the crusty blood on her neck, and she zigzagged through smashed melons, squashed peaches, empty polystyrene and cardboard boxes, the leftovers of Ridley Road Market. The East End barrow boys having gone for the day, only rats, pigeons and a couple of road-sweepers provided her with company. Her unsteady, scuffed purple boot narrowly missed the severed foot of a chicken. Cutting left and going down a passageway of graffiti, a mishmash of sprayed signatures, political slogans and empty-eyed cartoon figures, she entered a building of cracked and cobwebbed windows. She felt her way up a dark concrete staircase and, reaching the top-floor landing, swept aside a dusty, tie-dyed drape on a doorframe holed by woodworm. Four figures circled a small fire in the middle of an abandoned workshop.

'That you, Tam?' A man in the circle rose to his feet. The fire, a stack of burning fruit boxes, illuminated his naked and lean torso, the braids in his mullet, and a 'Z' tattoo on the back of his grimy neck.

'No,' the woman struggled to answer, entering the room and approaching the man, 'it's pizza fucking delivery.' She found strength to hug him. 'You silly tosser, Zeb. I got us some booze to celebrate with, didn't I?' Tam released him, shaking on her feet, and handed him the bag.

'Angel.' Zeb pulled her hair back and kissed her pale and freckly cheek. He pulled a can of extra-strength lager out of the bag. 'How's your head?' He ran his hand up her spine, passing the faded lipstick of the anarchy symbol and a patch of dried blood. She arched her back. 'If I ever catch that wanker . . .' He removed his hand from her and cracked open the can.

'It's a minor scar for the cause,' she said, kissing the 'Z' on his neck and taking the can off him. She leaned against a dusty wall. 'The banker looked more fucked up than I did. Really sad eyes he had. Weird he was.' She paused. 'But I'm fine.'

In truth, the short walk to the off-licence had been an ordeal. As if a slight loss of memory wasn't bad enough, the man and the pole a blur, she almost passed out in the rotten smelling market. Taking a swig of beer and returning the can to Zeb, she had no desire to burden the group with her bump on the head. There were more important matters on the anarchists' minds: like the arrests of Jamie and Stevo, who had stormed the atrium of a bank and got themselves locked up for the night. She certainly didn't want to be seen as a distraction to their leader, her boyfriend. Although Zeb earned respect from the majority, his posh background left a bad taste in a few pierced mouths.

'Any news on Jamie and Stevo?' she asked.

'No fucking word, Tammy,' the other woman from the riot replied, her red hair flashing orange by the fire, 'They're probably being steel-toed by a jackbooted pig. If you ask me, it serves the fuckers right for getting caught in the first place. I expect it was Stevo's doing. The dumb fuck.'

'That's enough, Jules,' Zeb put his bare arm, a scarred canvas of Celtic and aboriginal body art, gently round Tam's back, 'They'll be out tomorrow with a caution and a few bruises. I'd be surprised if they have to go to court – it's not like the pigs caught them red-handed.' He finished off his can of lager.

'Is that the fucking lawyer in you speaking,' Jules said, 'or is that what they taught you at fucking Cambridge?'

'Fuck off, Jules.' Zeb scrunched up his empty can and opened another. 'This shit about my past is getting tedious. The joke's dead. Anyway, it's times like this when we need a brain amongst us. If it weren't for me, you muppets would all be in the nick by now.' The fire dying down, it painting the room and anarchists a darker orange, he returned to his seat within the circle.

Not wanting her shakes to be seen by the others, Tam lay down behind him, away from the warm light and on the squat's cold wooden floor.

Knowing that Zeb spoke the truth, that without him they would either be behind bars or, even worse, restricted to handing out pamphlets on Upper Street, the figures round the fire went silent. In the last year, since Zeb was appointed leader of the 'East London Anarchists', they had upped their ante. His special weapon against the State, he had told them at the time his name was first mooted as leader, was his knowledge of the system.

It was in the unlikely setting of Cambridge University that Sebastian Townsend, as he was then called, first became obsessed with the anarchist and anti-globalization movement. In a crenellated tower at King's College, drunken rugby players for neighbours, he coordinated coaches of student activists to Parliament Square and led the charge against the Tories. Graduating with a 2:1, he moved to London to train as a human right's barrister, a decision made for him by parents he barely knew. At Bar School he isolated himself from the other students, preferring anarchist chatrooms instead, and two months into his pupillage, one of the worst experiences of his life, he dropped out of chambers. His parents disowned him and it was not long before he was on the streets, hanging out with society's other rejects. It was then that he met Tam: a pimp was beating her up behind King's Cross Station and he had to use a scaffolding pipe to save her. She took him to the Hackney squat, and it was there that they fell in love.

'You're the man,' a man round the fire squeaked, a cloud of marijuana smoke hiding his face. 'They must have lost shit loads, millions even, cos of us. Hell, we shut down half the city for half a day. You did us well Zeb.'

'We shut down a couple of banks,' Zeb replied, stoking the fire with a crowbar. 'Hardly half the city.' He turned round and looked at his angel lying on the floor, her face still in shadow. Facing the circle and the fire again, he raised his can. 'But well done anyway. Here's to a good day's work, some shit-scared wankers, and the safe return of absent comrades.'

'To Stevo and Jamie,' they all said, clunking cans together.

'Tam?' Zeb said, looking behind him again, 'Are you going to join in or what? You can sleep later.'

He crouched down, slipped a hand under Tam's sprawled out hair and lifted up her head. The only colour on her face was the red that trickled from her lips.

'Tam?' His fingers shaking as they absorbed her shivers, he looked into her vacant eyes.

The three colleagues ordered another round and the tide of conversation turned from Beth's date, to Tony Blair's new government, to the Brit pop battle between Oasis and Blur. Dan and Beth dominated the table's talk, while Justin just watched. It was not that he failed to harbour opinions over their bar-chat of pop and politics – he could have killed a whole evening talking about Blair's Third Way – but that he was too incapacitated to participate. He had slipped into weekend syndrome, when, removed from the strictures and routines of the office, he was mauled by loneliness. The others had plans, directions to their lives and loved ones to lean on. Dan would go home to his bourgeois existence on the leafy commuter belt, back to a pretty young wife and a meal kept warm for him in the bottom oven. Even Beth, the girl he had discarded, was reaping potential and pulling in dates as if they were mackerel. Should the architect disappoint, she would activate Plan B and lifelong friends would pick up the pieces.

Justin felt that he just had acquaintances, dope heads like Martin who would call him if they had nothing better to do on a

Friday night, and a mother's desperate pleas at the other end of the phone. He had read in some newspaper, probably *The Sun*, a story about some lonely poor fuck dying in his one-bedroom flat. Nobody missed him and a few weeks later it was the smell that finally prompted the neighbours to call the council. The police found him face-up on the kitchen floor, his face burrowed by maggots. 'He looked like Swiss cheese,' the reporter had relished.

'Justin?' Beth said, prodding a finger into his side. 'Are you OK?'

'What?' he said, startled. 'Sorry. Bloody work. Wish I could get it out of my head.' He wondered whether the woman with red dreadlocks called an ambulance for her friend. He decided to call the police, to complain about the Robocops' heavy-handed response, first thing tomorrow; before he drove to Gravesend and completed an only son's duties.

'Is my chaperone ready?' Beth slurred at Justin. 'If I drink anymore of these vodkas, I'll be dribbling my couscous all over Jeremy.'

'I wouldn't worry about that,' Dan said. 'He'll be the one dribbling, when he grabs an eyeful of what you're wearing.'

'One must respect the architect, Daniel,' she giggled.

'Yeah, I'm ready,' Justin re-entered the conversation, sober in comparison to his colleagues. 'I just need to go to the gents and give Martin a call. I won't be long.' He picked up his mobile phone, stood up and, catching his ghost-like reflection in the window, the crane outside resembling giant gallows, left them.

'Is he all right?' Beth asked Dan, Justin disappearing down a flight of stairs. 'Has Tania been in touch? He seems even quieter than usual tonight.'

'I asked him that earlier and he said no. He had a big row with one of his clients. Perhaps that's it.'

'It's not like Justin to let a client get him down. It must be Tania.'

'Trust me. He didn't bat an eyelid when I mentioned her name. And you know what he's like; he always keeps his problems to himself. He's a secret sod.'

Justin returned and, noticing Beth turn pink, guessed that they were talking about him. He asked Steph for the bill, tipped her with a tenner and missed her smile again. They collected their belongings from the cloakroom attendant and, the iron door slamming behind them, Dan caught a cab and Justin and Beth walked on alone. The road closures, the sealing off of the riot, had yet to be lifted and there was none of the usual north-to-south traffic. For a warm summer's evening, the streets were unusually empty.

'What's wrong, Justin?' Beth broke the silence. She was struggling to keep up with his longer strides.

'What do you mean?'

'I mean all this surliness. What's up?'

'Nothing's up.' He looked straight ahead.

'Is it Tania? Have you heard from her?'

'Not you as well.' He stopped walking and faced her. 'You know that I'm well over her. Christ, I must've bored you enough about her in the past.' His green eyes flashed orange under a streetlight.

'Is it me, then? You know that I'm cool with things between us. Really, I am.'

'No, it's not you. I'm fine.' He resumed his fast walk. 'Now where's this restaurant and this architect of yours?'

'Shit, Justin!' She pulled on his overcoat to slow him down. 'Will you open up for once in your self-pitying life? Or don't you do that to friends?'

'It's Mum, OK?' He stopped, faced Beth and immediately felt remorse at using his mother as an excuse.

'I'm sorry.' Beth released her grip on him. 'I shouldn't have snapped. I had no idea. Is she not better?'

'No. It's a few years since Dad died and she seems to be getting worse. I've got to go round tomorrow. She needs me. There's no one else for her.'

Saying no more, they reached the bottom of Upper Street and walked past Angel tube station. She steered them clear of the beggars and sleeping bags on the pavement, and yet he still managed to hear someone say '*yuppie cunt.*' He turned his head and saw a skinhead stroking a small puppy. The warmth of the evening attracted a migration of ripped denim miniskirts from the suburbs of north London. Peroxide plumage, tight crop-tops and white legs caught the attention of blokes with beer bellies and Bermuda shorts, the lads going continental and taking their pints outdoors. An ambulance screamed down the high street and he stopped staring at a woman with '*Take a closer look − if you're hard enough*' printed on her DD chest. The siren ringing in his ears, joining the abuse of the skinhead, the protesters, sweatshop workers in his in-tray, whispering colleagues and sobs on voicemail, he dragged Beth across the road. They halted outside Le Mercurie, a low-key restaurant of an architect's choice.

'Thanks for escorting me.' She examined her reflection, checking her hair, in a glass door.

'No problem.' He watched a fight break out on the other side of the road. A crowd poured out of a pub to watch and jeer as the men beat each other up.

'I'd better go inside,' she said.

'Sure.' He kissed her on both cheeks. 'Good luck.' He turned and walked away before she could look him in the face.

'Bye,' she eventually replied, taking one last look at him from the restaurant's doorway, 'and have a good weekend,' she called out after him. But the back of his overcoat had gone and a hen party, a boob-flashing bride-to-be leading a dozen or so fake-tanned friends, had taken over the pavement. The women and their bottles of Sea Breezers dangerously close, Beth went inside.

Justin woke up early the next day, before the end of Saturday morning's kid's TV, his meridian timeline for a weekend's activities. In his boxer shorts, he walked the short distance from his bed to the kitchen and pulled a face at the mouldy nectarines that he kept meaning to throw out. A bulb flickered above the designer oven whose brushed steel surface was stained by burnt grease, and dirty marks streaked the once white walls behind an Italian-made bin. He made a cafetiere of the strongest coffee that Sainsbury's supplied, a factor four, and poured the tar-like stimulant into a pint-sized mug. Dragging on a cigarette in between sips, he allowed the nicotine and caffeine to jump-start his body and mind.

For the morning after a Friday night, in fact most weeknights, he was abnormally refreshed. True to form, doped-up as usual, Martin had failed to materialize. Not that Justin had made exact plans with the fat advertising man. The phoney phone call in the Sky Bar was a ruse for his colleagues: a smokescreen for a night of cable TV and a warmed-up pizza on his lap. Dan would have crucified him if he knew the truth, that he had only retrieved a voicemail message from his mother. Besides, he knew that for him to have a hangover today, of all days, would have made him as mentally impaired as the patient that he was supposed to treat. He had promised his mother that he would arrive in time for lunch. First, though, as he switched on his phone, he had to lodge a complaint to the police.

Five years ago, after her husband died of cancer, Isabella Callaghan fled to Gravesend: she went there to be closer to her son and to escape the woe in the walls of her marital home. Running away had been a habit of Justin's mother. Born in Madrid, she rebelled against her strict Catholic parents, moved to London and became a model in the swinging 60s. Her dark and exotic looks had every designer and photographer queuing for a piece of her. With fame came a merry-go-round of male admirers, from pussycat rock-stars to stately lords a-leaping, and it was a surprise, therefore, that she chose Edward Callaghan, a humble accountant who revolved around the party circuit to laugh at well-dressed freaks on free bubbly. But Isabella's Catholic upbringing selected the man of simple means, even though he was Church of England. Sticking two fingers up at London's glitterati, the move to the countryside was apparently as much her idea as his father's. They both took jobs in Leamington Spa, an average market town in the middling Midlands: he in a small-time accountancy firm and she in a small boutique, which sold pastel-shaded wellington boots for Londoners in the sticks. When Justin was born, the Callaghans moved to the outskirts of Warwick and set up home in a timbered cottage, a quaint museum piece that excited coaches of Shakespearean groupies. Although he was an only child stuck in the middle of nowhere, with the Spanish side of the family denying their ungodly existence and not returning his calls, a teenager's attempts at reconciliation, there were at least the three of them then.

Showered and shaved, he threw on some clothes, picked up his mobile and locked the front door of his messy flat. He fired up the engine of his metallic blue BMW, a relic of his relationship with Tania, savings for an engagement ring going towards transport to Gravesend and the supermarket instead, and hid his eyes with heavily tinted shades. Past the Blackwall Tunnel, he picked up the A2 in Greenwich and, weaving in and out of two queues of traffic, saw families going off to DIY and flat-pack furniture stores, bored-looking faces staring out of SUVs and 4x4s.

The road opened up and he lowered his window. He accelerated through Kent's green Garden of England to the Prodigy's *The Fat of the Land*, the car stereo's volume at level sixteen and his black hair flapping in the wind. Punk rasps and six pumping cylinders of German technology had the desired effect of over-powering the driver's apprehension, but soon the exit to Gravesend, an aggressive green sign that pointed to an uphill sliproad, stole the comfort of the numbing motorway. He drove round the town centre, past grey pebbledash rows of retirement homes and solitary pensioners on the pavements. Out of respect for the funereal environment – he was seeing tombstones for houses and lost souls for pedestrians – he faded out the music and closed his window.

He parked in a cul-de-sac of semi-detached houses and walked past grey brickwork and identikit gardens, herbaceous borders neatly pruned and pansies in pots by the front doors. A cat gave him a death stare from under a hedge. He stopped at the house with a plot of weeds, empty crisp packets and beer cans, rang the doorbell and shook his head at an arrangement of dead geraniums in a hanging basket.

The door opened. A woman aged beyond her years in appearance stood in a dark hallway. Winged cheekbones, two fossils of former beauty, hooked up the flaccid skin of a once photogenic face, and her prematurely white hair blew in the soft breeze on the porch. Only her dark brown eyes, vestiges of her Mediterranean ancestry, had survived the weathering of grief.

'My darling boy,' her deflated lips puckered, 'how I've missed my boy.' He stepped forward and hugged her.

'It's good to see you Mum.' He held her tight as he whispered in her ear. 'It's good to see you.' As if they were a pair of invalids, they propped each other up and went inside.

Mrs Callaghan steered her son down a picture-less corridor, clasping his arm as if it was he and not her who needed treatment. Depositing him in her waiting room, a lounge of blank white walls, she went to the kitchen and made a couple of strong gin and tonics. Justin sat on a leather swivel chair, the one he always occupied when he made his weekly visit, and catalogued the objects on a mantelpiece above the electric fire, as he always did. A porcelain bull from a family holiday in Spain, his mother and father's wedding photo, a picture of him in his graduation gown and a postcard from Zanzibar, a reminder of Tania, decorated the otherwise bare room. His mother used to have a flair for interior design, but, like her diminishing appearance and her unmanaged garden, that was lost when they scattered his father's ashes on a Norfolk beach. He looked down at the floor, a dirty green carpet mottled by years of TV dinners, and the smell of embedded filth killed what little appetite he had.

She handed him his drink and placed a bowl of peanuts on the floor. On a peach sofa and slurping her G&T, she examined him with heavily made-up eyes. He crossed his legs, twitching his Timberlands, bowed his head and focused on a large stain on the carpet.

'Darling, you are looking terribly pale and thin,' she said, her drink shaking in her bony hands. 'I do hope that you are taking good care of yourself. Is that bank of yours working you too hard? I do wish that you'd find yourself a less stressful job.'

He admired her knack of shifting the focus onto him, but it irritated him when she used the subject of work to get at him. As a boy, he recalled, he had plenty of ambition. Between the ages of six and twelve it was all about fighting the bad guys, either imaginary Nazis in the hedgerows, usually in a costume that his mother had made for him, or the bullies that used to pick on the geeks and misfits by the swings in the playground. At secondary school he took his crusade a little too far, gave a nosebleed to a bully who picked on a fat Pakistani kid, and he was held back after classes to write an essay on 'Why I deserve to be punished.'

University, however, in hindsight, was responsible for where he was to eventually end up: it was difficult not to be affected by the race for adulation, and that was mainly in grades, girls and tolerance for alcohol. After a disastrous week of work experience at *The Birmingham Post*, shadowing a reporter of 'cat stuck up tree' stories, and with a girlfriend who didn't fancy moving to London with a tea maker in media, he abandoned the idea of journalism. Before he knew it, as graduation loomed, he was filling in application forms for the civil service and investment bank trainee schemes. His current predicament, a job analysing Third World sweatshops for a multinational retailer, was never part of a grand plan. It just turned out that way.

'I'm fine, Mum. Things really couldn't be much better for me.' He sipped his drink and managed a small smile. 'And how are you doing?'

'We're doing okay,' she replied, as if his father was somehow in the garden, pulling out the weeds round the front, and would come in and demand his lunch any second now. In the days of the cottage in Warwickshire, when the meat was ready to be carved, it had been his job to call his father in, and more often than not it was the Prince Arthur rather than the garden where he was to be found. In later years, after they had diagnosed the cancer, one sunny Sunday he joined his father. Over a pint in the pub's beer garden, the smell of freshly cut grass vivid in his memory, he promised that he would look after his mother. It was the only time that he saw his father cry.

'And how is Mrs Ellis?' he asked, trying to change the subject.

He was delighted when she had told him about Janet Ellis, a neighbour and a fellow-widow. It meant that at last she had someone else to look after her: a companion to take her to bridge nights, bingo, bowls, pub quizzes or whatever else widows do in order to kill time, before time in turn kills them. In the absence of family, when his relatives were dead or as good as dead, too bigoted and petty to speak to their fallen kin, his mother next to the Devil in Spanish eyes, his research on the Internet recommended people like Mrs Ellis.

'Mrs Ellis?' she replied, looking momentarily confused. 'Oh, yes, Janet is a wonderful woman, isn't she? We are both whipping the old boys at bridge, you know. She really is a wonderful old sport.'

'That's great, Mum. I mean it. You'll have to introduce me to her some time.'

'If she can fit you in her diary. She's quite booked up by strapping widowers, and it will be Zimmer frames at dawn if they know they've competition.' They both laughed.

'I wasn't exactly thinking of Mrs Ellis in that way, Mum.' He thought he detected a change in her, a sign of, perhaps, a recovery. His stomach began to settle and he reached down for a peanut.

'Why on earth not? There's nothing wrong with an older woman. Of course, you're with that lovely colleague of yours, the girl who you keep telling me about on the phone.'

'Beth?' He struggled to swallow the peanut. 'Yes, we're still giving it a go. We're just taking it slowly, that's all.'

'She sounds like a good girl.'

'She is.' He wondered how Beth's date with the architect had gone.

'Well I hope it works out for you both. I worry that you're lonely in that big city.'

'Me? Lonely? Coming from you, Mum, that's a bit rich.'

'You know it's different. I've had my time, married an amazing man and had a beautiful son. You have your whole life ahead of you, and I just want to make sure that you're happy when I'm gone.'

'Please, I didn't come all this way to hear this. And you're hardly past it: you've got a good few years ahead of you.'

'You don't know what's around the corner. Look what happened to your father.' She looked at the photos on the mantelpiece.

'I know Mum.' He stood up, joined her on the sofa and hugged her.

They continued their conversation in the kitchen, over roast chicken, new potatoes, lumpy gravy and soggy cabbage. She poured them both another glass of sauvignon blanc. Her hand shaking, she splashed a patched tablecloth. He mopped up the mess with his napkin.

'Mum,' he hesitated, 'do you think that you'll ever remarry? I mean, you are still young, and, well, Dad would've wanted you to move on.'

She looked down at her plate of food and skinned a chicken wing with her knife and fork.

'No, Justin, I shan't. My life and soul belong to your father. And one day we'll be reunited.' She poured herself another glass of wine. 'Anyway, look at me. I'm not exactly a catch even if I was on the market.' She speared a piece of chicken on her fork. 'Why do you ask?'

'You just seem so ... so much happier today. I guess that I wanted to know whether ...'

'Whether I'd moved on?' She chewed a mouthful of chicken. 'My loyalty to Edward, your father, does not stop me from indulging in a little sweet sherry with the merry widows of Gravesend. Does it now?' She swallowed.

'Of course not, Mum.'

After clearing the table, Justin doing the washing-up and his mother finishing off the dregs of wine and G&Ts, out of her son's sight, it was time for him to go. They went outside and he stopped her in the garden.

'I'll come round next weekend and clear this up for you,' he said, toeing an empty beer can amongst the weeds. 'Or I'll pay for a gardener, like I said I would. You can't have it looking like this. It's not right. I don't like it.'

'Stop getting at me,' she replied, as she pushed him towards his car, 'I've had enough complaints from my nosy neighbours. I know that the grass could do with cutting. I just haven't had the time to do it.' She steered him towards his car.

'Thanks for the lunch.' He opened the driver's door.

'It was the least your mad Mum could do.'

'Give me a call later if you want. I'm not doing much tonight.'

'Stop being so concerned about me,' she said, hugging him and then looking at his face. 'I'm sorry about the messages.' She paused and he looked down at his feet. 'Look, it's a Saturday night and I want you to go out and enjoy yourself.' She handed him a twenty-pound note and kissed him on his cheek.

'Don't be silly, Mum. I don't need that.'

She forced him to take the note.

'You can take that lovely girl of yours for a drink. And you certainly shouldn't be holding back because of me.'

They hugged again and he climbed into his car. He turned on the ignition, switched off 'Firestarter' on his stereo, the track on the CD, and put down his window.

'Love you Mum,' he shouted out over the engine. 'See you next weekend, yeah?'

'Love you too, darling.'

Her façade dropped as he drove out of the cul-de-sac, her dark brown eyes glazing over in the garden of weeds and trash.

'Look after yourself, my sweet boy,' she said to herself. 'You don't have to worry about me.'

Three

Maria Gomez bounced on a bench, a plank on a gas cylinder, in the back of an open-topped cane truck. The truck hurtled down a track of limestone chips, which dazzled in the morning sun, and it departed San Felipé in a cloud of chalky dust. Grass verges and overhanging branches turned white as it cut through the hillsides of Chenalho. Aged axles shuddered and Maria, gripping the plank under her bum, used her fleshy palms to compensate for the vehicle's ineffectual shock absorbers. For the journey, the importance of her assignment, she wore the traditional huipil of a Tzotzil Maya woman, a white sleeveless blouse with a collar of red and green embroidered flowers. A yard-long cortes, a finely woven red cloth, was wrapped around her waist and fastened by a cinch belt, while draped over her shoulders and worn only for special occasions was a dark brown cape with a pattern of white zigzags. Dangling over the cape and decorated with pink ribbons was her plaited tail of long black hair. Ten other men and women accompanied the grieving mother. Including Horatio, her eldest, each of them vied for a bit of the truck's cramped space, and they perched on sacks of corn, bundles of clothes and crafts, crates of vegetables, a spare wheel and canisters of gas and water.

The truck exited the track and joined the tarmac of the main highway. They drove through pro-Zapatista villages, down streets of wooden slatted buildings and past colourful murals of Subcommandante Marcos, Emiliano Zapata, Che Guevara and portraits of Mayan men and women in ski masks. Under yellow road signs warning of 'TOPES', speed bumps, children with baskets of fruit and buckets of tamales demanded pesos from braking vehicles. When a Volkswagen Beetle moved on, a pink arm waving out of the driver's window, the tiny highwaymen giggled at the gullible gringo who bought a plantain and not a banana. On the outskirts of the villages, leashed to stakes and in pockets of tree-shade on the sides of the road, goats grazed on grass and ginger-haired piglets snoozed in dried out puddles. In grass clearings, on the slopes of hills, women wove wool next to grazing black mountain sheep. Kneeling on their feet and slanting backs backwards, looms strapped to belts on one end and to tree stumps at the other, multicoloured threads spewed out of the women's waists.

Maria's concentration bypassed these roadside activities. Tears welling in her eyes, she rewound her memory to that night, when lightning struck over First-True-Mountain. Most of the village was asleep and only bony dogs patrolled San Felipé's streets. Thunder drowned out the roar of 4x4s and lightning masked the headlights that came through the pine trees. Skidding to a halt outside San Felipé's small church, a wooden hut painted in turquoise, all-terrain tyres kicked up dust and headlights lit up the Gomez home. As if they were conjured by the Death Lords themselves, four black silhouettes walked out of the illuminated cloud. Maria and her two sons stood firm in the mud-brick doorway. Horatio charged at the smallest of the masked Cardenistas, knocking his target down with a shoulder ram to the kidneys, but repetitive pistol-whips and the boot of Commandant Hernandez stopped further resistance. The fat tapir aimed his rifle at Maria and her eyes were shut when he fired. But she remained standing and, hearing her executioners laugh like the howls of wolves, she opened her eyes. Urbano was on the ground, by her feet; he had taken the bullet that was meant for her. Commandant Hernandez then pointed his smoking rifle at the head of Horatio, who lay unconscious in the Gomez orchard, spiky hair buttressing a banana tree. Threatening to send her first-born the way of her second-born, the paramilitary stated his terms. The next time that he visited, he told her, Urbano bleeding in a zigzagged blanket on her lap, he would take Horatio with him; her absent husband was spared on the grounds that he was 'too much of a wimp' to fight the Zapatistas. The Gomez home was doused in gasoline and Commandant Hernandez flicked a match at its thatched roof. The Cardenistas then roared off in their brand new pick-ups, stones and pebbles banging against steel doors.

Under a bandaged forehead and through black and swollen eyes, Horatio had watched his mother for most of the journey. From his sackcloth seat, a bag of squashed huipiles, he could read the sadness on her face. It made him all the more determined to succeed in his chosen course of action. Before they set off, while the others loaded up the truck to San Cristóbal de las Casas, he approached his father, who stood alone by the ashes of their home.

'Father,' he said, the dryness in his throat forcing him to swallow. 'I miss him as well.'

Lucio looked up from the ashes and slowly turned round. His eyes were as red as the crimson trousers that he still wore, the shaman's uniform caked in the dried mud of First-True-Mountain and the blood of Urbano. The glare of the sun too much, First Father torturing him further, he dropped his head again.

'I promise,' Horatio continued, observing his deflated basket-ball amongst the blackened wood, 'that we will see Urbano's killers brought to justice. The Zapatistas will help us.'

Remaining silent, Lucio looked at a trace of blood in the dust, the spot where he had found his wife and son not so many hours ago. Beneath a palm frond, a piece of half-burnt thatch, something caught his eye. He bent down and picked up Urbano's blowpipe.

'Yes,' Lucio said. He examined the blowpipe in the palms of his hands. 'We are all Zapatistas now.'

The truck descended into the Valle de Jovel, a vast basin cut into the mountains and a natural fortification for Ciudad Real, the former name of San Cristóbal de las Casas. Founded in 1528 as a regional command post, where foreigners were free to enslave and torture the local population, the city was nicknamed Villaviciosa, 'Evil City,' by the Maya in the Highlands. The villagers from San Felipé pulled up outside the church of Santo Domingo in the north of the city. Waiting for the others to disembark first, Maria looked up at the stone carvings on the church's ornate and pink façade. Faces contorted by centuries of rainy seasons, Spanish saints stared down at her, while two angels flanked the Host in a monstrance above the central window. Spread out in front of a large oak door and competing against tombstones for the space of a small cemetery were stalls of colour-ful textiles, tanned leather bags, Zapatista merchandise – ski masks, T-shirts and EZLN-embossed keyrings – and stone and amber jewellery. Arranged under canopies of white canvas, the souvenirs were manned by beady-eyed saleswomen, a gathering of Tzotzil, Tzetzal and Chol speakers. A couple of backpackers, more interested in groping each other than browsing handicrafts, were besieged by shouts of 'Good prices here', 'I find your pretty girl-friend a special gift', and a Latino youth whispering 'You need weed?'

Before the men took boxes of mangoes, bananas, papayas, tomatoes and red chillies to the food market, a maze of edible colours behind Santo Domingo, they helped the women unload their sacks of merchandise. The women then carried the weight of their work on their foreheads, leather head-straps tied to sacks on backs, and they walked through the stalls as if they were stooped hunchbacks. As they replenished the stock in their cooperative businesses, they discussed the terrible events of the weekend: a man-made storm, the plague of the Cardenistas, a brave young martyr, a fallen shaman and a broken father.

Maria and Horatio were excused from their usual duties. Instead, leaving the others behind, they walked south towards the central plaza and past a morning's traffic of Maya off to market and backpackers off to breakfast, the latter grabbing tables under Coca-Cola parasols and brushing off kids trying to sell them chewing gum and counterfeit cigarettes. Turning right and then left, they reached the street of 14 de Septiembre and stopped outside a former colonial mansion, with walls painted a brighter shade of yellow than neighbouring houses and whose red-tiled roof was in a better state of repair.

'Are you sure that you don't need me?' Horatio asked his mother. He touched a shiny brass plaque that bore the initials 'CONPAZ'.

'Of course I am,' Maria replied, nodding hard. 'You go and do what you have to do. This may take some time and I don't want it to disrupt your own plans.' She kissed him on the cheek and straightened the bandage round his forehead.

'OK Mamá.' He wiped his cheek on his WWF T-shirt, spiked up his hair, slanted his bandage again and looked around him. 'Only if you're sure.'

'I'm sure. And it's not as if I hold much hope here. A Tzotzil woman isn't going to change President Zedillo's policy towards us. Besides, you know how I feel about these patronizing peace observers. What do they know about our lives? Best to stick with our own people, our own solutions, right?'

'Right,' he nodded at her. 'I'll meet you back at the truck in about three hours.'

'Good luck.'

'You too, Mamá.'

His mother having gone inside, a thick wooden door closing behind her, Horatio walked on, his heart beating fast. He pulled out an old bus ticket from the back pocket of his jeans and read the handwriting of a Zapatista soldier, a boy of his own age called Adolfo, whom he had met by chance, about a month ago, in San Felipé's fields of maize.

'Carlos – un taxi – Bak Café – Insurgentes – Xibalba.'

In the confusion of a Zapatista stand-off against the paramilitaries, Adolfo had lost the rest of his patrol. While Horatio gave him water from his canteen and tortillas from his Tupperware, Adolfo talked of the repression of the Maya Chol people, the communities of Tila in northern Chiapas. He described how anyone who opposed the will of Mexico's ruling PRI Party was affected: Catholic Catechists, Zapatistas and members of opposition parties were either threatened or murdered. Forced to forfeit their homes, maize, beans and cattle, the boy's family hid in the mountains under bivouacs of torn bin-liners. Although the government promised to assist them, the Chol dissenters, the victims, were instead arrested by the police. Accusing them of crimes they did not commit, calling them terrorists and 'narcotraficantes', drug smugglers, the police jailed them without trial. When his father was sent to the Cerro Hueco State Prison, Adolfo joined the EZLN. With his new comrades, who only fired their guns in defence, he vowed to defend the refugees and the surviving Chol communities. Before he departed under the cover of forest, he scribbled down the name and address of Carlos. If the violence spread to San Felipé, the young soldier had promised that his godfather would help.

Aryans in disrespectful shorts blocked the arched walkway under the Palacio Municipal, a creamy colonial-style building to the west of the central plaza. Dispatched from an air-conditioned bus, they consulted maps and guidebooks for some inspirational direction, ignorant of the queue of straw hats and huipiles, the locals penned in by elongated bodies and Gore-Tex accessories. Horatio looked up at the giraffe-like aliens with their beards and badly groomed, long blond hair. Pushing his way past hairy white legs, he wondered how the ancestors of goofy wooden folk could have crushed the Aztec and ancient Maya elite.

He crossed the road, went past the budget hostels and craft shops on Insurgentes Street, and spotted the sign of the Bak Café. A white taxi-cab was parked outside the eatery's front of peeling orange paint, a menu of three Ts, 'Tacos, Tortillas and Tostados', scribbled on a blackboard in a dirty window. He checked the address on the bus ticket and, glancing back over his shoulder and roughing up his spikes of hair, entered the small café.

At the rear of a smoke-filled room and overlooking rows of empty tables, a double-chinned chef laboured over a charcoal grill. Like the fat off the chop that he tended to, sweat dripped on hot coals and fizzed. The door to the café opened and the chef looked up from the skewered meat.

Horatio's heart raced harder than it had done in any basketball match that he had played in. He avoided contact with the chef's piggy eyes and sat at the table farthest from the grill. On the table next to him and behind the sports section of *La Jornada* newspaper, was a grey-haired man, a Mestizo, the café's only other patron. Horatio quickly picked up a laminated menu to hide behind.

A waitress appeared from a door to the kitchen. A limp in her walk, she approached Horatio. The menu shook in his hands.

'Good morning,' she said. Her warmness surprised him and he lowered the menu.

'Hello,' Horatio replied. He picked at his bandage as he intermittently glanced at the man behind the newspaper, the dirty windows and the staring chef.

'What happened to you, then?' She pointed at his head.

Horatio removed his hand from his bandage and instead scratched the WWF logo on his chest.

'Basketball, señora.'

'Hmm, if you say so.' The waitress turned to face the chef and they both smiled at each other. She faced Horatio again. 'From your Yankee T-shirt and black eyes, I'd have said a fight. But that's none of my business. What do you want? We're not cheap here.'

He felt his heart beating hard again.

'Water . . . please.' The dryness in his mouth made him stutter.

'Anything else?' she asked, her eyes narrowing.

Horatio looked around him. The grey-haired man looked preoccupied with his newspaper, while the sizzling stove put the chef out of earshot. It was now or never for him to ask her.

'Yes,' he whispered. 'I'd like to book a taxi. To go to . . .' He pulled out the bus ticket. 'Xibalba,' he read the Zapatista's handwriting. 'I have friends there.' He searched her face for reassurance, but she gave him none.

'Xibalba?' the waitress replied, her abruptness making him drop the bus ticket to the table. 'Listen, boy, I'm no taxi service and, even if I was, I'm not the idiot to believe in a fictional place called *Xibalba*. Now I suggest you leave and stop wasting my time. You can get your water elsewhere.'

'But . . .'

'You!' A man's voice shouted out from behind him.

Horatio jumped in his chair. The newspaper lowered on the adjacent table and he saw a wrinkly face stare at him through a pair of round spectacles.

'What do you know of Xibalba?' the man asked, folding his newspaper. 'Who gave you that?' He pointed at the bus ticket, which was back in Horatio's shaking hand.

Horatio tried to swallow, but his dry mouth wouldn't allow it.

'Adolfo, señor,' he croaked, avoiding the man's stare by looking down at the table. 'He said that I could find Carlos here. And that I should ask for a taxi to Xibalba.'

'You saw Adolfo?' The man's voice softened. He stood up and sat down opposite Horatio. The limping waitress sat next to him and Horatio could smell the spice of chillies on her black shirt. 'When exactly did you see Adolfo?' the man asked.

'A month ago, in the fields of San Felipé, where I live.'

For his brave young brother, Horatio pulled himself together and recounted the encounter with the fugitive soldier. Adolfo, he told them, had said that if the paramilitaries were to attack his village, he should contact Carlos, using the password Xibalba. He pointed at his bandage and bruises and described the night of the full moon. Should he refuse to fight the Zapatistas, he repeated the threat of Commandant Hernandez, he would also be killed.

'What is your name, boy?' the man asked, his spectacles catching the sun that shone through cloudy windows.

'Horatio Gomez, señor.'

'I'm sorry, Horatio, but Adolfo is still missing.' The man took off his glasses and Horatio observed the sadness in his eyes. 'You are the last person, who we know of, to have seen him.'

'You know Adolfo?'

'He was my godson.' The man looked down at the table and at the handwriting on the bus ticket.

'You are Carlos?'

The waitress and the chef keeping an eye on some pedestrians outside, a small group of bearded backpackers, Carlos led Horatio into the kitchen, where it was safer to talk.

Maria leaned against the truck. The meeting with CONPAZ was as short-lived and as inconclusive as she had expected. A diminutive bureaucrat, an uninspiring Latino, greeted her from behind a large antique desk. Speaking to him over neat stacks of paper, an apparent obsession of the man, Maria repeated the story for the umpteenth time. In between bashing the keys of his typewriter and wiping the sweat off his bald patch, the man interrupted her: 'Are you sure that they were Cardenistas? Did you provoke the attack in any way? How old did you say your son was? Where exactly did they shoot him?' Maria responded as diligently as she could, resisting the urge to throttle the little man or probe him with her own questions: *'Is Mexico City nice at this time of year? Have you ever brought anyone to justice to justify your salary?'* What really maddened her were his doe-eyed, *'I can feel your pain'* expression, and a look that pinned his eyeballs to his eyebrows like a rabbit drunk on windfall. If the little man really wanted to know what life was like in Chenalho, she thought, he should have got his scrawny arse over to San Felipé to see the lifeless body of her boy, the blood in the dust and the ashes of her home. Observing him as he fumbled with the paper in his typewriter, she had decided against such a suggestion. All that the meeting had accomplished was a reaffirmation that Horatio was right. Outside the big wooden door, by the brass plaque, she wiped a tear off her cheek and hoped that her son had achieved more than she had done.

With the exception of Horatio, all the men and women had returned, with half-empty maize sacks and boxes, to the meeting point by the church. Maria circled the truck and mumbled to herself. She shuffled her thoughts and placed her concern for Horatio beneath the list of to-dos for the funeral: the candles, the copal incense, the flowers, Lucio's posh, *her* posh. When she returned to San Felipé, she would finish clearing out Urbano's clothes – what little of them were left, the fire destroying most of them – and she would check on how Lucio had fared with the construction of the open-faced coffin. The next day, the three Gomezs, followed by the rest of the village, would proceed through the streets with the wooden box raised on their shoulders, Urbano's face exposed to the heavens. To a wailing fanfare, they would lower him into a hole in the ground and she, the mother, would toss the confetti of her dead son's belongings into the grave. The other mourners, the entire village, would then take it in turns to throw in stems of yellow marigolds and gourds of holy water.

'Mamá!'

She turned round and saw her Horatio.

'Where have you been?' she asked, tapping her fingers on the truck's rusty bonnet. 'You've held everyone up, including me. Don't you realize that we have your brother's funeral to prepare for?'

'I have much . . .' he paused to catch his breath, 'to tell . . . The Zapatistas . . . they . . .'

'Shush. You can tell me what happened on the journey back. But you must keep it quiet from the others. Hear me?'

'Yes . . . Mamá.'

Bracing his hands and arms together, he provided his mother with a step into the back of the truck. Everyone else on board, he swung himself up and sat down on the bench beside her. The truck backfired and it rattled out of San Cristóbal de las Casas.

Located in the Zona Hotelera of Cancún, sixteen hours from San Cristóbal de las Casas by first-class bus, the Aquamarina Beach Hotel displayed a 'NO VACANCIES' sign in its tinted reception window. A coach pulled up and unloaded a cargo of day-trippers. Dressed in T-shirts and shorts, clutching day-glo rucksacks and bottles of water, the pink-skinned tourists had returned from a day of traipsing around Mayan ruins. Two teenage girls broke free from the group and ran a samba through the hotel foyer, their sneakers skating on polished marble floors as they neared a beachfront swimming pool. The taller of the two, her hair dyed black as opposed to her friend's blond, dropped her rucksack on a sun lounger and pulled off her Boston Breakers T-shirt.

'Hey, Erin,' the girl called out to her buddy, who was trapped around the ankles by the latest fashion for ridiculously long toggles and unnecessarily large pockets. 'Last one in has to kiss Jonathan, "the lotion", McCallister at La Boom.' No time to remove her black shorts and strip down to her bikini, she flicked off her sneakers and dived into the pool.

'Unfair,' Erin replied, working her way out of her shorts. 'That's not on, Rachel.'

'No, you're right.' Rachel spat out a fountain of chlorinated water. 'That's tonight's entertainment fixed.' Erin dive-bombed next to her and a wave knocked her under. She resurfaced and flicked her hair out of her eyes, 'Was that necessary?'

'There is no way in hell that I'm going to kiss that guy,' Erin said, also spitting.

'Hola, girls,' a man shouted out at the other end, the shallow end, of the pool.

Jonathan waded through the water as if he was an albino hippo, his blubber whitened by high-factor sun lotion. When he could no longer touch the bottom, he swam, or rather flapped his stubby arms, towards the two girls.

'You and the witch going to Ladies Night?' He doggy paddled around Erin. Waves crashed over the pool's edge.

'Well howdy, hippo,' Rachel said, gliding between them. 'Erin over here was just talking about you.'

'Lezzie Goth.'

'I see that you've been sucking up lotion again.' She pointed at the oily slick that ran off his shoulders.

'Aren't witches supposed to dissolve in water?'

'Yeah, but not greasy water.'

'Slag.'

'Slug.'

'Break it up you two.' Erin pulled Rachel back. 'Look,' she addressed Jonathan, 'if I say that we are going to La Boom, will you leave us alone? This is our vacation as well.'

'Hey, babe, chill. I promise.'

'Great. So you can now adios out of here.'

'Have yourself a deal there, honey puss.'

Jonathan paddled to the pool's steps. He heaved himself out of the water and, walking to a pina colada and a bag of potato chips by a sun lounger, puffed up his wet and clingy trunks. The girls, watching him from the safe distance of the pool, giggled at his tiny secret.

'Urgh.' Rachel closed her eyes for a second. 'He's so gross. Check out those tubas for legs and those bristles on his back.'

'I thought that you went for that pale look, Morticia.'

Rachel splashed Erin's smile.

'Hey, c'mon, before I hit twenty, turn serious, I can still behave like a teenager. Anyway, it's only a little experimentation with some hair-dye, nothing permanent. I kind of like switching identities. My dad always said that I'd make a great spy.' She raised an eyebrow. 'And black makes me feel sexy.'

'What?' Erin said, frowning as she wiped the water off her face. 'You feel sexy looking like an extra from the *Day of the Dead*? You're weird.'

'Well it sure beats being ordinary, Erin.'

'Hey, I'm not ordinary. I just think that you should maybe have, well, stuck with natural brown. Just take it from a concerned friend. You're more likely to pull the Prince of Darkness than Prince Charming.'

'Thanks for the advice, Oprah, but you conveniently forget that if it weren't for the Morticia look, I'd have to share slippery Jonathan with you. Besides, what is wrong with the Prince of Darkness? A dark and mysterious man sounds like a dream to me.'

'Well, he's going to remain a dream round here.'

'Too true.' Rachel observed the pale and pink bodies around the pool. 'The only brains in Cancún are the reefs of Brain Coral.'

'Come on,' Erin said, as she paddled away from Rachel, 'let's grab a couple of daiquiris here and then finish off that tequila back in the room. To survive the night I'm going to need all the help that I can get.'

They swam to the pool's bar, sat on submerged coconut shells under a palm-thatched shade, and Rachel ordered them one strawberry and one pineapple daiquiri.

'Your room number, señoritas?' the barman asked, passing them their drinks and trying to look cool behind bug-eyed shades.

'338,' Rachel replied in Spanish.

'That's just so good,' Erin said, sucking on her cocktail.

'The daiquiris or my Spanish?'

'What?'

'Nothing.' Rachel sighed. 'Do we have to go back to college? I say we drop out and go travelling round Mexico.'

'We could take the barman's job off him.'

'I'm not sure about that. Cancún isn't me. I could do with exploring a bit of real Mexico. I mean where's all that jungle the brochure said there was?'

'You and your darn jungle. I say we just relax and make the most of it. You can go backpacking and search for your soul another time – and then you can take someone else with you.'

The girls took a late-deal vacation, an all-inclusive trip, to cele-brate the end of their freshman year at Boston University. It was after watching the Red Sox suffer another defeat by the Yankees, when they were sitting with the 'Bleacher Creatures', the college kids in Fenway Park, that they decided upon a plan of escape. When the pasting was over, the Yankees stopped firing balls at the Citgo sign on the horizon, they trudged towards the bars on Lansdown Street. Using Rachel's ID card, a cut-and-paste job on her older sister's card, they ordered a couple of blueberry beers at Jillian's Bar. While Erin fingered a combo of mozzarella sticks, chicken wings and crispy potato skins, Rachel opened her rucksack. Between a book entitled *Neotropical Phyllostomids* and a paper on 'Indigenous Conservation Practices', she pulled out a brochure on Mexico.

'Here you go,' Rachel said, pushing the brochure across the table. 'Turn to page seven. It fits our budget, is available for our dates and has jungle.'

Erin opened the brochure to page seven. She looked puzzled.

'Cancún? You sure, Rach? Isn't that place like a real redneck den?'

'Yes, but we can use it as a base to go exploring from. And since when have you been put off by rednecks? Didn't you used to date one?'

'Very funny.' Erin looked at the photographs of white beaches and luxury spa hotels, and read the passage about 'unbeatable, 24/7 nightlife'. 'I kind of see where you're coming from. I'm only missing the piece about beaches full of intelligent, handsome and single guys.'

'Yeah, well, they have those and monkeys and snakes and all. Come on, sis.'

'OK, you have yourself a partner. But I'm not going on any jungle treks with you. You know how much I hate bugs.'

Apart from an urge for adventure, a chance to see and not just read about the tropics, there was another reason why Rachel wanted to get the hell out of Boston. At Scott Jackson's keg party, a jock's birthday celebration, she had one of her alcohol incidents. It was by a barrel of Old Milwaukee Best that she found herself slurring at Scott, who took a shine, a very intimate shine, to her new ebony hair. Somewhere along the hazy chain of events, she could not remember exactly when or where, was a kiss and a slap. Even though it was Scott who lunged first, took advantage of her inebriated state, Liz Butterworth, Scott's current squeeze, had slapped her and not him. The boys chanting *'Catfight, catfight'*, Rachel sobered up in record time and grabbed her coat. Not that she gave a damn, but Liz was still not speaking to her when she left for Mexico.

'At least you have Ecuador to look forward to,' Erin said, rocking on her coconut seat and squashing a slice of pineapple into the bottom of her glass. 'I wish that my course allowed me to bum off to South America. Us historians don't go further than the departmental library. It totally sucks.'

'And it can't come a day too soon.' Rachel smiled. 'Lectures in Quito, a whole month's research in the rainforest, ten days on the Galapagos Islands, two weeks on the Pacific coast, day-trips to Inca cities in the Andes. How's that for a programme?'

'It's unfair, that's what it is.' Erin slurped the dregs of her cocktail.

'I'm just training to conserve the world's fragile ecosystems,' Rachel had to raise her voice to be heard over her friend's slurping. 'You should be grateful. If it weren't for the likes of me, you'd be breathing fart in old age.'

'Nice thought, Rach.' Erin put down her empty glass. 'I suppose this hard training of yours will also have unpleasant side effects, like a healthy tan, a supermodel figure and a ruggedly handsome explorer as a boyfriend.'

'Do I detect some jealousy in my girlfriend?'

'Me? Jealous? Never. Why should I be, when I've got Tolstoy to read in cold and snowy Massachusetts, and only a mug of cocoa to warm me in bed?'

'If it's any consolation to you,' Rachel knocked back her drink before continuing, 'it's not going to be a picnic with the parrots. Think of my jungle amigos: bugs the size of Frisbees, vampire bats, man-eating crocs, venomous snakes, cannibalistic locals. OK, so I made the last bit up – at least I don't think that the Huaorani people have a taste for nineteen-year-old white girls.'

'OK, so it's going to be a little tough. But so is a keg party. And at those you don't get a tan.'

'Don't remind me.' Rachel rolled her eyes and Erin laughed.

The girls left the pool and went to their room. After they had showered and moisturized, tended to the day's sunburn, they laid out their wardrobes on their beds and chose what to wear to La Boom nightclub. Erin picked a white linen dress, something to show off her tan, while Rachel settled for a flowery sarong, something cheap from a Maya market, and a canary yellow shirt, the only smart top that she had packed.

'Wow,' Erin said, looking into a mirror and seeing her friend standing behind her, 'you look great. Now you just need to change your hair.'

'Thanks for the compliment,' Rachel replied, combing her hair with her fingers. 'You must appreciate that it's difficult trying to keep up with the princess. Nice dress by the way.'

'I can barely fit into it. Too many Domino's pizzas and blueberry beers.'

'Don't be a jerk. You look great.'

Picking up her margarita and leaving Erin to measure her imaginary tummy and bum in the mirror, Rachel walked over to the room's balcony and looked out across the Caribbean. The ocean was a larva of oranges, light blues and pinks, its rippled surface reflecting the early evening sky. Behind a large satellite dish on a flat roof, the dying sun cast light and shadow across the pool and strip of private beach. She lay down on a sun lounger, lifting up her head to stay with the view, and resembled one of the reclining Chac Mool statues that she had seen at the altar ruins, her laid out stomach primed to receive a sacrificial heart, a chilled margarita. In her daydream, closing her eyes and listening to the sound of lapping water, she saw Maya priests in feathered headdresses, chimneys of smoky incense, splendorous ceremonies atop pyramidal temples and warriors blowing conch shell trumpets.

A boom of music, more synthesized than a hooting shell, opened her eyes. A pirate's galleon, a crew of drunken teenagers on forty-dollar tickets, sailed in front of the hotel. Hollering like howler monkeys, they shot tequila shots on the decks and the guys dropped their surfer shorts at the coastline. She climbed off the lounger, turned her back on the underage conquistadors and spotted Erin in the doorway to the balcony.

'What is it?' Erin asked. 'You been dreaming again?' She sipped her drink.

'What?' Rachel replied, almost spilling her drink down her sarong, 'Oh, yeah, I was drifting off under the spell of the Caribbean, thinking of sacrifices on Mayan temples, when

Blackbeard and Jose Cuervo suddenly showed up.' She pointed at the booze-cruise sailing off on a fiery sea.

'I see.' Erin raised her glass. 'Here's to another week of your tripped out moments. To you, sis.'

They chinked glasses.

'To you as well, sis,' Rachel said.

Hoping to recapture the connection that she had felt and yet couldn't place, Rachel looked at the blood-red horizon, waiting to be bewitched again. The pirates had sailed on, and yet she could still hear the screams and the boom of bass. She finished her margarita, shook her head and followed Erin downstairs to the party.

Four

In Justin's local supermarket, a pensioner chased a paper trail of 'REDUCED TO CLEAR' labels. On the heels of a shelf stacker, who moved down the aisles as if he was the Pied Piper of bargain-hunters, a sticker-gun for a pipe, he pulled up his tartan trousers. An unwashed odour replaced the smell of freshly baked bread. Stretched at the waist in fatter years, the man's trousers were held up by a loop of garden twine, and his grey underwear ballooned out from under his concave belly. Through a magnifying glass tied to his waistband, he read the fresh prices on the not-so-fresh food. His false teeth whistled at the bargains he snatched, his basket overflowing with dented cans of cat food.

Justin slipped on a pool of liquid, the remnants of a bottle of gin, in the 'Beers, Wines and Spirits' section of the supermarket. Dropping his basket and his leather bag, his pinstriped body landed beside a pair of sandals and socks. The pensioner's hand dropped down to Justin's face. From the floor, Justin looked up at the hand's bulbous green veins and blackened fingernails.

'Thanks, but I'm fine,' he said to the pensioner, scrambling to his feet and brushing splinters of glass off his trousers. His knees and thighs were drenched in alcohol.

'Suit yourself, then,' the pensioner grunted, picking up his basket. He struggled with the weight of the cans of cat food.

'Can I, umm, give you a hand with that?' Justin pointed at the pensioner's basket.

'Eh?'

'The basket. Can I help? Those cans look heavy.'

'Don't patronize me!' The pensioner's raised voice prompted the heads of other shoppers to turn in the aisles. 'You're the clumsy idiot that fell, not bloody me.'

'What?'

'Got a hearing problem as well? Tough, isn't it? Give your ear a flick. Could be a loose battery connection. Usually works for me.'

Justin smiled and, diverting his eyes from the cataracts of his

55

companion, saw a woman browsing varieties of Highland mineral water. She reminded him of Beth: she wore her hair the same way.

'Not bad.' The pensioner wouldn't shut up.

'What?'

'Her. The bird checking out the posh water. Not bad looking.'

'You sure that you don't want a hand with that basket?'

'I'd get her phone number if I were you.'

'Really?' Justin wished that he had ordered a takeaway, avoided contact with people. 'How do you know that I haven't a wife or girlfriend waiting for me back at home?'

The pensioner pointed his dirty finger at Justin's basket: a lasagne for one, a half-litre of semi-skimmed milk, a bag of oven-roasted crisps, a copy of the *Evening Standard* and a single can of Grolsch.

'It's not like you're exactly thriving by yourself.'

'I was working late in the office. Anyway, what's behind your excuse of a diet?' Justin looked down at the content's of the pensioner's basket.

'My cats. The little bastards won't stop breeding. They'll only eat this posh stuff, which I can only afford on discount. Fussy little buggers they are.'

Justin felt a strange affinity with the pensioner. Their shared loneliness bridged the age and poverty gap.

'Here, don't be so stubborn. Let me help, please.' Not waiting for a reply, Justin took the basket off him and they walked to the checkout.

'Hi,' name-tagged Shirley said, 'are you paying separately or together?'

She addressed them, Justin thought, as if they were father and son.

'Separately,' the pensioner huffed.

'Together, please.' Justin placed the cans of cat food with his dinner and night's entertainment for one on the conveyor belt. At the other end and pushing his crisps, beer and a newspaper out of the way, the pensioner bagged his cans.

'I don't need handouts,' the pensioner said, noticing the crisp fifty-pound note in the checkout girl's hands. 'Spoilt the youth of today are – they don't know how easy they've got it. If it weren't for my lot, who grew up on rations and fought for your freedom, you wouldn't have that sort of money to flash about. I can tell you . . .' A faint and electronic jingle distracted him. 'That you making that bloody noise?'

Justin held his bag to his ear. He fumbled with the straps and pulled out a mobile phone from under a report on Central American Investments. 'Number withheld' flashed on the screen. He let it ring.

'It's probably work. Sorry.' He held the phone to his chest, but the annoying ring tone that Dan had selected as a joke wouldn't go away.

'Answer it or turn the damn thing off,' the pensioner barked, his teeth whistling. 'Bloody mobile phones, they should all be . . .'

'Leave him alone, will ya?' Shirley interrupted, pinching her nose because of the old man's smell.

Justin pressed the call receive button.

'Justin Callaghan,' he whispered into the phone, looking at the queue behind him. 'The police?' He saw the woman like Beth, two bottles of mineral water tucked under her arm, look at her watch and shake her head. 'If it's about the riot, the protester that was hit over the back of the head by one of your peacekeeping officers, I've already given my statement, made my complaint.' There was a pause. 'It's not about her? You're from Kent?'

'Your change . . . love?' Shirley raised a handful of notes and coins to no one.

'Weirdo,' Shirley said, exchanging her 'customer is always right' face for the 'customer is a stupid dick' face. She rang a buzzer and the stacker removed the abandoned goods. 'Sorry about that,' she said to the woman clutching mineral water and shrugging. 'Some people, eh?'

'Shame,' the pensioner said, picking up his bag of cat food, 'I wanted to thank him.'

Stumbling up Upper Street, his tears turning street lamps and shop fronts into a kaleidoscope of multicoloured light, Justin pushed his way past drunken and glum-faced commuters. He rubbed his eyes on his suit's sleeves, alternating left and right, and raised his elbows up and forearms down as if he was swimming the crawl along the pavement. The abrasion of wool on his wet skin turned his cheeks red, the blush and his streaming eyes attracting the stares of others. *Watch where you're going, arsehole!*' one shouted, after he nearly sent a kebab and baseball cap flying. *'Shit! You stupid, fucking moron!'* a man in a suit exclaimed, the clash spraying tears into the air. Stepping on a mongrel's crossed paws and kicking over a collection box of coins, a former McDonald's milkshake, he instigated a yelp and a *'Are you going to pick that up or what, wanker?'* from a moving sleeping bag. In Justin's head, a policeman repeated a textbook delivery of breaking bad news to the next of kin: *'I regret to have to inform you that,'* the copper had begun. He wished that it was just a night-mare, something for daylight to erase, and he held no conscience as he replaced actual suicide for imagined murder. *'Bring it on, Grim Reaper,'* he goaded in denial.

Past a queue of people at a bus stop, vomit burned the back of his mouth and he clung on to a lamp-post to steady himself. As a young mother cautiously steered a pram around him, he swallowed down the acidity and pushed himself off the lamp-post. Walking on, he tried to rationalize the irrational, interrogating circumstances with an unanswerable *'Why?'* and *'What if?'* Why hadn't she said anything to him on Saturday? *What if* they had discovered her earlier? *What if* he had been there for her? *What if* he hadn't been so screwed up himself? Lunacy is hereditary, right? The questions rolled through his head as if they were bullets in a spinning barrel, incomplete answers blowing his brains out in a no-win game of Russian roulette.

The constable had told him that his mother had been dead since either Saturday evening or early Sunday morning. Next to her body were empty packets of Diazepan, the antidepressants prescribed to her by her GP, and a half-drunk bottle of gin. They had found no note and the police doctor, the constable had said in a calm and matter-of-fact manner, believed that she had secretly de-medicated in order to save up enough pills. The suicide, therefore, as if it mattered, had been planned weeks in advance. But it was not until this morning, Tuesday, when her body was discovered. A neighbour – he suspected one of those who had complained about the state of her garden – who was collecting for some local children's charity, had visited her house and found the body on the living room's filthy carpet. The constable had asked Justin to identify her in the morning.

He crossed the road, a scooter swerving around him. *'Idiot, do you want to die?'* coming from behind a blacked-out visor, and bereavement turned to blame and anger. How could she have left him? *He needed her.* Was he not a good enough reason for her to stick around? *He'd stuck by her.* Had he failed her? *He visited whenever he could.* Did she not love him? *She was all that he had.* Ashamed at presiding over his mother's trial and execution, her suicide, he begged forgiveness. Adjourning the kangaroo court in his head, revoking its countenance to wash her blood from his hands, which he rubbed across his pale, drawn and wet face, he succumbed to her poison and ingested his very own escape. Like his mother, he wanted to asphyxiate his blood and numb the pain. But, unlike her, he knew that he would leave no one behind. There would be no notable next of kin, no number for the police to call, no kid having to abort his trip to the supermarket and take the morning off work to view his mum's corpse.

Walking down a street of terraced houses and stopping outside a converted Victorian pub, he pulled out a set of keys from his trouser pocket. His sight rinsed from his eyes, he felt for the front door key. After several failed attempts, the keyhole seen in double vision and his sense of touch as poor as his eyesight, he unlocked the door and punted his leather bag into a dark hallway. He switched on the lights and flinched at the whiteness of his flat. Unopened junk mail, bills and fliers for pizza delivery, cleaning and minicab firms, memos of life going on with or without him, littered a 'welcome home' doormat. He stepped on them and went straight to the kitchen. Dropping his gin-soaked suit jacket to a stripped-pine floor, he poured himself a pint of water and a tumbler of whisky. He carried his drinks and the whisky bottle to a glass coffee table, sunk into a leather sofa and lit a cigarette. Chaining his drinking and smoking, deaf to night buses and cats and drunks screaming and brawling outside, he stared at the blank screen of his widescreen TV.

'I know that you'll look after her,' his father had said outside the Prince Arthur, brushing a wasp off his pint of Speckled Hen and a tear off his cheek. He smiled, looked around the pub garden, at the kids playing tag amongst the daffodils, and then touched his son's hand on the table. 'You have done so well in life, made me such a proud a father. It makes it so much better to know that I'm leaving behind . . .'

'Please, Dad, stop it.' Justin gripped his father's hand.

'But I mean it. I couldn't have asked for a better son.'

'Dad . . .'

'There's no one else for her, certainly not her family. Once I'm gone, you will be all that she has.'

His head bowed, observing the weeds that grew round the table's legs, Justin looked up and saw his father's face and tears fade out on the blank TV screen.

From the inside pocket of his jacket, which remained crumpled on the floor, his mobile beeped twice. It teased him with the prospect of a message, words from someone that cared and who could be bothered to text. 'We found no letter. I'm sorry,' the copper repeated down the phone. He carried his jacket back to the sofa. 'LOW BATTERY', the mobile quipped. He scrolled through his address book: client, client, colleague, client, office, client, colleague, deceased mum, landlord, client, bank manager ... Pausing at 'BETH', knocking back the whisky and topping up his glass, he toyed with pressing the red or the green button. Even if she decided to take the call, he imagined her in candle-light with her new architect boyfriend, reminded himself that she was a work colleague and not a real friend, what good could she have done? The red button won: there was no one for him to call. There was a triumphant '*dah-dah*' when he switched the phone off. He looked at his watch, emptied and refilled his tumbler, and counted the hours till he should leave for Gravesend.

'You're sick,' Beth said, standing over Dan's bald patch and looking at an anatomical puzzle on his computer screen, 'What's that coming out of his backside? That's not his? No way. Is *it*?'

'Yeah, it's his anus,' Dan grinned. 'Read the instructions that came with it. Might stop the same thing from happening to you, when you're down that gym of yours.'

He called up the attachment's explanatory text and, in their own time, Beth trying not to look at the picture in the neighbouring window, they read how the unfortunate protagonist was a competitor in a Pennsylvanian power-lifting championship. Pulling in his stomach and pushing extra hard, the man had attempted to beat his personal best in the squat lift. At mid-stretch, the man giving it his all, including his arse, the lift was interrupted by a pop and a splatter.

'Forward it on to Justin,' Beth said, squinting at the picture, 'I've always worried about him in the gym. This might calm him down a bit.'

'Like it,' Dan said, spinning in his chair as he played with his mouse. He fired off the email and opened up a spreadsheet. 'So where is your Hercules? It's not like him to be late.'

'He's not my anything, OK? I've no idea where he is. He tells me nothing anymore. Perhaps he found a life.'

'Don't tell me that 'golden boy' was on the razz during a school night? Nice one, Justin.' Dan picked his nose. 'So are you seeing that Jeremy guy now?'

'What?'

'The architect – have you shagged him yet?'

'That's none of your business.' Beth glared at Dan.

'Have you told Justin?'

'Well, he knows that I'm dating again, if that's what you mean.'

'But you and him are still mates?'

'Justin doesn't do mates; you should know that.' She walked back to her desk and opened a Word document titled 'Lindo Conference Call'. 'I know that he has problems with his mum,' she continued, printing two copies of the memo, 'but he doesn't have to behave as if the whole world is against him. And it's not like he's the only one with family problems. I mean, I don't speak to my father anymore, and yet what's so rare about that these days.' She paused and looked out of the office's large windows. Rain pounded against the glass. 'But I do worry about him. Things mightn't have worked out between us, but I do consider him a friend, even if he doesn't think the same of me.'

'Of course he thinks the same of you.' Dan collected the two handouts from the printer and handed her a copy. 'And don't go worrying yourself about Callaghan. He knows how to look after himself. Shit, although I'd never say it to his face, I kind of admire the Spaniard for not wearing his heart on his sleeve. We all look after number one, right?'

'Yes, but . . .'

'Quiet.' Dan looked towards the lifts. A figure in a crumpled suit approached them.

Justin walked to his desk and switched on his computer. He put his suit jacket over the back of his chair and ignored the stares of his colleagues.

'Look who's Justin-time,' Dan smirked. 'Heavy night, lover boy?'

'What?' Justin replied, wiping the back of his hand over the stubble on his chin and the sheen on his forehead.

'Heavy night? I said.' Dan recoiled from the smell that sat next to him. 'Jesus, mate, you could have at least brushed your teeth and changed your clothes. You reek of booze and fags.'

'Sorry.' Justin cupped his hands around his mouth and sniffed. 'I was in a rush this morning.'

'Here, take a couple of these.' Beth passed him two mints from a tin on her desk. 'I don't want you fumigating any clients.' She didn't give him her usual morning smile.

'Thanks.' He crunched the mints between his teeth.

'If you get a moment and your hangover can face it, you might also want to look over the memo that I prepared at six this morning. You have remembered about the conference call?'

'Of course,' Justin replied, avoiding eye contact with her.

'So was she fit?' Dan said. He leaned over his desk and grinned at him.

'What?'

'The bird you pulled. Was she fit?'

'No, I mean, look, can you both just leave me alone and let me get on with some work.' He picked up a stack of papers, his psychiatric research on the Internet, and dropped it into a bin.

Dan returned to his spreadsheet, cover for surfing smut, and Justin caught his reflection, his unkempt hair and shadows under his eyes, on his monitor's screen. As his files loaded up, Word '97 welcomed him as a 'preferred customer', he saw his image mutate into the face of his dead mother, his black hair turning white and his eyelids closing. A nurse whispered in his ear and he nodded. 'Yes. It's her,' he confirmed. The job done, there being no doubt that it was his mother, he asked for permission to leave; he couldn't stand the smell of corpse and antiseptic for any longer. But he was told to stay. 'There are forms to fill in,' the nurse said; it came with dying, he learnt it all in one morning.

'I'm serious, Justin,' Beth said, creeping up behind him and tapping him on the shoulder. The ghost of his mother vanished from the screen. 'I don't give a shit what you get up to out of the office, but if your night of shagging and champagne screws up this deal.'

'You'll do what, exactly, Beth?' Justin looked up at her with his red eyes. 'Report me to that bitch in HR? Go on. Take me to the fucking cleaners. You'll be doing me a favour.'

'You're mad. I'll see you in the boardroom in five. Don't be late.' She turned her back on him and walked out of the office.

Dan sniggered and Justin stared at his monitor again. It was in the BMW, on the way back from the hospital, his mother's ashen face in the rear-view mirror, that he decided not to tell work. On the one hand was the stigma – a mother's suicide might make people question his own sanity – and on the other hand was the exposure to competitive sympathy, or *My experience of death is nastier than your experience of death.*' He dreaded the latter more than the former. In previous times of mourning, a Labrador at twelve and a father for his twenty-second, he had to put up with these professional mourners. Under an empathetically acceptable guise, they would use his tears to water boasts about their own morbid experiences. Imaginary points were scored for cause of death, suicide running a close second to murder, a father's cancer too common to be ranked, and one's creativity in the expression of grief: examples including a poem or a chintzy garden bench. The narcissistic narrators, at school, university or work, never cared much for what he had to say. They never listened; at least not properly. It was all about them and their own corpse, the living self-promoting themselves through sacrificial family, friends and pets. He imagined the bank, a place where every facet of one's life was entered into a tournament, from the size of your bonus, to the size of your house and your girlfriend's breasts, to be full of these necrophilious show-offs. The bastards would feed off his mother's body, alchemize Spanish flesh into golden stories for their line managers, who might secure them a promotion or pay rise because they like their teams to be tough and jolly good blokes. *'Fuck that,'* he thought, accelerating his BMW, speed cameras saluting him with flashes.

'Are you ready to fleece some diegos, then?' Dan stood up from his desk, stretched his arms and yawned.

'What?' Justin frowned.

'Oh, shit, I'm sorry mate. How is your Spanish mum?'

'I just want to check my emails.' He ticked Dan's forwarded jokes and jpegs for deletion.

'Whatever, Callaghan. Do what you want. I'll see you in there.' Clipping Justin round the back of the head with a notebook, Dan slouched off to the meeting.

'Hold on. I'll come with you.' He stopped deleting emails, the 'FW: power-lift shocker' saved from the trash bin, and took his file on Lindo's takeover bid of 'La Tela Maya'.

Sitting at the head of an executive-sized table, Beth looked up at her colleagues through thick-rimmed glasses. As if she was a teacher about to administer discipline, punish Justin for his unconscientious attitude, lack of team spirit, lack of any spirit, she tapped her papers on the table. Dan and Justin sat down either side of her, and the three of them huddled around a star-shaped speakerphone. Since the takeover bid was primarily Beth's baby, they all agreed that she chaired the call. So as to avoid participation in the setting out of their objectives, Justin volunteered to pour the coffee and distribute the chocolate biscuits. He was thankful that the meeting was a conference call: it freed the mentalist to pull silly faces away from the clients, and construct a checklist of things to do before the cremation. The burning was in the diary, on Saturday, in three days' time, and he was lucky to have got a slot. They had told him that they had a cancellation, someone's relatives considerately changing their mind and wanting a burial instead. The onset of autumn must be a popular time to die – a synchronism to the leaves falling off the trees – he pondered, pouring Beth a black coffee.

'Good morning, Miguel,' Beth said in Spanish, as she made contact with Lindo's HQ in Barcelona via the speakerphone.

'Good morning,' Dan shouted out in less perfect Spanish.

'Hi,' Justin mumbled.

'Are you sure that you're OK with that?' Beth asked, hanging up the call and beginning the meeting's post-mortem. 'Justin?'

'Sort of,' Justin replied, his mind still on what types of flowers to buy. He looked up at a clock on the wall before he faced Beth. 'From what I picked up, I mean, it seems fine to me.' He looked down at his notes, a Pollockesque scribble, and pretended to search for hidden answers in the maze of ink. He had no idea what he had volunteered to do. Something about a fact-finding mission to Mexico, scouting La Tela Maya, meeting some bloke called Hector Morales, the factory's MD, next week, were the limits of his comprehension. He found it hard enough to translate overexcited Spanish on a clear head, let alone a dead one.

'I know that it's not ideal, trust me, but this project means a lot to me and I'd be going if I could.' She sipped her coffee. 'If I'd known that this was going to happen, that Lindo would get cold feet over the purchase, then I wouldn't have booked my week off. But I can't cancel on Jeremy at this late stage. It was murder trying to book that cottage in the Lake District.'

'And the wife,' Dan said, 'would murder me if I was to miss our wedding anniversary.' He grabbed a biscuit. 'Though you have no sympathy from me, you lucky bastard. A trip to bloody Mexico? If I were single, I'd be jumping like a mad man at the opportunity. Plenty of your Latin types there as well. Have you ever been?'

'No. Can't say I have.' Justin finished his cold, black coffee and thought of who to invite on Saturday. The guestlist, so far, had stopped at himself, a priest, an undertaker and a corpse. When he had volunteered to fly to Cancún, Beth punching him in the arm to wake him up, Lindo having expressed concern over the bad PR that a sweatshop might bring to their 'globally responsible' brand, he was thinking of the bridge player, Mrs Ellis, the widow that his mother had talked of. He had decided to track her down.

'Well here's your chance,' Dan said, taking a bite out of his biscuit. 'Stop complaining,' he continued with his mouth full.

'I'm not complaining. You're the one who's complaining.'

'In a mood today, aren't we?' Dan flicked biscuit crumbs to the floor. 'Was she a dog, then?'

'What?'

'The girl you shagged.'

Justin ignored him and stood up from the table. As they walked out of the boardroom, grabbing files, papers, coffees and handfuls of biscuits, Beth took Justin to one side. She waited for Dan to leave before she said anything.

'Look, I'm not sure what your problem is, but if you're not up to this assignment, then say so now and we'll get back on the phone to Barcelona. Lindo are good clients of ours and I'm not having you screw things up out there. Our bonuses ride on this.'

'Are you questioning my professionalism, Beth?' Her face, he had spotted, was more venomous than sympathetic.

'No. But . . .' She moved closer to him, as if she was going to either slap or kiss him. 'So long as you know how important this is to me, that's all,' she said, her voice losing some of its icy edge. 'Have you thought about staying out there for a bit? A holiday might do you some good, and I know that they've got great beaches on the Yucatán.'

'Don't worry, I'll get the job done. And I'll give the holiday idea some thought.'

'You're a star, albeit it a very stinky star.' At long last she gave him that smile. 'But just watch yourself out there. If it really is a sweatshop, then I want to know. Lindo and the bank don't need that sort of adverse publicity. Best that we find out now, yes?'

'Sure.' He wondered if Mrs Ellis was listed in the phone directory.

'Oh, I suggest you check up on your jabs and start taking anti-malarial pills. I don't want you getting sick.'

'Sick? Oh, yeah, sure.'

The big day passed away as uneventfully and as quickly as the life it was supposed to celebrate. After watching some paedomorphic boy band on morning TV, who promoted their latest ballad to rob kids of their weekend's pocket money, Justin downed his third coffee, smoked his fourth cigarette and put on his black suit and tie. The drive to Gravesend was his third in only a week, a toing and froing record that he would never again have to repeat. He turned his car into the winding driveway of the crematorium, its furnace and chimney hidden behind evergreen trees, the smoke nowhere to be seen. It had rained the night before and the progenitive moisture, the smell of freshness, brought life where there was otherwise death. At the end of the drive and outside the entrance to an imposing redbrick building, he parked next to his mother's shiny new hearse. He patted down his hair, opened the car's door and breathed in the damp air.

A previous sitting left the chapel and sobbed by gaudy wreaths. Three generations forced their way to the front of the mourning line and read the prayers and tributes stapled to posies, prose and poems on flowery stationery, the 'in memories' of an old woman. In joyful ignorance of it all, a young girl skipped around a puddle and muddied her brand new patent leather slip-ons. Bored of the game of splash, she tugged on her mother's dress and whined *'Can we go now, pleeeeeaaase?'* The mother dabbed her tears with a silk handkerchief, stroked her daughter's head and promised her the new Westlife CD if she behaved herself.

'For granny's sake, darling, please.'

There was no such cavalcade or skipping child for Isabella Callaghan. Despite a good rummage through her house, a snoop through an empty address book and some research in Kent county's phone directory, he found neither a trace of Janet Ellis nor, indeed, a trace of any other friend or relative to see her off. He had thought, after a few whiskies and for not very long, about

66

calling his relatives in Spain. But why should they, he had silently debated by the water cooler at work, feel compelled to pay their dues to their fallen kin, who had prostituted herself to fashion and a Protestant? He was sure that his father's side of the family would have attended, if they were alive that is. For the late Edward Callaghan, like him, was an only child and both of his paternal grandparents were dead. The trifling turnout was a reminder of what awaited him.

'Good morning,' the undertaker said. 'You must be Justin.' Smiling as if it was a wedding and not a cremation, the man stretched out a white-gloved hand.

'Morning. Yes, I am. Pleased to meet you.' Forgetting the man's name, he shook the gloved hand. Because of his trip to Mexico, the preparations for the day had been done in such haste that he had little time to remember names. He had made most of the calls – to the priest, the florist and the undertaker – in cigarette breaks outside the bank, away from the ears of his colleagues.

'If you're ready, we can proceed to the chapel.'

Six pallbearers, who stood by the open boot of the hearse, shuffled their feet like they wanted to get a move on, hurry up their death-carrying duties so that they could go to the pub and watch football on satellite TV. Justin observed them as they grappled with his mother.

'Absolutely. You lead the way.'

The coffin on strangers' shoulders, feet marching in time to pre-recorded organ music, the tiny procession made a pitiful looking entrance into the chapel. Once inside, the pallbearers placed the coffin onto a raised dais – which was still warm from the cold corpse of the previous show – and, making sure that she wouldn't topple down and cause any embarrassment, pushed her on a bed of rollers. Sitting within her grisly reach and taking a front pew, not that there was a fight for a prime seat, Justin looked around the empty room. As if the chapel's interior designer was making an ironic link between saunas and crematoriums, the walls and pews were clad in cherry wood panels, and to what was otherwise a secular disposal unit, an altar, cross and lectern had been added as token religious features. He focused on a fake candle, a bulb on a plastic cylinder, which flickered intermittently under the cross.

The priest read from an abbreviated order of service: a set menu of prayers and tributes for those who had failed to construct their own, more personalized version. Since there was no congregation

– he didn't include the rent-a-mob of an undertaker and his six bored accomplices – Justin had felt it unnecessary to say a few words of remembrance; the priest had failed to convince him that God and the dead would still be listening. Settling for a Commendation without the trimmings, the service had barely started when it finished with The Lord's Prayer. A muffled 'Amen' cued the music and a hidden stagehand dropped the curtain, conveying Isabella Callaghan out of sight.

'Thank you both for your hard work,' Justin said to the undertaker and the priest, by the flowers at the exit. 'I really appreciate you both coming at such short notice. It was a lovely service. Delightful.' He looked down at a yellow-flowered wreath and the card that he had written the previous night: 'To Dear Mum, may you rest in peace with Dad. All my love, Justin.' He felt his eyes well up.

'It's such a shame that you couldn't contact your family in Spain,' the priest said, his ruddy cheeks suggesting a fondness for a post-funeral beverage. 'Do you not keep in touch with them?'

'I'm afraid that Mum fell out with her family. After dad died, it was just the two of us.' He prayed that the priest wouldn't suggest a pint down the road.

'You must have been very close to her.'

'We were.' He tried to smile. 'But there's no point in dwelling on the past. You've got to move on, right?'

'Yes, true, but you should also take time to grieve.'

'Of course.'

The priest and the undertaker hurried off to reset the stage for the next party, a small army of dark suits, black limousines and Mafiosi sunglasses in the car park. Justin punched his remote car key and watched the alpha mourners, the no-expenses spared cremation, rallying around the alcoholic priest. Running a hand through his uncombed hair and checking his mirrors for the image of his mother's mordant face, seeing only his green and bloodshot eyes, he started the engine. For background music, something to speed down the A2 with, he chose *One Hot Minute* by the Red Hot Chilli Peppers. The car accelerated down the driveway, jumping over speed bumps and splashing puddles, and he drove out of the evergreen forest and away from its smoky secret. With the riffs of 'Shallow Be Thy Game', the lyrics *'you'll never burn me, you'll never burn me, I'll be your heretic'* played at full volume, he left his mother's ashes to cool down.

Justin scrunched up the red-top tabloid that contained his half-eaten fish and chips. Ketchup and tartare sauce smeared over the bare breasts of a prostitute, he dropped the greasy package into the kitchen bin. He opened up a fresh packet of tissues, which he had bought for the funeral, and wiped his fingers and lips. A meal had seemed like a good idea when he was in the car, when he felt compelled to at least eat something, but the battered cod and soggy potato now stuck in his stomach. The pain deepened and he could not help but think of the topsy-turvy arse in Dan's email, the private soreness and the public humiliation.

He switched on the TV for some relief and companionship. A middle-aged woman, a teacher from Solihull who looked like she should really have known better, belted out a Celine Dion number on *Stars In Their Eyes*. He voted with his remote and the screen went blank. The quietness was stronger than ever – he was too uninspired to select a CD – and his stomach rolled over again. He ran upstairs, collapsing to his knees in a bathroom of Italian taps and mosaic tiles, dipped his head over the lavatory and puked. He flushed away the half-digested chips and tissue paper, dunked his head into a basin of cold water and, paranoid of catching his mother laughing behind him, looked into a mirror. Only a wet-haired sicko stared back.

Back downstairs, he hunted for activities to hurry along the evening. Fighting with the straps of his leather bag, he pulled out the tickets to Cancún and a *Lonely Planet Guide* to 'La Ruta Maya'. The book's cover, a touched-up photo of a palm tree on a beach and a jungle-strangled ruin, promised a destination of 'Tropical Beaches and a Land of Mystery'. He flicked through the pages and gave the pictures his own annotations: Indians in a market (*midget curios for amateur anthropologists*), a toucan in the jungle (*zoo*), white sands of the Caribbean (*watch out for the hypodermic syringes*), ancient ruins (*for modern despoilment*). Without his knowledge, let alone authority, Beth had added an extra week to his business trip. She had left the guidebook, with a silver bow wrapped around it, on his desk. On the inside cover, in red ink, she had scribbled:

'A perk from the company – go wild and have a great time, amigo.
With love,
Beth
xxx
PS: A box of fags and a bottle of tequila in and on return.'

Even Dan had bought him a going away gift. Yesterday, after smoking his tenth cigarette of the morning, four Marlboro Lights per break, he returned to his desk to find a new ring tone on his phone and a Swiss Army penknife by his keyboard.

'Sorry about the diego joke the other day,' Dan had said, 'I thought this might be handy for cutting limes or something. I can always exchange it for a Maglite torch, if you'd rather have one of those.'

Although he had no say in this enforced vacation, he thought that, perhaps, Beth was right, that his escape lay outside London. Determined not to go the way of his mother, burned by strangers, he skim-read the guidebook and paused at another montage of photos. One photo in particular arrested his attention. Pictures of a street market and a beached fishing boat passing him by, the pastel colours a blur, he gazed at a waterfall of bluish-green water, a cascade that tipped over a steep cliff face, an illustration to the chapter on 'Chiapas'. He could feel the coolness of the water on his irritable skin, the roar of the falls pleasantly deafening. As water seeped into his earlobes, the noise was replaced by silence. Submerged in the pool, flushed away like vomit, he at long last found the inspiration for his own exit; it was more fitting than an overdose in front of the TV. He immediately flicked to Chapter Three, to 'Chiapas', and read about a land of mountains, indigenous rebels, lost cities and deadly waterfalls.

When his eyes were dry and he could read no more, he closed the book and placed it on the coffee table, next to a line of empty tumblers and an overflowing ashtray. In a cupboard under the stairs and trapped under a vacuum cleaner, as well as a sports bag stuffed with a kid's collection of comic books, he retrieved his rucksack, a present from his father that he used to take on holidays in Norfolk. He slung it over his shoulder, dust rising off his back, ran upstairs again and raided his bedroom for some clothes for the journey: a pair of chinos and a collared blue shirt for business, and jeans and a lightweight fleece for a mountain trek. The clothes went in the mouth of the rucksack and Dan's penknife went in a side pouch. He lifted up his luggage, faltered downstairs and leant the rucksack against a wall in the hallway, next to his leather bag.

But he hadn't finished packing. There were more drawers to be emptied. He took a plastic bin-liner from under the kitchen sink and walked through to the sitting room. This time round, instead of a chest of clothes, he went for a cabinet. His hands in junk, personalized knick-knacks that he had accumulated over twenty-seven years, he first threw out what remained of his photos, family snaps at Christmas, old holidays with ex-lovers and envelopes stuffed with red-eyed university mates who he no longer spoke to. He dug up a diary that he had kept when he was seven years old. Illustrated in part by sketches of superheroes, it contained a folded-up 'A' grade essay on 'My Dream Career – Journalist'. Without reading any of it, including the essay, he dropped it into the bin-liner. A shoebox of love letters and cards from Tania, Jane, Emma and Rebecca followed, then a letter from his Spanish uncle's lawyer, a formal rejection from his mother's family to a twelve-year-old nephew.

The pogrom continued until all that was left was the sort of stuff that any normal person would have wanted to chuck out: a chewed pencil, a set of keys lost from its lock, an unused notepad, instructions for an unused video recorder and a broken alarm clock. But he saw these objects as safe. He felt that they didn't reveal an insight into his life, his fuck up, the secrets that he withheld and the ambitions that he had lost. After his death, the strangers could do what they liked with these objects.

He picked up the bag of memories and headed towards the front door. Outside, down a dark alley off the terraced street, he tossed the bag on to a pile of other refuse. The noise woke up a tramp, a bearded man nested in sacks of waste and cardboard boxes. On all fours, the tramp crawled to his new supplies and ripped open the bin-liner with his fingers. He poured out its contents on his lap and snorted at a few intact love letters.

Justin watched the tramp handle his life. 'Enjoy what you can of it,' he thought, watching him scatter the torn-up letters. 'See what good you can do with it.' He leant against a brick wall, shoved a cigarette in his mouth and lit up. A plume of smoke travelled in the direction of the stranger reading the diary of dreams, the holographs on the cover sparkling in dirty hands. He turned to go back inside, to rest before tomorrow's early flight, and left the tramp to cuss the *Fucking useless rubbish.*

Five

'Urrrggghhh,' Rachel groaned in her hotel bed, from under a sheet. Her sun-freckled face surfaced and she squinted at the sunlight in the window. She sat up and ran her fingers through her messy black hair. Her toes tickled the air with a web of cracked nails. 'One thing I won't be missing from here,' she yawned, 'and that's that darned dawn sun. You awake sis?' She kicked the sheet to the floor, wiped her face with the sleeve of her nightshirt, an old business shirt of her father's, and scratched the gunk out of her eyes.

'Oh no,' she said to herself, on seeing the empty bed next to her. 'You didn't did you?' She reached out to a bedside table and finished off a small bottle of water. 'Bad Erin.'

Counting to ten several times over, she rolled off the mattress, picked herself up from the floor and wobbled towards the bathroom. After donating much time to nature and little time to cosmetics, popping aspirins and killing the smell of alcohol with mouthwash, she put on a pair of khaki shorts and an old white T-shirt. She then squeezed her blistered feet into her deck shoes and, bouncing between two banisters, went downstairs for breakfast.

Most of the other hotel guests had already eaten and they lay on sun loungers by the pool, applying sun lotion before the day's big fry-up. Rachel hobbled past the marinating bodies and went inside an air-conditioned restaurant. She browsed the breakfast buffet, passing on the fruit salad, the banana a nasty shade of brown, and stacked her plate with hot cakes, crispy bacon and scrambled eggs. The protein and carbohydrates emulsified the cocktails of the previous night and she cleaned her plate. On her table was a copy of the *International Herald Tribune* and *La Jornada*. She opted for the latter, the local's choice, and tested her Spanish as she slurped her *café con leche*. Inside the Domestic News section, she read an article on Subcommandante Marcos, the masked leader of the Zapatista rebels, 'Mexico's latest sex symbol and T-shirt emblem.' Apart from the article's attempt to unmask Marcos

– 'Is he a foreign troublemaker, a scholarly professor, or a modern day Robin Hood?' – it described the recent murder of a thirteen-year-old boy. Shot dead in what the police called 'an inter-village dispute', 'Indian-on-Indian violence', the authorities, including the governor of Chiapas State, blamed the boy's death on the lawlessness that the Zapatistas had brought to the south-east of Mexico. The Zapatistas, on the other hand, blamed the authorities for arming the murderers, while Marcos blamed the wider impact of globalization.

Although Rachel had never indulged in politics herself, despising those phoney fraternity boys at college who aspired to the profession, she was a stickler for classing right from wrong. It was something that her loving, Christian parents had taught her from an early age. Her father, Tony Rees, had proved that it was hard work, not leftist laziness or Communist excuses, which lead to improvement and progress.

But there was an altogether different reason why Rachel had no time for Subcommandante Marcos and his balaclava honchos. During school break in the summer of '94, a gang of teenage boys with hosiery pulled over their heads had pulled a gun at her. She was in the wrong place at the wrong time; she had stepped into the path of an amateur bank heist and became a hostage in the trunk of a station wagon. One of the gang smacked her in the face, fracturing an incisor of hers. Thinking that she was out cold, saving the 'bitch for a going over later', the gang left her in the car and went to Bagelmania to grab coffee, snacks and a few sniffs of lighter fuel. Fortunately for Rachel, they had left a gap in a rear window. She took her chance and forced it down. Despite her hands bound by jumpstart leads and her bloody mouth silenced by gaffer tape, she found a state trooper munching doughnuts in a patrol car. The cops arrested the entire gang, polystyrene cups and hot coffee sent flying into the air, and a subpoena came in the post. As star witness, she faced gestures of popping guns and slitting throats as the gang was led out of court and dragged off to prison. The Rees family decided to leave the county on the bang of the judge's gavel.

She looked at the picture of the rebel in a ski mask and closed the newspaper on him. 'Masked heroes? A modern Robin Hood who fights for the poor? Sure.' She sipped her coffee and saw no difference between the Zapatistas, Marcos's merry band of Indians, and the gangs of her hometown. Instead, tapping a packet of sugar in her palm and watching a waitress clear the table, she saw heroes in the cogs of the machine. They were the spies and professors, the directors and writers, the architects and boat-builders, and waitresses. It was partly why she had chosen to study ecology and conservation, to go to the assistance of a polluted and dying planet. She took another sip of coffee.

'Well, well, well,' Erin said, behind Rachel. Ignoring the 'NO SWIMWEAR IN THE RESTAURANT' sign, she wagged her beach towel as if it was a tail.

'Do you have to go creeping up on me like that?' Rachel asked, turning round. She used a napkin to mop up the spilt coffee.

'What are you reading there? You're not going intellectual on me again? This is just soooo not the time or place for the brain.' Erin looked down at the newspaper on the table, under Rachel's elbow. 'In Spanish, huh? Jeez, that must be a riveting read.'

'Yeah, actually it is.' Rachel did not look amused. 'Now tell me what happened last night. I didn't hear you leave. Where did you go sneaking off to?'

'Jealous, huh?'

'Hardly, especially if it's who I think it is. His breath, Erin, *his breath.*'

'I was carrying mints; it was fine. Anyway, do you see that?' She pointed at the pool behind the restaurant's tinted windows. 'How about we have one final race?'

'You can't escape that easily.'

'It was our last night here, OK? And I've been doing more than reading a newspaper by myself.'

'Spare me the details.' Rachel put her face in her hands.

'I'll tell you what happened later,' Erin winked, 'but we've got a race now and the last one in has to get me a pina colada. Well, what're you waiting for?'

'I'm in shorts and T-shirt.'

'That hasn't stopped you before.'

Rachel jumped up from her chair and the girls sprinted out of the restaurant. They hit the pool's water, spraying the poolside and the bodies on sun loungers. Angry faces stared down at them.

'So have we got a lift with your folks?' Erin asked Rachel, who had just returned from making a phone call to her parents. She kicked a large suitcase into the corridor outside the girls' room.

'Yeah, it's fixed,' Rachel replied. She gave Erin a hand with another suitcase. 'Though Mom annoyed me. She's still giving me a hard time about Ecuador. Thinks it's going to be dangerous out there. I'm worried that she might speak to my professor and stop me from going.'

'Don't worry yourself about it.' Erin dropped the suitcase and put her arm round Rachel. 'Your mum loves you and only wants what's best for you. They nearly lost you – they don't want to risk that again.'

'I just wish that she'd trust me a bit more,' she said, dragging out yet another suitcase from the room. 'Statistically speaking, I'm probably safer in the Third World than I am at home.'

'Perhaps this trip will calm them down a bit. I mean, you survived your first trip abroad, right?'

'Hey, we still have the shuttle-bus to the airport and Duty Free to roam. Who knows what might happen between now and home-sweet-home.'

After checking out at reception and saying goodbye to the barman, who blew them kisses from across the pool, the girls loaded their suitcases into a shuttle-bus. They boarded with the other evacuees, whose fortnight's vacation had also elapsed, and grabbed window seats from which to salute and dismiss Cancún's concrete parade. Whereas Erin compared tans and fashion with a woman in the seat in front, gold to her bronze, Gucci to her Gap, Rachel peered out of her window and looked at the turquoise ocean past the hotel. The pirate's galleon had yet to set sail, plunder the horizon, and the water was more or less free from the razzmatazz of banana boats, sailboards and jet skis.

To the relief of all the sweating passengers, bar one, the engine started, the air-conditioning switched on and the bus accelerated along Boulevard Kukulkán to the airport.

'Bye Mexico,' she whispered to herself. She thought back to her evenings on the balcony, the sunset that turned the Caribbean into larva, and closed her eyes. Erin punched her on the arm. 'Ouch,' she said, opening her eyes.

'So do you want to hear what happened to me last night?' Erin asked, jumping about in her seat.

'If you must.'

Rachel stared out of the bus's window again, at a crowd of Mayan women who carried heavy sacks on their backs, and pretended to listen to Erin's tale of mischief at La Boom nightclub.

The two friends walked out of Duty Free. Rachel carried a bottle of Scotch whisky for her father and Chanel No5 for the jungle, a girl at college recommending it as an effective repellent against Ecuadorean bugs. Erin, who had been too giggly to shop, remained empty-handed. The airport's information monitor flashed 'FINAL CALL' next to their flight number.

'Were we really that long in there?' Rachel said, looking up at the monitor.

'Hey, I didn't buy anything.'

'Come on.' Rachel directed them towards the departures lounge. 'Mom will kill me if we miss our flight. She'll think that we've crashed or, even worse for her country club reputation, been locked up by customs for contravening our tax-free allowance. The shame that we could bring to the Rees' name.'

The girls walked down aisles of gift shops, neither of them tempted by saucy postcards, cheap lighters, T-shirts speech bubbled with 'I ♥ Cancún' and tacky replicas of ancient Mayan artefacts. Sales assistants stood at the entrances to their shops and facilitated the colonization of the world by cheap souvenirs. 'Good prices here,' they said, holding up T-shirts to their chests. In the departures lounge, the bar before take-off traded off a crowd of charter flight passengers, who downed pints and smoked cigarettes as if their flights were doomed and they had to overindulge in final requests. A barman served flaming sambucas to three sombreros, their wide brims hiding three red faces. 'Uno, dos, tres . . . wahey!' the men shouted, snuffing out the flames, raising their headgear and knocking back the shots. At the end of the bar and opposite the tipsy trio, a young couple shared a bottle of mineral water. They clasped hands as they anxiously checked out the other passengers.

A stampede of fresh arrivals moved along a travelator. White and tired, they reminded the departees, who travelled in the opposite direction, of what awaited them back at home and work. Rachel observed them as they glided past. She saw a mirror image of class and character to those on her travelator, the passengers on her flight, only without tanned and burnt skin, silly hats and empty wallets. The biologist in her observed a defensive mentality in the new invaders. She recognized a behaviour that drove prey to cluster into herds of family and friends: a safety in numbers attitude, with kin and kind sticking together.

One specimen, however, a Caucasian male, defied her theory.

Standing alone, his hands in his pockets and with a leather bag slung over his shoulder, he looked set apart from the others. At first, she deemed he must be a Mexican, a Latino: his dark hair and disdain for the tourists matching the phenotype and social organization of an aloof native. Yet his skin was as white, if not whiter, than the rest of the Anglo-Saxon rabble, and as for his clothes – a bright blue shirt and khaki chinos – he looked far too Banana Republic to be anything other than an American or, pushing it, a European. He moved closer to her and she saw no sulking girlfriend, wife, friend or anyone else who he might have had a tiff with. She concluded, therefore, that he was travelling solo, that he had rich friends waiting for him past customs, a luxury suite in the Hilton International, a base from which to lure bimbos on the beach to. She had seen his type in the last two weeks and she classed them with the wasps that circled the rim of her cocktail glass before they entangled themselves in her hair. *'Jerk.'*

Satisfied with her hypothesis, ready to turn her attention away from him and ask Erin for the bottle of water, she caught him staring back at her. Their positions on the two travelators were near level, as if they were two knights well placed for the joust, and he looked at her face-on. She flicked her eyes up and to the side of him, feigning interest in the toilets that passed behind him. In no mood for horseplay, especially not with a jet-setting playboy, she waited for the sexual innuendoes to cross the no man's land that separated them. But he said nothing. Thinking that he must have passed, it seemed like an eternity as she watched the walls speed by, she lowered her eyes. She mistimed her drop; the man was opposite and still studying her. Out of curiosity, she decided to stare back.

It was not what she had expected to see: his expression was too blank for a loose lothario and too pained for a predator. Green eyes locked on to her and she thought she saw sadness, perhaps a broken heart, but she was not sure. Part quizzical and part cognizant, unshielded and yet strong, the face was too impassive for a clear-cut decipherment. She wanted to help him, but really to learn. *'If only he'd darn well say something,'* she telepathically pleaded, forgetting her earlier fear of unwelcome attention. Whereas she was lost on him, she was convinced that he could read her. As with the molten sea, the connection that she had felt on the balcony, she was no more the wiser as to what it was exactly that she was drawn. She wanted to press the emergency stop button, bring them to a standstill and interrogate the opaque specimen. *'Hey, do I know you?'* But he looked away and bowed his head. Twisting her neck to follow him, she watched the leather bag on his back coast away.

'What is the purpose of your trip, Señor Callaghan?' the immigration official asked. The man took off his mirrored sunglasses and pinched points into his waxed moustache. He compared the photograph in the passport to the pale face in front of him.

Justin had queued for at least twenty minutes because of the official's retardant going by the book, the treatment of every jet-lagged tourist as if they belonged to a cartel, hyperactive kids stuffed with drugs scarier than Sunny Delight. There was no way in hell that he was going to mention business, a foreign acquisition of a sweatshop, let alone the other purpose of his trip.

'I'm on vacation,' he replied, 'to do a bit of diving.' He lobbed the Saddam Hussein look-alike a fake smile.

'You bring equipment?'

'No. I'm a beginner.'

'I see. You travel alone?'

'Yes. I'm alone.'

'I see. Your first visit to Mexico?'

'Yes.'

'OK, Señor Callaghan.' The official stamped Justin's passport and tourist visa card. 'Cheer up and have fun diving.'

'Thanks.' He picked up his documents and put them in his leather bag.

In Baggage Reclaim, waiting for his rucksack to pop out of a chute, he watched a pink bag go round a conveyor belt. The merry-go-round of luggage stirred a turkey steak, three gin and tonics, two red wines and three cognacs, and the time-killing meal, which he ate while watching the in-flight movie, *George of the Jungle*, buckled up for a connecting flight. A woman picked up the pink bag and his rucksack came into view. Holding in the contents of his stomach, he leant over the conveyor belt and grabbed the rucksack by its straps. He paced through customs, withdrew a few thousand pesos from an ATM and went outside to search for a taxi.

The afternoon sun, a haze above a verge of palm trees and

tarmac, made him blink and his eyelids stuck to his dry eyeballs. He took off his rucksack, placing it by his feet, and pinched his shirt off his sweaty back. Desperate for a cigarette, he pulled a carton of duty-free out of his bag and bit off the cellophane packaging. He lit up and smoke hung over his head. A hangover had set in and, combined with jet lag, too much reading of a guide book on the plane and the concrete bunker of Cancún airport, an anticlimactic welcome to Mexico, he was too exhausted to contemplate what lay ahead of him. Death, he thought as he inhaled deeply on his cigarette, deserved more than the sterility of a car park full of Volkswagen Beetles and people carriers.

'May I?' A Spanish-accented voice interrupted his questioning mind. He turned round and saw a man in a white shirt and grey flannels. The Mexican pointed at his cigarette.

'What?' he replied. 'Oh. Yeah.' He handed the man a cigarette and the lighter.

'Thank you, señor. Where you from? United States? Canada?' The man lit the cigarette and returned the lighter to Justin.

'No. I'm from England.'

'Ahh, England. Good. You like Princess Diana? Sexy woman, yes?'

'Eh?' Justin thought of the image of the waterfall, the peace and quiet that it held for him.

'Many señoritas in Cancún. You have good time here.'

'Right.' He wondered how high the drop would have to be to be effective. It was something that had bothered him on the plane; it had prompted him to order another cognac off the stewardess.

'You want taxi?'

'Yes,' he replied. 'How much to the Le Meridien Hotel?'

'Ah, good choice of place to stay. Best I do is fifteen US – special price for you.'

Before he could haggle, not that he would, the man had picked up Justin's rucksack and walked over to a clapped-out Volkswagen Beetle. The taxi driver wiped a half-eaten pastry, boiled sweets and the loose pages of an adult comic book off the back seats, squeezing in the rucksack. Justin scraped a Hershey bar wrapper, cigarette ash and an empty bottle of Pepsi off the front passenger's seat. He ducked under a pine-scented Virgin Mary, the air freshener hanging from the rear-view mirror, sat on a hot plastic seat and slammed his door shut.

'So you like Mexico?' the taxi driver asked, hitting a speed bump at speed. The car's chassis rattled and the swinging Madonna crossed herself in a net of cotton thread.

Justin stared out of the Beetle's windows. To the sides of the road were concrete blocks of automotive retailers, building suppliers, electricity plants, factories and fast-food outlets.

'Yeah.'

A dog sat three legs and a stump on the sidewalk. Waiting for a gap in the traffic, it scratched its ribs and followed the speeding taxi with a scabby muzzle. *'What the fuck are you doing here? Weirdoooooo,'* Justin heard the mutt whine. He turned round and looked through the rear window. The dog hopped to the other side. *'Ha! Missed!'*

'You OK, señor?'

'Yes thanks.' Justin rubbed his eyes and, facing ahead again, saw a montage of family photos taped to the Beetle's dashboard. Smiling faces stared back at him and he glanced at his driver, at the grin on his face and at the yellow armpit stains on his nylon shirt. He wound down his window a little further to let out the smell.

'Are you here on business or pleasure?' the driver asked.

'What?'

'Business or pleasure. What are you doing here?'

'Oh, a bit of both.'

'What do you do mister? What is your business in Mexico?'

Justin tried to think of a safe answer.

'I'm a writer,' he invented, 'inspired by your scenic country.' He observed the architectural hash of concrete and corrugated iron that they passed.

'No way!' the driver screamed. 'I write myself.' He took his eyes off the road and addressed his frowning passenger. 'I write many poems. About love, my dreams, my history. But I have shown my poems to not a single person, not even to my wife. They are for me and me alone. Understand?'

'Yes.' Justin wondered how far the hotel was. 'There's nothing wrong with that.'

'You are a fellow-artist.'

Justin put on his sunglasses.

'Maybe one day,' the driver continued, as Justin continued to look out of the Beetle's windows, 'when I am nearly dead, then perhaps I will show someone my work. But, for now, I could not face the criticism of others. They're my thoughts, personal to me. You understand?'

'I think I do.' He removed his sunglasses and faced the driver. His mind stopped wondering. The last time he felt like this was in the supermarket, when he met the pensioner and before he took the call from the police. Since he last spoke to his mother, it was the last time that he had properly listened to anyone.

'So where in Mexico are you going for inspiration, for the juice of your writing? Surely not Cancún?'

'I was thinking of Chiapas,' Justin said, less automated in his response.

'You really are a crazy man. There are many bad things happening there. Indians killing each other, road bandits, drug smugglers, all kinds of bad shit. Not a good place for a gringo tourist.'

'I'm not a tourist.' He reached back and pulled the guidebook out of his leather bag. The book opened at a page with its upper corner folded down. 'This, or something similar, is what I want to see.' He held up the picture of the waterfall over the steering wheel. 'It must be quiet though. Not full of tourists.'

'Very pretty.' The driver glanced at the falls under the hanging Madonna. 'What sort of story takes you there? Romance?'

'I'm afraid I can't say.'

'Of course, señor; we must be careful with our ideas. Hey, listen, I may be able to help you find such a place. A friend of mine in Palenque, he runs tours and . . .'

'I'm not going on any rip-off tour,' Justin replied, sinking back into his hot plastic seat and rubbing his temples. 'It has to be quiet. No crowds.'

'No, señor.' The taxi driver's yellow teeth flashed at Justin. 'These tours are special. My friend only takes small groups into the mountains, and with him you see places no other gringos see. He will find a pretty waterfall for your book. I'm sure of it.' His hands off the steering wheel and his foot firmly on the accelerator, the driver raked the junk in his car for a pen and paper. He rested a Pemex fuel station receipt in the centre of the steering wheel and wrote down a name and telephone number. The pressure of the applied nib sounded the horn. Justin silently watched him scribble away, gripping his guidebook in his sweaty palms. 'Here, take this.' The driver handed him the receipt. 'Give Manolo a call. He will help you find your falls.'

'Thanks.' Justin bookmarked the chapter on Chiapas with the receipt.

Twenty minutes later, on Cancún's Boulevard Kulkulkán, the Beetle pulled up outside Le Meridien Hotel, a palatial honeycomb of marble suites, tiered swimming pools and palm-shaded tennis courts. A doorman ran towards the taxi and opened the passenger door. Justin stepped out of the car.

'Thanks for the lift,' he said, passing a twenty dollar note to the driver.

'Thank you, señor. You're very generous. Give Manolo a call and have a safe journey to your falls.'

The Beetle backfired, the driver chuckling to himself as he punched his horn, and it screeched out of the hotel's driveway. Justin followed the doorman into a marble-floored foyer and cooled down in the air-conditioning. At the reception desk, a man in a tuxedo turned his nose up at him, stepped over his rucksack and marched towards the 'Lord Pacal Ballroom and Conference Centre'. His team's PA had forewarned the hotel of his arrival and he just had to fill in a form, drop off his passport and book an 8 a.m. wake-up. Before he went to his room, dosed up on melatonin and tried to sleep, he had a phone call to make. He asked the doorman for his leather bag.

'Yeehaw!' the taxi driver screamed. Blood clots for eyes and a tongue as forked as a snake's, he put his foot down and the Beetle thwacked into a human speed bump. A white dress wrapped around the wheels, and tyres mashed bone and entrails on hot tarmac. Justin, gripping a sticky plastic seat, smelt the rotten meat as it rattled in the wheel wells. 'Bang! Oh yeah, we got her *reeeal good*.' The driver activated the wipers to remove the droplets of blood on the windscreen.

'Jesus Christ!' Justin screamed back. 'What the hell have you done?' he looked behind them, over the rifles and machetes on the backseats, and stared out of the rear window. A page of an adult comic book, a storyboard of impish oral sex, was stuck against the reddened glass. From where they just came from, the scene of the murder, he saw a bulimic mongrel feed on the victim's detritus. Fur sticking up on its back, the dog choked and hurled up a pink blancmange of hair and bone. 'No!' he shouted. 'Please leave her alone,' he wept.

'Well, if you're going to be like that.' The driver leaned over, chilli and garlic on his snake's tongue, and he kicked open the passenger door. 'Fuck you!'

Justin rolled onto a grassy verge. He picked himself up and ran as fast as he could through jungle. Thorns and prickly leaves shredded his clothes and, stripped down to a pair of *'Jungle Justin'* briefs, blood trickled down his arms and legs. He tugged at a vine, a giant beanstalk promising a happy-ever-after ending, which dangled from an ancient tree. The creeper was longer than he had expected and he coiled the wooden flex by his feet. When the vine was taut, he climbed towards the top of the tree. About halfway up, he heard a woman whimpering beneath him. He stopped his ascent and slid down the beanstalk. It was the girl from the airport.

'You're bleeding,' she said, as they relived their lover's trance. 'Here, let me take a look.' He felt her hands stroke his body. The massage drained the pain, stemmed the blood that flowed down his limbs, and he felt his heart beat faster. Naked, they walked hand in hand to a clearing in the forest, to a four-poster bed of mown grass and palm trees. Flies fed on their salty skin, but the lovers were desensitized to the bites. They were blind to what else was around them.

Justin lay on his back, alone in the grass: he was too fast asleep to see the girl leave and too late to ask for a name and number. A tickle on his side interrupted his regret. As if they were sabres drawn on a battlefield, the blades of grass rose up and buried him in a mass of spiky shoots. Growing thicker and thicker, the grass turned into a pool of water and he was sucked into its dark green depths. He gripped aquatic weeds and roots to slow down his descent, but it was useless. His muscles wasted away and he resigned himself to an inevitable end.

Above him, silhouetted by the light from the sky and clouded by murky water, he saw the girl. As if she was choosing a lobster in a tank, she looked at the pathetic creature in the pool and pushed him down further. He cried out to be saved, but she shook her head, her black hair flicking across her face, and laughed.

A phone rang and he jumped out of the water.

'Good morning. Buenas dias. This is the Le Meridien Hotel's comple-mentary wake-up call. The time is 8 a.m. We wish you a . . .'

He banged down the receiver. Resuming his sleeping position

and propping his neck up with pillows, he looked for the dark-haired girl. He wanted to give her another opportunity to save him, to conclude the dream his way. All he saw, though, were the curtains at the end of his bed, an image of a girl in pleats, material flicking as if it was hair in air-conditioning, the silhouette effect coming from the sunshine outside. He raised an arm and confirmed the time with his watch. It was time to start the day.

Despite recent distractions, plans for Palenque and the height of waterfalls among them, he had not forgotten about the promise that he had made to Beth, the reason that he was sent to Mexico in the first place. For her sake, if not his own, he had to assess whether La Tela Maya was a PR disaster in the making. His mission was to search for malnourished urchins chained to sewing machines, and/or pregnant Indians stirring vats of dye. Should Lindo purchase a Third World sweatshop, throw scrutiny on their profitable claim to have 'a clean human rights record', Beth would take the rap. He didn't want her to posthumously blame him for screwing up her bonus.

'What do you think, Mr Callaghan?' Hector Morales, the Managing Director of La Tela Maya, asked Justin in his smoke-filled office. He leaned his tubby body back in his chair, put his cowboy boots on his leather-lined desk and lit another cigarillo. The smoke drifted upwards and choked a portrait of President Zedillo, the one piece of decoration in the MD's cell of an office. A ceiling fan removed the smoke before it reached Justin, who sat on the other side of the desk in chinos and blue shirt. 'You think the Spanish will be pleased with our results?'

'I've seen these figures before,' Justin said, placing his file on the desk. He lit a cigarette and hoped that the bus to Palenque had air-conditioning. The receptionist at the hotel had provided him with a list of departure times for first-class buses. 'They are certainly impressive,' he continued, looking at a clock on the wall, 'and they are why Lindo, my clients, have paid me to fly out here and visit you.'

'Thank you for your compliment. I keep my costs low and the craftsmanship high.' He spoke in an Americanized accent.

'They probably are.' Justin looked at Morales and used him as another reason for catching a bus to the mountains. 'And in return, Señor Morales, Lindo can make you a very rich man. Still, if it's all right with you, I'd like to visit the factory floor before I finish my report.'

'Absolutely. I was going to insist on it anyway.'

The two men left the office, Justin following the tiny man with the big ego and big belly. They walked outside, crossed a dusty courtyard and headed for a silo of corrugated iron. As if it was a giant beatbox, the building amplified the sound of machinery and the chatter of workers from inside. Morales opened a small door and they entered a large, hangar-sized room. Under a ceiling of dangling light bulbs were rows of tables and benches, cramped workstations for the mainly Indian and female workers. They inspected the production line, from stitching to packaging, and Morales explained the start to finish of a crop-top's creation: from a reel of cotton to a Californian girl's midriff.

Justin nodded and tried to remember what it was like when he last took mushrooms. It was at a blazer and tie drinks party in Devon, hallucinogens turning a consultant, who hand-chopped as he talked about himself, into a wind-up soldier. The guidebook suggested that they wouldn't be too hard to score; mushrooms, after all, he had read on the plane, were once worshipped by the ancient Maya. He thought they might be useful at the top of the waterfall.

They stopped to talk to an employee, a scared-looking woman behind a sewing machine, and Justin assumed that she had been auditioned and rehearsed before his arrival. Sure enough, she remembered her lines as if her job depended on acting and not needlework ability. 'Señor Morales, he treats us very good. Yes, he is a good man to us. We *verrry* much like working for Señor Morales. La Tela Maya is a nice place to work. Yes, yes.' It was a good show: far from convincing in its stage management, but enough to warrant a tick from Justin, who had a bus to catch and a tour group to join. Unless the kids were under the floorboards or operating the internal organs of the machines, he could also vouch for the factory not using child labour; a bonus for the kids and a bonus for his colleagues.

'Are you married, Mr Callaghan?' Morales asked, dismissing the Indian woman with the back of his hand.

'What?' Justin looked behind Morales and watched the woman's face turn sad. 'Umm, no.'

'A girlfriend, then?'

'No.' He watched the woman sob into the palms of her hands.

He wanted to help her, but what good could he do when he couldn't even help his own mother. It was just the way the world was, and he had at least planned his exit strategy.

'Shame, since you probably won't have a need for one of these.' Morales pulled a baby blue T-shirt from a pallet marked 'WALMART'. Justin looked away from the woman and read '*Miss Bossy*' printed across the T-shirt's chest.

'No. I can't see what I'd do with one of those.'

'How about your colleague? Beth?'

'I don't think . . .'

Morales threw the T-shirt at him.

'Thanks,' Justin said, looking at the T-shirt in his hand, 'but I won't be seeing her . . . I mean . . . Never mind, I'm sure she'll just love it.' He folded the T-shirt into a square and tucked it into his bag. It was best to take it, he thought, rather than to risk questions over why he wouldn't be returning to the bank. He decided to dispose of the shirt discreetly, when he was on his travels.

'So are you happy with what you've seen?'

'I'll need to speak to my team in London,' Justin replied, scanning the sweatshop's cramped workforce, 'but I can't foresee any problems in closing the deal.'

'Excellent.' Morales hugged him. Justin pushed him away and wiped the sweat off his forehead with the back of his hand.

'Do you have a phone that I can use?' Justin asked.

'You can use the one in my office.'

They left the factory, the can of people and machines, and returned to the office.

'If you'd like,' Morales said, standing in the doorway, 'my secretary can book you a taxi. It can be ready for you when you have finished your call.'

'Thank you. I shall be going straight to the central bus terminal.'

Morales closed the door and Justin sat in the Managing Director's chair. He dialled Beth's mobile number.

'Hello? Can you hear me? Beth?'

'Justin?' Beth answered. There was a delay in the connection. 'Hi! How the hell are you?'

'How's the Lake District?

'How is it going over there? Pretty hot, yeah?'

'Beth? There's a delay. Slow down.'

'We're doing fine . . . Oh, yeah, see what you mean.'

'Yes, it's very hot. Listen, I must be quick as I'm on Morales' phone.' The bad connection at least made him stick to the point. It stopped him from saying anything that he shouldn't; it stopped him from going beyond the simple results of a factory inspection. 'You can close the deal. The factory is as good as you can expect from that sort of place.'

'That's fantastic news Justin. Once I'm back in the office, I'll call Barcelona and get the ball rolling . . .'

'What?' He struggled to hear her through the crackly line. Swallowing hard, he tried to be strong, to stop the silent pauses down the phone from making his mind wander. He felt his throat constricting. 'You deserve this deal,' he struggled to say, 'I'm really happy for you . . .'

'What, Justin? Hello? Can you hear me?'

'Bye Beth,' he said, his head in his hands. He lowered the phone's receiver. 'Take care of . . .'

Incapable of finishing his sentence he hung up. For a few minutes he just sat there, the clock on the wall ticking loudly, the ceiling fan beating like a chopper's blades. Finally he stood up. He wiped the moisture off his cheeks and eyes and opened the door to the office. Morales stood outside, as if he had been eavesdropping.

'Well?' Morales asked. 'Is everything OK?'

'Yes,' Justin replied. He swung his bag over his shoulder. 'Is my taxi ready?'

'It's ready when you are.'

'Thank you.' Justin went to the corner of the office and picked up his rucksack. 'Beth will be your contact from now on.'

Justin walked out of the office. He was now free to deal with matters more important than Spanish takeovers of Mexican sweatshops.

It was dark when the taxi stopped at the bus terminal. Justin tipped the driver with a wad of pesos before he harnessed his rucksack to his back. He walked past a traffic jam of fast-food trolleys, taco and tamale vendors, and entered a brightly lit bus station. Joining a queue of backpackers, who modelled humps of mountaineering technology, he looked up at the timetable of departures on the wall above the ticket office. His eyes were dry again and he had to blink continuously to see the times. If the backpackers hurried, stopped evaluating the costs of tickets to the times of departure, he could, he reckoned, catch the next bus. Relieved at completing his obligation for his colleagues, seeing the back of Hector Morales, he was in no mood for further delays and distractions.

A woman behind the ticket desk called him over. He asked her if there were any seats available on the next bus to Palenque. Tapping a keyboard, she looked at her computer screen and nodded. She asked for his name and reserved an aisle seat for 'CALLAGHAN' on the 8 p.m., ADO run first-class bus. He paid, grabbed his ticket and change and rushed towards the gate, another queue of backpackers. An ADO porter stowed his rucksack in the bus's hold and the driver, who wore shades in the dark, tore the corner off his ticket.

'Excuse me,' Justin said, standing in the aisle of the bus and addressing a seated woman, 'but you're in my seat.' The woman sucked a tamale, maize and mince dribbling down her multilayered chin, and she ignored him. 'Excuse me,' he repeated, louder, 'but that's my seat you're in.' He tapped her on the shoulder and showed her the stub of his ticket.

'Eh?' the woman finally replied. She looked up at the ticket. 'Son of a bitch,' she said in Spanish, as if Justin didn't understand. She put the tamale in her handbag, stood on his toe and pushed him out of the way.

When the woman had stolen someone else's seat, he brushed the maize off his armrests and sat down. The bus moved and he closed his eyes and ran through tomorrow's itinerary. As they drove out of the terminal, went down streets of smoky cafés and cantinas, a blast of music and sound effects shattered the silence. He opened his eyes and saw a small TV lowered from the roof of the bus. The opening credits of *Men In Black*, in English and with Spanish subtitles, flashed at his face. He closed his eyes again and thought of a waterfall's soothing waters.

Six

Rush hour hit San Felipé early, in the darkness of pre-dawn. Illuminated by handheld and flaming torches, the streets were busy with the traffic of every man, woman, child and beast of the village. Each family manned a small mound of possessions, from mum's cast iron griddle pan and dad's machete, to a kid's basketball and a tethered pig, sad sentries to empty mud-brick homes. The headlights of a convoy of open-topped trucks, on loan from neighbouring and friendly villages, lit up the refuse of Tzotzil Maya and the dust of activity. When a truck was packed with people and belongings, bodies squashed up against sacks of clothes and clutter, it went into low gear, turned out of the village and rattled up the steep limestone track that connected San Felipé to the main highway. In the back, the cramped human contents looked eastwards and hoped to see the sun rise above the mountains for one last time. Another truck rolled forward and it too loaded up. The process would continue until all that was left of San Felipé were the shells of former homes, the refuse heaps of a lost life and another Maya ruin.

The decision to go was by no means unanimous. It took two long days of debate, in a stuffy concrete community centre, to reach a consensus. Some of the villagers, including Lucio, wanted to wait for international peace observers to arrive. A shield of foreigners armed with cameras, they argued, had a record of preventing attacks; the paramilitaries didn't like to upset their political paymasters, a government wanting to attract foreign investment, by becoming subjects of gruesome holiday snaps. Others, like Maria, had hoped that the EZLN, the Zapatista army, would defend them. For the majority, though, the two options were considered to be either too uncertain or too violent. Most of the families, it was agreed, would travel to Polho, an autonomous refugee camp, or San Cristóbal de las Casas. They would stay in the highlands of Chenalho and return home when, or if, the paramilitaries departed. Other families chose to move farther afield, to seek work in the factories and plantations of Villahermosa, or build homes in the south, planting new communities in the Lacandón rainforest.

'Please, Lucio,' Maria had said to her husband in the candlelit cemetery. Lucio knelt beside a freshly dug grave. Incense smoke passed over his face and it wafted through limestone tombstones and wooden crosses. 'You can't keep blaming yourself for what happened.'

Lucio lit a candle in a jam jar and placed it under a small cross, next to a bunch of yellow marigolds and Urbano's blowpipe.

'When peace returns,' she continued, handing him a bandana to wipe away his tears, 'we'll be able to visit him anytime we want.'

He kissed the cross, stood up from the grave and put on a white straw hat. His wife wrapped her big arms around him.

'Apart from our brave son,' he said, his sad eyes connecting with his wife's, 'there is no other reason for us to return to San Felipé. The government is welcome to this cursed land. I shall be pleased to see the back of it.'

'We can make ourselves a lovely new home.' She hugged him again.

'Yes,' he replied, as he looked down over her shoulder at the blowpipe on fresh soil.

Lucio wanted to go as far away as he could from Chenalho, First-True-Mountain, the sacred landscape and the shrines that he gave and lost his soul and son to. He wanted to save what he had left, namely his marriage, and prove to Maria that he was young enough to start again, that he was no longer tied to the will of the mountain gods. To Lucio's surprise, she had agreed. The loss of her home had given her no incentive to return to San Felipé, should the hostilities ever end, and she had too much pride to be a refugee for the rest of her life. After the option to stay and fight was overruled, she thought it best to start afresh and to build a new home in a new land. They had both decided, therefore, to go in the truck headed for the Lacandón rainforest.

The fire had left the Gomez's with a meagre starter pack for a new life. From the ash, charcoal and blackened mud-brick, they salvaged a few cooking pots, a granite pestle and mortar and a steel griddle for tortillas. The entire kitchen was packed in a wooden banana box and labelled 'GOMEZ' and 'LACANDÓN' on the lid. For clothes, the village's collective spirit filled a rice sack with shirts, pants, blouses, sandals and boots.

Maria picked up the sack of clothes in one hand, a paraffin lantern in the other, and walked out of the community centre, the Gomez's home for the past week. Saluting a goodbye to Emiliano Zapata, the moustached revolutionary painted on a wall outside, she went into the central square of San Felipé and joined the crowd of other evacuees. She placed the sack and lantern on the edge of a basketball court and looked behind her, through a swarm of people. Lucio, who struggled with the weight of the banana box, eventually caught up and dropped the kitchen utensils by the sack of clothes. The shaman's knitted and zigzagged backpack, the only other item to have survived that night, was slung over his shoulder, and the gold-painted cross stabbed him in the back.

'Are you sure that we have time?' Maria said to him. She observed the headlights, dust and silhouetted figures at the end of the street. 'Is it really not safe for Horatio to meet us here?' She raised her red bandana over her mouth to filter out the dust and the smoke of burning paraffin.

'We have plenty of time,' he said, waving the smoke and dust away from his sore eyes. 'We have a few hours of sunlight before they'll be leaving for the Lacandón, and there is at least an hour to go until dawn.' He pointed at the cool blue light past the eastern mountains. Then he looked around them, at the anxious looking faces in the queues to the convoy of trucks. 'Horatio has to be careful now. Not everyone supports the Zapatistas. It's best that we meet him in the forest.'

With the exception of the shaman's backpack, which remained attached to Lucio's back, they left their belongings in the square and walked towards the crowd and headlights. Lucio looked up and saw a boy cradle a puppy in the back of a truck. The vehicle was fully loaded and ready to roll on out.

'Goodbye, Alonso,' Lucio called out to the boy who was one of the shaman's helpers and a friend of Urbano's. The boy smiled back at him and, reminded of his loss, Lucio felt the muscles in his throat tighten.

'Goodbye, Señor Gomez,' the boy replied, waving his hand.

'Is that you, Lucio?' the boy's mother said, turning round from her seat in the truck.

'Yes, Gloria, it's Lucio.' He found it difficult to speak. The smoke in the air stung the back of his throat. It was a sensation that he had last felt on his return from First-True-Mountain, the body of his son in his wife's arms and flames consuming his home.

'I heard that you and Maria are going to the Lacandón.'

'We are.' Lucio turned to look at his wife who stood some distance behind him. Maria did not like the other women witnessing her tears, and under the shadow of a palm tree she waved at Gloria.

'Where is Horatio?' Gloria asked, nodding at Maria. 'My eldest daughter is very upset that he didn't say goodbye.'

'Oh, he is fine.' Lucio picked a speck of dust out of his eye. 'He went on ahead of us. Horatio is not good with goodbyes. There is also . . .'

'I understand,' Gloria said, saving Lucio from having to publicly explain his son's Zapatista predicament. 'We'll miss you all.'

'And we'll miss you. Good luck at Polho.' Lucio faced the small boy again. 'Alonso,' he said, his throat tightening again.

The boy's face popped up over his mother's embroidered shirt.

'Remember me as a friend, and not for what I taught you.'

Lucio watched the truck disappear out of the village, its headlights lost to the trees as it made its way up a windy and chalky road. Beside Maria again, he guided them towards the northern edge of the village, down empty streets and past abandoned homes and barren orchards of mango, banana and papaya trees. Leaving behind the torches of the remaining villagers and the headlights of revving trucks, only the light of a pale moon and a young sun, the sky luminous behind the mountains, spotlighted the way. When they reached the path through the field of maize, Maria tugged the bag on her husband's back.

'Down there?' she asked, frowning at the dark tunnel in the stems of maize, the route to the Pool of the Paddler Gods.

'It's OK,' Lucio reassured her, 'I know the route well.'

They walked through maize, coffee and forest, and dragged their feet through maize cobs, twigs and then pine needles. On the path of the black mountain sheep, their sandals slipping in dark brown mush, they heard a rustle in the shadows, the trees and brush that bordered the path. They both froze.

'What is it?' Maria whispered into Lucio's ear.

'Quiet,' he replied, his heart beating hard.

The snap of twigs grew louder and Maria looked for a weapon. Finding nothing, she clenched a fist and peered into the blackness of the trees.

A figure burst out of the bush and skidded to a stop on the path. Maria sprung back her fist and lunged.

'Mamá!' the figure cried out, sidestepping Maria's fist. 'It's me, Horatio, your son.' Horatio raised his arms in surrender. Maria's fist quickly unclenched.

'Horatio!' Maria hugged her son.

Lucio watched on and smiled.

'It's good to see you mamá,' Horatio said, when Maria eventually relaxed her grip on him. 'It's so good to see you.' He then walked over to his father. 'And you, father.'

With the birth of a new sun and a new day, night's cold blue rotated to dawn's warm orange. Definition returned to the trees, dew sparkled on pine needles, and birds sang morning grace before they breakfasted on grubs and fruit. While Maria and Horatio chatted on a log on the side of the path – the Zapatista rookie talked about his new friends – Lucio sat on a wet patch of grass and thought of Urbano, the son that he should have been with. He tried to shake off the symbolism around him, the traitors of dawn who had misled him, the beliefs of an ordered cosmos. He wanted to reach up and confront First Father, smite the sun that gloated at a boy's death and a fallen preacher, and to remove the gizzards of the songbirds that sang as if nothing had ever happened. His back itched under his lightning-streaked backpack.

'Come,' Maria said, holding Horatio's hand and walking him to a stretch of path that was clear of shadow, 'let me see you in the light, my handsome son.'

Dressed in a black shirt and combat pants, a crimson bandana tied around his neck, Horatio wore a Zapatista soldier's uniform. A belt of bullets crossed his chest and a hunting rifle was slung over his shoulder.

'Look, Lucio,' Maria addressed her husband on the ground.

Lucio stopped scraping his muddy sandals with a twig and slowly raised his head.

'Look at the man your son has become,' she continued, as she patted down her son's waxed hair.

'Mamá, please,' Horatio said, using his fingers to return the spikes to his hair. 'What do you think father?'

Lucio poked the twig between his toes and flicked mud into a clump of weeds. He looked up at the soldier in the dawn sun.

'I approve,' Lucio said, squinting at the rays of sun that pierced the branches above him. He looked at his son's rifle and the bullets strapped to his chest. 'The gun is for defence only, I presume?'

'Of course.' Horatio slapped a hand on the stock of his rifle. 'They don't just give these to anyone.' He gave his father a sheepish smile.

'I know.' Lucio dropped the twig by the shaman's backpack and he briefly looked down at them both. Birds cackled in the branches above him. He stood up and placed his hand on his son's shoulder, moving the nozzle of the rifle out of the way to find space for his shaking fingers. 'I'm sorry if you ever thought I neglected you.' The loose skin under his eyes creased as he faced his son. 'Things are going to change from now on. You and your mother are all that I have now.'

Maria raised herself up from her seat on the log. She joined her son and husband. Forming a small circle, the three held each other close.

'Do you know where they're going to send you?' Maria asked Horatio. She looked down at the dewy ground.

'No, not yet,' Horatio replied. His grip tightened round his mother and father. 'I have requested to be in a patrol near to you both, in the Lacandón forest, in Montes Azules.' He paused and scratched the adolescent stubble on his chin. 'But I should stay in Chenalho for a bit longer. The Cardenistas are attacking more villages each day and . . .' he paused, ruffling his hair, 'I feel that I should stay here for a bit longer. For Urbano.' Maria wrapped her arms around her son.

'How can we find you?' Lucio whispered within the Gomez's circle. His hands shook as he looked down at his shaman's backpack. 'Can you tell us where your camp is?'

Horatio stepped back from his parents. The low sun highlighted the spikes in his hair and the metal of the rifle's barrel on his back.

'We are camped in the cave . . .' Horatio hesitated, 'the cave in your mountain. It was my commandante's idea.'

Lucio looked up from the ground, the shaman's backpack by his sandals.

'It's OK,' Lucio said, 'it's about time that place was put to better use by a Gomez.'

On the top of the Temple of Inscriptions, the main pyramid at the Mayan ruins of Palenque, Justin peered into a dark hole set between stone slabs. Steps went down into the heart of the temple and he waited for Anne, a French archaeology student, to spoil the peace.

'This is so amazing,' Anne shrilled. She poked Justin in the back with her guidebook. 'No?'

Anne, the only other solo traveller in the small tour group, had latched on to Justin in the minibus to Palenque, the first leg of '*Manolo's Mayan Adventures*' While he closed his eyes and tried to think of ways to speed up his death, guarantee that the waterfall would do the job, she sat down next to him and read out her guidebook's account of Pre-Columbian history. She mistakenly believed that his silence did not equate to a lack of interest in her. She even found his sombre attitude, the lines that kept reappearing above his green eyes, attractive. Too preoccupied to put her straight, the word according to the *Rough Guide*'s appendices followed him out of the minibus, across a platform of skulls carved into stone and then all the way up to the top of the temple. It now threatened to march him all the way down the sixty-seven steps to Pacal's sarcophagus, down a not-so-very secret passageway of front-to-back tourists and through a strobe of camera flashes.

'Remarkable,' Justin replied, looking at his watch and counting the minutes till they had to return to the minibus and set off to the mountains. Irritated by the heat, mosquitoes and Anne's useless information, he looked to infiltrate a group of Japanese tourists, whose hi-tech accessories might help him fend her off. Unable to enter their ranks, forced to wait in line at the top of the tomb's steps, he instead felt her rub up against his back. Her breath cooled his neck and, catching a glimpse of her out of the corner of his eye, he felt bad about being harsh to the pretty French girl. It was not as if she knew what was going on inside his head. In single file, Justin leading the way, they descended a dark and slimy stairway to Palenque's pièce de résistance.

'You know that this tunnel was discovered as late as 1952. I read all about it.' Anne held up her *Rough Guide* as a footnote to her authority. 'It was found by chance by a Mexican archaeologist. A loose slab, and voila – they found the stairs and, with it, one of the greatest discoveries in Central America.'

She babbled on with her litany of regurgitated facts, while Justin distracted himself by looking at the contraflow of ascending tourists. Wearing blank faces under Nike golf visors or 'I ♥ Tequila' baseball caps, they seemed more excited about paying respects to a margarita in a five-star hotel, than to a dead king in a urine-smelling vault.

The stairs levelled out inside the belly of the temple. Over the head of a Japanese woman, who was stuck to the eyepiece of her camcorder, Justin got his first view of Pacal's sarcophagus, a limestone tablet of softly lit inscriptions. Pushing his way forward and dissuading the pint-sized Spielberg from continuing her multi-angled heresy, he saw an engraved image of the king falling into what appeared to be water. Tentacles and other strange beasts broke the dead ruler's fall, a fanged monster in the depths beneath him, while above him was an extravagantly plumed bird perched on a cross-shaped tree.

Anne joined Justin by the sarcophagus.

'What's he doing?' he asked her, the deceased's splashdown representation too coincidental to be left unexplained. This time he genuinely wanted to hear her facts. 'It looks like he's in water.'

Anne smiled at the first bit of interest he had shown in her. She swept back her black hair and stood on her toes to take a closer look at the tomb.

'Let me see,' she said, holding his bare arm to steady herself, 'if I remember rightly, he is falling down the World Tree, into the throat of the White-Bone-Snake and on to the Maw of the Earth.'

'Of course he is.' In all honesty, he wanted to hear more about the diving king.

'You see that?' She pointed at a few squiggles on the head of a fanged monster. 'That is the glyph of the sun. The Maya believed that the king would rise again in the east, after his journey through Xibalba, the watery Otherworld, like the sun does, at dawn, every day.'

'What do you mean "Xibalba and watery Otherworld"?'

'The Primordial Sea, the place of Creation, where First Father raised the sky and First Mother modelled flesh from maize and water. The temple itself symbolizes the first mountain, land that the gods summoned from the sea. We are inside the mountain itself and the great plaza that we walked across, from the site's entrance, is the "Lakam Ha", the "Big-Water".' For no apparent reason, she started to snigger.

'What's so funny about that?' He frowned and she stopped sniggering.

'I'm sorry,' she said, squeezing his arm and smiling. 'In order for the dead king to rise, his sons had to cut their penises. I'm not kidding. The sacrifice of blood was needed for their parent's resurrection. Quite a sacrifice, no?'

'Yes,' he replied, thinking of the urn of ashes that he had left at the crematorium, the mother that he, the only son, had failed to bring back from the dead. He looked back down at the sarcophagus and attempted his own critique of the engravings.

Dressed in a hatched skirt and a feathered headdress, with thick bangles on his arms and legs and sandals strapped to his flailing feet, the expressionless king seemed strangely passive to his fate. It was as if he was in a chemical trance, the sculptor leaving a vacuum in his eyes to artistically prove the point. To Justin, the entire scene resembled a nightmarish LSD trip: a royal space cadet flying past goblins and half-human, half-beast chimeras, the tripping corpse looking up at a foliated cross and a cackling parrot. The surrealist treatment continued beneath the king's falling backside. Feline and serpent fangs, the jaws of the White-Boned-Snake that Anne had referred to, rose out of lily pads, ready to catch him and transport him under water. Hieroglyphs framed the tablet, words composed of an amalgamation of animal faces and human skulls, while the sides of the sarcophagus displayed figures sprouting up from plant shoots. He wanted to ask her who the individuals were, but he thought better of it: '*His family reserving him a place in Xibalba*', his mother and foreign relatives overseeing proceedings. He empathized with poor Pacal.

A yell of 'Hey mister!' distracted him. A large pink-skinned man in below-the-knee shorts and a Dallas Cowboys baseball cap, his headdress worn back to front, huffed over a camera strapped to his chest.

'Are you gonna move on or what?' the big Texan drawled. 'We want to take some pictures as well, you know.'

Justin saw the queue of flabby clones stretch up the steps.

'Sorry,' he said to the man. Anne made her ascent up the stairs and, after one last look at the falling king, he followed her to daylight.

Outside again, free from the cramped queue and the tetchy Texan, they sat down on the top step of the temple, some twenty-five metres above the 'Big-Water' plaza. Justin lit a cigarette and Anne puffed on her filter-free Alitas, the cancer stick of choice for a backpacker in Mexico. They flinched at the brightness in the clouds and at the ruined buildings in the jungle clearing. People clambered over the ancient walls and causeways as if they were investigative ants, while others congregated by the cafeteria and gift shop, Mayan children pouncing on the tourists with baskets of handicrafts. They both looked out in the direction of The Palace, a multi-storey complex of buildings, arched walkways and an observatory tower, crumbled masonry leaving rooms without walls. A breeze from the lush mountains around them teased goose pimples out of their bare arms and legs.

Justin stubbed out his cigarette on the temple. He watched the butt skip down the steps that the bodies of sacrificial victims had once tumbled down. Anne passed him a bottle of water and he took a swig. He returned the bottle to her and again felt remorse at the way he had ignored her. Whether it was the heat, the primordial setting, or just the way that her lips touched the bottle, he began to fantasize that she could do more than translate tombs for him. As Anne dabbed her tanned skin with a handkerchief, removed the perspiration off her neck and forehead, he began to appreciate her company in his remaining days.

'We'd better go,' she said, snapping him out of his trance. 'They're probably waiting for us back at the bus.'

'Yes,' he replied, reminded again of the real purpose of his tour to Chiapas. 'You're right. We should go.'

On all fours and feet first, they climbed down the narrow steps of the Temple of Inscriptions.

'You have two hours for lunch,' Manolo informed his passengers, the eight Europeans who had been sleeping off the run around the ruins in the back of his shabby minibus. 'We meet back here, in the central square, OK, amigos?'

Stopping in the town of Ocosingo, a bit of 'real Mexico' according to Anne's speaking guidebook, the minibus parked opposite the white-painted church of San Jacinto. It was the last stop before they set up camp in the mountains. Justin opened his eyes and saw the girl's head on his shoulder. Her hair tickled his chin.

'We have to get up,' he whispered into her ear and gently pushed her off him.

'Where are we?' she grunted, pushing her hands down on his thighs to sit up. She rubbed her eyes and looked out of the bus's dirty windows. In the foreground, seated on a low wall in the shade of an olive tree, two Mayan men stared at her from beneath their straw Stetsons. Chewing sunflower seeds as they watched the world go by, their skin wrinkled like leather, they spat the shells onto the sidewalk and continued to say nothing. In the background, small children chased each other and disturbed mangy dogs that sunbathed in dried-up fountains and flowerless flowerbeds. Street vendors pushed trolleys of fried plantain chips, barbecued maize cobs and helium-filled balloons, shiny Disney characters on string. Overhead, crisscrossing electricity pylons and tangled cables, faded bunting flapped a vestige of a carnival and the paraphernalia of an undemocratic election.

'But where are the mountains?' Anne asked, to an unresponsive Justin.

The minibus emptied and the group split up. The two German couples opted for the food market. While the inseparable pair of Dutch romantics, their hands rarely seen apart, strolled to a nearby pizzeria and ordered the 'Zapatista Special', a snack with a *'fiery flavour'* to it, or so the blackboard outside proclaimed. Anne suggested to Justin that they lunched together. Although he wanted to be alone, to collect his thoughts and gather some remaining kit for the waterfall, he didn't want to abandon her. Also, after the time he spent with her at the temple, he no longer felt irritated by her. So long as she didn't distract him too much, the comfort she gave him, he thought, feeling her hand on his arm, removed some of his anxiety.

'Hey, you two,' Manolo called out to them from a street cart selling soft drinks, 'two hours, remember.' He cracked open a Pepsi, rubbed his belly under a purple string vest and winked at them from behind his Oakley shades. Justin waved his hand in acknowledgement and dragged Anne down a street of open-fronted shops, past racks of machetes, black rubber boots and red bandanas.

'So,' she said, struggling to catch up with him after pausing to sniff the fresh bread of a bakery, 'where are you taking me? And, please, slow down.'

'Lunch,' he said, walking faster. 'This will do.' He stopped at a

101

restaurant that welcomed American Express and Visa cardholders.

'I can't afford that.'

'You don't have to,' he replied. The return of his abruptness confused her. 'I'm sorry,' he continued, seeing her put-out expression, 'I'll pick it up. Now just go inside. We can fatten the cow on my company credit card.'

'What fat cow?' she asked.

'It doesn't matter. Look, just go and get your derriere inside, please.' He opened the door and pushed her inside.

'Señor?' A boy's voice called out from behind him.

Justin paused in the restaurant's doorway and turned round. A Maya youth, a teenage boy leaning against a bicycle a few sizes too small for him, stared at him from a gutter of splat mangoes and squashed turkey giblets.

'You want some stuff for you and your pretty lady?' The boy moved closer to him. 'For your vacation?'

'What?' Justin replied, his hand on the restaurant door.

'You want some weed or pills?' the boy whispered to his back.

His body half in the restaurant, Justin stopped and turned round again. Looking at the dealer, whose screwed-up face advertised the effects of his supply, he recalled the tomb of Pacal: the king's eyes left blank, the trippy monsters breaking his fall into the watery Otherworld.

He let go of the door and struck a deal with the boy: hallucinogenic, must be Mayan, in half an hour, payment on delivery, meet him at the restaurant and be discreet. They shook hands and the boy cycled off. Justin went in the restaurant and pulled up a chair next to Anne.

'What do you do?' Anne asked Justin, while she mopped up her plate with a tortilla. 'And how come you are travelling alone? Are you meeting up with friends later on? I'm going on to Oaxaca and Mexico City to meet friends.'

'I work for a bank.' He put down his knife and fork. 'As for your second question, I like to travel alone.'

The hereditary migraine, the poison passed from mother to son, throbbed in his skull. He looked at his watch; there were only twelve hours to go.

'Good,' Anne said with her mouth full of maize and minced

beef. 'I mean no, that's cool. I'm like you, single and travelling by myself. Not a banker, mind. Why did you want to be one of them?'

'I don't know.' He rubbed his temples. 'It just sort of happened.'

'If it's any consolation, you don't look like a banker. And you can always change your career.'

'And I suppose that will make me fit in?' He didn't want to sound harsh, but the small talk wound him up. The last thing he wanted to do was talk about his fucked-up life. He wondered when the drug-pedalling boy would show up again.

From behind a beaded curtain, the entrance to the kitchen, a cleaver slammed down on meat and bone.

'After our trip to the mountains, where will you go?'

'Somewhere quiet,' he said, lowering his voice and trying to give Anne a polite smile.

'Sounds good. Perhaps I can go with you?'

'No.' Another thud came from within the kitchen. 'Waiter,' he called out to the back of the room, 'the bill please.' He mimed pen-to-paper to a man watching a black and white western, a waiter glued to a toaster-sized TV.

The waiter dragged his feet off a table. Keeping one eye on a fuzzy shootout, the cowboys giving it to the Indians, he randomly punched the buttons of a calculator and wrote down the standard fee charged to a couple of gringos for two beef stews and two cokes. He walked to their table and handed the bill, on a silver saucer of complimentary mints, to Justin. His top price provoking not so much as a raised eyebrow, he scampered off with Justin's Amex card and disappeared behind the beaded curtain. Three minutes later, the sound of gunshots, whooshing arrows and howling Indians blocking Anne's attempts at conversation, the waiter returned for a signature.

'Mister,' the waiter said, returning the card and taking the signed chit, 'there's a boy in the kitchen who wants to see you. Do you want me to get rid of him?' Raised voices, a row in Spanish, replaced the thuds in the kitchen. The beaded curtain shook.

'No. Don't worry. I'll see him.' Justin stood up, pushed his chair under the table and picked up his leather bag.

'What is it?' Anne asked him.

'It's fine,' he said, gently touching her shoulder, 'I'm just picking up some provisions for the mountains. I won't be long.'

He followed the waiter and swept the strings of wooden beads to one side. A pile of plucked and jaundiced-looking chickens, on a cutting board by an oil-fuelled stove, greeted him at the kitchen's entrance. Heads still attached and beaks opened wide, screams fixed at the point of slaughter, the birds perfumed the room with a smell of rotten meat. Flies, activated by the scent of decay and stopping via an ultraviolet zapper, dropped to the floor and whizzed in circles in sawdust and crumbs. A sandy-coloured kitten skidded into view and, after much toying and prodding, munched on the fried and currant-like snacks. In the corner of the room, where the pots and pans were hooked up to drip-dry, was the human action. Too stoned to register the danger of fighting a man with a cleaver, the boy from the street argued with the chef. The waiter pulled the boy back and pushed him towards Justin.

'What have you got?' Justin asked, pointing to a brown paper bag in the boy's hand. The chef sulked off and the waiter stood by the butchered chickens and watched.

'I get what you wanted, man,' the boy said, catching his breath. 'Shit, man, that dude was about to chop my hand off. You came just in time, man.'

'Yeah, well, let's see what you have then.' Justin flinched at the boy's breath, the whiff of bad egg on black gums. He opened out his hand to receive the contents of the paper bag.

'Hojas,' the boy said, spittle rattling between his decayed teeth. He emptied the contents of the bag, a package of cellophane-wrapped leaves, into Justin's palm. 'The best shit that I have. Sacred shit, from the Mazatec companeros of Oaxaca. Nothing like it in Maya lands. You like?'

'I'm sorry, but I don't want these.' Justin sniffed the leaves and returned them to the paper bag. 'I asked for Mayan drugs, what the ancients used.' He desired authenticity, a proper Pacal-style sending off.

'No, man. This is much better than Maya shrooms. This is medicine for the soul. Trust me.'

'And how am I supposed to take these?' He put a hand in the bag and re-examined the leaves wrapped in cellophane.

'Smoke the hojas, you do.' The boy pulled a small wooden pipe out of his pocket. 'Here, you buy and I give you my pipe for free. Deal?'

'It alters consciousness, right?'

'No understand.'

'Never mind.' With the minibus leaving in ten minutes and

104

with Anne by his side, he knew that he had little choice in the matter: there was no time to browse Ocosingo's alleyways for 'By Royal Appointment', King Pacal warranted, hallucinogens. 'Medicine for the soul' was at least the right prescription for him. 'How much do you want for it?' he asked the boy, as he opened his wallet and paged his last wad of pesos.

'Umm,' the boy mulled, looking at the cash.

'Tell you what.' Justin looked at the notes and then at the set of smiling brown teeth. 'Why don't you have this. It should be enough.'

'Gracias.' The boy took the bulk of Justin's wallet, fanned his face with the notes and stuffed them into his pocket. Justin put the hojas into his bag and they shook hands. 'Have a good vacation, man.'

The boy left via a door at the rear of the kitchen, raising his finger at the chef before cycling off, and Justin followed the waiter through the beads and back into the restaurant.

At the table, refusing to sit down, he asked Anne if she was ready to go and she replied 'Yes.' She rose up from her chair and together they walked towards the door.

'Señor?' the waiter said, pushing an empty silver tray into Justin's chest. Anne was already on the pavement outside.

'Yes?' Justin replied. He slung his bag over his shoulder,

'Many police between here and your bus. It's not good for a foreigner to be caught with drugs – it's highly profitable for the cops in Chiapas. You pay and I'll see to it that they hear nothing.'

Justin dropped one peso on the silver tray. He slammed the door behind him.

The minibus braked hard. Tyres skidded on loose chips of gravel and the tour group pulled over. His eyes wide open and yet blind to the journey so far, the blade of Dan's penknife opened up in his hand, Justin bolted back to reality. He sucked the blood that oozed from his finger. The blade had proven its worth, its sharpness, and he examined the neat incision in his skin. His face pressed against the window, his breath misting up the glass, he saw the sun setting behind the mountains, pinky red streamers above peaks of dark green forest. Bereft of town and streetlight, his final frontier was a barren land of pine and rock. It was perfect, even better than he had imagined. Then a man in a camouflaged helmet walked past. Smoking a cigarette and fingering the trigger of a semi automatic rifle, the green man disappeared round the back of the minibus. Justin heeled his bag and its herbal contents under his seat.

'Army checkpoint,' Manolo declared to the anxious faces in the back. Despite the low light, the tour guide still wore his Oakley sunglasses. 'Don't worry. Just don't mention the "Z" word and you'll be fine.'

'What's the "Z" word?' Justin asked. Everyone stared at him; he had not participated in any of the backseat banter, marvelled at the sunset and the mountains, pointed at the pretty Maya villages and black mountain sheep, at any point during the journey.

'Zapatista,' Manolo replied, grinning, 'the army is fighting them in the highlands.'

'Are we safe?' Anne asked, sitting next to Justin and looking concerned.

'The Zaps won't harm you. They like foreigners. Gringos pity the Indians and treat Subcommandante Marcos, the Zaps' leader, as the new Che Guevara. It's the army you got to watch out for.'

Two soldiers, who brandished guns and chewed tobacco, ordered the tourists off the minibus. They told them to form a line, pointing their rifles at the side of the road, and to have passports and visa cards ready for inspection. There were about a dozen soldiers in total; Justin counted them. A couple scaled the roof of the minibus and searched the rucksacks, tents and provisions strapped to the roof. Another two went inside, crawled through empty chip and sweet packets, water bottles, backpacks, guide-books and day bags. In the back of an olive-green pick-up, a plain-clothed slob, who wore jeans and a black T-shirt, sat his fat arse down on a bench. Commandant Hernandez looked at the line of foreigners from behind his mirrored shades. Justin stared back and shook his head.

'You!' Commandant Hernandez bellowed. He jumped up from the bench, bounced off the pick-up and approached Justin. 'Passport.' Although he was gifted in girth, he had to stand on his toes to address his taller victim. 'Passport,' he repeated, shouting up at Justin.

Justin handed over his passport.

'What interest do you have in Chenalho, Justin Callaghan?' Commandant Hernandez flicked through the pages of Justin's passport.

'I don't know.' Justin stared at the white face and red eyes, his reflection, in the man's shades.

'You're here as a tourist?'

'Yes.' Justin looked down at the finger stabbing his chest.

'You look Mexican, gringo. You really a tourist?'

'I said, yes.'

'Good.' Commandant Hernandez spat at the road. 'You make sure that you remain a tourist, Englishman. That you don't go straying from your faggot camping trip, outstay your welcome, do more than shake your head to piss me off. You hear me?'

'I hear you.' Justin glanced at Anne, who looked terrified as she watched his interrogation. When Commandant Hernandez wasn't looking he gave her a small smile as a way of reassurance.

'Now fuck off and get back into the bus.' Commandant Hernandez slapped the passport into Justin's hand. 'All of you. I don't want to see any of you again.' He turned on his shiny boots and strutted back to the soldiers in the pick-up. The vehicle keeled over as the soldiers heaved him up.

'Not the brightest of ideas to upset Commandant Hernandez,' Manolo said, stopping Justin at the door to the minibus. The Germans, Dutch and Anne were already inside. 'That man's pride is as big as his butt. You're lucky he didn't arrest you. What were you thinking?'

'I didn't do anything,' Justin replied. Ignorant to all that was around him, he was immune to the bullies in tight jeans and vests.

'With his paramilitary dogs, Hernandez has the police and the army eating out of his hand. That man has his own law out here.'

'But I didn't . . .'

'That son of a bitch can easily take away my business. You and your selfish stunt could have lost me everything. Next time, señor, think about others.'

Justin bowed his head, his face hidden under his fringe, and he entered the minibus. He took his seat next to Anne and ignored the stares as he squeezed past her legs. Folding his fleece into a pillow, he leaned against the window and looked outside. The sun was now fully tucked behind the mountains, the streamers had gone and the sky had turned blood-red. He saw his eyes, a watery reflection in the glass, float over the burning forest. Should the gods turn him into a ghost, he looked at his projected eyes, the fat commandant would be the first to be haunted.

A knot of naked feet toed Justin's clothes and his leather bag. Twisting and kicking, the feet pushed his sacrificial garments, his jeans and a blue shirt, against the tent's zipped-up flaps. The grave goods in his leather bag rattled and Justin, who chose to lie on his back and guide her on top, tensed his neck. He lifted his head up and, not going for a breast, looking over a sweaty thigh instead, checked that they hadn't kicked anything out of the tent and onto the wet grass.

It was not going well, but he blamed himself and not her. He was stupid to think that he could perform and he was ashamed with himself for leading her on. She sat down on him, her eyes squeezed shut and her body embalmed blue by the moonlight on an aquamarine flysheet, while he thought of dinner, barbecued chicken and more tortillas, which they had eaten around the campfire. He had thought about smoking some hojas, to gee himself up and numb his head for the act, but decided that he should save his medicine for the next day. Overall, it was a stupid idea and he regretted it.

'This feels so good,' Anne moaned.

The pull was easier than the erection: one of the tents was missing. 'Fallen from the minibus roof or stolen by the soldiers,' Manolo had made his excuses. Justin and Anne, whom everyone thought were lovers anyway, the French girl treating him like he was hers, were forced to share. But neither of them resisted the order: she bagged her man, was rewarded for putting up with his surliness, and he had something to add to his last rites. She had caught him weeping under a palm tree, his face in his hands away from the fire, tears for his mother trickling down his face. She kissed him on an unshaven cheek. A crate of Dos Equis beers and a bottle of rum removed the need for foreplay.

'Ah!'

Her nails scratched his chest and his skin burned under her touch. He licked a breast to fake affection. Sweat and insect repellent stung his tongue and he quickly withdrew from her nipple.

'Ummm . . .'

He wondered whether she had already come, whether he could now will an ejaculation and set his alarm clock, was free to do one last rehearsal before bed. The matter of waking up on time, not to mention departing from the camp without anyone noticing, preyed on his mind as she slid up and down on him. Searching for a distraction, forgetting that he was having sex, he heard the rustle of leaves and the harp of crickets from outside. It was as if every nocturnal creature had come to watch and laugh. She drew his face into her chest and, his ears muffed by her breasts and her heartbeat overpowering an owl's hoots and distant thunder, he wanted to thank her.

'Oh.'

Coming up for air and with something else to think about, he visualized the path at the edge of the campsite. His fingers on her bottom and his thumbs moving towards the fringe of her pubic triangle, he reckoned that it wouldn't be too difficult to find his way. After dinner, Manolo had run through the next day's itinerary and kindly pointed out the path to the falls, the mountain sheep trail that led out of the camp's clearing. Later, while the others played a game of poker and bonded without him, Justin sneaked off to take a closer look. Sure enough, in a gap in the trees, a black tunnel that he shone his torch at, the sheep had marked the way with hoof prints and droppings. So long as the shit and mud didn't run out, he couldn't envisage there being a problem.

'Oh! Oh! Oh!'

Quiet Beth, neighing Tania and one or two faceless one-night-standers replaced Anne. He thought about constructing an all time 'Top Ten,' do what his colleague Dan did: be a wanker and bestow honours on the movers and shakers in his sexual history. But the joke was always on him. It was always his fault, whichever way he looked at it. He was the one that always fucked up, not her or her or her.

He came and she fell off him. They lay side by side, saying nothing and a good inch apart. He looked up at the shadows of branches, the skeletal limbs and fingers that clawed the canvas ceiling. Before he caught sight of his mother, the shadows of her bony hands reached out for him, he picked up his alarm clock and set it for 4 a.m.

'Goodnight,' Anne said, kissing him on his chest.

'Goodnight,' he replied, placing the clock by his ear.

Seven

Justin lay on his back and stared up at the tent's canvas ceiling. His head felt like it was about to explode. It was still dark and, as he had been doing all night, he checked the time on his alarm clock. '03:22AM', the clock's digital numerals seemed to barely change. In his head he once again went through the procedures that he would need to do at the waterfall. He recalled the sarcophagus at Palenque, the image of the falling King Pacal indelibly marked in his mind, and Anne's description of blood sacrifices for dead parents and watery Otherworlds. The coincidences that had confronted him on his journey were too great for him to ignore. His imagination stoked by Pacal, to kill time he even attempted to read more about ancient Mayan sacrifices in his guidebook, under his sheet and using Anne's torch. What began with a photograph of a waterfall in his London flat, started off as a simple jump, now included a knife and hallucinogenic drugs.

Eager to get on with the job, tortured for too long as he waited for the light of dawn, he turned over to check that Anne was still asleep. She was curled up in her sleeping bag and her back faced him. Satisfied by her lack of movement, he slowly pulled off his sheet and moved towards the tent's flaps.

'What time is it?' Anne groaned, stirring in her sleeping bag. He froze. She was too groggy to prise her eyes fully open. 'Why are you getting up now? It's still dark.'

'It's OK,' Justin replied, trying to sound calm, 'I'm just going for a pee,' he stuttered, 'you can go back to sleep.' He wanted to tell her the truth, to allow her to hug him and say goodbye properly, but he knew that was impossible.

Anne turned over in her sleeping bag and he unzipped the tent. He picked up his clothes and bag and went outside. The moon had disappeared and darkness greeted him. Borrowing Anne's torch, his hands shaking a beam by his bare feet, he put on his blue shirt, jeans, socks and shoes. When he had refreshed his haggard face with icy water, stuck his head under the rusty tap of

111

an old oil barrel, and rinsed out his dry mouth, he waved the torch through his bag for a final roll call of equipment. His pupils darted from side to side as he saw Dan's Swiss Army knife, the wrap of hojas leaves, the pipe, the guidebook and his passport, his body's ID. The rest of his possessions, mainly unneeded clothes and paperwork on La Tela Maya's takeover, he cleared up and stored inside his rucksack's pouches; they were someone else's worry now. He abandoned the unwanted luggage by the ashes of the campfire and, following parental example, left no note. Almost ready, he opened his wallet and placed his remaining pounds and pesos back in the tent, at the end of Anne's sleeping bag.

'Take care,' he whispered to her, gulping. He used the same words that his mother had said to him. Only Anne was a sleeping stranger, nothing of real significance to him.

He gently zipped up the tent and hid her from sight. His heart beat so hard that he found it difficult to breathe. The leather bag on his shoulder and the torch avoiding the small cluster of tents, he swallowed the cold mountain air and headed towards the path at the edge of the camp's clearing.

Turning trunks and branches pale, the beam of torchlight transformed trees into holocaust victims, subjects of a grizzly black and white photograph. When the sun eventually emerged, through a morning mist and above forested mountains, Justin threw the torch in the bushes and moved even faster. A breeze rushed past him and the veins on his arms and wrists, which had up until now been prominent and promising, disappeared under goose pimples and raised hairs. He shivered and blew on his cold hands. His fingers still reeked of Anne, her salty scent stuck under his nails, and he hoped that she wouldn't blame herself for what he was about to do.

A rumble of thunder restored his focus. Laughing at himself for thinking that his resolve could be shaken by a one-night stand, that Anne actually cared, he broke into a jog. Like the impatient kid at the crematorium, he skipped over puddles to speed up the funeral. The rumble grew louder and he realized that it was too continuous for thunder. He stopped and listened. 'The waterfall?' he asked himself, spinning around and seeing nothing but pine trees. He started to panic and a sudden fear entered his head. Manolo, full of a tour guide's bullshit about secluded waters, had suckered him into a trip to the '*Niagra Fucking Falls*' of Chiapas. He imagined coaches of honeymooners, who had woken up early to picnic by the cascades, cooing over their breakfast hampers as he attempted to come to terms with his own personal demons. But he couldn't face a postponement, he could not wait a day longer, and he decided to keep going. If necessary, he could continue on through the mountains until he found a peaceful and private setting. The avoidance of people was his very reason for being there.

The noise faded out, birds sang and insects screeched encouragement. Mother Nature had him to herself again and he felt his confidence return. Beyond the tops of the trees, past cobwebs that bridged branches and glistened on pine needles, the sun burnt a hole in the clouds. The heat charmed his pulse and he prodded the returning veins on his wrists with his finger. He plucked a cigarette from his pocket. Inhaling deeply, a slipstream of smoke followed him through the forest.

He had walked not far, when once again he was forced to stop. This time it was his body that was responsible. Dropping the butt of his cigarette, coughing as he gasped for air, he caught sight of his reflection in a boggy puddle. He had become obsessed about his cleanliness, about how he was going to be perceived wherever he was going to be going, and he picked up a stick and poked the mud off his shoes, scraping the drier bits off his shins. Country living, getting dirty, was not unfamiliar to him and he tried to pull himself together, snap out of his paranoia. He picked up the pace again and reminisced over his childhood, the fun he used to have playing a mudded-up boy Rambo. Hiding in a field's foxhole with a plastic machine gun, he would wait for dog-walking gooks to cross a meadow of daisies, pretending that it was a matter of life or death whether he was spotted or not. The scariest missions, however, were those which he performed at dawn. Fully camouflaged up, he would spy on the Callaghan's neighbours, who had a barn of screaming pigs and who collected smashed up cars in their backyard. He never understood his school friends and their obsession with boring computer games.

He threw the stick back to the trees and ignored the puddles, splashing his feet in them like he was a child again. The path left the forest and he zigzagged up a steep incline, up a largely treeless slope. He gripped onto volcanic rocks and dead roots to maintain his balance. At the top of the slope and in the thick of the mist, he saw a grassy plateau on a mountain's edge. There was another rumble. His heart jumped.

113

'Damn it!' he shouted out. His echo answered him back in the fog. He did a 360 degree turn and, his paranoia returning, he expected to catch the guys with the hot dogs, candy floss, racks of postcards and throwaway T-shirts, small businesses by a sign to *The Falls this way, folks!* But he saw only mountain-grass, grey-green blades swaying in a breeze, and solitary boulders, shiny and black from the wet. The occasional dead tree, the last men standing on a smoking battlefield, wooden comrades already uprooted, decayed and committed to soil, were his only companions. Then he heard the roar in the mist again. It was neither thunder nor a coach's engine. His heart pounding, the whites of his eyes exposed, he ran towards the source of the noise, the fog growing thicker. The ground squelched, slurped and burped. He floundered to stay upright.

The mist curled into his mother's white dress, stark folds inflating and deflating, her cuffs craned up and ready to catch him. As he clumped towards her open arms, the air grew damper and his clothes stuck to his skin. The strain of exercised muscles threatened to rip his shirt off his back, and his jeans, sodden as well as filthy, rubbed his thighs and the back of his knees. Visibility was reduced to a few metres and he slowed down. Ready for another step forward, he oozed a foot out of the mud and watched the water fill the footprints that he left behind. His pupils dilated and his green irises tinged with red, he saw the water beneath his leading foot. He stopped in time. He had reached a stream, one of the sources of the waterfall.

Taking short and sharp breaths, he followed the stream in the direction of its current. The mist was too dense to see the stream's conclusion, the start of the falls, but from the ear-splitting roar, he believed it to be not far. Water seeped into his shoes and the wet leather squeaked against his toes. Every so often the spectre of his mother would reappear, her vaporous hand urging him on, her white body gliding over the river before she reverted back to shapeless spray. Her presence spurred him on and he waded through the mud and water faster. Eventually the mist cleared to reveal a dawn sun. He swept his wet hair out of his eyes and at long last saw his destination. He felt his stomach roll over and he thought he would be sick.

His body tense and his eyes fixed to the ground, he shuffled towards the river's drop. Going down on his hands and knees, the leather bag on his back, he crawled over a large stone slab and stretched his neck over the cliff's edge. He estimated the fall to be at least twenty metres, although the spray made it difficult to be certain. Height, however, was an irrelevance. The real trick, he knew, as he rolled up his shirt's sleeves, was in the wrists.

A rainbow illuminated the way down. The band of colour, which rose up from the bubbles below, was pricked by the treetops on the banks and the boulders that scaled the length of the falls. His head pounded almost as hard as his heart, and he surveyed the forest, water and rocks for gatecrashers and have-a-go diplomats, people who might have a crack at changing his mind, waste his and their time. Clarity was poor, but he figured that if he couldn't see any of them, then they, whoever they might be, couldn't see him. Reality beating the picture in the guidebook and everything going to plan for a change, he crawled back along the stone.

He hooked his bag on a branch of a diseased tree, trying to be as methodical as he could; it helped him to remain focused. Shorn of its limbs, bar two branches at mid-trunk, the tree was weathered into the shape of a cross. With the stone platform adjoining it, the drop only a couple of metres away, it also made a convenient diving station. The bag secured on the cross, he undid its straps and first picked out the penknife, Dan's gift. His knees weakened and he had to grab the tree's trunk to stay upright.

He flicked open the larger of the two blades, the one between the nail clippers and flathead screwdriver, the one which he had tested on his finger in the minibus. The blade's shiny steel reflected in the low sun and he examined it. He carefully placed it on the slab of rock, his operating-cum-altar table, and then pulled out the pipe. Tapping it in the palm of his hand, clearing its bowl and passageways of charred narcotics, he wiped its mouthpiece on his jeans to remove any trace of the bad-breathed dealer. A pain stabbed him in the stomach and he had to pause for a bit. He repeatedly swallowed to stop himself from vomiting.

The pipe joined the knife and he searched for his anaesthetic. Thinking that he had found it, his fingers touching a cellophane-wrapped package in the bag, he instead pulled out the 'Miss Bossy' T-shirt. In the rush to go, he had forgotten to dispose of it.

'Fuck it,' he said. Since it had come this far, eluded his earlier inventory check, and since he was increasingly obsessed by fate, he decided to keep it with him. The T-shirt, he thought, would be a useful piece of evidence in the coroner's inquest, when it came to identifying his corpse. Thinking about extra weight to carry, it also gave him an idea. When he had removed the hojas and returned Miss Bossy to the guidebook, watch and passport, he picked up some pebbles off the streambed. He dropped the stone weights into the bag and refastened the straps.

'Yes!' he shouted out, as he weighed the bag's ballast in his hands. Worried that he might have attracted unwanted publicity, his mind playing tricks on him again, he ducked down and grazed his knees on the slab. He looked around him. In the fog of the plateau, he saw only the solitary trees, sad-looking and leafless, and the shiny black boulders that poked out of the marshland. But an ensuing racket, so close that he nearly jumped before time, seemed to confirm his fears. He was not alone.

'*Wah!*' a bird squawked. Hopping on the cross of the tree, the bird flapped its grey wings and flashed its yellow eyes and speckled belly at him. '*Wah!*'

'Shoo,' Justin whispered, 'piss off.' He lightly clapped his hands, his shoes squelching and squeaking on the stone slab, but the bird just tilted its crested head, blinked its fiery eyes and stuck to its perch on the cross. It continued to stare at him and he resigned himself to the fact that he would have a feathered undertaker as a witness. He surveyed the fossilized trees and prehistoric rocks for further intruders. As certain as he could be that the plateau was free from any other unwelcome guests, he removed the hojas from its cellophane packet and crushed the leaves in his palm. Scentless and identical in appearance to the sage he used to douse on tasteless pizza in front of tasteless TV shows, he worried about the strength of the hojas. He packed the pipe with as much of it as he could, leaves spilling out over the bowl's rim, and returned it to the stone altar. With his back facing the tree and the bird, the latter observing silence like it knew what was to come, he kneeled before the scalpel and potion.

It was a good few minutes before he did anything else. He just sat there on the stone slab, thinking and not thinking, looking down at the drop and then at the sky. Water dripped down his pale and furrowed face, his eyes not blinking. In this state of limbo, between life and death, he altered the order of service and lit the last of his cigarettes. He puffed smoke into the mist. Woolly hoops flew over the cliff and disappeared into the foam of the falls, and he reflected upon the appropriateness of a verbal dismissal. Recalling his mother's low-key cremation, he imagined his epitaph.

The poetry was not forthcoming. Pointless years left him not a stanza's worth of material to celebrate in his curriculum vitae. He tried to do an 'end of term report' and praise a young boy's *'teamwork on the playing fields'*, his *'good grounding for a successful future'*, his *'determination and his sense of good'*. Instead he highlighted the man's *'need to get his act together'*, the *'wasted potential'*, the *'doesn't really mix in with the rest of his class'*, the *'you won't make a living doing that sort of job'*. There was nothing to credit.

Foundering on a no comment for himself, the knife beckoning him on the stone, he tried to imagine who might have bothered to show up at his funeral. There were his two work colleagues, who had brought him gifts of a treasure map and a multipurpose dagger, supplements to a statutory *'We'll miss you in the office (joke!)'* Hallmark card. As for school and university friends, he could think of no one that could prise themselves away from their busy lives of work, girlfriends, wives, children or, in the case of Martin, druggy parties. His Spanish relatives ruled out, he thought about plane tickets to London for the shepherds in Mexico, who gave him a tour guide's telephone number, mythological inspiration and a sacrifice for his last night. Even now, on the precipice of death, sleeping with Anne preyed on his mind. She only added to his lifelong list of guilt.

But it was his mother who had led him to the brink. It was she, the one person that he had placed his trust in and the only incentive to stick around, who deserved a special mention. Her suicide, he dragged hard on the cigarette, had proven that even she didn't give a shit about him. Because she was the final push, her ghost now baying for him in the spray of water, it was only right that he dedicated his fall to her.

Now the stage was set and his mind was free from sentimentality, the time had come. The pipe in one hand and a disposable lighter in the other, he torched the hojas and sucked down the flame. Hot smoke burnt his lips and scorched the back of his throat. He managed to hold the smoke in his lungs for three seconds, what he would normally do with weed, before he coughed up a black cloud and gasped for some of the muggy air. Repeating the process, emptying the ash on the stone slab and refilling the pipe, he smoked until the last of the wrap was burnt and vaporized hojas stung his lungs.

Far from being hallucinogenic, the first hit sobered him up. He looked over the cliff's edge, his route down, and started to be all rational about how quick it would be to die. He almost wished that he had done what his mother had done and gone with an overdose, put up with the ignominy of being handled by strangers. Feeling slightly bemused by it all, he looked around him, at the dead trees in the clearing mist, and began to have no issues with an uncelebrated funeral.

The next hit was hardly an improvement. His humour fanned and his predicament ribbed, dribbling and sweating in laughter, his tragicomedy toppled him from his stone prayer mat and he nearly rolled off the cliff. In gut-wrenching hysteria, coughing uncontrollably and spitting black phlegm off the edge of the cliff, he giggled at the knife before him and the characters that had led him to the waterfall.

'I don't want to see any of you faggots again. Especially you, Englishman,' he mimicked the commandant at the roadblock, laughing with the parrot on the tree at the soldiers struggling with his fat arse. 'Thought you could cut some limes with it,' he looked at the Swiss Army knife on the stone slab, 'Your diego type as well,' he copied Dan's smirk. Giggling at the mist over the falls, the fact that the bank actually paid for his one-way plane ticket, he saw his mother standing in her garden of weeds and empty beer cans. 'You certainly shouldn't be holding back because of me.' He went into hysterics and wiped his sweat and tears on his sleeves.

Still laughing, he drew on the last of the hojas. Prior to the full effects of the final hit, the third stage of alteration, he rubbed his forearms and wrists, grabbed the penknife and felt for the fattest veins. Slicing right and then left, skin hissing on each laceration, he fell back against the tree and dropped his bleeding wrists to his knees. The hojas kicked in and the trip began.

Roots squirmed in the shower of blood, the drops that dribbled down his red and brown streaked jeans. They wove a cradle for their host to lie in, a wooden throne for a deceased king, while vines slid into his flesh and gorged on his nutrients. Leaves unfurled from newly nourished buds and the cross-shaped tree, which woke up from the dead, burst into a rainbow of blossom. On the two branches, the cross's crossbeam, a supporter's gallery of ghouls and Spanish relatives mingled. Nibbling on cucumber sandwiches and sipping sweet sherry, like he imagined you do at a proper funeral, they chatted about the wee boy's coming of age and the poor lad's descent into loneliness. They concluded, chinking crystal glasses together, that it was '*All for the best: for his sake as well as for everyone else's.*' A bird, with a long turquoise tail and a speckled belly, like that on Pacal's tomb, shrieked spells from the top of the foliated cross. It dared him to catch a wave and to surf down. '*Go on – be a man!*'

He stood up and unhooked the extra-weighted bag off the tree. The blood from his wrists splashed on the stone altar and, smiling up at the priestly parrot, he stepped up to the edge of the cliff. His green eyes, as vacant as those carved on the sarcophagus, looked down at the drooling fangs of Anne's description of a White-Boned-Snake, the water that crashed beneath him. Blood coagulated on the stone and the hardened drops turned into files of red ants. Forming into garrisons, the ants charged off the cliff, launched a kamikaze assault on the snake and showed the first-timer how it was supposed to be done. Out of the pit of the snake's jaw, his mother twirled a crash mat in her white dress, her bloodlust circumnavigating the entrance to his watery tomb. Obedient to her as always, the boy slung his heavy satchel over his back and, assuming the dive position, tipped his toes and stretched his arms above his head. Blood trickling down his forearms, pattering on his pale face, he leapt into her arms.

He glided downwards, his hands skimming the curtain of water, a trail of life's slop demarcating his fall with two rusty tramlines. The ants skydived next to him and, unfairly opening tiny parachutes, they waved him goodbye, drifted to the rainbow in the sky and left him to fly solo. But he was not alone for long. The streaming water had plenty of gargoyles to bid him adieu. Soon he flew past Pacal himself. Memorialized in rock, a face eroded into a boulder that jutted out of the falls, the drowned antecedent laughed at his protégé. An arm bashed against a beaked nose, stigmata exploding, and he crowned the king with a ruby headdress. Then he saw the fangs of the white snake, which sparkled in the sun. On the creature's forked tongue was a billowing white dress, a coffin lining spread across the pool.

The force of impact and the icy water lowered his drug-induced temperature. He thrashed his red armbands in the maze of currents, flaring bloody spirals around him, and expended life's last drops until his arms turned limp. A vertical eddy sucked him down. Playing with him as if it was a child abusing a doll, it threw him around a bit before it grew bored, teed him off on a helter-skelter course and putted him for a hole-in-one on a green of reeds and pebbles. Shunted to a weightless standstill in the depths of the pool, he saw, through the murk of muddy water and blood, a glimmer of light on the surface.

Bubbles from his mouth, clothes and leather bag floated upwards and fuddled his vision, but he was certain that he saw a pair of altar candles float by. The source of the light, a gold crucifix, then drifted above his head. Beyond the thunder of the falls and the echoes underwater, he heard a voice bless him in an other-worldly language. With his last reserves of strength, the water tasting alcoholic, he reached out and touched the gold-painted wood. Hung beneath the cross, the World-Tree-Centre, he shut his eyes and surrendered to Xibalba.

Eight

Lucio used the altitude of the sun to estimate the time that he had remaining. He had left Maria and Horatio by the maize fields, chatting about Horatio's graduation to an AK47, his plans to be a commandante, and the long-haired Lacandón Indians, who were to become their neighbours. The shaman's backpack slung over his shoulder, he had one last errand to run before they could say their goodbyes to Horatio, walk back to the village and catch the truck to the Lacandón forest. The ground, the path to the Pool of the Paddler Gods, was soft after the storms and he had to tread carefully. Mountain sheep had tilled the ground to a piste of sludge and, at this rate of progress, he feared that he would be late. Scared of his wife's response to them missing their truck, he left the path and took an alternative, less muddy route. Ahead of him, a spiky ceiba tree signed the exit to an overgrown logger's track, a diversion that would take him past the ancient ruins on the riverbank.

It was Lucio's father who had introduced him to his first ruins, the remains of a small temple and tomb near the banks of the sacred river. They stopped there for lunch, to eat tortillas before he made his debut as a six-year-old helper, and assisted his father in constructing an altar out of saplings. His first impression of ancient Maya achievement was a huge disappointment. For although he had yet to see the sites of Palenque, Tonina and Yaxchilan, young Lucio had heard of pyramids towering above the jungle as America's first skyscrapers, and he had high expectations for San Felipé's own contribution to the great civilization. Instead he was shown a heap of moss-covered stone, a mound that was no more than three metres high, the combination of man's neglect and destructive roots disguising its man-made origins. Loggers had realized the ruin's significance when they tunnelled their way to its centre. Colourfully painted burial pots, jade necklaces and even human skulls made good money on the black market. Most of the tunnel had since collapsed, but enough of it remained to allow a boy to pretend that he was a Maya Lord, who rose from the grave and cursed the looters for disturbing his sleep in Xibalba. It did not take long for the young Lucio to forget his initial disappointment. He soon appreciated the ruin's modesty and dilapidated state, qualities of which made it an ideal den.

More recently, two weeks ago, he had visited the ruins with Urbano. His son had created a new den out of the trench and Lucio would take him there to play. Whereas he used to act the vengeful spirit, sworn enemy to grave robbers, Urbano played the academic: bagging shards of ceramic for the rituals of his apprenticeship and creating heroes out of fragments of bone. When he found something of interest, he would climb up to his father, who read aloud the sacred book of Maya Creation, a tatty paperback of the *Popol Vuh*, on a stone slab on the mound's summit. They would take it in turns to tell the stories that the artefacts spoke of.

With Urbano no longer by his side and the *Popol Vuh* turned into ash, burnt with his home, Lucio arrived at the mound. Sweat mixed with tears and he wiped away the moisture from his unshaven jaw-line, the stubbly beard that he had grown since his journey to First-True-Mountain. Taking a deep breath, he gripped a vine and climbed up a slippery stack of loose stones. When he had reached the top, he removed his backpack, sat down on the stone slab and rested his tired legs. As he slipped off his muddy sandals, looked down at a new set of blisters, he saw his son's collection of ancient artefacts. Ordered into categories as if it was a museum display, with human bone separated from animal bone, polychrome from unglazed ceramic, the artefacts were now an archaeological deposit of his son's life; they were no longer about the ancestors.

His vision blurred by grief, Lucio ran his hand through the pieces of ceramic. The chips fell off his callused fingers and a rusty-red shard caught his attention. He picked it up from the pile and examined its painted decoration, an outline of a wiry spider monkey. The monkey, he remembered telling Urbano, was considered to be a talisman of good luck to the ancients, a moniker for ingenuity and industriousness. As Urbano scratched dirt off the shard, Lucio described how the ancient Maya scribes and the half-brothers of the Hero Twins, Hunahpu and Xbalanke, were all depicted as monkeys. But there was another side to the monkey. Quoting from the *Popol Vuh*, reading from a page in his paperback that had come loose from the book's spine, he repeated the story of how the gods destroyed the wooden people. Because of their unfeeling and uncaring nature, the gods turned the wooden people into monkeys.

Lucio put the shard in his trouser pocket. He wiped his eyes with his grimy hand, put on his sandals, returned his backpack to his back and descended the mound. Through the noise of a breeze in the trees and the chirps of crickets, he could hear the roar and gurgle of water. A barrier of bush blocked his route to the river-bank. He withdrew his machete from its scabbard and swung the blade through immature ash, palm and pine, milky sap released into the air with each swipe. The cull of nature continued until he could see, a few metres ahead, the brown and obese river. In all the times that he had visited it, he had never seen the water look more violent than it did then. It seemed to share his anger with the land, impatient to burst its banks and fed up with its proscribed and meandering course. Hanging on to roots, branches and creepers, which arched over a narrow riverbank, he walked upstream, turned a bend in the river and saw the Pool of the Paddler Gods. In the distance, high up above the pool and shrouded in mist, was the waterfall that drained brown blood off First-True-Mountain. He leant against a tree to rest. Observing the violent water and the mountain beyond it, its peak hidden behind cloud, he berated himself for the devotion that he had bestowed on the place.

Behind a rainbow captured in the spray of the falls, he spotted a blue dot at the top of the cliff face. He quickly ducked down and moved behind the tree, his eyes fixed on the intruder above him. His heart beat raced as he thought of the Cardenistas, drug smugglers and even Zapatistas. The sun shielded the object's identity and he blinked at the rainbow, trying to identify what the blue thing was. A fly circled his head, distracting him with a loud buzz, and he swatted it away. He dabbed his sweaty forehead on his sleeve and looked up at the cliff again. The rainbow contin-ued to bridge the pool with a spectrum of colour, but the blue dot at the top of the falls had vanished. It was probably an old maize or fertilizer sack, he thought, trash carried down the mountain and now submerged in the river. He stood up from his crouch and double-checked the cliff face again. Certain that the blue thing had definitely gone, that he was alone, he walked on to the Pool of the Paddler Gods.

Scum, bubbles and mini whirlpools waltzed on the pool's surface. A berg of spittle joined the dance and Lucio wiped a hand over his lips. His phlegm rode an eddy, spiralled out of control and was sucked out of sight by a vertical and downward current. He looked up at the joke of a guardian, the boulder's beaked nose sticking out of the curtain of water, and cleared his throat for another insult. The spit fell well short of target and, turning his back on the meaningless lump of rock, he dropped his backpack on the grass bank and took a deep breath.

Two altar candles splashed into the pool. As if they were a drowning man's white hands, raised up in a hopeless plea for help, they bobbed up and down before an unseen force sucked them to Xibalba. Satisfied that they had gone and impatient for another dunking, he turned the backpack upside down and tipped the rest of the shaman's tools on the bank. Picking up a plastic canteen and a squash gourd, he poured alcoholic posh and cane liquor into the swirling cauldron. He scattered the copal incense and maize husks over the diluted drink, returning the empty freezer bag to his backpack, and watched the cosmic mixture dissolve away.

The gold-painted cross, the 'World Tree of the Centre' and the pivot and pillar of the cosmos, was all that remained of his former life as a shaman. He bent down and picked up the wooden carving. The gilt caught the sun and his wide eyes reflected the fiery cross. He threw it at the pool and it flew in the air like a golden dagger. Stabbed by the cross, as if the shaman had wounded the Earth Lord himself, the brown water turned a deep shade of red. Bubbles rose up from the depths and the floating cross shook about. Lucio's heart beat faster as the water grew louder and redder. He dropped to his knees and stared at the bloody message from the gods.

'Forgive me,' he whispered, crossing his heart. 'But you took away my boy,' he cried out to the falls. He buried his head in his hands and wept. Blood continued to bubble up from the depths of the pool, and he began to murmur his prayers in Tzotzil.

Nine

Five years later

'Ten bucks on Speedy Gonzalez,' Bruce said. The geographical information systems specialist, a hi-tech cartographer with a marine's crew cut, tapped a large tank of leaf-cutter ants. His wager was directed towards a small green foresail, on a hull of six sprinting legs, which led hundreds of leaf-lugging workers down a log and towards a nest under construction. For certain employees of Conservation International (or CI as they preferred to call it), typified by the likes of boyish Bruce, weekends began with ant racing in the staff-room. It was a way of readying themselves for the race to their own nests, the commute home through the busy streets of Washington, DC. At least that is how Rachel, a junior bat ecologist and a top graduate from Boston University, viewed it.

'Yeah?' Rachel replied, desperate to leave the building. 'I reckon he's going to stall at that chicane of twigs. My ten bucks go on the wee guy on the low road.' She pointed at a smaller log, a stick hidden under the main causeway, the leader of the ants who chose to take the most indirect route to the nest.

'What would you know of ants, Batwoman?' Bruce peered into the tank, his smirk stuck to the glass.

'A darn sight more than you and your pie-in-the-sky satellites.' She watched the ants over his shoulder. 'Look, there you go.' Gonzalez stopped at a spaghetti junction of twigs. The hare of the ant kingdom stalled, the leaf too large for the chicane, while Rachel's tortoise and its pea-green cargo dived into the nest, snatching victory by a ducked antenna. 'Told you,' she said, smiling.

'Little . . .'

'Ten dollars, please, Buzz Lightyear.' Rachel opened out the palm of her hand.

Bruce delved into a pocket of his combat pants and pulled out two five-dollar notes.

'Go and buy yourself some antihistamine, landlubber.' He put the notes into her palm, the smirk returning to his face. 'You're going to need it over the next few months. You'll be eaten alive on the forest floor while I'm safe in my chopper.'

'Not with my own army of ants on the ground and my babes in the sky.' She put the notes into a back pocket of her jeans.

'So I'm your babes now? The pilot's finally got to you, huh?'

'I'm talking about the bats, Bruce. The bats.'

Rachel joined Conservation International six months ago. It was her thesis, on '*Avian Extinctions in the Neotropical Forests of Ecuador*', that clinched the job as an intern in the Center for Applied Biodiversity Science. Although she couldn't say that bat conservation was always a dream career of hers, the job gave her a fast-track entry into one of the world's leading environmental agencies. And after the events of the last year, the attacks on New York and DC, her urge to do something more beneficial to the planet than law or banking, careers that most of her BU contemporaries had chosen, had only increased. On a more personal level, her knowledge of bat ecology was also her plane ticket to southern Mexico. The following week she was to finally fulfil the promise that she had made five years ago, when she watched the sunset in a boozy Cancún, and join a reconnaissance team travelling to a designated 'hotspot' in biodiversity in Chiapas.

'Of course,' Bruce responded, his fingers tapping the ant tank again. 'You and your bloodsucking, flying rodents. How can I possibly compete?' Bruce, a specialist in aerial mapping and a qualified helicopter pilot, was also looking forward to the expedition. His hotspot, however, was narrowed down to a twenty-four-year-old intern, whose contours he had remotely mapped in the office and pinpointed for field inspection.

'The only flying rodent that I'm aware of is about six-foot tall, takes out-of-focus photographs and migrates to the Mile High Club to mate. So don't even go there.'

'What has the boyf to say about you going away?' Bruce winked at her. She avoided eye contact with him by looking down at the ants. 'Guess he must be nervous about letting you loose in the jungle. I mean, you fell for him in the bush. Perhaps you might meet someone else this time, upgrade your fella in a real man's jungle.'

Rachel and the 'boyf', Todd Walker, became an item in the Tiputini Biodiversity Station, during their Sophomore Ecology

Program in the Amazonian rainforest. Brought together by the picking of ticks off each other's bodies, romance incubating under bat-catching mist nets, the relationship blossomed in junior and senior years at Boston University. For the last six months, however, since her move to DC and his decision to stay in Boston, to do a Ph.D. on Massachusetts's marine life, the long-distance phone calls had grown shorter and less frequent. The 'Miss you so much babes' had changed to 'Speak to you soon.' Rachel was not in the mood for Bruce's badly veiled flirtation.

'I hear that you're the one with the reputation,' she said, not knowing quite how far to push it, Bruce being marginally senior than her. Two female lab assistants, who eavesdropped by the coffee-machine, nodded their heads. 'Todd and I are inseparable,' she lowered her voice, noticing that they had company, 'he's the only guy I've loved and ever will love. OK?' A lie, she excused herself, seemed like the only option to discourage him.

'Yeah, sure Rachel, but he's not going to be there for you in the Selva. And, believe me, it won't be the three-star research station that you students were used to in Ecuador. In Chiapas, babe, we've some pissed-off locals to deal with.' He put his hand on her shoulder. 'You'll be grateful for having an old hand like me about.'

'I'd rather be served with rice and beans,' she said, removing his hand from her, 'than commit myself to your protection.' The two eavesdroppers laughed, spilling their coffees on the floor and on their lab coats.

The brief for the Rapid Assessment Program to the Montes Azules Biosphere Reserve, the Selva Lacandón, had warned her about the likelihood of a hostile reception. Pro-Zapatista villages, mainly displaced communities from the highlands to the north, were the 'squatters' whose impact on local bat species she was to investigate. Conservation, these masked Mayan rebels believed, was used to brand them as 'eco-terrorists', perpetrators of defor-estation. They blamed groups like Conservation International for handing over land to multinational companies, the sponsors of Rachel's research.

'Anyway,' she continued, checking her reflection in the glass ant tank, 'the brief says that they don't attack gringos.' She patted down a few strands of her dark brown hair; she felt that she should at least make some effort for poor Todd. 'I mean, in '94, on the night they stormed San Cristóbal de las Casas, they even had their photos taken with tourists. And it's not as if we'll be doing the actual evicting. We're just notifying the authorities of the damage that they're doing.'

From the NASA satellite images in her project folder, the correlation between forest fires and illegal settlements, as well as eyewitness accounts from friendly Lacandón Maya, Rachel rejected Zapatista claims of innocence. She would rather be unpopular to a few misguided guerrillas, who were going to reject American assistance in any case, than allow a natural wonder, a place that she had spent years wanting to visit, go up in smoke. As for multinational investment, as far as she was aware it didn't go beyond the construction of eco-lodges for granny and grandpa eco-tourists. It was not like they were handing over the management of the rainforest to Ronald McDonald.

'Yes, but they're not idiots, Rachel,' Bruce said, looking serious for a change. 'Our names will be on the research that evicts them.'

'You sound scared.' Rachel took her turn to put a hand on his shoulder. 'Aren't you manly enough for your real man's jungle?' As a group of young men in an Illinois State Penitentiary would have testified to, it took more than a few masked bandits to scare Rachel Rees. 'Look, I really must be going.' She removed her hand from his shoulder. 'Todd will be waiting for me.' She picked up her rucksack, pushing in the brief on Montes Azules, and zipped up her fleeced parka.

'Hey, I'm sorry,' Bruce said, opening the door for her, 'I didn't mean to be an arse. It's just, you know, me fooling around a bit. Trust me, I know what a bitch this profession can be for relationships: just look at my pitiful scorecard. But, as a friend, the offer to be your Chiapas protector stands. You just have to ask, that's all. No strings attached. I promise.' He smiled and she pitied the guy who spent his entire life, both professionally and personally, in the clouds.

'Don't worry about it. I'm also sorry: for being a bit uptight. I'm a little nervous about this evening. To be honest with you, the whole distance thing has been tough on Todd and me. But that is no excuse for me flexing my emotions on you. And thanks for the offer to look after me in Mexico, but I really can take care of myself.' She smiled back at him and then looked at her watch. 'Shit. I've got to go.'

'Good luck.'

'Have a great weekend. I'll see you on Monday.' The staff-room door closed behind her.

'What are you looking at?' he said, to the two lab assistants giggling in the corner.

Rather than wait for the elevator, she ran down the stairs of the fire escape. She rushed past reception, trailing a hand to wave goodbye to the security guard, pushed open a glass door and exited the building. Outside, streetlights and car headlamps reflected on wet tarmac, the rain pounding on platoons of umbrellas as office workers and late-night shoppers poured onto the sidewalks. She played with the collar of her coat, dropping a fluffy hood over her head, and tailed a man in a suit, who barged his way up Connecticut Avenue, his briefcase knee-capping the pedestrians in his way. Ahead of her, past the pinstriped plough and a queue to a stand of soggy pretzels and hot dogs, she saw Dupont Circle. Among the couples and waiting other halves, who were magnetized to DC's marble meeting point, an illuminated fountain, she spotted Todd sitting alone on a park bench. She crossed the road, slipped through a jam of cars and jogged up to him.

'Hey,' she said. Todd jumped. 'I'm sorry I'm late,' she continued, looking at the frown under his navy blue hood, his hunched body shivering on the bench. 'We've been up to our necks in meetings and packing equipment. The whole office is going berserk over this project and then a colleague collared me on the way out. I had no idea it was this late. Please forgive me. Honey?'

'You could have called my cell-phone,' he said, as he stood up and shook off the dammed water on his raincoat. In the orange light of the Circle, she saw his blond fringe stuck to his forehead, water dripping off his red nose. She removed their hoods and she kissed him on his cold and wet cheek. 'I guess you're sort of forgiven.' He kissed her on the lips.

They ignored the rain, which grew thicker and steadier, and embraced by the fountain, did what the other couples were doing. Water streamed down their wrapped-up bodies and they both said nothing. The rain, the fountain, car horns, kids on skateboards and an echo of 'love you – love you too' surrounded their silence. She loosened his grip around her waist and, pushing him slightly back, looked at his varnished face and dripping eyes.

'It's good to see you,' she finally broke their silence.

'How can you eat that?' Todd asked. He pointed over a candle in a pint glass and at Rachel's half-pound burger on a haystack of fries.

The taxi had stopped outside Smokey's, an affordable jazz 'n' blues bar on the recreational strip of Adams-Morgan, and she had led him to a balcony table that overlooked the stage. As a pre-expedition treat, a stomach lining for three months of chicken, rice and beans, she had ordered 'The All-American Works', the biggest burger on the menu. Todd, a vegetarian since college and a convert to fanatical conservation, had chosen the tofu burger and a butter-bean salad.

'I know,' she said, cutting into the burger, 'it's a filthy habit.' She skewered more than a mouthful onto her fork. 'But there's no point in me giving up meat before Mexico. I heard that the research station's chef, a Lacandón woman, is quite a carnivore. I'd starve if I turned veggie.'

'Don't you realize that your burger is the very reason that your rainforest and bats are going extinct?'

'What?' She dropped the fork and food back onto the plate. They had covered this debate before and she expected another stalemate. 'Come on, honey, this is pure American.' She pointed the fork and beef at him. 'The cattle ranchers, who are chopping down Montes Azules, or any other rainforest for that matter, are not responsible for this.' She bit into the minced ruminant and chewed furiously. 'A Big Mac, perhaps, but not a Smokey's Special.'

'Whatever.' He picked up his pint and took two swigs of organic wheat beer, a brew that was as blond as his hair. 'So how long are you going to be in the field for? One month, two months, six months, a year?'

A three-piece band – a guitarist, a bassist and a pianist – entered the stage below. Hands started to clap around the smoky bar and Rachel joined in. Todd watched her from across the table, waiting for the applause to stop.

'I'm sure that I told you on the phone.' She stopped clapping and faced him again. 'Three months, that's all. It will fly by.'

Todd pushed a discoloured butter-bean to the side of his plate.

'At least it's Mexico,' he said. 'It's like Texas, right? Safe, stable and yet not so boring.'

'Yeah, suppose so.' She glanced down at the band on the stage. No longer did she feel the compulsion to tell him everything about her life. The man that she once wanted to marry now felt like an old friend, someone whom she cared for deeply and yet felt distant from. She didn't want to bother him with stories of guerrillas in the jungle. She just wanted to clear the air between them.

'So what's the big deal out there?'

Rachel sipped her glass of wine before she replied. She blew her hair out of her eyes and made a mental note to have it cut before she went to the tropics.

'Just some squatters in the rainforest. CI is assessing the damage they've done.' She hoped that would be enough on the subject.

'Are the squatters indigenous?' Todd raised an eyebrow at her.

'Yes.' His accusative look annoyed her. She finished off the dregs of her wine and shook her wet hiker's boot under the table. 'It's not a question of us against them, Todd. We're just helping them to care for their heritage, the planet's heritage. Jeez, you know the score as well as I do: it's freshman year ethics in conservation.'

'Hey, I didn't say anything.' He raised his hands as if in surrender. 'There's no need to go all defensive.'

What she used to find endearing about him, the look of innocence he would put on when an argument was about to break out, she now found irritating. The change in her feelings made her feel guilty, like she was somehow being unfaithful to him.

'This project comes from the top,' she continued, her face hardening. 'The United Nations has designated this year "the year of the mountains". Mountains and forests, from Chiapas to Afghanistan, are now declared a matter of international security.'

'Don't tell me that you're involved in the 'War on Terror'. After all that agonizing of yours over careers, all those anti-war marches we went on after 9/11, you finally chose to be a spy and not an ecologist.' He took another swig of beer and shook his head.

'It was your idea, not mine, to go on those demos.' She looked down at the band and wished that they would hurry up with their tuning, get on with it and play a song. 'You were always the political one, not me,' she muttered over the balcony.

Another carafe and a pint of blond beer appeared on the table. They drank and listened to a Dr John cover, 'Shut D Fonk Up', from beginning to end. A couple at the table next to them, who had reserved a cosy alcove, licked ketchup off their lips and scrunched up each other's hair with greasy fingers, lubricated by a basket of drumsticks.

'Todd?' Rachel said, turning away from the couple and touching his hand on the table. Her palm covered his knuckles and she tried to calm his fidgeting.

'Yeah?' he replied, his sad face rising up from the table.

'What shall we do?' she asked. She felt her lip trembling slightly. She still loved him, just not in the same way as before.

'I don't know. Finish the wine, pay the bill and go back to your place? That's if I'm invited.' He looked at her eyes, which were almost as dark as her hair, and the faint wrinkles and freckles that come from working in the sun.

'Of course you're invited.' She squeezed his hand. 'Don't think that I'm enjoying the separation.'

'Look, why don't we both think things through while you're in Mexico.'

'Right.' She looked at the half-eaten food on her plate.

'And you'll look at our stars, at the Big Dipper, and think about me? Remember those great times that we had under the Ecuadorean night sky?'

She leant over the table and kissed him on the cheek.

'Of course I will.' She sat back in her chair and watched the couple snog in the alcove.

Contriving chatter in between sips, the standing of the Red Sox in the MLB considered a safer topic of conversation than field-work, she finished her wine and he struggled with half a beer. They took the Metro to Pentagon City and walked in the rain to her apartment in Arlington, a studio flat littered with textbooks, photographs of bats, notes on phyllostomids, a brand new rucksack and takeout pizza boxes. 'It's been a crazy week,' she excused the mess. Sitting side by side on a sofa, their cold bodies wrapped up in a multicoloured blanket from downtown Cancún, they drank green tea and watched *The Tonight Show with Jay Leno*. For the first time in their three years, they made love under the cover of darkness, neither a candle nor a low-wattage light bulb to see each other with.

Ten

A nurse pushed an empty wheelchair along a strait of sickly green linoleum. Her shoes and the wheelchair's new tyres squeaked on the sterilized floor, the rubber squeaking loudest when she braked and took a right-angled corner. Signs to the Neurological Rehabilitation Unit, Homerton Hospital's section for brain injuries in north-east London, directed her above her head. She went down a corridor and weaved in and out of a convoy of porters, who chauffeured trolleys of patients to 'drive-thru' treatment. An overflow of walking wounded, a spill of red from the 'Accident and Emergency' section, slowed her down with a barrage of bloodied and bandaged bodies. The corridor clear again, she turned left and went down a few other corridors until she arrived at the Neurological Rehabilitation Unit. She pushed the wheelchair through a ward's swing doors and went down a line of full beds.

'Here you go,' the nurse said, docking the wheelchair at the end of one of the beds. 'Brand new it is. So mind you don't go losing it like the last one.'

'Thank you,' Zeb whispered, rising up from a chair beside Tam's bed, rubbing his eyes. He kissed Tam's pale cheek. With the exception of her twitching eyelashes, Tam remained motionless. Zeb watched her intently. Despite the odds, his hope for movement, his faith in her recovery never wavered. He rubbed the back of his shaved head. His fingers scratched the 'Z' tattoo on the back of his neck.

'I don't know,' the nurse said, shaking her head, 'how anyone could go so low as to steal a wheelchair, eh? The East End never used to be like this. There were the gangs and all, for sure, like the Krays, but they didn't go stealing bloody wheelchairs. There was none of these asylum-seekers from God-knows-where-a-stan, nicking things like . . .' she paused, looking at Tam's paralysed body on the bed, 'wheelchairs.'

'Please, Mary,' Zeb said, still looking down at the fixed

expression on his love's face. 'We don't know who the thief is. Don't go blaming just anyone.'

'You're too bloody forgiving. I admire you for that.'

'Well you shouldn't.' He held Tam's hand in his palm, caressing her limp fingers. 'It's my fault that she's in this state.' He still blamed himself for not being by her side at the riot.

'You know that's not true.'

Zeb kneeled down beside the bed. He stroked back Tam's hair and looked into her staring green eyes. While the nurse ranted about the police siding with 'Johnny Foreigners', asylum-seekers building bombs in council flats, he thought about justice himself. Five years after the banker had destroyed his life, robbed his angel of the ability to speak and walk, the pain and the rage had not diminished. The coward might have run away, leaving the pole by Tam's neck and escaping into the chaos of the riot, but Zeb knew that he could not hide forever. He gently kissed Tam's fingers.

'How did she do in classes today?' he asked the nurse, more out of habit than a genuine desire for an answer. The doctors had told him that a trip to the States, treatment from a specialist, offered the best chance of curing an extra-dural haematoma. It was a cure that required more money than could be made through begging and courier work.

'No change, I'm afraid,' the nurse replied, like she always did.

'That's Tam: defying convention as usual.' He smiled awkwardly. Now that they had a replacement wheelchair he wanted to take her home. He loathed the weekly trip to therapy classes; it seemed pointless. The only reason for going was to ensure that they didn't take her away from him. 'We'd better be going.'

'Wait.' The nurse opened her purse and stuffed a five-pound note into Zeb's hand. 'Go and get yourselves a cab.'

'I can't take your money,' he said, his deep frown lines making him appear older than he actually was.

'I insist, Sebastian. For Tam if not for you.'

'You're very kind.' He took the money and put it in the inside pocket of his leather jacket. A piece of paper fell to the floor. The nurse picked it up before he could.

'Is this yours?' the nurse asked, holding up the paper, a printout of names.

He took the paper out of her hand and returned it to his jacket.

'Thanks. It's for courier work,' he lied; the list was evidence of a traitor within the squat.

They both transferred Tam from the bed to the wheelchair. He tucked a tartan blanket behind her back and around her wasted muscle.

'Before I forget,' he said, holding the handles of the wheelchair, 'you should know that I'll be going away for a couple of months. Jules, a good friend of Tam's and someone I can trust – I think that that you met her once – will take her to therapy classes as normal.'

'Two months, eh? Going anywhere nice?'

'Central America,' he replied, massaging Tam's shoulders.

'Well you go and enjoy yourself. Don't worry about Tam. She'll be just fine. I'll see to that.'

He nodded at the nurse and then pushed Tam towards the ward's double doors.

'Sebastian,' the nurse called out, stripped sheets already under her arm. Zeb and Tam halted at the doors. 'Why would anyone want to steal a wheelchair?'

'I don't know,' he said, facing the doors and not the nurse. His mind was preoccupied with what he had to do back at the squat. Rick and Jamie were waiting for his return. Stevo would soon show up.

'Eh?' She looked at the graffiti on the back of his jacket, a skull painted over a Mobil logo, and the 'Z' tattoo on his neck.

'Bye, Mary.'

The ward's doors slammed shut.

Using his jacket to shield Tam from the rain, Zeb pushed the wheelchair into the shelter of the anarchists' squat. He double-checked Ridley Road Market for suspicious individuals, plain clothed police, before he closed the rusty doors of an old furniture factory. In a dark and dusty hallway, he wiped the raindrops off her cheeks with the back of his hand, meticulously making sure that her freckled skin was dry. Past a concrete staircase, an even darker passageway, he led them towards the light of a room at the back of the building. Due to Tam's condition, after the paralysis was confirmed, Zeb had made the anarchists tidy up a ground-floor room. Walls were painted white, floors were cleaned and, with the money he made from courier work, her parents uncontactable, they had a proper bed, electricity, an old TV set and a loo that worked. He gently picked her up and moved her from the wheelchair to the bed, propping her up with pillows and switching on the TV. A badly tuned Tom and Jerry cartoon flickered on the TV's small screen. He kissed Tam on the forehead, pulled the piece of paper out of his jacket pocket and left the room.

'Jules,' he called out in the dark hallway, 'we're back.' He went up the concrete staircase.

The rest of the squat had seen little change since the anarchists first moved in. Candles were still used to illuminate communal sleeping areas, sleeping bags sprawled out over old factory floors, and crumbly walls were daubed with graffiti and anarchy symbols. So long as Tam's environment remained clean and comfortable, an order that no one dared to disobey, Zeb felt that there was no need to interfere with the décor upstairs. It was the home of the East London Anarchists, a squat in Hackney, and he wanted to keep it that way.

Zeb stopped at the second floor. He took in the old factory's musty air. In the semi-darkness, dust sparkled in the streaks of daylight that seeped through boarded-up windows, the council's feeble attempt at keeping squatters out. With Tam safely home and in her own bed, the nurse informed of his departure, he was free to correct the wrongs of the world. Only, in contrast to previous missions, where anarchism for the greater good inspired his protest marches, it was his own personal world that needed his assistance. Having swapped his family and their country house for a ragged mob of anarchists, he placed his loyalty to Tam above everything else. His parents' refusal to pay for an operation in the US sealed his divorce from them; only he could help Tam. He ducked under a black drape nailed to the frame of a doorway.

Two men sat on the floor of a small room. A circle of candles lit up their contrasting faces: Rick, a baby-faced version of Zeb, a new recruit without the shaven hair, scars and tattoos, and Jamie, a skinhead with labourer's muscles and with piercings in protruding eyebrows. They looked up when they saw Zeb. Jamie grinned and Rick looked slightly anxious. Zeb waved the piece of paper at them and told them to be ready for Stevo's arrival. He told them that they were dealing with a traitor, someone who could jeopardize their trip to Mexico, someone who had the gall to betray Tam. He expected them to act without mercy. At the back of the room, next to a roll of black bin-liners, was a crowbar. Zeb picked it up and pointed its tip at the darkest corner of the room, where the outline of a wheelchair, a stolen wheelchair, could be faintly seen in the shadows. Rick stared at it, the candles on the floor lighting up his wide eyes. Jamie's grin broadened.

'I want that fucking thing in the centre of the room,' Zeb said to them. He used the crowbar to swipe back the drape and went back downstairs.

'Come on, angel,' Zeb said, sitting on the bed next to Tam. He opened Tam's mouth with a finger and thumb, his palm supporting her locked jaw and chin. A spoon of baby food passed through her shaky lips and the honey-like pulp trickled onto her neck brace. He removed his hand, her mouth closing, and wiped away the mess with a clean cloth. The early evening news crackled on the TV set in the background. Terrorists grabbed the headlines again.

'Don't know why you get her that crap,' Jules said, the teenage girl from Belfast sitting at the end of the bed and watching the TV. She poked a fork into a can of baked beans and sipped from a can of extra-strength lager. 'When he's gone to the jungle,' she said, referring to Zeb, putting her hand on Tam's leg and addressing her friend's static face, 'I'll get you some proper food.'

'Nurse Mary recommends the stuff,' Zeb said, taking the can of lager off Jules and taking a swig. 'It's what's best for her.' He looked at Tam. 'Isn't it, angel?' He missed the support that she once gave him.

'Christ, I can't believe you're still listening to that racist bitch.' Jules stood up from the bed and switched off the TV. 'Fucking fascist news.'

'She'd do anything for Tam,' he said, handing back the can of lager to Jules. 'Remember, if it wasn't for her, Tam would be in a care home. We would have lost her forever. Fuck knows what would have happened to her.' He put his arm round Tam, carefully lifting up her neck brace and kissing the back of her neck, the spot where she was struck.

'But where are your principles these days?' Jules returned to the end of the bed. She opened up another can of lager.

'My principles?' He looked up at a bare light bulb that hung above the bed. He paused before he lowered his head to look at Jules. His eyes twitched. 'Don't talk to me about principles, Jules.' His arm was around Tam again.

'But we're anarchists, Zeb. We don't cut deals with the enemy, especially if it means fucking over a group like the Zapatistas. I mean, they're Zapatistas, the very people we support. Subcommandante Marcos is a bloody hero.' She shook her head. 'How can we trust these Americans anyway? How do we know they'll pay up? They're the fucking CIA.'

Zeb gently released Tam, returning her to the support of pillows, and he stared at the floor. The crowbar was by his feet and he kicked it under the bed, disgusted by the very sight of it. Two months had passed since the Americans had contacted him and made their offer. One of them had showed up at the squat. It was a cold and drizzly morning and the man came with a brief-case full of evidence, including photos from the Bishopsgate riot and newspaper clippings from Mexico. Zeb was surprised by how much they knew; they had even unearthed some shit about his father once working for MI6, doing some espionage job in Russia in the days of the cold war. It was while he studied the photo of Justin Callaghan that they mentioned money, the offer of treatment for Tam. All he had to do was to volunteer as a peace observer in Chiapas, infiltrate a Zapatista patrol and assist the authorities in identifying a man called Hunahpu. As an anarchist from Europe, the man said, the Zapatistas would look upon him favourably. The man told him to think about it, leaving behind the photo, a business card with the name Agent Decker on it and a contact number.

'It's her only hope,' he said to Jules, looking at Tam's blank face, thinking of the man that had paralysed her on that summer's day. 'We have to trust them.'

Footsteps echoed in the hallway outside. The sound grew louder as running feet approached Tam's room. Jules dropped her head, her red and curly hair flopping over her white face, and Zeb stopped stroking Tam's cheek. He reached for the crowbar by his feet.

'What's going on?' the man gasped, entering the room. He ran his hand and a joint through his brown dreadlocks. The bulb above Tam's bed lit up his bloodshot eyes. 'I got your message and came as soon as I could,' he said to Zeb. 'It sounded pretty fucking serious: something about the plans for the Chiapas gig.' He sucked on the joint, screwed up his face and coughed.

'Stevo,' Zeb said, rising up from his seat on the bed. His hand behind his back, he walked up to his panting comrade. 'How about we go upstairs and talk about it there.' He didn't want Tam to see what he was about to do.

Jules held Tam's hand. She watched Zeb with concerned eyes. Tam dribbled out chicken broth.

'Can't see a problem with that, mate,' Stevo replied, grinning, unaware that only Tam wasn't watching him, that no one else was smiling. He put his tobacco-stained hand on Zeb's shoulder.

'Good,' Zeb said, looking at Stevo's grubby hand on him.

'Let me guess.' Stevo paused to stub out his joint on the floor. Zeb looked down at the litter as if it was a personal insult. 'You got the fucking maps to the military bases? No, wait, you heard that the rebel camp is run by a Salma Hayek double. Wicked.'

'Shall we go?' Zeb pushed Stevo towards the entrance to the room, into the dark hallway outside.

'Not bad, Tam.' Stevo saw Tam's new wheelchair by the entrance to the room. 'It beats that tatty old one. I reckon those thieves did you a favour there. What do you reckon, Zeb?'

Zeb didn't reply. Instead, he hurried Stevo out of the room and followed him up the dark staircase, his hand still behind his back. They stopped on the second-floor landing, by the black-draped doorway. Zeb whispered something into Stevo's ear and showed him the crowbar in his hand. Stevo nodded, grinning even more, and Zeb pulled back the drape.

Candlelight rippled shadows over exposed brickwork and dark wood flooring. A curtain of cobwebs, dulled by dust, plaster and age, flapped in the draft of a blackened out window. In the centre of the room, circled by candles, was the stolen wheelchair.

'Cool,' Stevo said to Zeb, looking at the wheelchair, 'why didn't you tell me that you found it? Where was . . .'

Stevo's body thudded down on the hardwood floor. Zeb dropped the crowbar by his feet, making it look as if he had just struck Stevo. He briefly covered his face with his hands, in conflict with himself as adrenalin pumped through his body. Breathing in hard, he nodded at Jamie.

'I'm telling you, man,' Stevo screamed, his wrists bound by gaffer tape to the wheelchair's armrests. Three figures looked down at him. 'I never told anyone anything about Mexico. You got to fucking believe me. We're friends. I'd never dob you in. I'd never betray Tam.'

139

'How much did they pay you, Stevo?' Zeb asked, rubbing the 'Z' tattoo on the back of his neck, the crowbar swinging by his side. He walked round the wheelchair, impressed by Stevo's follow-up act to his dramatic fall.

Jamie and Rick stood opposite the seated Stevo, the former frowning his thick eyebrows and the latter wiping the sweat off his forehead.

'The last I heard,' Zeb continued, glancing at Rick, 'was that the going rate for an activist's name was two pounds and twenty-five pence.' He pulled out the printout of names from the inside pocket of his jacket. 'I count eleven names on this shopping list. Was it really worth it for twenty-odd quid?' The tip of the crowbar tapped the hardwood floor by Stevo's feet. 'Of course. How stupid of me. There was I thinking that we're all worth the same amount. I don't imagine your buddies in the Special Forces Club and multinationals care much for equality. Did I reach a fair price? Did I pay for that joint you were smoking?'

'The joint was off a dick-head mate in Stokey,' Stevo spluttered. 'Trust me, Zeb, I've never seen that list before.'

'Never seen it?' He screwed up the piece of paper and threw it into the corner of the room. 'You can't remember the Internet café? I'm sure that you were there last Tuesday. You must know the one. It's the one I use, run by that Nigerian family. Loyal they are. But you don't understand loyalty, do you, Stevo?' Again he glanced at Rick, trying to ascertain his reaction to what was going on.

'Internet café? You mean the one by Dalston junction?' Stevo laughed. 'I was looking up Chiapas, Montes Azules, reading about fucking macaw parrots, the nature, man. Rick will tell you. He was with me. Rick?' He directed his plea at one of the two figures in the shadows.

'Rick?' Zeb turned round and stared at his youngest accomplice. 'Is Steve shitty Irwin telling the truth?'

'I don't know,' Rick said, the candlelight catching his pupils dart about. 'Sorry, I didn't see what he was doing on the computer.' He stepped back towards the drape.

'Please, Zeb, I . . .' Jamie slapped Stevo's cheek. Stevo looked up at Jamie, then at Zeb, as if the slap in the face was not part of the script.

'Come on, Stevo,' Zeb said, trying to remain composed, looking anxiously at Jamie, 'don't give me shit about you giving a toss about parrots. What else did you tell them? Did you tell them about our Zapatista comrades?' He turned round and glared at Rick, his heart beating fast. 'Here, young Rick, why don't you do the honours?' He thrust the crowbar into Rick's hand, trying to stop the shakes of his arm. 'Help him out. Shut him up. Let him get used to that fucking wheelchair.' He looked away, focused on the wall behind him, his entire body reacting against what he was doing and saying. It was the image of Tam's unflinching face that kept him there.

'No,' Stevo screamed, 'Zeb, listen . . .' He wriggled about in the wheelchair. The gaffer tape dug into his wrists.

'It's OK, Stevo,' Zeb said, his calm voice belying his discomfort, 'don't worry about it. Sit back, get used to the silence and let the surgeons do their work.' Rubbing his shaved head again, he swallowed, tried to justify the necessity of what he was doing; the treachery was against Tam, not him. 'We know what we're doing. The infliction of paralysis is both an art and a science.' He glanced behind him at Rick. 'And there is a thin line between a masterpiece and a right old hash. So keep still.' He grabbed Stevo's dreadlocks, trying not to hurt him too much, and exposed a spotty neck for a target. 'You're right-handed, aren't you? In which case, Rick, for maximum effect you want to hit him on the left-hand side.'

Rick stepped up to the wheelchair, the crowbar shaking in his left-handed grip. Zeb could barely watch him; he now almost felt sorry for the treacherous bastard.

'Don't fucking do it, Rick,' Stevo shouted out, 'I'm fucking innocent.' Zeb pulled Stevo's dreadlocks a little harder.

'I can't do it,' Rick said, backing off from the wheelchair. 'I'm sorry, Zeb.' He handed the crowbar back.

'Oh dear.' Zeb released Stevo's dreadlocks and looked at Rick. 'And to think that I had high hopes for you. How long have you been with us?'

'A month,' Rick said, stepping back further.

'It was exactly a month ago. You came with a personal recommendation. Slimy son-of-a-bitch he was. I met him at that rally in Finsbury Park, and he told me that he had a good lad for me, someone with the balls for direct action, who wanted a just world at whatever cost. I saw a bit of me in you, Rick.' The crowbar was shaking in his hand, as if the steel bar had a life and will of its own. 'It's why I invited you to Mexico, so that we could fight together.' Zeb squinted at Jamie, who blocked the draped doorway and took something out of his pocket.

A black bin-liner fell over Rick's head. Tripped up, his fingers and nails scratching at the bag on his face, Rick fell to his knees. Steel-capped boots kicked in his sides and his desperate breaths vacuum-packed his open mouth with the bin-liner. His body folded in on itself and his suffocating head dropped to the floor.

Zeb remained frozen while Jamie did his stuff. Unable to watch anymore, he looked away and helped Stevo take off the tape wrapped round his wrists and the wheelchair.

'Give him some, Jamie,' Stevo shouted out from the wheelchair, while Zeb set him free. When he could stand up he took his turn to boot Rick. 'Fucking traitor.'

Zeb pulled Jamie back, looking uneasily at the crumpled body on the floor. Handing the crowbar to him, he told him to do what he had to do in order to find out who Rick was working for. In particular, he wanted to know whether Rick had told anyone about who was funding their trip to Chiapas. 'No one must know about the Americans,' he said, his back facing Jamie and Rick, the latter now taped up in the wheelchair, a breathing hole popped in his bin-liner mask, 'Decker will call the whole thing off if he hears we've been spied on.' He left the room before they began the interrogation. Behind the draped doorway, he leant against a wall and took a breath. In the darkness he listened to Rick's screams coming from inside the room. Covering his face with his hands, he slid down the brick wall and slumped to the floor.

'Now, Rick,' Stevo said, Zeb listening outside, 'why are you here?' He raised his voice. 'What is it? Work experience for one of those risk analysts? You look like a fucking student.'

Zeb could hear Rick's sobs. Clenching his jaw, he put his hand in a pocket of his jacket and pulled out the photo that Decker had given him. He examined the photo of Justin Callaghan in a beam of light, holding it up towards a starry gap in a boarded-up window.

'What did you tell them about Mexico?' Jamie said, taking the role of interrogator. 'That we're going to fuck up their development plans? That we're going to help the Indians defend their land from the men in suits, stop the evictions?'

'It's conservation work,' Rick whimpered, 'they don't care about peace observers.'

Zeb lowered the photo from the light, trying to hear what Rick had to say.

'They just want to protect the rainforest,' Rick continued, his sobs punctuating his words. 'Please, Stevo, Jamie, we're on the same side. They are conservationists.'

Zeb returned the photo to his pocket and stood up. 'He's just a kid,' he thought to himself, facing the draped entrance to the room, not knowing whether to intervene or not. Then he thought of Tam back downstairs, felt relief that they had exposed the spy in time.

'No, Rick,' Stevo said, 'we're not on the same side.'

There was a brief period of silence in the room. Taking one last look at the draped entrance, Zeb bowed his head and slowly made his way down the stairs. He tried to block out Rick's screams as he made his way back to Tam.

Eleven

A lancha, a long and canoe-shaped riverboat, motored up the jade-coloured highway of the Río Lacantún. The wake of full throttle washed steep banks of silt and submerged beached driftwood, fragments of mahogany and palm. Swarms of butterflies took flight from the beach, their sapphire wings reflecting in the water, and the wave lapped the twisted roots that anchored the edges of the Montes Azules Biosphere Reserve, a tropical wilderness that stretched across lowland Chiapas. Tall and overhanging trees and vines absorbed the buzz of the outboard engine, and the forest's dark green depths echoed back with the shrill of insects, the chatter of birds and the burps of amphibians.

Under the shade of a tarpaulin canopy, with her skin tinted blue by the plastic above, Rachel dropped her arm over the lancha's side and soothed her sunburn in the cool water. Behind her wraparound shades, the type a field operative need not worry about losing or breaking, she observed the banks for Morelet's crocodiles and tri-coloured herons. Bruce sat on a bench opposite her, his Converse boots squashed under bundles, carrier bags of luxuries – from razor blades, processed cheese and Snickers bars, to bottles of rum and Dos Equis beers – and sacks of maize and rice. He pointed a camera in the direction of Rachel's profile, magnifying his vision of her through a fully zoomed lens, and panned her tail of dark hair to the tip of her pink and freckly nose. The shutter clicked and the film whirred on its spool. She looked away from the bank and stuck out her tongue. He rested the camera on his lap and shrugged.

'Do you have to keep doing that?' Rachel shouted over the buzzing engine. 'We've only been here a couple of days and you must've wasted two whole films on me. What is it with me? Have I got a tarantula creeping on my back? Or a beefworm on my neck?'

'You make a pretty decent foreground,' he shouted back, 'and you add scale to the scenery behind you.'

'Well do you have to do so many close-ups? I hate having my photo taken.'

'Don't worry. No one else has to see them. They're for my private collection.'

'Great.'

She returned to face the riverbank and saw a Mexican military outpost, a small hut guarded by a couple of adolescent soldiers, and a machine gun on a tripod, its line of fire covering a bend in the river. Beneath large, green helmets, the soldiers clocked the passing boat and its three passengers: two gringos and a Lacandón boatman, the latter in a plain white smock, his black hair grown traditionally long and with a droopy moustache to match. Rachel waved at the soldiers like an unabashed tourist. Their fingers on triggers of machine guns, they refused to wave back and she shook her head. 'Great buddies,' she thought, pushing up her shades and imagining the sort of reception she might receive from her enemies, the Zapatistas, the bad guys whom the army was supposed to protect them from.

The boatman cut the engine and the lancha glided across the water. Shifting his weight to one side and pushing down on a pole, he steered them to an unsteady-looking jetty, a series of poles and planks that linked a forest clearing to the waterside. He caught a rope thrown by a young girl on the bank, whose hair was as long and black as his, and pulled the mooring line taut. The lancha scraped a set of uneven steps and stopped. Rachel threw her backpack onto the jetty, pushed down on a solid-looking mooring post, avoiding the rickety steps, and lifted herself out of the lancha. Missing out on the opportunity to push her in, his feet trapped under a bag of lime to flush the latrine with, Bruce balanced himself and handed her the carrier bags of luxuries. At the lancha's stern, by the cooling engine and a rusty fuel can, the boatman passed sacks of rice, maize, beans and a block of news-paper-wrapped ice to the girl.

'Hey,' Rachel called out to the girl, 'how about I give you a hand with that?' She spoke in Spanish and pointed at the package of ice on the jetty. The girl let go of the package's string handle. The ice too heavy for her, she exhaled in short bursts and tensed her grubby cheeks. She frowned at Rachel.

Sensing disgruntlement in the tiny face that stared up at her, Rachel admonished herself for interfering in the girl's duties, for daring to question the girl's way of getting things done in *her* world. The last thing that she wanted to do was to sound patronizing to the locals. Since they arrived two days ago she had been so busy setting up her lab, unpacking boxes of equipment and removing scorpions from her wooden hut, that she had only talked properly to one of the Lacandón staff at the research station. Yet with the exception of Josita the cook, who had introduced herself to them on their first night, she didn't even know the name of the boatman. It made her feel bad and she wanted the Lacandóns to feel as if they were part of the team. Given that the team consisted of just the Professor and Bruce, it was also in her best interest to make new friends. Naturalization, though, the girl's face told her, didn't come with shifting ice.

'Sorry, señorita,' the boatman said, climbing out of the lancha. The jetty shook and the boatman's movements sent out ripples across the water. 'Ofelia, my daughter, knows only a little Spanish.' He said something in Lacandóne, a language beyond the grasp of the American, to his sulking daughter.

'Sorry,' Ofelia mumbled with her chin stuck to her neck, as she stared at the melting package by her feet, pages of *La Jornada* newspaper going soggy in the sun.

Rachel rested her brace of carrier bags on the bank and walked up to the girl. She smiled and offered her hand to shake. The girl raised her arm above her head and, a tight grip taking the larger of the two by surprise, they shook hands.

'Nice to meet you, Ofelia.' Rachel spoke slowly in order to be understood. She let go of the girl's hand and wiggled her sore fingers. 'My name is Rachel. And this, sorry, that, is Bruce.' She pointed at a hunched figure under the sack of lime, her colleague walking towards four cabins on a small hill and already past a sign that said 'PRIVATE PROPERTY: RIO LACANTÚN BIOLOGICAL RESEARCH STATION. TRESPASSERS WILL BE PROSECUTED'.

The girl's eyes reflected in Rachel's shades. Her father stepped off the jetty and she dropped her chin to her neck again.

'Good evening, señorita,' the boatman said, patting his daughter on the head and flicking his long black hair out of his dark brown eyes, 'I am Guillermo. Señor Bruce and the Professor have yet to introduce us.'

'Rachel Rees,' she replied, smiling at him. 'Pleased to meet you, Guillermo.' She removed her shades and shook his hand. The girl, she noticed, as she stuffed her shades into her backpack, was still staring at her. 'You have a very pretty daughter. How old is she?'

'She's just turned eight. She's a little firefly, as untamed and as free spirited as the forest that she was born in. But she means well and she works hard.' He picked up the block of ice and held it to his chest.

'I hope that I didn't offend her. I only wanted to help. The ice looked kind of heavy.'

'There is no offence, señorita. It's our first season here and she is not used to seeing foreigners, especially gringo señoritas.' His hand ruffled the hair of his daughter. 'We moved from the Laguna Lacanja. She loved it there, where it's isolated, but there's good pay in the Lacantún station, for all of my family. You are good people to us. We need you to protect our forest.'

'I hope we can help,' she said, watching a flock of yellow-headed Aztec parakeets fly over the clearing. 'Well I guess it's up to me to prove that we gringos don't bite.' She smiled at the girl's small and unamused face. 'I don't know what you think, as her father, but it might be fun for her to join me on a night of bat tagging. I start work tomorrow, so perhaps she can join me at the end of the week? That is, of course, if you agree to it and she is interested.'

'Ah, so you are the famous bat catcher. I was expecting a man.'

'Sorry, but we come in all shapes and sizes these days.'

Guillermo looked confused.

'The Professor has asked me to be your guide and machete bearer,' he said, smiling again. 'Did he not mention me to you?'

'Not by name. But he did promise me some help; I don't really fancy going out there alone.' She looked at the wall of trees and jungle that surrounded the cleared hill. 'It's good to have you on board.'

'It will be an honour to work with you, Rachel Rees, and it is very kind of you to invite Ofelia. I am sure that her mother, my wife Josita, can excuse her from kitchen duties. At least for one night.' He patted his daughter on the head again and she ran behind his legs, using the cover of his smock to spy on the leggy Lokin who caught bats.

'And I look forward to working with you, Guillermo,' she said, smiling and putting on her rucksack. 'Now I think that you'd better deal with that ice – or else it will be warm beers and sodas. The Professor would never forgive me.'

'Ah, yes.' He spotted the wet patch on his smock, water seeping out of the package in his hands.

'I'll see you bright and early tomorrow morning. We begin with sieves of bat poop at 4.30 a.m.'

He raised his eyes heavenward.

'It's just the start, you wait,' she said, seeing his face. 'I'll meet you outside the equipment shed.'

'OK, señorita. Till tomorrow and "bat poop".'

'Goodbye, Guillermo. Goodbye, Ofelia.'

The two Lacandóns walked up the path to a cabin with a plume of smoke rising up from a thatched roof. Ofelia skipped behind her father, swinging two bags of beans beside her, and turned round every so often to gawk at the tall and pink stranger on the riverbank. Rachel waved and, as with the soldiers, there was no response. Shrugging, she picked up her carrier bags and took a gravel path to a different cabin, a pine-slatted dormitory that housed cubicles for biologists and eco-tourists. There was time, she reckoned, for her to snatch a siesta before dinner. From now on, she had to adopt the sleeping hours of a bat.

The beating blades of a helicopter woke her up. Dried palm, the cabin's loosely thatched ceiling, rustled in the artificial wind and the mahogany beams creaked. Rachel swung on her hammock and looked up at the flapping fronds, a woven pattern of fishbone-shaped stems. The afternoon sun pierced cracks in the slatted walls and fine white beams cross-hatched the dingy dorm, the light catching the termite dust that fell off the ceiling. Some palm debris landed on her face and she coughed. She rolled off her hammock and rubbed her mouth and eyes with a towel pegged to her door. Still wearing the clothes that she wore to the shops, khaki combat pants and a T-shirt with a scarlet macaw on it, a memento of Boston's field school in Ecuador, she peered out of one of the cracks in the wall.

Bruce jumped out of his new toy, the chopper on loan from the Agency for International Development, 'USAID' stencilled in black on olive-green doors. He perched his Ray Bans on his head. A man in khaki shorts and chequered shirt, the expedition's Professor, ran across the clearing. His long grey hair streaming in the wind, he ducked his white beard down and shouted at Bruce through cupped hands. He looked inside the cockpit and stuck up his thumb.

Rachel stepped back from her spy hole and looked at her watch:

there was at least one hour until dinner. Going down on her hands and knees, she swept her ten-foot square cubicle for her bottle of perfume, a surprisingly effective form of bug repellent. She looked under her bedside table, a block of wood on two stacks of bricks, and saw a spider, which she at first mistook for a mouse. The spider stood guard over the bottle of perfume. Six eyes sparkled as if they were sequins, while pincers flexed and bristles pricked up on the back of a fat abdomen. As her hand neared the perfume, the spider reared up, lifting two hairy legs off the ground. She flicked its belly and watched it fly across the wooden floor. Finding its feet again, neatly bending eight knees on landing, the spider scuttled down a gap in the floorboards.

Rachel squirted the perfume on her wrists and forearms, then rubbed the scent on her neck, ears and forehead, perfuming any exposed skin that might tempt a mosquito. She upturned her jungle warfare boots, which she bought from an army outfitter in DC, and shook them about to dislodge any sleeping scorpions. Her boots free of traps and safely on her feet, she picked up her sketchbook, a soft-leaded pencil and a pocket-sized torch off the table. She smiled at the photo of her mom and dad by her project folder. Outside her room, she flipped over a paper sign pinned to the door, a black marker penned 'DO NOT DISTURB: BAT HIBERNATING' switching to 'GONE FORAGING'. She walked past a line of doors to identical cubicles, most of which were unoccupied. Since there were no other research teams or tourists in the station, the large cabin currently housed only the three employees of Conservation International; the Lacandón family were housed in a couple of rooms in the kitchen cabin. As much as she enjoyed the peace and quiet, she found the deadness of the place eerie. She left the cabin and stretched out her arms in the grassy clearing.

An orange sun skirted the tops of palm trees, a satellite dish and shiny solar panels on the western horizon. Clouds of midges popped up from the grass that she stepped on. The swarm grew larger as she crossed the clearing and she fanned them away with her sketchbook. A topless Bruce and a pony-tailed Professor swigged bottles of beer on the kitchen's veranda. She waved at them, not wanting to interrupt their discussion of aerial surveillance, the merits of a loaned chopper and a few well-placed contacts in the Mexican military. A whiff of spicy cooking came from the rear of the cabin, whetting all manners of appetites in the species-rich clearing. She felt her stomach rumble.

An upside down bucket, normally used for seed flotation and washing laundry by hand, made do as a stool. She placed the bucket next to a coconut tree, checking the furry bark of her backrest for ants and millipedes, and settled down to her end-of-day wind down. Her sketchbook opened at a half-drawn cabin and a pressed mosquito. The bites of dusk, the previous evening's battle of the bugs, had postponed the drawing's completion and she wanted to finish it. She cleared the desiccated mosquito off the page, leaving a smudge of dried blood and guts on the paper, held up her pencil to the figures on the veranda and measured their scale with a sliding thumb. Pencil in motion, she scratched out an interpretation of the Professor's beard, pony-tail, round spectacles, socks in sandals, beer in hand and pipe in mouth pose. For Bruce, she used the stain made by the squashed mosquito to illustrate his quiff, lightly shading in his pale, topless body. After attending to the clouds in a late afternoon sky, the low sun dropping long shadows into the composition, she signed off the drawing with a few squiggles and rested her hand. She held the sketchbook up to reality, the kitchen cabin, and compared her impressionistic record to the flesh and beer in the foreground. At the bottom of the drawing she wrote: '*Lovers on the kitchen balcony (the boozy Prof., Buzz Lightyear Bruce and talk of a chopper) – Valentines Day, 2002, Lancantún Biology Station, Chiapas*'. She closed the sketchbook, stood up from the bucket and walked towards her male models.

'Hey guys,' she said, stepping up onto the veranda, 'you left any beers for me?' She went for the igloo by their feet, pulled a Dos Equis out of slushy ice and used the edge of the veranda's banister to uncap the bottle.

'Drawing again, huh?' Bruce pointed his beer at the sketchbook under her arm. 'Hope you managed to fit in my chopper.'

'Afraid not. It was just too big.' She swigged her beer, shaking her head.

'Hey,' Bruce said, grinning, 'it's good to see that you've got your sense of humour back. Does this mean that you are finally over that guy?'

'What?' She swatted a fly on her perfumed neck.

'Come on, Rach. You haven't exactly been your normal self out here.' Bruce scratched his chest, his skin reddened by too much sun. 'What's with all this wandering off with your sketchbook and going all darned quiet on us? What happened to the girl who gave as good as she got? You've been weird ever since you met up with him in DC.'

'No I haven't.' He reminded her to write a letter to Todd. 'I've just been soaking up the environment. I like it here.'

'May we take a look?' the Professor asked, pointing his pipe at the sketchbook. He exhaled a puff of smoke and gripped his bottle of beer as if his life depended on it. Prior to arriving at the station, Rachel had met the Professor only a couple of times; it included an interview in a bar in DC, the Professor slurring his questions and plying her with doubles of Jack Daniel's. He taught at Harvard, was one of the world's experts in botanical research, and CI drafted him in on a project-by-project basis. She had heard that one of his stipulations for working in the field was a ready supply of alcohol. A friend of hers from Harvard said that he even had it written in his contract.

'Do you mind if you don't, Professor?' She remembered, in time, the caption that she gave her sketch of him. 'It's just that I haven't drawn for ages and, well, it's pretty bad.'

'Oh, go on Rach,' Bruce nagged, 'stop being so modest. The Prof. and I have appointed you as our field artist. You'd better get used to showing us your skills. I have high expectations of you.' He coughed.

'Field artist?' she said, raising an eyebrow. 'More like war artist.' She looked at the chopper, the orange sun and pink sky reflecting on its windscreen. 'What are you going to do with that? Pick a fight with a few Injuns?'

'Isn't she a babe?' Bruce beamed at his chopper. 'USAID left it for me at the San Quintín army base. I got a call on the sat-phone this afternoon. Picked it up while you were taking a siesta. You missed out on one helluva ride over the reserve.'

'Why are USAID giving us ex-military Hueys?' Rachel asked him, also looking at the Professor. 'Come on, Bruce, what favours have you promised those development bozos?'

'We've promised nothing,' the Professor interrupted, opening up another bottle of beer, 'at least nothing to add to our original mission statement. The Agency wants to see the back of the squatters as much as we do.' He removed a fly which had tangled itself in his long grey hair. 'If we can positively link the settlements to deforestation, we'll be speeding up the whole relocation process. USAID can then drop in their investors and protect the forest in the long-term, taking care of your bats and my orchids.'

'Yeah,' Bruce said, his Ray Bans dropping onto his nose, 'we should now be able to get a great shot of every fire started by the rebels. If we present that sort of evidence in our report, we might actually see the Mexican government do something – before it's too late.'

'Umm,' Rachel paused to sip her beer, 'have you considered, Bruce, the fact that your terrorists might want to take a shot at you? It is, after all, a lovely chopper.'

'Yeah,' Bruce hesitated, 'anyway, they wouldn't dare. It has USAID written all over it.'

'Urrr, precisely.'

'It would be suicidal of those monkeys to try anything.' Bruce said, spitting out over the veranda, 'The US government would kick arse if anything happened to us.'

'And like suicidal martyrs are so not in fashion right now. And those US government markings, well the Zapatistas will just love those cute initials. After all, everyone loves Uncle Sam at the moment. Still, rather you than me in that hovering hearse.'

'What would you know about terrorism?' Bruce toyed with his blond and sweaty chest hair. 'You're just a manicured bat fancier. Why don't you stick with your mist-nets and leave the real work to the boys.'

'OK, kids,' the Professor said, tipping burnt tobacco out of his pipe's bowl, black ash dirtying his sandals and white socks. 'You may have noticed that there is only the three of us on this rapid assessment, in this research station. If you can't stick each other, I suggest you both get on the next plane out of Tuxtla and I'll call for replacements from DC. We must work as a team. This is a job, not an excuse for out-of-office horseplay. In the field, and especially here, we must count on each other's support.' He finished off his beer.

'I'm sorry, Professor,' Rachel said, 'Bruce and I like to joke around a bit. It's all very harmless. Honest.' She squinted at Bruce. 'If it's OK with you both, I might just go and see if Josita needs a hand in the kitchen. I'm assuming that it's just the three of us for dinner.'

'So you didn't hear?' Bruce grinned again.

'Hear what?' she asked, pausing by the entrance to the kitchen cabin.

'About our guest of honour, is what.'

'No. Should I have done?'

'I figure not.' Bruce puffed up his chest. 'Although it's not every day a sexy anthropologist who's lost her way in the jungle drops by. My valentine's fixed. How about yours, Rach?'

'Give me a break. I'll catch you and your pith helmeted sweetheart over dinner. Can't wait to meet her.' Clutching her beer and sketchbook, she pushed open a mosquito-proofed wire-meshed door and entered the station's dining room. The door closed on squeaky springs and she ignored Bruce's shouts of 'You missed your chance.'

The dining room consisted of long tables and low benches, solid pine furniture arranged in parallel lines as if it was a summer camp's canteen. To the front of the room, from the direction of the doorway in which she walked through, an open window of mesh ran the full length of the wall, providing a panoramic view of the clearing, the fiery helicopter and two silhouettes of men and beer on the veranda. Until the generator started at 6 p.m., the room had to make do with the light from outside, and the chicken-coop-styled interior was at its dimmest before dinner. Shelves on all four walls were piled high with books on neo-tropical taxonomy and Maya archaeology, and with falling apart paperbacks, trashy bestsellers for bored academics on humid evenings. In the corner of the room and on three separate shelves, was a display of artefacts from forest walks: a clay incensario, a jaguar's skull, a peccary's tusk, green tail feathers of a quetzal and a fer de lance viper in formaldehyde, poisonous fangs biting into a glass bell-jar.

'Hello?' Rachel called out to a small door at the back of the room. 'Josita?' Voices, trumpets, Spanish guitars and banging objects shook the walls. She clicked the latch and slowly opened the door.

'Señorita,' Josita shouted out, seeing Rachel in the doorway. She had to raise her voice above marimba music, a small but loud radio, and her daughter, who banged a cauldron with a ladle. Wearing an apron of Disney characters over a white smock, her long black hair identical to her husband and daughter's, the Lacandón chef attended the cluttered surfaces of a gas stove. Her face was lost in the steam of boiling broth. 'Stop that banging Ofelia and say hello to our guest. It's your new friend, the bat lady.'

Ofelia stopped drumming and ran for cover under her mother's apron, her big brown eyes stalking the giant from beneath a print of Minnie Mouse. Josita leaned over a bowl of severed chicken feet and switched off the radio.

'That's better,' she said, tipping the feet into the mist of the cauldron, putting in the final touch to the biologists' dinner.

'Smells good,' Rachel said, as she leaned over the stove and sniffed Bruce's romantic meal. 'What is it exactly?' She observed what appeared to be eyeballs and claws floating on the surface of a black stock.

'Chicken feet and boiled eggs in a black bean sauce. You like? It is Ofelia's favourite. You want to try some?' She lifted out a spoonful of the tarry substance, a chicken foot gripping onto the ladle by a long claw, and passed it to her.

Rachel knocked the foot back into the pot. She pulled her hair back over her ears and slurped the ladle.

'Hmmm, it really is good.' She looked down into the pot and at the unpromising looking, and yet surprisingly tasty, black broth. 'Ofelia has good taste.'

She felt something tug at her combat pants.

'Can I still watch the bats with you?' Ofelia said, in perfect Spanish. She stared up at Rachel.

'Ofelia, where are your manners?' Josita spoke to her feet, her daughter under her apron again. 'Wait until you're asked. Really now. What would your father have to say?'

'But mamá. The señorita said . . .'

'Shush.' Josita then looked at Rachel. 'I'm sorry. Your arrival here has had her excited for days. She can be a little pushy sometimes.'

'No, no,' Rachel said, shaking her head and smiling at the girl's half-hidden face, 'you don't understand. It was I who invited Ofelia to join me. I cleared it with your husband, on the way back from the market in Benemérito. I'd love her to come along.' She sensed a small ally in the making, but the girl went even further beneath her mother's apron.

'That's very kind of you, señorita, but you shouldn't feel that you have to. I don't want her distracting you from your good work. My youngest can be a handful at the best of times.'

'I promise that she won't be in the way. And your husband will be there in any case. It will be fun as well as educational. The two of us, I'm sure of it, will have a real blast.' Rachel crouched down and lifted up the apron. Ofelia moved behind a flea-bitten shin. 'Hey . . . you . . . want . . . to . . . still . . . help?'

'Why do you speak slowly?' Josita gave Rachel an odd look.

'I thought that she couldn't understand much Spanish.'

'Ha,' Josita exclaimed, patting her daughter's head, 'Ofelia not understanding Spanish? She's the brightest in her class; she speaks better Spanish than both her parents, the little gibnut.'

'No kidding.' Rachel frowned at the little rodent, the gibnut, under the apron. 'Been taking language classes all afternoon, have we kid?'

Ofelia giggled from behind her mother's shin.

'What day do you want to punish yourself?' Josita asked, stirring the cauldron on the stove. 'I'll need to plan her kitchen duties for another time.'

'How about Friday? That gives me a week to cut the paths with Guillermo and set up the points for the nets. Is that OK with you?'

'I should survive; she'll just have to make extra tortillas on Thursday. More to the point, let's hope you survive with this little terror on your tail.'

Ofelia emerged from the cover of Minnie Mouse. They all chipped in to finish preparing dinner: Josita heating tortillas on a griddle, Rachel struggling to carry vats of rice and chicken talons, and Ofelia branding the Lokin a 'weakling'. In this play-ground of rolling pins, boiling cauldrons, chicken feet and boiled eggs the biologist and her new pupil talked about Friday. Ofelia squirmed at the mention of bat poop and girl-eating vampires. By the time dinner was ready to be served, the sound of chatter coming from next door, Rachel felt that the ice of earlier had finally melted.

'So what are you doing out here?' Rachel asked Liz, Lacantún station's guest of honour and Bruce's squeeze-to-be, at the dining table. 'Bruce tells me that you're an anthropologist. How very exciting for you.' She picked what little meat there was off a scaly chicken foot.

'Bruce flatters me,' Liz replied from the opposite side of the table. Apart from her environmentally unfriendly florescent pink T-shirt, which Rachel thought was more San Fran than Selvá Lacandón, the social scientist bore an uncanny resemblance to the dark-haired conservationist. 'I'm still doing my doctorate and I'm here for research. Well, that and the beaches on the Yucatán. You can't come all this way and not get a tan. Right?'

Rachel watched Liz play the Lady to Bruce's Tramp, her doe eyes raised over a spoon, an egg on a nest of black beans. The Tramp slurped a tortilla and a candle on the table flickered.

'How nice for you,' Rachel said. 'What kind of research are we talking about?' She dipped a fork into a pot of salsa and painted a red sock over a white claw.

'Conceptions of the female orgasm in Lacandón communities.'

Bruce grinned like a lottery winner and Rachel felt him nudge her knee under the table. The Professor, who was now on spirits and fully inebriated, wiped away a black bean moustache with a paper napkin.

'Fascinating,' Rachel eventually responded. 'Have you found some good material?'

'It was all going great until . . .'

'The villagers kicked her out,' Bruce blurted out. 'The Indians felt threatened by a beautiful and liberated woman. They thought she might steal their men.'

'As if I would,' Liz said, smiling at Bruce, who couldn't keep his eyes off her chest, 'I'm twice as tall as most of them. But Bruce is right: the women were the ones who hated me the most. And the little girls were especially nasty, bad behaviour of which was no doubt encouraged by their paranoid mothers. The little shits would go into my bedroom, without my permission, go through all my stuff, steal my cosmetics and try on my clothes. It drove me crazy.'

'You poor thing,' Rachel said, pretending to be sympathetic, 'it must've been very traumatic.' She pushed a plate of inedible cartilage out of harm's way, put her elbows on the table and rested her chin in her folded hands.

'They even stole my favourite mascara. It was from Clinique's new range. Do you know the one that I mean?'

'Can't say that I do. Sorry.'

Liz shrugged.

'Anyway,' Liz continued, 'things got so bad that I just had to leave. Tomorrow I'm flying back to New York to recuperate. Hotel cocktail bars here I come.'

'What a shame that you have to go so soon,' Rachel said, turning to look at Bruce. 'We could do with an extra pair of hands to help out. Isn't that right, Bruce?'

'Eh?' Bruce said, his game of footsie with the anthropologist not evading the radar of the bat expert; it had put Rachel off her chicken feet.

'I said,' she raised her voice, 'it's a shame that Liz can't stay to help out.'

'Too right,' the Professor slurred, dropping his napkin, his beard finally clear of broth. 'I could do with someone else to take cuttings. Do you like orchids?'

'I just luuuurve orchids. What a marvellous specialism you have.'

Rachel leaned further into her hands.

'But I have booked my flight and I really can't change it.'

'Please at least allow me to fly you to the airport,' Bruce said, pushing the drunken Professor out of play, 'we can't have you going home without a chopper ride over the Reserve.'

'You'll really take me with you? Awesome! I've never seen the jungle from the sky.'

'Hey, it's no problem.' Bruce's nudges turning into punches, Rachel's thigh took a pounding. 'I'll enjoy it. It will be like my first time as well – it always is when I'm up there.'

'It must be so incredibly romantic up there,' Liz swooned at the pilot.

'Yeah,' Rachel said, yawning, 'though you'd better watch out for the stingers. They can be *real* nasty.'

'Stingers?' Liz said, playing with the fringe of her hair. 'There are bees that high up? *Really?*'

'I'm talking about stinger SAMs – surface-to-air missiles – launched by some pissed-off rebels who don't take kindly to being spied upon.' Rachel smiled at Liz. 'A hit from one of those is slightly worse than a bee sting. But you probably knew that already.'

'Don't listen to her,' Bruce said, scowling at his colleague, 'Rachel has read too many Tom Clancy novels. The girl likes to think that she's in 'Nam; it's her first season in Montes Azules and her imagination is running wild. In reality, it is as safe as Disney World out here.'

'Complete with the cartoon characters. Right, Goofy?' She pinched him under the table.

'You guys crack me up,' Liz said. 'You have a family vibe going on, a nuclear focus to withdraw to. It's something I miss in my own field studies. It's so cute.'

'I don't know if I'd call my relationship with Bruce "cute",' Rachel said, 'but you're not wrong about the nuclear bit.' She picked up her bottle of beer off the table. 'I'm just going outside for some fresh air. It's too stuffy in here and I can barely breathe. Please excuse me Professor. Nice meeting you, Liz.' She stood up from the bench, her fist colliding into her colleague's back. 'Sorry Bruce.'

'I'll see you tomorrow morning,' the Professor said, his inebriated state delaying his response. 'I'll help you get things started with whoever that guy is. We meet at the usual time, right?'

'Guillermo is his name. Yes, we R/V at 4 a.m. Goodnight all.'

'Blow some kisses to the bats from me,' Bruce said, to the rattling mesh of the cabin's door and the figure disappearing into the dark outside. 'I've seen her do it,' he whispered in Liz's ear. 'I was reading my book, having a quiet beer on our first night here, when I saw her on the veranda. She was blowing kisses to the sky and, I guess, at the bats. It's kind of odd, don't you think?'

Rachel walked past the helicopter and caught her ghostly reflection in the cockpit windows. Light from the cabin and distant galaxies, the stars in a clear night sky, lit up her khaki combat pants and the parrot on her white T-shirt. Dew on the grass wet-wiped the dust off her boots, returning browns and greens to camouflaged Gore-Tex, and her sodden turn-ups cooled down her lower legs. A large bug, a beetle with the wingspan of a small hummingbird, did a kamikaze dive at her head. Trapped in her hair, its belly up and its legs kicking out, the beetle screeched down her ear. She calmly plucked it free. Clamped between her finger and thumb, the beetle wriggled about as if it was a maggot on a hook. She relaxed her grip and watched it fly up into the sky, the feeding ground of her bats. A patrolling insectivore, which she identified as a Microchiroptera, darted down in a shadowy flash and tucked into its hand-fed dinner. The screeching abruptly stopped.

Above the beetle's last stand she saw the Big Dipper. Tracing the inverted saucepan with her finger, she transported herself, via Washington, DC and the Amazon rainforest, to Boston. She toasted the constellation with the dregs of her beer.

'Happy Valentine's, Todd.'

She blew a kiss to the stars and headed for the dormitory.

Two scorpions scurried about in the thatch above Rachel's hammock. Pincers picked through the palm as they swept the cabin's rafters for a midnight snack, a crunchy moth or a juicy pupa. They hooked their legs over fronds so that their heavily armoured bodies wouldn't fall, saving themselves from crashing onto the insomniac underneath.

Lying on her back, sweat pouring down her forehead, Rachel had watched the acrobatic scorpions for the past two hours. Her body was trapped inside a sleeping-bag liner, a cotton barrier to any mosquito that may have infiltrated her cubicle. She tried to cool down by remaining still, the venomous and precariously placed trapeze artists pinning her rigid. The noises of her neighbours amplified in her head. Tiptoes on floorboards had progressed to panting and hushed gasps; the coming to fruition of Bruce's hard work over dinner. She could also hear the Professor snoring, his rattling lungs broadcasting a health warning against pipe-smoking and alcoholism. She longed for a good night's sleep before the first day in the field, but it was her thoughts, rather than the background noises, which really kept her awake. It was the knowledge that she was an unwelcome hero, an enemy to the people whose land she wanted to save, which kept her tossing and turning.

Faint laughter, husky and high-pitched, came from two cubicles down. She rolled over in her hammock and sighed.

Ofelia, Josita and Guillermo had given her some comfort: Guillermo had even praised her for protecting the forest. The Lacandón Maya, her new friends, were, after all, the legitimate owners of the forest. Sure, the brief had said that they weren't the direct descendants of the Selva's ancient residents, the pyramid builders of the Petén, but then neither were the Zapatistas; she went through the argument again. Originally from the Yucatán and called the Carib, a peaceful people from Campeche and Merida, they had moved to the Lacandón rainforest way back in the 1700s. The rebel communities, the squatters, however, had come much later. Tzotziles and Tzetzales had arrived in the last few years, and had no idea how to live in a rainforest. Their lives, the forest's life, would, she thought, be better off for what she had to do. She lay on her back again and wiped the sweat off her forehead with her nightshirt's sleeve.

Pincers acting as if they were grappling irons, a dangling scorpion swung up and resumed its search of bugs in the palm thatch. Rachel closed her eyes. Mountaineering scorpions turning into Zapatistas, she fell asleep.

Twelve

Five miles north of the research station, under a moonless sky and corozal palm branches, camouflage against satellites and choppers, twelve men congregated around a campfire. All cross-legged and dressed in black, red bandanas tied round necks, they whispered in Tzotzil and passed a cigarette round the circle. One of the men stood up and the others went quiet. Broad shoulders sporting a leather gun belt, spikes of hair catching the firelight and flickering like flames, he paced the perimeter of the camp and pounded a ski mask in the palm of a hand. Squinting up at him from the ground, politely refusing the communal cigarette, Lucio tapped his pipe against his thigh. Lucio waited for the Zapatista Commandante, his son, to address the patrol.

'Where are they?' Horatio asked his men. He kicked a log back into the fire. Sparks shot up into the air. 'Who saw them last?'

All heads dropped. Every face sought refuge in the fire's embers and a firework display of spitting sap. Only Lucio dared to continue looking up.

'Listen,' Horatio softened, sensing the agitation around the fire and catching his father's disapproving look. 'There is nothing to be scared of. These people are on our side. We are in a global struggle and we are no longer alone on the frontline. The war has many frontiers, even in distant lands where the wooden people live.' He paused to look at his father, expecting at least his backing when it came to foreign support. 'The English companeros want to help. They too are in resistance to their bad governments. Father, tell them, please, you of all Tzotziles must understand.'

Lucio unfolded a page of newspaper, a pocket of tobacco, and filled up his pipe. He struck a match above the pipe's bowl and puffed out smoke rings. All eyes were on him.

'Well?' Horatio said, annoyed by his father's prolonged silence, the ritualistic pipe-smoking.

'My son,' Lucio replied, as he rested his pipe on his knees. Smoke rose up over his tanned and wrinkled face. 'Over the last few years you have done us proud, especially me. Our trust is in you. My confidence, the Lord and the gods' confidence, is with you. And your patrol is as loyal as always.' The circle of men nodded. Lucio took another puff of his pipe.

'And the foreigners?' Horatio continued, as if he needed reassurance himself that he had done the right thing by inviting them. 'Do you trust them? Surely you must.'

'You know my position on the foreigners,' Lucio said, looking at the faces round the fire, no longer having to justify his own decision to bring an outsider into their ranks. He wondered where his adopted son was; of all the nights he should have been there. 'If they can report on the Cardenistas and the federal army, shield the villages from attacks, do what Hunahpu has done, then we must regard them as fellow Zapatistas.' He touched a red pottery shard, an ancient painting of a spider monkey, which hung from a leather cord round his neck. Five years had passed since Urbano's murder and Lucio was now a fully fledged Zapatista supporter. He had even found a successful role for Hunahpu within his son's patrol.

The circle murmured various grunts of agreement. Horatio dabbed his forehead with his scrunched up ski mask, scratched a spot on his cheek and ran a hand through his spikes of hair. He nodded at his father and they exchanged small smiles.

'They will tell us about their plans this evening,' Horatio said, his confidence returning, 'they have intelligence for us to act upon and an idea to stop the expulsions.'

Lucio fanned pipe smoke away from his face and looked up at Horatio again. The smile had gone from his face.

'Where is Hunahpu?' Lucio asked his son. 'Shouldn't he be here if these men have knowledge of the expulsions?' Everyone watched Horatio, to see how he would react to Lucio's question.

Horatio threw another branch onto the fire. The young sapling hissed in the flames.

'He is on a patrol of the Rio Lacantún.' Horatio hesitated. 'A new chopper, another Huey from San Quintín army base, was spotted near the biological station. Hunahpu volunteered to investigate. He'll be back soon.' Although he treated Hunahpu as a brother, appreciated his ability to translate Zapatista struggles to foreigners through the Internet and friendly journalists, he wanted his father to see that he could also bring in help. It was almost as if he had to prove his worth to him, just like he had to as a boy, when Urbano was the shaman's apprentice. His father had discovered Hunahpu, and he had discovered allies in the London anarchists.

'But you did brief him on what was happening?' Lucio asked, not believing that Hunahpu, of all people, would have missed out on the opportunity to greet their new guests. The fact that they were English and had information on the expulsions of Zapatista villages, including Nuevo San Felipé, made it all the more imperative that he should have been there. 'You did tell him who they are and where they are from?' The orange light of the fire rippled over his wrinkles and his look of concern. His shiny black fringe and dark brown eyes were highlighted by the flames.

'Hunahpu will be notified in good time,' Horatio snapped back, 'when he is back from his patrol. Is that OK with you?' As a young Commandante he hated it when his father put him on the spot in front of his men, the majority of whom were older than him.

'Yes, son.' Lucio sucked on his pipe.

Horatio did one more lap around the campfire. The sound of English voices and trampled foliage stopped him from starting another lap. He gazed into the forest's moving shadows and saw three figures emerge out of the trees. A shaven-headed man pulled back a curtain of vines.

'Companeros,' Horatio addressed the circle, pointing at the three approaching white men, 'stand up to greet our friends. They have travelled far to be with us.'

Lucio shifted about. He placed the pipe on a bed of leaves by his feet and sat up to look at the new arrivals.

The Zapatistas rose to their feet and the shaven-headed foreigner stepped into the light, his two cohorts behind him. Lucio, the last to stand up, observed a Z-shaped tattoo on the back of the man's neck, above the skull that was painted on his black leather jacket. One of the man's companions, a man with greasy dreadlocks, flicked a cigarette into the trees. The third man, the biggest of the three, behaving as if he was a bodyguard to the man with the 'Z' tattoo, hid a liquor bottle in his green poncho.

'Thank you for your warm greeting, Commandante Horatio,' Zeb said, his education giving him a good grasp of Spanish. He smiled down at his shorter host. 'Please, everyone, sit down. We are all Zapatistas.'

The circle did another chorus of grunts and the Zapatistas returned to their seats on the forest floor. The newcomers sat next to Horatio at the head of the fire. Lucio sat down last, opposite them and on the other side of the fire.

'Amigo,' Horatio whispered into Zeb's ear, 'perhaps you should introduce yourselves before we discuss the business of why you are here.' He glanced at his father through the fire, seeking some sign of approval. Lucio was too busy tending to his pipe to notice him.

'Of course, Commandante,' Zeb said, as he observed the expectant faces before him, a small army of Maya men, a line of impressionable teenagers and moustached adults. 'Companeros,' he said, silencing the chit-chat and leaving only courting insects as disturbers of the peace. Fireflies speckled the backdrop of his auditorium and an owl hooted as if it was a heckler. 'My name is Zeb. I am the leader of the East London Anarchists, an organization dedicated to resisting the oppression perpetrated by the governments of globalization. Like you, we fight for democracy, freedom, rights, dignity and respect.' He bowed his head. 'To our shame and regret,' he spoke to the fire, 'we come from a country that is a slave to the bankers that butcher your people, destroy your culture and traditions.' He looked up from the fire. 'It is with this noose around our necks, the sins of our own bad government, that we have come, in the name of civil society, to visit you.'

The circle remained silent. Lucio fidgeted on the other side of the campfire. He struck a match and relit his pipe. He wished that he had left the village earlier, met up with the patrol before Hunahpu had gone on his recce.

'Two of my most trusted friends,' Zeb continued, 'fellow anarchists from London, have joined me on this pilgrimage to your war-torn land. Jamie,' he gestured at the rock of a man by his side, 'and Stevo,' he looked at the stern face under dreadlocks on his other side. 'They both share the burden that I feel.'

Lucio raised his hand. Horatio frowned at his father.

'And what,' Lucio asked, as he held a flame over his pipe, 'if you don't mind me asking, do you want from us, East London Anarchists?' The interruption set off a Mexican wave of startled faces. 'Do you expect us to lift this burden, this guilt, of yours?' There was something about the visitors that made him distrust them. They were not like the foreign peace observers he had seen Hunahpu interview. They seemed too cool.

Zeb smiled and shook his head.

'No,' he replied to the group as a whole, unflustered by the elder puffing smoke rings from across the fire. 'Our burden is our responsibility. We are not here to ask for any favours from anyone. It is more a question of what we can do for you. That, amigos, is why we are here.' Stevo and Jamie grinned with him.

'Who says that we need your help?' Lucio asked.

'Father,' Horatio shouted out over the fire, 'please, it was I, through Carlos and the high command in San Cristóbal, who invited our guests, accepted their kind offer to act as peace observers. These men bring intelligence, information on the evictions, news of plans to destroy Nuevo San Felipé.' He turned to face Zeb. 'I apologise for my father's questions. He is a good man – just a little paranoid sometimes.' He glared at his father.

'I understand,' Zeb said, eyeing the older man through the flames. 'There's nothing wrong with a bit of paranoia.'

'Fucking troublemaker that one is,' Jamie whispered into Stevo's ear. Stevo responded by tossing back his dreadlocks.

'Do continue, Zeb,' Horatio said. 'Tell us what you have heard. And without further interruption.' He stared at his father.

Bunching up the tails to his leather jacket, the sweat on his forehead and the painted skull on his back glinting in the light of the fire, Zeb stood up. He flicked a soldier ant off his sleeve and a collage of leaves fell off his black combat pants. The earthy confetti continued to fall as he walked around the circle, as he retraced Horatio's earlier steps, the patrol looking up at him this time.

'Your Commandante is correct,' Zeb eventually said, scanning the faces below him, 'we do have information on the expulsions. As I'm sure you're far more aware of than I am, Montes Azules, with its green and black gold, biodiversity and oil, has become a landing strip for multinationals.' He spoke in fluent Spanish and kept the patrol's attention. 'For many years, the combination of the forest's inaccessibility, its lack of roads, and Zapatista resistance has prevented foreigners from stealing and exploiting your land. It has just been too much of a hassle to get a hold of.'

'Vive Zapata,' Horatio shouted out.

'Vive Zapata,' the patrol, with the exception of Lucio, echoed their Commandante.

'Whereas the War on Terror gave the West an excuse to take oil from the Middle East,' Zeb continued, resuming his walk around the circle of men, the fire crackling in the centre of them, 'the Zapatistas and the Maya of Chiapas are not so easy to class as

165

terrorists. You guys don't go around shooting people or blowing up skyscrapers of bankers. It's very frustrating for them.' The air still and the humidity claustrophobic, Zeb took off his leather jacket and hooked it on a branch. All eyes were mesmerized by him. The script that Agent Decker had provided him with seemed to be working.

'We defend,' Horatio said, looking up at Zeb, 'we don't shoot first and we never target civilians.' He looked across at his father and saw him nod in agreement. Small signs of approval like that made a big difference to Horatio. After listening to Zeb's wise words, he hoped that his father now realized that he was right to have invited the anarchists to the camp.

'Well you might not target humans,' Zeb said, touching the green trunk of a tree, 'but you do cut down the forest. And if you do that, just think about all those cute animals that you are wiping out.' He paused and looked up at the stars behind the upper branches of the tree. The circle of men muttered to one another. 'Think of all the international support the Mexican government will get for sorting it out,' he said, looking down at the men again, 'for looking after the environment.'

'It's lies,' Horatio said, jumping to his feet. 'We are the true guardians of the forest. No Tzotzil or Tzetzal would ever rape the sacred land of his ancestors. It's the army, the Lacandóns and the corrupt government that run the illegal timber trade. They are the ones who supply the convoys of trucks, not us. There is no evidence to suggest that it's us.'

'With all due respect, Commandante,' Zeb said, scratching the 'Z' tattoo on the back of his neck and facing Horatio, 'who needs evidence when you have science on your side.'

'What do you mean?' Horatio looked confused.

'Where do you think these academics and conservationists find the money for their research?' Horatio shrugged and Zeb continued. 'You go to the big boys for cash: Pulsar, Pemex, BP, Coca-Cola, all the usual suspects. They give you a wage to study the mating wails of tapirs while, in return, you give them carte blanche to go in and replace eco-terrorists with eco-tourists and bio-pirates.'

'And that is what the conservationists at Lacantún are doing?' Horatio asked, glancing down at his father, feeling totally vindicated in bringing the foreigners to the camp. 'They are using their research to evict us?'

Lucio's deep worry lines flickered with the flames of the fire.

'Yes, Commandante,' Zeb said, sensing that he had won over Horatio's trust. 'After we received notice of the planned expulsions, the email sent to Zapatista supporters by Carlos, and after the approval of our delegation to Chiapas, we unmasked an informant. He was a risk analyst for an environmental agency.' It was Decker's idea to use Rick's infiltration to their advantage; it justified the course of action they were to propose to the Zapatista patrol.

'Do you know which agency it was?' Horatio asked.

'No. He wouldn't talk.'

'Yeah,' Stevo said, waving a cigarette in his hand. The smoke in his eyes forced him to blink repeatedly as he looked up at Zeb and Horatio. 'And he didn't say much when he left, either.' He spoke in English.

'What?' Horatio looked down at the dreadlocks in smoke. 'I'm afraid my English isn't great, companero.'

'Neither is Stevo's,' Zeb said, glowering at the ruddy-cheeked face of his comrade. 'The informant was a low ranker, someone who had nothing better to do than spy on a few anarchists in his spare time. Unfortunately he gave us no names.'

'You let him go?' Lucio asked from the ground. The question passed under his arched eyebrows and it left a trail of exhaled pipe-smoke from his mouth. The other men looked at Lucio and then at Zeb.

'You could say that,' Zeb replied, still ashamed by what had happened to Rick. 'I'm worried that he may have had time to tell others of our expedition.' He faced Horatio. 'Of our plans.'

'What are your plans?' Horatio asked, avoiding Zeb's wide and staring eyes, noticing a scar under the white man's lower lip.

'They're not exactly plans. Not yet, anyway. Right now, they're just a few, well, suggestions.' Zeb paused and turned away from Horatio and the men on the ground. He scratched the back of his neck again. 'You see we need your approval first.'

'So you do need us, then,' Lucio said, looking at the 'Z' tattoo on Zeb's neck.

'Smart arse,' Stevo whispered to Jamie.

'You're right,' Zeb turned round and stared at Lucio. 'We do need you.'

'And what is it that you would like to suggest?' Horatio asked, watching Zeb pace around the circle of men.

Zeb stopped pacing. A bat swooped over his head and caught a large moth.

'I suggest that we do something to scare them off, create a deterrent of sorts, if you know what I mean. I suggest we take the fear from your villages and kick it back to these new agents of globalization, these spying conservationists, so they will go back home screaming like their protected primates, crying 'no more' to their multinational backers. I suggest, companeros, Commandante Horatio, we bag ourselves a hostage.'

'Well that wasn't the fuck-up I was expecting,' Stevo said, benchrocking on a felled mahogany trunk and passing a bottle of tequila to Jamie. After the Zapatistas had sanctioned Zeb's motion with raised hands, Tzotziles shaking hands with east London anarchists, the two cultures separated and prepared for bedtime in different ways. While the Tzotziles sang Zapatista hymns around the campfire, Stevo and Jamie decided to get drunk and smoke weed by the river.

Jamie took the bottle off Stevo and took a large gulp.

'Wonder how long they're going to sing for,' Stevo said, looking behind them, the campfire glowing through the trees. 'It's going to be hard enough sleeping out here, let alone with them warbling all night long.'

Jamie, as usual, said nothing. Instead he picked up a pebble by his feet, from a stockpile of boredom-busting stones, threw it and watched it skip and skim across the Río Lacantún, starry phosphorescence bridging the river's banks. The last of the tequila dribbling down his double chin, he tossed the empty bottle along the same trajectory as the pebble. The bottle bobbed downstream, its gold-foiled neck swaying about like the head of a drowning man.

'Do you think Zeb's OK?' Stevo asked Jamie, as he watched the bottle fill with water and sink.

'Yeah,' Jamie replied, throwing another pebble into the river, 'he's with the Commandante.'

'I mean do you think he's OK up here?' Stevo pointed at his head, at his temples hidden under dreadlocks. 'That shit with the wheelchair and his obsession with paralysis. You don't think he's starting to lose it, do you?'

'Zeb's fine,' Jamie said, shaking his head and smiling, 'you don't know him as well as I do. He's close to fixing things up for Tam, so, of course, he's going to get a little excited. Thought he handled it pretty well back there.'

'Suppose so.' Stevo dipped his hand into a freezer bag full of fresh marijuana and rolled a joint. He lit up and a large flame singed the greasy knots of his fringe. The smell of burning herb and hair joined the other unpleasant odours that lingered around the two men.

Through the trees, behind the riverbank and the anarchists' wooden perch, the orange glow of the campfire silhouetted the singing Zapatistas. Smoke drifted between tree-trunks, palm fronds, thorny thickets and vines, and random bursts of torchlight sliced the darkness with lines of cloudy beams. A guitar, finely tuned in spite of the humidity, played an upbeat rendition of the Zapatista anthem. Competing against the crickets for the forest's acoustics, the Tzotziles sang the anthem's Spanish lyrics.

Now we can see the horizon
– Zapatista combatant –
The change will mark
Those who come after us.

Forward, forward, forward we go
To take part in the struggle ahead
Because our country cries out for
All of the efforts of the Zapatistas

Men, women and children
We will always make the effort
Peasant and workers
All together with the people.

'Na, nah, na-naah, na-naah,' Steve hummed, unable to translate, let alone understand, the lyrics of the tune. 'Na, nah, na-nah.'

'Forward, forward, forward we go
To take part in the struggle ahead
Because our country cries out for
All of the efforts of the Zapatistas

Our people demand an end
To exploitation, now!

169

Our history says . . . now!
To the struggle for freedom.

A twig snapped behind the two anarchists. Jamie spun round and jumped off the uprooted tree. A clenched hand, fingers bent into an imitation firearm, prodded Stevo between his hunched shoulder blades. Stevo dropped his spliff.

'Christ, Zeb,' Stevo said, pushing the triggered fist out of his back and moving a tattooed forearm off his shoulder. He swept a hand through his dreadlocks and shuffled about on his perch like a troubled hen. 'Why do you have to do that?'

'A bullet moves faster than a crowbar, that's why,' Zeb replied, his stern face visible in the light of the stars. 'It might not be fucking Dalston, but it's not bloody Center Parcs either. Stay on guard. It's why I brought you here.'

'When are we going to get the guns?' Jamie asked Zeb.

'Give them a bit of time,' Zeb said, patting Jamie on the back. 'We need to build their faith in us first.'

'Wonder what I'll get,' Stevo said, picking up his spliff off the ground. 'Hope it's an M16 or an AK47.'

'Probably a water pistol,' Jamie snorted.

'Grow up.' Stevo swayed on the trunk.

Zeb looked out across the black and windy river. Blocking out the bickering on the bank, he thought of the squat and Tam as he watched phosphorescent bubbles and reflected stars on the water. He had never been apart from her for longer than a day, let alone gone abroad, and even though he trusted Jules, he worried about how Tam would cope without him. On top of that, there was the double-edged guilt he felt. First there was Tam, the daring doer of old and the paraplegic of now, who was left behind while he was with the Zapatistas in the jungle. Tam would have loved to have joined a Zapatista patrol, been with the true champions in the resistance against globalization. For an anarchist, it didn't come much better than to be on the frontline with the famous Zapatistas. Then there was the even deeper guilt he felt about working for the other side. Decker had promised him that no harm would come to the Zapatistas, that it was only about unmasking Hunahpu, and yet he was torn up about manipulating the Commandante and his men.

'To you, angel,' he said, looking down at the river, toasting Tam with the rum he had decanted into an empty water bottle, reminding himself of why they were there. 'I won't fail you. I promise.'

'Eh?' Stevo said, to the skull on the back of Zeb's jacket, 'you got some more booze?'

Zeb wiped the moisture away from his eyes before he turned round.

'Go easy on the drinking, Stevo,' he said, handing him the bottle. 'The Zapatistas don't drink. So far we have the Commandante's confidence, but it's not exactly going to help if he sees any of us drunk, especially with that father of his on our case.'

'Who the hell does that old man think he is?' Jamie asked, taking the bottle off Stevo. 'What's it got to do with him what we get up to?'

'He's the village shaman,' Zeb said, still agonizing over the dilemma he was in, about having to manipulate the Zapatistas.

'He doesn't do voodoo, does he?' Jamie asked. He chuckled to himself.

'No, Jamie, they don't do voodoo.' Zeb smiled at the idea of it, trying to forget about his guilt. He took the bottle off Jamie. 'Anyway, it's not the shaman who I'm worried about. It's Hunahpu we have to watch. I tried to find out some more about him, but no one was willing to say much, even our friend Horatio.' Zeb finished off the rum in the water bottle before continuing. 'When he eventually shows up, I want you both to keep a close eye on him.'

'No problem,' Jamie said, 'I'll see to it that he keeps his nose out of things.'

'Thanks, Jamie. But on no account are you to touch him. Understand?'

'Sure mate. I'll save him for you.' Jamie grinned.

Zeb tossed the empty water bottle into the river. The three of them then walked towards the campfire and the Zapatista chorus of:

Vamos Vamos Vamos Adelante . . .

A tray of candles illuminated a porcelain statue of a madonna and child. The icon's blue blouse flashed on an open-air altar of arched and bound sapling. To the right of the madonna and in the centre

171

of a quadrant of maize stalks and pebbles, a calloused hand placed a gold cross, its painted gilt flaking off wood. A black cloud rose up from crackling copal incense, crystals of which were placed at the base of the altar in corn husks and strips of bark. The cloud masked the stars in the night sky. With the moon of First Mother yet to make an appearance, darkness continued to preside over Montes Azules and the rituals of the shaman.

Lucio bowed before the Sky Tree altar and, mimicking First Father's 'raising of the sky,' washed his raised hands in the perfumed cloud. Satisfied that he was alone, taking one last look around the forest to make sure, he prayed to the ancestral gods first. He recited Tzotzil prayers in a monotonous hum, his palms rubbing the pebbles and maize shoots to unlock the portal to the Otherworld. Finished with the old incantations, he opened his mouth wider, coughing in the smoke, and said the Lord's Prayer in Spanish. His pleas for supernatural guidance ending with a whispered 'Amen,' he kissed the shard of pottery round his neck and crossed his chest.

The call to evening prayer, the fulfilment of a shaman's duties, had given Lucio an excuse to retire from the sing-along by the campfire. It wasn't that he disagreed with the lyrics of the songs, for he had converted to Zapatismo five years ago and was as vocal as Horatio in the *'lucha de liberación'*. Nor was it the father–son spat over the patrol's direction. The invitation to foreigners, for assistance, was an action which he and Hunahpu fully supported; it was almost flattering for him to have his son recognize his policy and his example. And, as all Zapatista councils would have attested to, the Lacandón and paramilitary threats going unabated, more foreign observers were needed in the Selva. But hostage taking . . .

'Father,' Horatio called out, interrupting Lucio's thoughts. Horatio pushed away a branch from his path to the altar and his father. 'Couldn't you have found a better place for the altar? Why didn't you put it on the riverbank, like you used to do in Chenalho, where the men can at least find it? It's jungle in here.'

'And allow it to be defaced by a passing patrol boat?' Lucio replied, facing the racket of breaking foliage, his frown accentuated by the flickering candles. 'And did you not learn anything from me when you were a boy?' He pointed at a large tree with bright green bark, its branches sheltering the altar.

'Ah, a sacred ceiba tree.' Horatio looked up at the tall tree.

'It's the Wakah-Chan, the World Tree Centre, the site of regeneration and order for our people's universe.' Lucio touched his son's cheek. 'Do you remember what I taught you about the Wakah-Chan?'

'You mean how First Father went up to the sky by growing a tree out of sacrifice? Sure, I remember the story of Creation. I listened to you, then, father. And I still do.' He smiled and then hugged his father.

'Then you'll know that it is through the tree that our world is centred,' Lucio whispered to his son, holding him close to his embroidered shirt, a hemline of red and black zigzags. 'Without the Wakah-Chan, there would be chaos, the destruction of the Maya.' He stepped back and looked at his son's young face with his aged eyes. 'Why, Horatio? Why did you invite those wooden idiots into our camp?'

'I thought you'd be pleased.' Horatio looked down at the candles on the altar. 'Now we have more foreign companeros to fight alongside us.'

'Those men are not companeros,' Lucio said, his curt voice making Horatio look up. 'They will bring violence to our sacred land. They don't care for Zapatista principles.'

'Don't preach to me about Zapatismo.' Horatio shook his head, smiling sarcastically. 'You need to wake up, father. The violence has been here for centuries. It has been here ever since the Spaniards first set foot on our soil, and evicted our ancestors from their homes. Only a few years back, the Cardenistas robbed us of our *own* home, as well as *my* brother, *your* son. We were humiliated, forced to flee, and I am not going to stand by and watch them take Nuevo San Felipé from us. This time, with me in command, we will do whatever it takes to resist them. That is our only objective.'

'No, Horatio, your objective is to command by following your men. It is not by following the lead of those unprincipled, foreign terrorists.' Lucio put his hands on his son's shoulders, slightly shaking him despite being the weaker of the two. 'Have you not thought of the consequences of this crazy plan of theirs? It will give the federal troops the justification they are looking for – and have so far been lacking – to evict every Zapatista sympathizer from the Selva. What would Subcommandante Marcos say of your warmongering? Do you honestly think that he would condone hostage taking?'

'You mean our gone-to-ground Sub?' Horatio removed his father's hands from him. 'What good is he when he is either too scared to show his face, or too involved with selling T-shirts and keyrings of himself on the streets of Mexico City, marketing his cult to tourists and teenagers? It is time we used force again, like the Marcos of 1994 did, like Emiliano Zapata in the Revolution.'

'Times have changed.' Lucio watched the incense smoke rise up over the altar. 'They changed even more after the strikes against New York and Washington.' He looked at his son. 'If we attack civilians, as you propose, they'll have no qualms in classing Zapatistas as terrorists. All forms of indigenous resistance, including peaceful protest, will be suppressed. Your action will finish us all. Would Urbano have wanted that?'

'Who says it's *my* action?' Horatio raised his voice, upset that his father had used Urbano in his argument. 'Who says it is *my* plan to take a hostage?'

'I don't understand.' Lucio picked up a candle from the tray on the altar. He held up the light to his son's face.

'It's simple, really,' Horatio said, trying to calm down and remove the image of his brother's lifeless body from his mind. 'You had the right idea to invite outsiders to our struggle. You know that I admire you for what you did; you inspired me; even made me believe in your gods. It was amazing how you found Hunahpu.' His face softened towards his father. 'But Hunahpu's reports to the media can only take us so far. At the moment we are receiving a little coverage in *La Jornada*, parcels of candy and baggy clothes from middle-aged Texan women. We are Zapatistas, not a charity.'

'And you think that three foreign mercenaries are going to scare the bad government?' He placed the candle closer to his son's face, looking at him hard. 'Those monkeys from England couldn't even shoot Teresa, your mother's lame Turkey.'

'Let me finish, please.' Horatio moved back from his father's candle. 'There won't be any killing. This is just a kidnap of a conservationist spy. As Zeb said, this is an opportunity to scare the big companies. You should see our hostage – who we'll free in any case – as a scarecrow to the bankers. It is a warning for them to stay away from our homes and leave us in peace.'

'But . . .'

'Please, father, there is more that I wish to say. Because the kidnap will be perpetrated by a group of foreigners, no Maya man, woman or child will be implicated.' He paused to catch his breath. The image of his dead brother had returned to his head, making it difficult for him to speak. 'Hunahpu can even send out a report to the foreign press, condemning the anti-globalization vigilantes, the unwanted interference of outsiders, thus ensuring that we are safe from any retribution.' He paused again, fidgeting with the spikes in his hair, and hoped that the inclusion of Hunahpu into the plans would reassure his father. 'But the result will be the same: there will be pressure to recall the conservationists, investors will panic, and we'll receive more publicity over the injustice of the evictions. How can the wisest Tzotzil, my own dear father, fail to see the merits of this action?'

Lucio turned away from his son and faced the Sky-Tree altar. He opened his lightning-patterned backpack, which was wedged between two spiky roots of the ceiba tree, and started to clear away the Christian and pre-Colombian offerings.

'Please tell me you support me,' Horatio pleaded, as he watched his father pick up the pebbles from the altar. 'Father?'

'I support you.' Lucio dropped a pebble into his backpack. He then looked at Horatio, thinking back to the day when his son had helped him carry Hunahpu away from The Pool of the Paddler Gods. 'Because you once supported me in my decision. Like you, then, I shall try to find faith in your decision. As for the cooperation of Hunahpu, you should speak to him yourself. It was wrong of you to send him out on a patrol tonight.'

'Well, he's back now,' Horatio said, hesitating before he continued, 'I've already spoken to him.' He stepped back so his father wouldn't see his face.

'He agrees with the kidnap?'

Horatio continued to walk away.

'He does.' Horatio ducked under a branch and out of a proper response. 'He agrees that we need more publicity,' he called out, his tripping figure out of Lucio's sight and the range of the altar's candles.

'Where is he now?' Lucio asked, to the moving trees and snapping branches, 'Horatio? *Horatio*?'

Horatio failed to reply. Only the ring of crickets and the rustle of leaves, nocturnal lovers and hunters in games of jungle chase, surrounded Lucio, the green-barked ceiba and the half-cleared altar table. Lucio cussed the Earth Lord and spat at the ground. He picked up the porcelain madonna and wrapped it up in a red

EZLN neck scarf, Maria's latest product for the tourists in Palenque, and put it in his backpack. Reaching for the cross that he had rescued from the Pool of the Paddler Gods, the icon that had conjured up another son, he could not believe that Hunahpu had agreed to the kidnap plan. He disbelieved the contradiction to his teachings, the loss of reason in the reborn, the deviation in his discovery and responsibility. 'Urbano would have seen sense. He wouldn't have agreed to it,' he thought of his brave little apprentice. Without any care, he forced the cross next to the stuffed scarf and wiggled it inside the backpack as if he was gutting a rabbit. On the sound of a cushioned crack, the cross went down and the porcelain madonna crumbled. Lucio fastened his backpack's straps and spat again. He swore and turned his angst to the husks of melted copal resin, stamping the embers into a layer of peaty topsoil and kicking leaves over burnt bark.

'How could he agree to this madness?' he asked out aloud. 'Damn his publicity.'

'Whose publicity might that be?' an unseen voice replied. Branches shook in the shadows and Lucio jumped.

A toucan flapped its wings against the upper branches of a beech tree. The woken bird thrashed its yellow bill from side to side and squawked at its noisy neighbour, the clumsy bipedal creature that was making a racket under its roost.

'It wouldn't be the shaman who spits at the ground and shouts "shit" at the trees, would it?' the voice said. The moving bush stopped at the ceiba tree. A silhouette of a man leant against the green tree-trunk.

'Do you have to go creeping up on me like that?' Lucio looked at the man who reclined on the World Tree Centre.

'And do you have to go swearing your head off to the Selva's all-and-sundry?' The man stayed in the darkness, his features obscured.

'You woke the toucan up. Not me.'

'Ah, well, you see, Lucio, the toucan and I go back a long way. She'll forgive me in time. She always does; she's not like the quetzal.'

'How can you joke, Hunahpu? Can't you see the danger ahead?'

'You mean the conservationists?' Hunahpu sighed. 'A Yankee prom queen and her evil Lacandón guide, a small girl whose list of interests includes tagging bats and stealing peanut butter sandwiches?' He picked at the ground with the tip of his machete, as if he was bored. 'Yeah, they are really scary. I saw them this evening. It was terrifying, especially with those big nets that they waved about.'

'An American woman and a Lacandón girl? This is terrible.' Lucio put his head in his hands. 'How could you Hunahpu? It's a woman and child.'

'How could I what?' Hunahpu returned his machete to its leather sheath. 'What has got into you tonight?'

'And you have spoken to Horatio about who you saw and who we are dealing with?'

'Yeah. I told him. So what? He seemed to be happy that they were unarmed.'

'And what about that man Zeb? What did he have to say?'

'Who the hell is Zeb?' Hunahpu examined his ski mask in his hand. He picked out a cluster of small burs that had attached themselves to the black wool. 'Please don't tell me that CONPAZ have sent us another gap-year student to entertain. You know how I hate having to wear my ski mask in camp. Couldn't they have sent him or her to Nuevo San Felipé? Maria's great with those kids – she could also sell them some of those new scarves of hers.'

'You haven't met Zeb? Or the other two?'

'No,' Hunahpu exclaimed, his silhouetted head looking up at the sky, 'and what do you mean by "other two"? Don't tell me that Horatio has decided to branch out into eco-insurgent-tourism. What have we got to do? Give them a tour of a few army checkpoints; show them around a refugee camp before sitting them down to a traditional Zapatista meal: rice and beans as a surcharge and bring-your-own soft drink, please. Great amount of good that's going to do to us and the villages.'

'Horatio didn't speak to you about the hostage?'

'Hostage?' Hunahpu's voice suddenly turned serious. 'What hostage?' He released himself from the tree. Loosening his red neck scarf, he straightened up and stepped forward. Apart from the stubble on his pale chin and his green eyes, which caught the light of the altar candles, his face remained in shadow.

'So my son didn't tell you?'

'What's going on, Lucio? What happened here tonight?'

Thirteen

'How're you doing over there?' Rachel asked, watching her young Lacandón apprentice crane her neck over a microscope's eyepiece. 'Found anything of interest?' She put her laptop and spreadsheets to sleep and walked the few feet to the other end of the wooden shed, the research station's pre-fab laboratory. Ofelia rocked on a tall stool, one of her father's creations. Rachel steadied her, wrapping her arm around the girl's white smock, leaned over her shoulder length black hair and adjusted the microscope's lens. 'Now turn this,' she said, turning the fine focus knob for her. 'Do you see anything now?'

'Yes!' Ofelia screamed, jumping up and down on the stool. 'The seed has grown bigger.' The stool wobbled on one leg and her bare feet dangled over a dusty concrete floor. 'The machine is magic!'

'The seed isn't actually bigger,' Rachel said, smiling at her young protégé, 'it just appears bigger. It's magnified by the lens.'

'No, I tell you, it is bigger,' Ofelia responded, her wide eye attached to the microscope's sights. 'It looks all funny. It's yucky!'

'Hey, watch what you're saying. That's my research, our evidence. You'd look kind of funny yourself if you were put under a microscope.'

'Can you *really* make me bigger? I want to be as tall and strong as you, so I can fight the big bad jaguar in the forest and chase him away from us.'

'I'm not sure it was a jaguar that we heard last night,' Rachel said, trying to make light of the incident the previous night, 'and, take it from me, you don't want to go wishing away your child-hood. Being an adult, being "big", is not what it's cracked up to be. Trust me: you're better off staying small.'

'Mamá said you were magic people, related to the wooden folk in Creation. She said that you steal Maya children lost in the forest, and I tell her that she is wrong, that you protect me. You would never harm me, would you?' Ofelia removed herself from

179

the miracle down a tube and looked up at her teacher, pulling a face of distrust and putting her hands on her tiny waist.

'I catch only the naughty children.' Rachel bared her teeth. 'Like the ones that distract me from my work, pretend they don't speak Spanish and go stealing my peanut butter sandwiches in the field. Why, do you know of any? I'm feeling kind of hungry.'

'Stop it!' Ofelia giggled and put her small hand over Rachel's open mouth.

'OK. But only on the condition that you stop calling me a Lokin. It's not a name I take kindly to. Is that a deal? Partner?'

'Yes, señorita.' Ofelia returned to the microscope and the marvel of the miraculously expanded seed. 'If it wasn't a jaguar, what do you think it was?' she asked, her voice cupped by her hands on the arm and body of the microscope.

'I don't know. It was too noisy for a rodent or a snake, and jaguars, pumas and ocelots are just scaredy-cats when it comes to humans. Perhaps it was a tapir, or perhaps it was a *Lokin*, who had sniffed out a young Lacandón for a scrummy dinner.'

'No!' Ofelia yelled. 'I don't believe in nasty Lokins. It was just a silly fat tapir.' She looked up at her teacher for reassurance.

'Exactly.' Rachel ruffled the girl's long black hair. 'So I don't want to hear any more about your scary stories and cruelty towards us whiteys. We gringos are not so different to you. Are we now?'

'But you are magic. You can make things bigger.'

'I give up.' Rachel shook her head, smiling. 'If you still want to be a biologist, Ofelia, you have to believe in science and not in magic. Have you not learnt anything from me this past week?'

'Yes!' the young girl shrieked. 'You are a good teacher. Now I can tag my own bats, yes?'

'Well, I'm not sure about that. If you give me the scientific name, in Latin, for your favourite species of phyllostomine, then I'll think about it.'

'You mean señor Stripy who we caught last night? But that's unfair. I don't understand strange Latin words.'

Rachel leaned over her pupil again and reached up to the laboratory's bookshelf, a warped plank above the work desk, which was cluttered with textbooks, stationery and a cardboard box of freezer bags. From among the biologists' bric-a-brac, she pulled out a book, *Neotropical phyllostomines: A Field Guide*. The humidity and the analyses of her predecessors had loosened the book's pages, and she had to hold it together as she handed it to Ofelia.

'That should help you to classify him,' she said, as she watched Ofelia flick through the book's fragile pages. 'Think carefully about his distinguishing features: his four white facial stripes, his greyish brown fur and his appetite for fruit. If you do that, you should, I hope, be able to identify and name little stripy face. Classification is very easy; it's just logic, really.'

With her face buried in the book, Ofelia was too busy with tracking down the badger-faced bat to listen to her teacher. Rachel left her to it. She shut down her laptop and cleared away the trays of seeds and other plant residues, the fibrous spoils of a dawn-time harvest, the faeces that fell from the night sky. After two hours of washing, filtering and logging the information-rich poop, attempting to create a correlation between bat species and deforestation, she was ready for her main meal of the day. As a bat conservationist, whose routine included a sleep in the morning and a midday wake-up call, she missed the station's lavish breakfast of scrambled egg, crispy bacon, refried beans, tortillas and French toast; Josita's calorie-packed specials. It wasn't until 3 p.m., after lab duties and before another night of prowling the forest for specimens, that she could finally sit down and take her own turn to replenish lost energy. One week of field-work had passed and the routine, not to mention the heat, bugs and lack of companionship, little Ofelia excepted, had already begun to wear her down.

'Hey, Earth calling Ofelia.' She tapped the studious Lacandón on the shoulder. 'Come on, you must have found señor Stripy by now?'

'Shush,' Ofelia replied, playing peek-a-boo from behind the fanned and disintegrating book, her face squashed between photographs of a big-nosed frugivore and a big-eared insectivore.

'OK, then, how about I leave you to your detective work? I've got to write a couple of letters to my folks and friends back home. I thought I should let them know that the locals are real friendly and polite.'

'Shush!' Ofelia remained fixed to the book.

'Right, I see. I'll be outside if you need me.'

Rachel left the shed, picking up her sketchbook, two envelopes and a pencil on the way out. She walked across the clearing to the upturned bucket under the coconut palm. The sun was at full power and it coaxed a heavy sweat out of her unacclimatized glands. Above her, soaring and screeching in a blue and cloudless sky, oblivious to the spy on the ground, a triangular formation of parrots went about their daily commute over the Selva, their yellowy green plumage gleaming in the sun. Back to earth and outside the kitchen cabin, tending to a border of flowers and weeding with a machete, Guillermo swept back his long black hair and waved at the American 'boss woman'. She waved back and admired the results of the Lacandón's hard work, a colourful display of yellow marigolds and red and white frangipani, *Flor de Mayo*. She recalled his description of the flower's symbolism: the yellow 'flower of death', the red and white frangipani representing the sun and the moon. Smiling at the superstition over such beauty, she checked the bucket for lurking ugliness, poison-sacked spiders and scorpions, before she sat down.

She opened the sketchbook at a fresh page, sharpened her pencil with a penknife and thought of Erin first:

22nd February
Rio Lacantún Research Station
Chiapas

Dearest Erin,

Sorry it's taken me so long to write, but things have just been crazy since I arrived in Mexico. I can't believe that I've already been here two weeks! It seems just like yesterday when I was back in freezing DC, sitting uncomfortably in Smokey's and having a teary drink with Todd (the joy that was . . .).

How's Law School? Have you met any good-looking guys yet? Any future husband material? You must write and tell me all your news, sis. I just hate being kept out of the Boston sorority loop. How are the Red Sox doing? Did we beat the Yankees?

It's great to be back in the jungle again. It's difficult to say why, but it almost feels like a second home to me; somehow, even the ticks, mossies and other bugs are starting to feel like family. Unlike the station in Ecuador, which was a real student dive, CI have given us our own rooms in a palm-thatched cabin, a great cook and weekends to do as we please – I'm hoping to go to the highlands this weekend, to check out some of the Maya villages up there. The only thing that is lacking, is the company. The place is DEAD! Do you remember me describing Bruce to you on the phone? He's the jerk who works in geographic surveillance and who has been trying to jump my bones for the last six months. Well, out here, the heat and the isolation have made his hormones doubly worse. He picked up a chopper last week, his 'blades' as he calls it, and has already used it to trap one of the station's female guests; she was some floozy anthropologist; think of Liz Butterworth on HRT and you've got her spot on. Apart from him, the only other gringo is the Prof.: a bearded, socks 'n sandals, beer swilling and pipe-smoking academic. As much as I admire and respect him, it's kind of dull talking about his boring orchids all the time. After all, they're not quite like my cute bats :))

To be honest, my only genuine friends are the Mayan family that services the station: Josita the cook, Guillermo the handyman and their daughter, Ofelia. The girl is a sweetie. You'd love her, sis. She's a little madam – but then aren't the best of us – and yet, for an 8-year-old, she's incredibly bright and knowledgeable. And get this: she wants to be a biologist! Isn't that cool? Tonight I'm going to allow her to tag her very first bat. I'm not sure who's more excited, her or me. When I get home, I'm going to try to persuade CI to sponsor her education in the States. Wouldn't that be amazing for her?

I'm sure that it is nothing to worry about, but something strange happened last night, while I was out checking the mist nets with Ofelia. Although we've had no direct contact with hostile locals, I think that someone might be spying on us. We had stopped for a snack of Happy Cow cheese (the processed stuff – it's really gross, but it keeps well) and peanut butter and jelly sandwiches, when we heard something move about in the bush. Thinking that it was a jaguar, Ofelia panicked. But it sounded more like two clumsy feet than four agile paws. I'm also positive that I saw a flashlight in the trees, yet I suppose it may have been a firefly, there was a plague of them that night. And it sounds silly to me now, because it was so dark then, but I think that I saw a figure. I haven't made a big deal about it to anyone, for fear of scaring Ofelia, and I haven't even told the Prof. yet. I know that it's nothing, so I don't know why I'm even telling you about it. Please, please, PLEASE don't tell my mom. I'll be on the next plane home if she hears.

Have you seen Todd at all? I have yet to write to him. To be honest, I don't know what to say to him. The longer I spend out here, the more distant I feel towards him. He's a wonderful guy and all, don't get me wrong, but I just can't see it working out between us. It's not the distance; it's the other old chestnut of moving on after school. I'll try to write to him this weekend and tell him how I feel. If you do see him, would you see how he's doing for me? You guys always did get on well. Thanks, sis.

I'd better go now and check on my little lab assistant, before I'm charged for child labor offences! I can hear her screaming for attention in the background.

Please send my love to your folks.

WRITE BACK COWGIRL!

Love,

Your dearest, bug-busting buddy,
Rach.
X
PS: Will try to email from the tourist spots in the highlands. No disrespect to our vacation, but I don't think I'll be going back to Cancún!
PPS: Yet to find you a souvenir: Tarzans, sadly, are in short supply in the Lacandón forest.

A sudden and piercing scream interrupted her writing. She quickly turned round and faced the hut, in the direction of the scream. Her smile dropped as her sketchbook, pencil, letter and envelopes fell to the grass. She looked out towards the wall of jungle that surrounded the station's clearing, her eyes wide and her pupils darting from side to side. Her heart raced as her mind flashed back to the previous night: the flashlight, the figure, the footsteps, the forest's hidden eyes, *her hunch.*

'OFELIA,' she shouted out towards the hut, knocking over the bucket and breaking into a sprint. Adrenalin and terror topped up the redness of her perspiring face. 'OFELIA,' she cried out again, glancing intermittently at the blackness behind the trees, her imagination filling in the darkness with human eyes.

Guillermo jumped out of his 'flowers of death', activated by the scream in the hut and Rachel's screams in the clearing. He chased after Rachel, his machete raised like a sword.

Too tense and pumped up to wait for Guillermo's armed back-up, Rachel stopped ten yards short of the hut. She picked up a spiked surveyor's pole and took wide strides forward, narrowing the gap between herself and the open door, using the pole as a probe and spear.

'What the . . .' she paused in the doorway and looked into the shed, 'are you doing?' she lowered her voice, embarrassed by what she saw and by her earlier reaction. She withdrew her calibrated spear from a petrified Professor and a semi-naked Bruce. Blood poured from a gash on Bruce's shoulder.

'LOKIN!' a high-pitched voice screamed. A sheepish face peered up from the floor, from under the safety of the work surface and a whirring table fan. 'You *are* a Lokin,' Ofelia confirmed to the crazy-looking woman with a spear, before giggling behind the book on bats.

'Shit, Rach,' Bruce pitched in, looking uncharacteristically coy in his topless state.

'Put that down,' the Professor said, pushing down Rachel's pole with a jar of peanut butter, blood-stained tweezers in his other hand.

'What's going on?' Guillermo asked, addressing no one in particular. He struggled to look past Rachel's sweaty back, to check on his daughter's safety.

'It's my baby beefworm,' Bruce whimpered. He held up a freezer bag that contained a bloody, half-inch-sized grub.

'I thought . . .' Rachel said, having to pause because of Ofelia's giggles, trying to pull herself together, 'that . . .' She dropped her spear to the floor, briefly looking back at the wall of jungle, the darkness that surrounded the station. Her heart was still racing. She returned to face Bruce. 'That's gross.' She tried to make light of the situation, banish the image of terrorists lurking in the trees.

'Hey,' Bruce said, looking proudly at the grub in the bag, 'that's my baby you're talking about.' He swung his offspring's ziplock cot in front of Rachel's face. Knocked against the sides of the bag, the grub curled up a tail of black bristles.

'Is that its head or its anus?' she asked, breathing in hard as she took a closer look at it.

185

'You mean that moving hairy bit?' Bruce replied, closely inspecting the creature, 'That's his anus, although he breathes through it as well. Neat, don't you think? It was his spiky hair that was digging into my shoulder. He was a resistant little rascal. Weren't you beefy?' Bruce poked his finger into the bag.

'I see.' Rachel felt her heart restore itself to a normal beat rate. 'It must be nice knowing that he takes after his father: bald, stubborn and lets his arse do the talking.' She turned to face the Professor, forcing a smile, slowly forgetting the image of the shadows in the trees. 'I think I can guess the purpose of the tweezers, Prof., but what's the deal with the peanut butter? Don't tell me that you're already starting to wean him on solids? And I mean the beefworm, not Bruce.'

'It's an old trick that I picked up in Belize,' the Professor said, appearing to enjoy his moment as a proud wet-nurse. 'One season, it was a survey near the Guatemalan border, we had a terrible time with the blowfly. I remember one poor botanist incubating up to eight in his scalp, all in one go. Out of all the methods for removing them, and we tried many, we found a smear of peanut butter over their air hole to be by far the most effective.'

'You mean their arsehole,' Bruce said, stroking the hairy maggot.

'Yes, I suppose so, Bruce.' The Professor gave Bruce a strange look; Rachel wondered whether he had already started on the beers. 'Anyway, starved of oxygen, the maggot rises to the surface of the skin, thus allowing one to gently free it with a pair of standard bathroom tweezers. Peanut butter beat the petroleum, Vaseline in a beer cap and the gaffer tape, in terms of speed of surface re-entry that is. It's quite clever really.'

'Genius.' Bruce faked a yawn behind the Professor's back. 'Although, from personal experience, I can hardly say that it was an easy birth.'

'LOKIN!' Ofelia screamed, from her position on the floor.

'Yeah, Rachel,' Bruce nodded at the girl under the work desk, 'what's with you barging in and threatening us with my surveyor's pole? What's got into you? You scared the hell out of us.'

'I'm sorry,' Rachel said, looking behind her again, surveying the impenetrable bush which surrounded the clearing, 'it doesn't matter.' She then looked under the work desk in the hut and saw Ofelia smiling up at her. 'Please, Ofelia, get up from the ground. The joke's over now.'

Ofelia crawled out of her den under the work desk. She patted her white all-in-one smock, smacking dirty brown patches on her knees and elbows, and released a cloud of dust into the hut.

'Is everything OK?' the Professor asked Rachel.

'Do you mind if we speak alone?' Rachel replied, not looking at his face, still ashamed by her reaction to the screams.

'Hey, that's not right,' Bruce said, 'remember what your buddy Liz the anthropologist said? We are one happy family. And that means we share secrets.'

'Haven't you got a maggot to feed, dada? And that woman was never my buddy.'

Rachel and the Professor went outside, leaving Ofelia and Bruce to wet the beefworm's head/anus, while Guillermo, who laughed under his moustache, returned to the symbolism in his flowerbed. On the veranda of the kitchen cabin, by two sloppily assembled chairs, Rachel stopped the Professor.

'I'm really sorry about that,' she said, looking back at the hut, then at the jungle beyond it.

'Don't worry about it,' the Professor said, wiping the sweat off his forehead. 'What did you think was wrong?'

'I haven't been sleeping too well. Tiredness can play havoc with my nerves. There's nothing wrong. I'm just being silly. I'm sorry.'

'Stop apologizing.' He flicked a fly off his beard. 'If it really is nothing, why do you want to speak to me in private?'

'My imagination led me to believe that we were watched last night, in the field and God knows what by. It's crazy and really not worth you worrying about.'

'Did Guillermo see anything?'

'No. He was asleep. I told him that he wasn't needed and that he should take some rest in the pick-up. He'd been gardening all day, it was only fair.' She looked back at the shed. 'Although Ofelia thinks that she heard something. But since when has the jungle been without strange sights and sounds? It was probably the shadows of trees and the noise of a harmless lizard or rodent or something.'

'They do sound larger than they actually are.' The Professor smiled at her. 'Still, if it makes you feel safer, I'm sure that you don't have to go into the field tonight. Why don't you take an early weekend? Weren't you going to go to San Cristóbal? You could catch a bus from Comitán and be there for dinner. I can recommend you a nice hotel and restaurant.'

'That's very kind, Professor, but I'm not chickening out of my job. I need tonight's data if I'm to hit schedule, and it takes more than a few rustling leaves to scare me off.'

'How is your research going?' the Professor asked, pulling out a chair for her. They both checked the chairs for signs of unwanted life and sat down.

'It's going well. We're finding a large number of *Desmodus rotundus.*'

'Vampires?'

'Yes. Last night we caught six, out of a total of twenty. The night before we captured eight.'

'What does it mean?'

'It means we have our evidence. The vampire thrives in defor-ested habitats. It lives in symbiosis with human populations, where it has a plentiful supply of blood in livestock, especially cattle. Their unusually high abundance, as a ratio to the other phyllostomines, indicates high levels of habitat disturbance, perpetrated, no doubt, by our squatters and their cattle ranches.'

'That's great news.' The Professor patted her on the arm.

'If you're a vampire, yes.' Rachel remained stony-faced. She didn't see the destruction of the forest as something to celebrate.

'Of course.' The Professor realized what she meant and dropped his grin. 'Still, you've got what you came for. I haven't had as much luck with the flora. Everything is as it should be.'

'If Bruce stops using his chopper to seduce stranded anthropol-ogists, and instead takes some in-focus photos of the settlements, finds these hidden cattle ranches, we must surely have enough evidence to show CONAFOR and the FAO?'

'It might be enough . . .'

Two tiny feet crashed onto the veranda. Rachel and the Professor turned round. Ofelia, gasping and shaking, the whites of her eyes widened, her lips trembling, ran towards Rachel.

'Ofelia,' Rachel exclaimed, instinctively standing up. Her chair fell over and off the veranda. She crouched down and caught the child in her arms. 'What's happened? Are you OK?' Ofelia held her tight. She looked back towards the trees.

'Yes, señorita.' Ofelia released her grip and looked up at her teacher. 'It is *Vampyrodes major.*' She handed back the tatty taxonomy guide and smiled. The book fell open at the page of the 'Great Stripe-faced bat'. Rachel sighed.

Hunahpu dug his boots into the flanks of Itzamna, a silvery mule, the name of his transport synonymous with the Paddler Gods and transportation to the Otherworld. He pulled on the reins of rope and disappeared into the trees. Lucio watched his adopted son from his own, smaller and sandy-coloured mule. He moved off in the opposite direction, down an old and overgrown logger's track, cantering towards the village of Nuevo San Felipé.

The patrol's tortilla dominated breakfast, usually a time for social guzzling and daily vows of resistance, statements more often told in sing-along satire and jokes about an obese Cardenista, a 'tyrannical tapir', was a subdued affair that morning. Segregation, marked along the lines of allegiance and conviction, as opposed to race and colour, split the patrol and created cliquey pockets of diners. Hunahpu and Lucio ate on the riverbank, Jamie and Stevo doted on Zeb by the hammocks, and Horatio and the Zapatistas discussed strategy by the campfire.

Knocking back a mug of heavily sweetened and lukewarm coffee, which was served from a cast iron pot on warm ashes, Horatio asked his men if they were in agreement with the proposal to the English. The circle having given him a unanimous nod, he waved at Zeb and invited him to join them round the fire. Zeb poured himself a mug of coffee, while Horatio used a stick on silt to draw a map of the evening's operation. In answer to Zeb's questions, he pinpointed the presence of military outposts, the defensive network of streams and the strategic merits of a cave. The latter, Horatio informed a studious Zeb, would prove to be effective in securing the prisoner. Zeb nodded as the young Commandante spoke. It was local knowledge like that which Decker said he needed. It was what Tam needed.

There was only one point of the plan that Horatio wanted Zeb to clarify. Thinking back to the conversation that he had with his father the night before, he wanted Zeb's reassurance that the anarchists did the actual hostage taking. He wanted Zeb's word that the Zapatistas' role would be confined to that of guides only. Zeb assured his shorter partner that no Mayan would be implicated. The guilt inside him was growing stronger; the lies were becoming harder. His target was the one they called Hunahpu; only he would be implicated by the hostage taking.

'Thank you,' Zeb said, avoiding eye contact with Horatio, 'your assistance is much appreciated, Commandante. Taking us to the location and guiding us past the army is, really, all we ask for.' He scratched an insect bite on his shaved head; the insects and the heat were becoming unbearable. 'If it's OK, though, we could also do with three ski masks and a rifle.' He paused and looked at Stevo and Jamie by the hammocks. 'And a standard-sized crowbar,' he said, lashing out at a fly, staring at two other figures hidden behind the reeds on the river bank.

'Of course,' Horatio said, following Zeb's stare and looking worried. One of his men scurried off into the forest to source the weapons. 'If you are ready, I can introduce you to my brother, Hunahpu. It is he who will release our denial of involvement to the media.'

'We've already met,' Zeb said, still staring at the figures by the river.

On the riverbank, sheltered from the campfire's connivance by a curtain of vines and reeds, Hunahpu and Lucio formulated their plan of counteraction. Forced to wear a mask, still not trusting the foreigners with his identity, Hunahpu believed that an early warning was the best means of preventing the kidnap. It was considered too risky to warn the research station itself, the route riddled with military checkpoints, so they agreed on placing a note at the site of the nets, near the location of the intended kidnap. Hunahpu had noted the movements of the bat catchers the previous night and he knew of a good spot. That afternoon, they decided, Hunahpu would ride Itzamna to the conservationist's sampling paths, going inland from the Lacantún and deep into the jungle, avoiding the old timber routes favoured by the army and its armoured Humvees. If the woman took heed of the warning, they calculated that she would have two hours to evacuate the area and return to the station. The hostage takers would arrive to find nothing and the mission of the misguided Maya and the foreign terrorists would be aborted. It was the best that they could do. There was little time available to them.

'Are you still going back to Nuevo San Felipé?' Hunahpu asked Lucio. He fiddled with his ski mask, lifting it up every so often to ventilate his overheating skin. Sweat and salt bees tickled him on his sore neckline.

'Yes,' Lucio said, watching Hunahpu's discomfort. He blamed Horatio for forcing Hunahpu to wear the mask; his son knew that it was dangerous for Hunahpu to reveal his identity to strangers. 'I promised Maria that I'd return yesterday. She'll throw my chair out of the house if I don't show up tonight.'

'Will you speak to her about Horatio? About the foreigners and the hostage?'

'If our plan works and the biologist has any sense,' Lucio said, handing Hunahpu a fresh bandana to wipe away the sweat off his neck, 'I don't see any need to worry Maria. Even if she agreed to help, to speak to Horatio, she would never make it here on time. The village is four hours away by mule and, let's face it, Maria is hardly the lightest of passengers.'

'Hunahpu,' Horatio called out from the bushes behind them.

Green eyes narrowed in the slit of Hunahpu's ski mask. Leaving Lucio by the river, Hunahpu clambered over the bank, his leather bag over his shoulder. He swept aside a net of vines and headed for the campfire.

Introductions were not required. Hunahpu had briefly met the English the night before, after leaving Lucio at the altar and hearing what madness had entered the camp. It was by the hammocks where he first spoke to them. He gave them his Maya name of 'Hunahpu' and apologized for the mask. Anonymity, he explained, uncomfortable by the way the shaven-headed man stared at him, stopped the authorities from using his foreignness, his non-Indian roots, to discredit his work and allegiance to the campesinos.

'Good morning,' Hunahpu said in Spanish, saluting Horatio and the Zapatistas. He nodded at Zeb and helped himself to the pot of coffee. 'How did you boys sleep last night?' he asked Zeb, in English. He leant on his leather bag. The only man to hide his face, he looked as if he was the black sheep of the patrol. Only, in contrast to Zeb, he was a Zapatista, with nothing to prove.

'Fine,' Zeb said, wondering how the hell the masked man had ingratiated himself to a Zapatista patrol.

Stevo and Jamie sat either side of Zeb. They eyeballed Hunahpu.

'Well it's a lovely sunny day for a kidnapping,' Hunahpu said, breaking the silence. His green eyes caught the early morning sun as he looked up at the blue sky. 'We couldn't have asked for better weather. It's lucky you English didn't bring that dreary, national weather of yours.' He looked at Zeb, smiling through his mask. 'This must be a break for you. On your way home, you and the kids should stop off in Cancún. They like to serve tourists there.'

'You mean foreigners,' Zeb said, trying to remain calm, thinking of the man's face on the photo that Decker had given

191

him. 'Aren't you yourself a foreigner to the Maya? You are from the city, right?'

Hunahpu looked down from the sky, his eyes now fixed on Zeb. He rubbed the wool that covered his jaw.

'It matters not where we come from,' Horatio said, sensing the tension between Hunahpu and Zeb. 'We are all in resistance. We are all Zapatistas.'

'Vive Zapata!' the patrol shouted. It was followed by more silence and more eyeballing across the smoky fire.

'It's good to see that you've brought the heavies with you,' Hunahpu said, referring to the two men sitting next to Zeb. With their expressionless faces and black outfits, Stevo and Jamie resembled a pair of minders, Zeb being their celebrity client. 'After all, we are talking about a particularly vicious couple of individuals to kidnap.'

'You mean Stevo and Jamie,' Zeb said, putting his arms round his men, 'they wouldn't harm anyone.' He looked directly at the green eyes in the mask.

'Why don't you join us?' Horatio asked Hunahpu, trying to diffuse the tension again. 'Then, my brother, you personally can make sure that the conservationist is cared for.'

'Yes,' Zeb said, 'what a great idea Commandante. As the scribe-in-residence, Hunahpu can write the spy's confession.' He tried to look beyond the mask, to see what sort of man he was speaking to. The grip that the man had over the Commandante was trying his patience. 'I was going to do it myself, but it makes perfect sense for Hunahpu to do it.' He then reverted into English and faced Hunahpu again. 'What do you say masked man? Will you give us a confession?'

'What confession?' Hunahpu asked Horatio, ignoring Zeb, annoyed that he hadn't been told about this additional component to the plan. 'No declaration, nor any other document for that matter, should leave the camp without my authorization.' Although he treated Horatio as the brother that he never had, it was Horatio's father, Lucio, who he was closest to. It was times like this when he understood why Lucio found it difficult to trust Horatio. It was times like this when he felt as if he was an older brother.

'Umm,' Horatio hesitated, prodding the ash of the campfire with his machete, 'I'm sorry, Hunahpu, I forgot to tell you that Señor Zeb wants the conservationist to confess to being a spy.

Since she will be his hostage, I agreed that it was probably best for them to draft the confession.' He glanced over his shoulder towards the river, where his father was, then looked at Hunahpu. 'I'd feel far better, though, if you wrote it.'

'Go on, Zorro,' Zeb said in English, addressing Hunahpu, trying to push him further, 'come and join the party and pen a confession for her. All the woman has to do is talk and sign the confession, a document that you would have drafted and approved, and we'll release her.' He looked at the faces of the Zapatista soldiers. They looked as if they had no idea what he was saying, his fast English incomprehensible to them, and so he continued. 'You don't have to worry about her, Hunahpu. She'll be back in her flat in Virginia by Monday.'

Hunahpu didn't reply. Instead he reflected on what Zeb had said and stared at the campfire. He watched a cloud of ash take off in a warm breeze. A giant millipede crawled over his powdered combat boots and he kicked it off. The millipede landed on its back and sizzled in the hot ash.

Zeb stood up and nodded at Horatio. Stevo and Jamie followed his example. Hunahpu looked down at the frying millipede.

'How do you know that she has a flat in Virginia?' Hunahpu asked, raising his head from the ashes and observing the Z-shaped tattoo on the Englishman's neck.

'What did you say?' Zeb turned round. He looked at the green eyes that stared up at him through the mask.

'I said . . .'

'I heard,' Zeb interrupted. 'It was a guess, seeing that Conservation International is based in Washington, DC, in Virginia. Let's hope that your lack of geographical knowledge hasn't given us duff coordinates for tonight's little adventure.' He examined the masked face and imagined the soft features that remained hidden, the coward that wouldn't reveal himself to him. The bait was there and now all he had to do was to reel in his catch. 'How impolite of me, I almost forgot to thank you for your invaluable report, the location of the conservationist. If it weren't for you, we wouldn't have ourselves a hostage and a confessor.' Flanked by Stevo and Jamie, Zeb retreated to the hammocks.

The Zapatistas watched the three anarchists disappear into the bush. They argued amongst themselves about the kidnap, about having to follow the lead of a foreigner and take their chances with a stranger. Hunahpu bowed his head and focused on the burnt remains of the millipede. Horatio stood up, walked to the other side of the fire and sat next to him.

'You should come tonight,' Horatio said to Hunahpu, scared of what he had potentially unleashed, 'I'd like you to watch them closely for me.'

The Zapatistas spent the rest of the morning packing away the camp. Empty maize sacks were stuffed with hammocks, blankets, food rations, cooking equipment and boxes of ammunition. They strapped the full sacks onto three donkeys with rope and strips of leather, while Lucio's altar and the campfire were dismantled and camouflaged, ash and cosmic stones committed to the river. A line of black-uniformed and gun-belted litter-pickers then scoured the camp. Carrying plastic bin-liners, they stooped down to collect an assortment of English cigarette butts, roaches and Rizla papers.

Stevo and Jamie sat on their rucksacks and watched the activity around them. Zeb had instructed them to wait for him by their bags. He told them that he had to make a call on his mobile phone, to check on how Tam was doing and to give a report to Decker. The height and thickness of the trees blocked his reception in the camp, so he went down to the river, to a spit of sand that gave him clearer access to the sky.

'He's been gone ages,' Stevo said to Jamie. He rocked back and forth on his rucksack. 'You think things are OK? I don't trust that American.'

Jamie didn't reply.

'Well I'm going to look for him,' Stevo said, as he watched the Zapatistas tie the last bag of trash onto a donkey's back. 'You wait here.' He picked up a crowbar by his side and walked towards the river.

Jamie nodded and dragged on a rolled-up cigarette.

On a sandy headland, a walkway into the jade waters of the Río Lacantún, Zeb paced up and down. He had his phone by his ear. Stevo spotted him through the rushes on the riverbank.

'Don't give me that shit,' Zeb shouted down the phone, unaware of Stevo walking towards him. 'You fucking sort it out or I am going straight back to London. I don't care about your bloody bureaucracy. Transfer the money, make the appointment with the specialist for Tam . . .' He paused as he listened to the voice down the phone. 'How should I know if it's him? The fucker keeps wearing a mask. You just look after my Tam and let me worry about things out here.' He paused again. 'Of course I'm fucking calm. Of course we won't hurt the conservationist.' He hung up, rubbed his temples and put the phone in a pouch of his black combat pants.

'Problems?' Stevo asked, standing behind him. Zeb turned round. His face was red from the phone call.

'No,' Zeb snapped back, taking the crowbar off Stevo, his other hand swiping the flies round his head. 'Fucking insects,' he said, digging the crowbar into the sand, twisting it about as if he was killing something. 'Come on. We should get back to the others.' He scratched the back of his neck as he looked towards the forest.

Zeb leading the way, his crowbar skimming the sand, they walked up the beach in silence. At the foot of a steep bank and startling a small lizard, a brown tail slipping into a crack in dried mud, they grabbed handfuls of roots and hauled themselves up from the riverbed.

'How is she?' Stevo said, trying to make conversation as he wiped the sand off his clothes. He caught his breath on the top of the bank.

'What?' Zeb looked for the clearest route back to the camp. He smashed down a few plants with his crowbar.

'Tam – is Jules looking after her?'

'Shush.' Zeb slapped his hand over Stevo's mouth. He heard voices through the trees. They stopped where they were and hid behind a tree. It was Lucio and Hunahpu.

Zeb peered round the tree's green trunk. He spied on the two men through a net of creepers and parasitic plants, watching them saddle up their mules in a small and shaded clearing. Hunahpu was not wearing his mask, but he had his back to them and Zeb was unable to see his face. All he could make out was that he had fairer skin than the Mayan man and that he had black hair. He watched them jump onto their mules. Lucio then reached out from his mule and handed a piece of paper to Hunahpu.

'What do you think?' Zeb heard Hunahpu ask. He watched him fold up the paper and put it in his leather bag. 'Do you think that she'll listen to what it says?' Hunahpu swung the bag over his shoulder and gripped his mule's roped reins.

'Let's hope that she finds it first,' Lucio said, 'then we must hope that she has some sense and leaves.'

'Do you know how long you'll be in San Felipé for?'

Zeb tried his hardest to see Hunahpu's face, but he still had his back to him and he couldn't risk moving further away from the tree, without being seen.

'Maria wants me to fix the roof to the house, so at least a few days.' Zeb saw the old man smile at Hunahpu. It angered him that they seemed so close, that the Zapatistas treated the coward and criminal as one of their own. 'When the mess here is cleared up, you should come and stay with us. Maria would like that. '

'It would be nice to see her again. It's been a few months.'

Lucio leaned out of his saddle. He gripped Hunahpu's arm and looked at him with his compassionate eyes.

'Good luck, my son.'

'Thanks,' Hunahpu said, 'but Itzamna's doing the tough bit. He's the one carrying a wooden load like me.' Zeb watched Hunahpu pat his mule's silvery mane.

'Then may the Ancestral Lords bring him speed and you the body of Mayan maize.'

'Goodbye, Lucio.' Hunahpu put on his ski mask.

'Goodbye, Hunahpu.'

Zeb moved back behind the tree. He crouched down and whispered into Stevo's dreadlocks.

'We go an hour earlier than planned,' he said, his grip tightening round the crowbar. 'Let's tell the Commandante.'

Fourteen

Headlights flashed through the trees. The research station's battered white pick-up pulled over on an old logger's track, stopping at a wooden stake with a florescent tie around it. An assortment of nocturnal insects, large and small, ugly and graceful, bounced off the vehicle's headlights, their lacy wings beating a strobe effect in the man-made light. The driver's door opened, its hinges squeaking, and Rachel waved a flashlight at the muddy ground and entangled vegetation that lined the track. Attracting her own collection of flying bugs, she switched off her torch and jumped out of the pick-up. Her human companions, Guillermo and Ofelia, joined her at the rear of the vehicle. She pointed out what was and was not required from the trunk, helping Guillermo unload two large canvas bags, three backpacks and a cardboard box. The equipment laid out on the track, she returned to the driver's seat, turned off the headlights and, out of habit rather than necessity, locked the pick-up's doors. Starved of the headlights' beams, the insects dispersed, only to regroup around the three beams of torchlight that pointed at a cutaway of foliage, the start of a tunnel-like path. The three of them then picked up the equipment, fanning the swarms of insects with their spare hands and torches, and squeezed through a gap in severed branches. Guillermo led the way with his machete.

Although Rachel had told the Professor that she would be behind schedule if she missed tonight's sortie, it was the promise that she had made to her young disciple that made her decline the offer of a night off. For tonight was not so much about her research, as it was the night her protégé came of age and tagged her first bat. She forced herself to press on for Ofelia's sake, trying to forget about the shadowy figure from the night before. As they walked deeper into the jungle, though, her anxiety would frequently return. It made her flash her torch at every unidentifiable noise that they passed, a reptile's or a rodent's rummaging through leaves turning into a predatory human, tiny steps

197

turning into a man's steps. She took Ofelia's hand and held it tight.

'How much further?' Guillermo asked Rachel, throwing down his machete and loosening the bandana around his neck. He pulled a flask out of his backpack, passing the warm water to Ofelia before he took a swig for himself.

They had walked, skipped and tripped for over thirty minutes. Their flashlights animated the shadows of the trees and under-growth, and they required all their concentration to stay on course along the straight and south-easterly path. The path had been cut and cleared only a week ago, but the weeds had regrown and the restrained branches, which Guillermo had woven together and pinned back, had wormed their way loose.

'It's not far now,' Rachel replied, taking a swig of water from her own flask. 'Look out for the next marker. That's where we put up the first net and catch our first bat.'

Guillermo picked up his machete, rummaging his hand through the dead leaves to find the handle and gently flicking away a large caterpillar. He hacked at the obstructive plants with mulish deter-mination. Rachel and Ofelia followed him, Rachel shining her torch under her chin and pulling a scary face. Ofelia giggled and Rachel forgot all about the rebels; she stopped shining her torch at every patch of darkness that resembled a man.

'What are you two laughing about?' Guillermo called back, smiling to himself. He was happy for his daughter and the bond that she had with Rachel. It pleased him to see her learn from the American scientist. 'You sound like a pair of howler monkeys.' As he spoke, his torch's beam and concentration strayed. He tripped up over a tree stump and landed in a bed of giant ferns.

'You OK?' Rachel asked the moving ferns.

'Yes,' he said, Ofelia now giggling at her father. He levered himself up with his machete. His white smock puffed spores into the air. Back on his two feet, he shined his torch ahead of him and illuminated a tree trunk of inch-long spines. Something pinned to the tree caught his attention. 'Señorita?'

'Yes,' Rachel said.

'I think we've found the first marker.'

'Excellent.' She exchanged smiles with Ofelia.

Guillermo cut away a vine and revealed a florescent tie wrapped around the tree. 'There is something with it,' he said, as he pulled a folded sheet of paper off one of the tree's spines.

'What?' Rachel asked, letting go of Ofelia's hand as she squinted in the direction of Guillermo. She took off her backpack and dropped it by a coil of speckled and zigzag-patterned roots. 'What have you got there?' She failed to see the roots moving.

'I cannot read it. It is in English.' Guillermo held up the piece of paper above his head.

Rachel walked up to him, Ofelia following her, and she took the damp paper out of his hands. The message was written in red ink:

TO THE CONSERVATIONISTS AT LACANTÚN STATION:
LEAVE THIS AREA IMMEDIATELY. YOUR MOVEMENTS HAVE
BEEN WATCHED AND YOUR LIVES ARE IN DANGER IF YOU
DON'T LEAVE WITHIN THE HOUR. YOU MUST RETURN TO THE
SAFETY OF THE STATION. YOU HAVE BEEN WARNED.

Rachel felt her heart pounding. She scanned the trees and the thick bush with her torch, taking her time to see if it really was a face that stared at her through the leaves, spinning around if she thought she heard something from elsewhere. The branches above them began to shake and, gasping, she quickly looked upwards. Two eyes caught the light of her torch, their reflective glow beaming down at her from a tall tree. It was nothing but a spider monkey, disturbed from its sleep by the rays of light below. She breathed in hard and noticed Ofelia's anxious face looking up at her.

'What does it say, señorita?' Ofelia asked, standing on tiptoe to look at the note in her teacher's hand. Her tiny frown was captured in Rachel's torchlight.

Rachel screwed up the paper and put it in her combat pants' pocket. She tried desperately to think of an alternative source of the note, a less sinister reason for it. Her heartbeat slowed down as she thought of Bruce. She shook her head.

'It's Bruce and his idea of a joke,' she said to Ofelia, trying to believe that to be the case, 'it's not worth the honour of a translation.'

Apart from mocking her embarrassing incident in the lab, Bruce had kept up the intimidation over Josita's staple meal of chicken, rice and beans. The onslaught of gags culminated in a dismembered chicken's claw, which he had stolen from the dining table's bowl of scraps, laid to rest, voodoo style, on a pillow in her hammock. He had left her a far from humorous calling card:

'*Here's an extra foot to help the chicken run away from the Bogeyman*'. She found it difficult to believe, though, that he would have visited the sampling paths alone, just for a joke. The softened-up gringo was more used to travelling the Selva by chopper; he was not the type to risk his life by going solo on the jungle floor. Shaking her head, her deep breaths turning into muted laughter, she tried to convince herself that Bruce was as insane as he was unfunny.

'OK,' she said to Ofelia and Guillermo, her head nodding repeatedly as she tried to shake out the image of Zapatistas in the shadows. She flashed her torch around her before she continued. 'Let's get to work and catch ourselves some bats.' She retreated from the marked tree and pointed her torch at her backpack on the ground.

'Snake!' Ofelia shrieked.

Frozen by the warning by her side, feeling a small hand and arm wrap itself around her, Rachel felt her heart race again. She stared into another pair of glowing eyes, this time on the ground and by her rucksack. The snake's eyes widened as they focused on her. She looked into its forked pupils, as if she was staring at the Devil himself. The zigzag patterned root slowly came to life. She observed the snake's flickering tongue as it slowly raised its neck in her direction.

Guillermo instinctively bucked the bags off his back. His machete above his head, he leapt past Rachel and his daughter. In one clean swipe, the blunt edge of the blade crashed down on the back of the snake's neck. Guillermo grinned at the scaly spasms by his boots.

'Very dangerous,' he informed Rachel, who was still frozen by the spiny tree, the serpent's eyes engrained on her vision. Ofelia clung onto her leg. 'It's a four-nose. A young male as well: the worst.' He grinned at the dead snake hooked over his machete's blade. 'They like to pick a fight with anything that moves, even man and machete. You are lucky that he was half-asleep.'

Rachel shone her torch at the snake's disjointed mouth. Blood and poisonous froth dripped from its fangs. She put her arm around Ofelia.

'It's a fer de lance,' she said, feeling Ofelia shake under her arm. She gripped Ofelia tighter, trying to mask her own shakes. The responsibility of looking after her pupil lessened her own fear. 'Not very nice.' She smiled and tried to make light of their encounter with the venomous viper. Spider monkeys, snakes and bugs she could just about deal with. They were the original inhabitants of the forest, justified in their defensive actions and under her protection. Instead it was the two-legged creatures that hid in the shadows, those that left cryptic notes on a palm's spines, who made her bolt around at every snap of a twig or swish of a branch. Bending down, her hand passing a bloody leaf, she pulled an olive-green poncho out of her backpack and laid it out on the ground. She sat down on the poncho, Ofelia sitting beside her, and hoped that the capture of a bat would help her to pull herself together.

'Señorita?' Guillermo waved the dead snake about in his hand as he tried to catch Rachel's attention. Breathing in the humid air as she attempted to normalize her heartbeat, her elbows on her knees, Rachel looked up. The snake's cold and fixed stare made her shiver. 'He'll make a nice belt, no? How about I skin him for you?'

'Sure.' Rachel swallowed, not really registering what Guillermo had said. Observing him with his machete, his muscular arms and Central America's most dangerous snake dead in his hands, she was grateful to have him there.

'Do you mind if I take him back to the pick-up? I don't want the ants to get to him. They'll eat through him if we're not careful.'

'Do you have to go back to the pick-up?' she asked, her raised voice followed by another unseen crash of animal and foliage. She flashed her torch in the direction of the noise.

'I won't be long. The blood might attract other predators. We don't want to have to deal with a jaguar as well as a four-nose in one night.'

'Jaguar!' Ofelia shrieked.

'OK,' Rachel said, giving Ofelia a disapproving look, 'we all need to calm down a bit.' She looked up at Guillermo. 'Ofelia and I should be able to cope with the mist nets. Don't be long, though.'

She watched Guillermo and his torch's beam bob along the path, as he headed back towards the pick-up and the logger's track. The screeches of the bugs and the rustling of leaves seemed to grow louder as he disappeared into darkness. 'Don't be long,' she shouted out after him.

Man, snake and torchlight were lost to the forest, their presence replaced by fireflies, which sparkled in the bush like imitation stars, a mirror of the celestial landscape in the sky. Half-heartedly, Rachel pulled another silly face at Ofelia, as if that would somehow remove her increased sense of vulnerability. Ofelia didn't giggle this time. Rachel unzipped one of the canvas bags, set out four aluminium poles onto the poncho, and hoped that her work would ease her nerves. Assisted by Ofelia, who was only too eager to put her hands to everything, she slotted the poles together to create two nine-metre lengths. They then rigged a black nylon net between the upper halves of the aluminium supports, trying not to snag the net's delicate slack, its bat-catching pockets, on the abundance of spiky branches. Taking a pole each, they extended the net either side of the marked tree, the map coordinates to be surveyed, and anchored it with guy-lines tied to two palm trees. Once completed, the mist net looked more like a badly placed volleyball net than a treetop-level trap. Rachel beat it with a spare pole, imitating the struggles of a large frugivore, to test its strength. Noticing the excited look on Ofelia's face, playfully batting away the moths over her torch, she felt at one with the forest again.

'Not bad,' she said, as she put down the pole and shone her torch up at the black sail that billowed above them. 'Next time I can sit down and you can do it by yourself. How about that, partner? Do you reckon you can handle it?'

'Of course I can handle it.' Ofelia looked up at the net and picked at the drawstring ties of a sample bag. She squashed a few soldier ants under her tapping sandal. 'Waiting is boring.'

'Be patient,' Rachel whispered, gazing up at the stars beyond the net and its cradle of branches. 'Patience is the greatest skill of a conservationist. You'd better learn it if you want to become one.' She went to her backpack, took out some foil-wrapped sandwiches and handed a peanut butter and jelly distraction to Ofelia. In between mouthfuls of tasteless Happy Cow cheese, she tested her student on the checks and measures for a captured bat. Throwing bread crusts at a termite nest, a giant cocoon of dusty brown tree pulp, they then prepared the rest of the equipment: setting up the scales, selecting a red beaded collar and labelling the sample bag with the date and coordinates of the mist net. Nothing else left to do, quietly waiting for the commotion of a snaring, intermittently looking up and spot-checking the gauze that turned a bright moon grey, Rachel suggested a game of 'I spy'. She gave them both thirty seconds to scan the forest with their torches before they began.

'I spy,' Ofelia whispered, 'with my little eye, something beginning with the letter T.'

'Did you say P or T?' The crickets seemed louder and Rachel struggled to hear.

'T!'

'Shush!' Rachel flashed her torch at the trees, the muddy ground and the equipment on the poncho, smiling as she did so. She finally shone the torch down the path, the route back to the pick-up. 'Is it termite nest?'

'No.' Ofelia grinned.

'Transect line?' She went on to describe the scientific benefits, the best means of ensuring a representative sample of ecology, of arranging mist nets along a T-shaped layout of interlocking paths, or transect lines. 'No? I give up. What do you see, smarty pants?'

Ofelia pointed her torch at a patch of exposed soil, a gap in the groundcover of rotten leaves, by the roots of the spiky tree that had the white marker on it. 'Tapir tracks,' she exclaimed, referring to the boar-like and lumbering inhabitants of tropical Mexico.

'Really?' Excited by the find and impressed by her student's sharp eye, Rachel moved across the poncho to look at the spot highlighted by Ofelia's torch. She scraped back the leaves on the ground with the spine of her notebook, cautious of toxins in the topsoil and pincers in the peat, and unveiled a U-shaped impression in the soft mud. The hoof print was not of a four-toed tapir. Her smile dropped and she felt her heart beating erratically again. She found it hard to breath, as if her lungs had shrunk and she could only exhale and not inhale. The research station had no horse and Bruce couldn't ride.

'This is a horse's, not a tapir's.' She struggled to speak as her finger circled the crescent pressed into the mud. 'It looks fresh as well, perhaps just a few hours old.' She looked over her shoulder and saw a tiny frown on Ofelia's face. Breathing in hard, not wanting to pass her fears on to the girl, she recalled a conversation that she had with the Professor, over a beer and outside the kitchen cabin. The Professor had told her that some of the Lacandóns had given up farming to go into tourism, and that a few of them ran horseback expeditions to the Selva. Trying to forget about the note in her pocket, the warning in red ink, she screwed up her face and stuck her tongue out at Ofelia. 'Sorry, can't give you that, as it doesn't begin with the letter T. I win.' Looking around them, seeing dark human shapes in between twisted trunks and palm leaves, her mind deceiving her again, she wished that Guillermo would hurry up.

A high-pitched shriek, followed by a crash of bush and branches, made them both jump. Rachel whizzed around on the poncho, the beam of her torch slicing through the trees. There was another shriek and she quickly flashed her torch upwards. As if it was a storm cloud in the sky, the mist net shook, its guy-lines tugging taut and rustling palm fronds. The relief was so over-whelming that Rachel laughed.

They lowered the trap, unclipping the net from hooks on the poles, and located a tiny brown and grey ball of fur in a pocket of nylon. The bat stuck in its flight position, its leathery wings and sharp claws pinned back, Rachel handed Ofelia a pair of garden-ing gloves and pliers. While Rachel carefully held the bat still with a finger and thumb, Ofelia disentangled its claws with a pair of pliers. The bat's wings sprung shut and its body, which was not much larger than Ofelia's gloved hands, dropped away from the net. Rachel carried the specimen to the equipment on the poncho and asked Ofelia to switch on a specially adapted lantern, its bulb sensitive to a bat's nocturnal vision. She then held up the bat for identification.

The bat's long tongue licked a coat of pollen off its pronounced snout, the yellow powder dusting its silvery-grey belly and its black whiskers. Rachel told Ofelia that the bat was a handsome example of a Phyllostomid flower-eater. Its beady eyes were set low over its snout and its fine eyelashes tickled smiling lips.

'Isn't he gorgeous,' she said, dabbing a tissue on his snout and cleaning specks of pollen away from his eyes. 'You know that he is very rare.'

Ofelia studied the small creature, speechless.

'He feeds on the nectar and pollen of flowers high up in the trees. From the messy state that he is in, we can assume that this little bambino has just had his breakfast.' She removed more pollen off the curly whiskers of his chin, and placed the tissue in a plastic sample bag. Pollen was forensic evidence in the assessment of the squatters, an indicator of deforestation, and she would analyse it under a microscope back at the lab. She saw bats as the unsung heroes of conservation work, the information that they carried invaluable to saving countless numbers of other species. The only mammals to fly, she considered them to be tiny superheroes, their mysterious lives, nocturnal habits and the unwarranted suspicion that they provoked making them even more attractive. Despite catching hundreds since she discovered her passion for them in the

Amazon, the thrill of the catch was as strong as ever. 'He is called *Hylonycteris underwoodi*,' she said to Ofelia, as she looked into the bat's small black eyes, 'Underwood's Long-tongued bat.' Do you want to hold him? He is yours.' She passed him to Ofelia, who was already on her knees beside her, as entranced by the creature as her teacher was. They took care not to damage the bat's paper thin wings in the transfer. 'Have you got him?'

Ofelia stroked the downy fur on the bat's domed head, her fingertips ruffling the fuzzy growth between two rounded and button-shaped ears. She cooed at the softness and coveted her very first catch. Leaving bat and girl to bond, remembering the excitement of when she held her first bat, Rachel went to the cardboard box and pulled out a small cotton bag. It was time to weigh the specimen.

'Must we put that nasty thing over señor Tongue?' Ofelia asked.

'Our little friend has some information to tell us. It won't hurt him. I promise.' Rachel bagged the bat, the cotton muffling its squeal, and she placed the shaking bag on a set of digital scales. 'He's a male all right. He weighs just six grams; a female would be nearer eight or nine.' She recorded his weight in a notebook and then gently tipped him out into her hand. 'Hey, calm down.' It wriggled about and she had to clamp her fingers round it to stop it from flexing its wings. 'Ofelia, check the bag to see if he pooped. I'd like to get a sample if we can.'

Ofelia found no poop and so instead Rachel asked her to measure the bat's body, tail and forearm length with a pair of blunted callipers. Finally, following Rachel's instructive commentary to the tee, Ofelia attached a red beaded band to its neck. She snapped the buckle into place once she was sure that it was neither too loose nor too tight. Rocking back on her knees, a big smile going from cheek to cheek, she admired her pet and his pretty red bandana.

'Do you want to hold him before he goes?' Rachel asked. The joy that she took from Ofelia's enthusiasm had made her forget all about the note. She had no idea that Guillermo had been gone for over an hour.

'Yes please.' Ofelia handled the bat again.

Outfitted like a true campesino, a slash of red round his neck and whiskers like a droopy moustache, the bat relaxed in the child's gentle grip. Motionless and with its tongue hanging out like a sleeping kitten, it seemed in no rush to escape.

'Must he really go?' Ofelia's smile disappeared from her face.

'Who's to say we won't catch him again?' Rachel patted Ofelia on the head, gently doing the same to the bat. 'Anyway, for the forest's sake, I hope that we find more of his type; his species only live in undisturbed forest. And since you did such a great job with the little one here, I can't see why you can't tag a few more. How about that?'

'But I like this one.'

'He is kind of cute, I agree, but he belongs to the wild. Come on, now, let him go.'

Ofelia was about to open her hands, set the bat free, when they were emblazed by light. A flashlight shone at them from the path to the pick-up. It dazzled their eyes and the bat twitched in Ofelia's hands. The light grew brighter and the bat began to beat its wings, squealing as if it was being tortured, biting and clawing at its human-fingered straitjacket. Ofelia juggled the bat between her hands and squealed herself.

'Put the torch down,' Rachel shouted at the light in the trees. Blinded by the beam, she shielded her eyes with her hand. The light down the path was getting closer, a ring of darkness bordering an increasingly fiery epicentre. 'Guillermo? Can you hear me? You are scaring the bat and your daughter. Put the torch down.'

The bat beat its wings harder and faster. Ofelia screamed again. Her hands opened and the bat took off. The creature soared up to the moon and Ofelia held out her bleeding index finger; the bat had left her a ring of ruby red droplets.

'Guillermo!' Rachel shouted louder.

The light was almost upon them. Although no footsteps could be identified in the noise of trounced brush and the snaps of stems, a metallic thud on wood rang out through the forest. Rachel removed her gloves and, forgetting her earlier vow of maintaining calm, felt the rush of panic come over her, the piece of paper in her pocket. Blinking repeatedly and shielding her eyes with one hand, the flashlight X-rayed her skin, flesh and bones.

'Ofelia,' she called out, grabbing the young girl and holding her close to her side. The beam of light split apart. There were three torches and they all pointed at her face. The slaughter of vegetation stopped, the last creeper to fall landing by her boots, and the crickets, until now drowned out by the crashing advance, resumed their tuneless chorus.

She held tightly onto Ofelia, both of them still blinded by the torches. The little girl's head was in her chest and she could feel her shaking with fear, her heart beating furiously through her ribcage, like the bat that they had caught earlier. As the central beam of light lowered, the torch resting at the waist of a figure clad in black, her blind spot was removed. She saw a crowbar spear the leaves by her boots. Her pulse now accelerating, she saw the masked face. Ofelia whimpered in Spanish into her shirt.

'Who are you?' she managed to say, before two men grabbed hold of her and Ofelia, ripping them apart as they kicked and screamed. Ofelia bit the hand of her captor and the man yelped in pain. He released his grip on her white smock and she sprinted away, disappearing into the jungle. The other man whipped Rachel's hands behind her back, immobilizing her with lashings of twine, and shoved her head into a mule's sackcloth nosebag. She coughed at the dust and wool of her scratchy hood as they spun her round. Then a sudden pain exploded on the back of her neck. She fell down and momentarily forgot where she was.

'Find the girl,' Zeb said to Stevo, who was nursing his bleeding finger. Zeb pointed at the trees behind him, at a small white dot fleeing through the forest, then fell to his knees, landing beside Rachel's hooded body. 'What have I done?' he whispered to himself, the crowbar shaking in his hand as he looked at Rachel.

Stevo dived into the thick bush and low branches to search for the child. It was futile, though; she had vanished. He leaned against the trunk of a young tree, its waxy black sap sticking to his clothes and bare arms, and scanned the trees one last time with his torch.

'Sorry, Zeb,' Stevo said, as he made his way back to the path, foliage slapping into him, 'can't find her anywhere.' He looked at Rachel on the ground, shocked by what Zeb had done to her.

'Leave the girl alone,' Rachel slurred under the sackcloth.

'Forget her, Stevo,' Zeb said, still looking at Rachel, his body shaking. 'Let's move out before she alerts the station.' He stood up and handed the crowbar to Stevo, not wanting to see it again.

Taking an arm each and following Zeb, Stevo and Jamie lugged Rachel down the path to the logger's track. 'Stay calm,' Rachel thought, seeing stars in the blackness of her hood, 'the brief said to stay calm.' She took short and sharp breaths, inhaling the dust that filtered out of the sackcloth, spitting out the grit that stuck in her mouth and which grinded between her teeth. 'I'll be rescued soon. Stay calm.' The pain at the back of her head throbbed in waves. She felt groggy, as if she was drunk, her legs without strength. 'It will be over soon.' Her mind worked in brief bursts. She registered that her captors, supposedly indigenous insurgents, were speaking English. Then she blanked out and thought she was back in Illinois, a student again, being dragged away by a gang of bank robbers. She spat out more dust and gasped for air.

Five Zapatistas, all on loan from Horatio and wearing ski masks, kept watch over the mules by the pick-up. Guillermo was tied to the pick-up's towbar and in a tyre rut, the fer de lance coiled round his neck as a joke, his mouth gagged by thick rope. He groaned and squirmed in the mud when he saw the three men and their hostage emerge from the jungle. The Zapatistas helped Stevo and Jamie to lift up Rachel and put her on a mule. Guillermo looked around for his daughter, the snake bouncing under his chin as if it was a rubbery and zigzag-patterned necklace, but she was nowhere to be seen.

'What're we going to do with him?' Jamie asked Zeb, pointing his machete in the direction of Guillermo.

'We leave him,' Zeb replied, double-knotting Rachel's bootlaces to the stirrups of her mule. 'He'll be fine.'

One of the Zapatistas approached Zeb. His rifle slung over his shoulder, Horatio patted the nose of Rachel's mule.

'She came without resistance?' Horatio asked, watching Zeb tuck the ends of her bootlaces under the saddle's leather girth tabs. 'You didn't hurt her, did you?'

'Of course we didn't.' Zeb stopped what he was doing and faced Horatio, his eyes wide and staring. 'Just lead us to the cave, OK?' He looked up at the hostage on the mule, her hooded head bowing down. Horatio also looked up, fearful of what the Englishmen had done to her.

As a punishment for allowing the girl to escape, Zeb ordered Stevo to take the hostage's reins and to travel by foot. The rest of the patrol mounted their mules and, led by Horatio, Zeb and Rachel, the convoy left behind Guillermo and the pick-up. The patrol disappeared round a bend in the logger's track, the sound of their chatter and the light from their torches replaced by the shrill of insects and darkness.

Two small hands peeled back a palm leaf at the side of the logger's track. Her white smock camouflaged by splotches of mud, Ofelia left her hideout. She ran towards her father at the back of the pick-up.

Fifteen

Rachel was stretched out on a tarpaulin sheet, on her back and in a position of minimal pain. The warmth of her limp body had condensed on the cold plastic, and she felt pools of water between her fingers. Still groggy, she believed that she was floating in the sea, waves lapping over her neck and anaesthetizing the burning sensation. In the dirty orange sky of the cave's candlelit ceiling, she saw small black objects hanging upside down. Looking as if they were cantankerous gargoyles, with pug faces and devilish wings, they hopped about on their inverted perch and skipped between columns of stalactites, a portcullis of spikes that imprisoned her. She pulled her hand out of the sea, water dripping from her white and wrinkled fingers. Biting her lip to override the painful cramp in her joints, she extended her arm towards the bats, calling on them to help her. She passed out again. Her fingers slapped down onto her hot and wet forehead.

'I don't believe this,' Hunahpu said to Horatio, standing at the entrance to the cave and putting on his ski mask. He pinched the mask's eye, nose and mouth holes into place. 'What happened to commanding by consensus? Zapatismo principles?' His throat sore, he paced the hearthstone of the catacomb, a pebbly ledge on a steep hill-slope. 'You had no right to leave an hour earlier than planned. I should have been there. Can't you stand up to him?' He looked out across a defensive palisade of treetops and orchids, bright-red flowers blossoming in the moonlight. Horatio looked down at the ground.

His mission accomplished, the warning impaled on a thorn next to one of the conservationist's white markers, Hunahpu was surprised to arrive at an empty cave. He couldn't understand it; Itzamna had made good time and there was another hour to go before the agreed time of departure. The explanation lay in an empty rum bottle by the cave's entrance. A scribbled note poked out of the top of the bottle.

GONE HUNTING
We had enough of waiting.
Z

Seven hours later, voices woke him from a nightmare of his former life; a flashback inspired by the loneliness that engulfed him as he waited, alone, on a cliff-face, mist in the trees like the spray of the falls. While he rose to his feet outside the cave, the patrol tethered their mules in a secret paddock, a nearby and tree-covered plateau. The three anarchists untied their hostage from her saddle and lifted her off the mule. Stevo and Jamie carried her down a hill to the cave, the navel of the mini mountain, dragging her feet over rocks and roots. The nosebag worn as if it was a blanket over a criminal's head, the conservationist stumbled into a cavernous courtroom. 'Batwoman's Lair,' Stevo christened it as he pulled the nosebag off her head. Rachel blinked the dust away from her eyes. Her vision blurred, she saw a ring of candles around a tarpaulin sheet. She collapsed down on it, but Hunahpu could only stand by and watch. A scene of internal discontent, he knew, would only encourage the new arrivals. He had decided to speak to Horatio when the others were asleep.

'I can stand up to him,' Horatio said, looking up from his muddy boots, 'I don't understand your problem anyway. They did a good job – she came without a fight.'

'What did they do to her?'

'Nothing. They gave me their word. Perhaps she is just tired.'

Hearing enough, Hunahpu decided to inspect the damage for himself. He ducked under the lipped rock of the cave's entrance and entered the orange glow of the conservationist's cell. Inside, forced to crouch down, the top of his woolly mask buffing a calcite ceiling, he dismissed the Zapatista sentry, a stand-in for the Englishman who paid his way out of his nightshift with a carton of cigarettes.

Hunahpu shuffled to the rear of the chamber, towards the light that shone from a crevice in the rock, the natural doorway to the cave's inner sanctum. Centuries of build-up, the waste of former cave dwellers, burnt maize husks and desiccated bat droppings, crunched under his boots. Holding a stalactite to pull himself through the foot-wide gap, algae lubricating his tight passage, he squeezed into the second chamber.

Surrounded by candles and presented as if she was a corpse in a mausoleum, her dark hair swept back from her pale face, he saw the results of this supposedly 'good work'. Too scared to touch her, to check if she was alive and determine whether he was an accomplice to murder, he leant against the damp walls of the woman's tumulus. His breath smoked in the cold air as he slowly slipped down to the dirt on the ground. There he stayed and stared, hoping for movement, candles and sociable bats teasing him with an illusory light and shadow show.

Seated in shame, he thought back to the innocence that he had intruded upon on the night of his patrol. He watched the Lacandón girl hustle the gringo woman for sandwiches, peanut butter propagating a play-fight and their laughter echoing in the trees. He remembered the excitement at a lowered and chirping net, the young Lacandón displaying great fondness for her brave, American friend: 'Vampire Whisperer,' 'Tamer of blood-suckers,' they sniggered. Standing behind a broad tree trunk and avoiding the light of their torches, he heard of the woman's teenage visit to Cancún, the frustration that she felt at the denigration of Mayan land, the feeling that, one day, she would return and do her bit. It was the last and only time that she had visited Mexico; 'five years ago,' he overheard. The girl asked about home in the USA, who and what awaited her teacher's return, and giggled at the subject of men and marriage, demanding why someone so pretty wasn't married already. He peeked round the tree to confirm this spoken-of beauty, his body spring-loading a branch as he looked through gaps in the leaves. The branch sprung off his back and crashed into the leaves around him. He quickly ducked into scrub, beams of light pinning him down, the girl screaming 'jaguar, JAGUAR!' He retreated into the bush and returned to the patrol, to deliver his report to Horatio. Watching her as she now lay on the cave's floor, her skin white and her limbs in puddles of water, he blamed himself for what had happened to her.

Rachel's eyes opened. She tried to sit up, raise her head even, but the pain in her neck was too bad. She managed to turn her face to one side, to look at the hell-hole that she was in. A masked man came into focus. His face was so close that she could feel the warmth piping out of his woollen breathing hole.

'Who are you?' she whispered in Spanish, focusing on his green eyes. 'What have you done to Ofelia?'

'The girl is fine,' he replied in English. 'She escaped.' He paused, his eyes locked to her eyes, his game different to her game. 'How are you?'

'What do you want from me?' she managed, at last, to find the strength to demand. His accent confused her; it was not like the English of the others, yet he looked too tall to be Mayan.

'You will be free soon. I promise,' was all he could think of saying.

'I said, *arsehole*, what do you want from me?' She was so weak that she felt sick.

'They want to question you about your work.'

'What do you mean? Who are you? You've got the mask, haven't you?' She noticed that he was unarmed. *If only I could sit up and check the exit*. She assessed and then rejected the stupid idea.

'They are . . . It doesn't matter.' Again he didn't know what to say.

'It might not matter to you, but you're not the one who's been hit over the back of the head.'

'They hit you?' He moved closer to her, his hands held out and wanting to help.

'Get away from me,' she growled at the two giant palms that occupied her field of sight.

Hunahpu put his hands to his sides.

'I only want to help.'

'Then why don't you just go? And take your buddies with you.'

'They're not my friends.' He wanted to show her his face, harness her trust, but he couldn't risk it. 'At least not all of them.'

'Yeah, right,' she said, sarcasm unaffected by the neck wound. 'Just tell me who the hell you are, you and your masked men, and what are you going to fucking do to me?'

He wanted to put her straight and reveal his true stance on the foreigners. Instead, though, he scratched the bridge of his nose, a layer of knitted wool, and looked away. With a bounty on his head and in his thoughts, the truth had to remain masked. For the sake of his family he had to keep quiet.

'I'm a Latino, a Mexican, I'm not with the men that did this to you. I'm with the Zapatistas.'

'A Latino Zapatista?' She rolled her eyes. 'Don't tell me that I have the privilege of speaking to Subcommandante Marcos himself.'

'No, I'm not Marcos.' Noticing blood on her nostrils, he took off his red bandana and put it in her shaking hand. To his surprise she stayed silent and accepted the bandana.

Perhaps, she looked at the fidgety figure, noticing the avoidance of eye contact, there was some truth in what he said. She blew her nose in his bandana.

'Who are they if they are not Zapatistas?' she asked him.

'They are anarchists from London. That's all I know. You must understand that this is not our idea.'

'But you thought you'd tag along for the ride anyway, right? I bet you are real proud. I wonder what your mommy would say if she could see you now.'

'My family are all here. I'm here, talking to you now, for their protection, not yours.'

'Like I give a shit,' she croaked, touching her throat. 'You don't have any water, do you?'

He jumped to his feet and unclipped a water bottle off his belt.

'I'm sorry.' He passed her the opened bottle. 'Please, it is fresh.'

She took a large gulp of water. Her hand shaking, the water spilled down her front as much as it passed down her throat.

'Next time you can get me something stronger,' she said, as she rolled the bottle back to him. He picked the bottle up and reattached it to his belt. 'What do these anarchists have in store for me? What do they need to know about my work? I'm assuming they don't want to know how to extract seeds out of bat faeces.'

'They want a confession.'

'So hey, what's the big deal?' The water was already making her feel stronger. 'I confess: I handle bat shit. Now can I please go?'

Hunahpu shook his head and paced the perimeter of the woman's stone cell. He put her spirited performance down to shock. It was best, he thought, if he left and said no more; she needed her rest for the morning's inquisition, and he needed to write a sensitive confession for her.

'I have to go. I could find you some fruit. Would you have some fresh papaya?'

'I'm not hungry,' she whispered. She looked up at the big blur standing above her, wailed with frustration at being so helpless, placed at his feet and at his mercy.

Seeing her shiver, he took off his fleecy black poncho and tucked it under her bare arms to keep out the draft. 'That should at least keep you warm,' he said, bent over her, her closed eyelids shaking beneath him and blocking him out. Affected by her trembles, the effect he had upon her, he stood up to go.

'It was you, wasn't it?' She opened her eyes when his shadow departed from her shuttered pupils. She rolled her head to one side and saw his silhouette behind the candles on the floor.

'What was me?' He was half out of the chamber.

'The note. It was you that left me the note. Wasn't it?'

'Try to sleep now,' he said, as he slipped away through the crevice.

She heard his crunchy footsteps fade out in the neighbouring chamber, hushed voices indicating a change in guard. The squeals and squeaks of the bats filled the cave's vacant space, their familiar noises offering some comfort to her. Caped as if they were lawyers, their wings collapsed into gowns, she watched them bounce about above her. She pleaded her innocence to them, wished that they could defend her like she had done them. The pain returning to her neck, she lolled her head to one side and closed her eyes.

Sixteen

Three Mexican soldiers sat on the veranda outside the research station's kitchen cabin. They ate sandwiches as they kept out of the midday sun, their guns propped up beside them under over-hanging palm thatch. Inside the cabin, Ofelia cringed at the table manners next to her. She was seated, for questioning, beside Commandant Hernandez and his bowl of drumsticks, while the cabin had been converted into an interrogation room. Every so often she had to duck to dodge the chicken grease that spurted from the Latino man's mouth. Also present was a man going by the name of Agent Decker, an American dressed in a beige linen suit and Ray Bans, with his gaze fixed on his mobile phone. Lastly, seated opposite her and cramped together on a wobbly bench, were the remaining inhabitants of the Lacantún research station: the Professor, Bruce, her bandaged father and petrified looking mother.

The Professor had radioed the US embassy shortly after a blood- and mud-splattered Guillermo had banged on his cabin door, waking him up with the news about Rachel and the Zapatistas. An embassy official had informed him that there was a representative of the US army in the area, a drug enforcement agent training local forces, a man that could quickly put together a search and rescue team. As soon as it was light Bruce flew his Huey to San Quintín army base and picked up Agent Decker. Commandant Hernandez and a small group of soldiers joined him.

'So, young Ofelia,' Decker said, putting his hand on Ofelia's shoulder, 'Do you think that the man was a foreigner? Was the man that hit your friend too tall to be Mayan?'

Ofelia just stared at her plate of uneaten food, trembling. From across the table her father reached out and held her hand still. He sat in frustrated silence as he could remember very little of what had happened.

Commandant Hernandez shook his head. Helping himself to

one of Ofelia's tortillas, he mopped up the juices left on his plate and wiped his greasy hands on his camouflaged combat pants. He scratched his belly under a tight black T-shirt and rocked on the bench. The prospect of catching the Zapatista patrol, capturing the foreigner who meddled with his affairs, had stoked his appetite. He had grinned all the way on the flight to the station, as he looked out of the chopper's windows and at the sea of green below. With the Zapatistas and the squatters gone, the land sale could begin. Commandant Hernandez, leader of the Cardenistas and a former slum-dweller of Mexico City, would become one of the richest men in Chiapas. His stomach now full, he wanted to get a move on, go out into the jungle and hunt Hunahpu down. He couldn't see Decker getting anything else out of the Indian girl, who snivelled next to him.

'Please, Ofelia,' Decker said, having to bend down to look at the young girl's quivering face. 'He wasn't just a tall Mexican? A Mestizo, perhaps? They can, you know, look like us gringos in a lot of ways.'

Ofelia remained silent. Her wide eyes were now focused on the man's mobile phone.

'Ofelia?' Guillermo expressed fatherly concern from across the table. 'Be brave. Tell the señor what you saw and you can help him to bring her back. Was the evil man a foreigner? It's important that you remember.' He picked at his white bandana, a blood-stained neck bandage, while everyone waited for a response.

'They were not men,' Ofelia said. She looked up from the table, as did everyone else. A tear trickled down her cheek. 'They were Lokin.'

'Lokin?' Decker asked her, confused.

Commandant Hernandez shook his head. He couldn't understand why Decker was wasting their time with her.

'They are evil creatures of the forest,' Guillermo said, reaching out across the table and wiping the tears off his daughter's face, 'tall monkey-like beings that snatch people away.'

'Right.' Decker sighed. He picked up his mobile phone and put it in his jacket pocket. It was evident to him that the girl was too traumatized to be of any use to them; he needed a credible witness to pin Hunahpu and the Zapatista patrol to the kidnap.

'The three Lokin spoke English,' Ofelia continued, catching Decker's attention again. 'They had Mayan friends. I think they spoke in Tzotzil.' She told them that she saw the Lokin and the

216

Tzotziles tie Rachel to the back of a mule. 'They disappeared down the old logger's track, in the direction of Nuevo San Felipé,' she tried to be as helpful as she could.

Decker smiled and nodded at Commandant Hernandez.

'Nuevo San Felipé is a squatter community,' he said to the Professor, his face turning serious. He glanced at the Commandant, who was licking his lips. 'They must be using her as a human shield, to stop the evictions.' He pulled out a bag of candy from the breast pocket of his suit. 'Thank you, Ofelia. You have been very brave and very informative.'

Ofelia took the bag of candy off him and stood up from the bench. She dashed over to her father's side on the opposite side of the table, hiding her face from the American and Commandant Hernandez with her cupped hands. Gripping onto her father, she whispered something into his ear before she buried her face in his white smock.

'My daughter,' Guillermo said, as he stroked his daughter's head, 'has reminded me that we found a note, by the point that we were ambushed. Señorita Rachel didn't say what it said. She said that it was something from señor Bruce.'

'I left her a stupid note by her hammock,' Bruce said, horrified that he might have inadvertently played a role in Rachel's kidnap. 'It was a joke, that's all.' He put his head in his hands and scratched the insect bites on his scalp. 'I certainly didn't leave her anything in the forest.' He looked up and rubbed his eyes. His pale face pleaded innocence to the Professor in particular. 'Christ, I wouldn't dare go into the forest at night.' He looked away and out of the cabin's meshed wire windows, the bright sun silhouetting the soldiers on the veranda. 'Poor Rachel.'

'Excuse me for interfering,' the Professor said to Decker. He brushed back his long grey hair. 'But you said that you were looking for only one foreigner amongst the Zapatistas. Ofelia said that there were three Lokin.'

Commandant Hernandez stopped picking his teeth with a dirty fingernail. His piggy eyes squinted at the Professor, the bearded academic opposite him. He cleared his throat and spat a slimy speech impediment into a tissue. The scrunched up tissue was deposited into his bowl of gnawed bones.

'There is only the one foreigner, Professor,' Commandant Hernandez said, his upper lip slightly curled up as he stared across the table. 'Our sources are quite certain of this. Given what the poor little Lacandón girl has been through, she cannot be certain of exactly what she saw. It was dark and her little brain must be confused. Lokin indeed,' he snorted.

Guillermo frowned at the sneering Commandant. He put his arm round his daughter and kissed her on the top of her head. Her face was still tucked up in the safety of his smock.

'We will investigate Ofelia's claims,' Decker said to the Professor. Commandant Hernandez slurped water from a plastic beaker and Decker waited for silence before he continued. 'However, Professor, we are really after the terrorist that calls himself Hunahpu.'

'Yes,' Commandant Hernandez interrupted, slamming his beaker down onto the table. His fat neck rippled over his tight T-shirt as he leaned forward. 'This man is very dangerous. For over a year we have tried, with the help of the police, army and our North American friends, to catch this villain Hunahpu.' He picked up a jug and refilled his beaker. Ofelia sneaked a look at him and quickly hid her face again. 'Hunahpu poisons Maya minds, NGOs and busybodies in the newspapers with his ridiculous accusations against the government and my men. He makes people believe, through his reports and foreign friends, that there is still a war in Chiapas. It is his slanders that stop investment, the flow of money to our impoverished state, the improvement in the quality of life for us *real* Mexicans, like your Lacandón friends here. Like me.' He took a swig of water and ironically toasted Guillermo, Ofelia and Josita, the Mayans in the room.

'We did not realize,' Decker said, sounding sombre in comparison to the ebullient Commandant, 'that he would go so far as to take a hostage. Up until now, the EZLN, unlike their counterparts in Colombia, the ELN, have never kidnapped any foreign or US nationals. One must assume, now that Subcommandante Marcos is rarely seen or heard of anymore, that Hunahpu is taking advantage of the Zapatistas' loss of centralized command.'

'The Indians think of Hunahpu as some saviour,' the Commandant snarled, 'as, the blasphemy of it, a Christ-like figure. The story goes that he rose from the dead, came to this world out of a sacred river, and was summoned by a shaman's spells up a fucking mountain. These Mayans,' he grinned, as Guillermo shifted about uneasily on the bench opposite, 'are simple people. They like to believe in crazy myths, anything that justifies their stealing of land.'

'What will you do next?' the Professor asked Decker. There was uneasiness in his voice.

'Thanks to Ofelia, we have a good idea of where the rebels were headed for. We've already done one flight over the region and, if it's OK with you, Bruce, we'd like to use your Huey again this afternoon.'

Bruce turned away from the sunshine and soldiers in the wired window.

'Of course,' he said, facing Decker. 'If those men touch her . . .'

'Try not to worry too much,' Decker said. He picked up his sunglasses off the table. 'I'm sure that Rachel is fine.' He smiled.

'How can you be so sure?' the Professor asked, nervously rubbing his beard.

The Professor's question provoked a short pause from the other side of the table. Everyone looked at Decker, including the Commandant.

'I'm sure,' Decker said, smiling at the Professor as he stood up. 'Now can someone take us to the location where Rachel was captured?'

Stevo fiddled with the telescopic sights of his rifle. Lying next to Jamie outside the cave's entrance, with his rifle pointed at the adjacent jungle, non-retaliatory wood and leaves, he swung his blistered forearm and the battered firearm. The cross-wires of the rifle's sights rested on a red smudge in a distant tree. Stevo tried to focus the sights to see what it was that he had targeted. His indelicate finger and thumb required a few fumbled attempts before he succeeded, eventually, in clarifying, partly, his stoned vision.

'It's a bloody scarlet macaw parrot,' he exclaimed, stubbing out the last of his joint on a rock.

Zeb had ordered Stevo and Jamie to guard the conservationist, while he went further up the hill to find a signal for his mobile phone. Their captive unlikely to escape by herself, her wounded neck keeping her immobile, they were instructed to look out for the masked man. The rifle, a bag of weed and the wounds on their limbs helped to stifle the boredom.

'It'd better not be one of them beefworm things,' Jamie said, more interested in the white spots on his forearm than whatever it was that Stevo was looking at. He squeezed one of the spots and wiped the pus away with his finger. 'I'm not playing host to an ugly maggot.'

'He's a real beauty.' Stevo continued to admire the magnified parrot. 'Even better than the ones I've seen on the Internet.' He laid down his rifle on the rocky ground, untangling his dreadlocks from the safety catch and trigger, and tapped Jamie on the shoulder. 'Are you bloody listening? It's a scarlet macaw, an *Aramacao*, and you're missing it.'

'Piss off, Stevo.' Jamie pushed him away. 'This is serious. I can feel the little shit eating me from the inside-out.' He held his wrist up as if, somehow, the internalized flesh-eater could be spotted through his hash of surgery, a volcanic-looking crater, and the thick black hair that covered his Neanderthal-like appendage.

'Stop being such a wimp. There's nothing there and, if there is, it'll only crawl out when it's ready. Anyway, check this out.' Stevo rolled up his ex-German army shirt's sleeve and exposed a weeping wound of black pimples and white blisters. The disfigured skin ran up the entire length of his arm. 'And that was from a fucking tree. According to Horatio Hornblower, it's poison ivy. I got it when that damn kid ran away.' Stevo waved his arm in front of Jamie's face.

'Stay away from me, you infected freak.'

A hail of small rocks fell from the upper reaches of the slope above them. Set loose by descending size eleven boots, it drew a dusty curtain on the tropically diseased freak show. The chips of limestone ricocheted off the sentries' viewpoint and landed on the red orchids in the treetops. Two steel-capped boots skidded to a stop beside Stevo and Jamie. A crowbar pinged on the upper lip of the cave's entrance. The scarlet macaw took flight in a flash of red.

'Everything OK?' Zeb asked Jamie. He wiped the sweat off his forehead.

'No sign of the prick,' Jamie replied. His loud and stoned response caused startled faces, some under ski masks and others part covered by red bandanas, to pop up from their positions around the hillside. The Zapatista patrol was placed around the craggy fortress, hidden behind roots, ferns and boulders and on the lookout for Federal troops, paramilitaries and choppers. Still shocked by their guests' lack of restraint, the volatility of the skinhead with the 'Z' branded on his neck, the Zapatistas tried to catch a glimpse of what was now the problem.

'I'm sorry again about last night,' Stevo said to Zeb.

'Forget it,' Zeb said, biting his fingernails like it was compulsive.

The day was not going well for Zeb. It had begun with him finding Stevo fast asleep, passed out with an empty bottle of rum by the mules and nowhere near his designated post. Zeb ran to the cave as soon as he found him, beating back the branches in his way with the crowbar, immune to the thorny trunks that cut through his clothes and skin. His heart pounded hard as he ducked under the cave's lipped entrance. If the conservationist had gone then he would have failed Decker and therefore Tam; she had to be there for him to destroy Hunahpu. Fortunately for Stevo there was no evidential damage to the mission. The conservationist was still lying down on the tarp, only now with a woollen cloak wrapped around her. She screamed at him and he left her alone. Later, however, while talking to one of Horatio's teenage soldiers, he heard how Hunahpu had entered the cave and spoken to the prisoner.

'Yes, señor. He was in there for some time,' the boy had said, not knowing what the problem was with a high-ranking Zapatista, a brother to the Commandante and a son of Lucio, wanting to speak to the señorita. Zeb found Hunahpu on the banks of a small stream, the camp's washbasin at the bottom of the hill. Hearing the fall of rocks and the snap of twigs, Hunahpu masked his face and cocked his hunting rifle.

'Hey,' Zeb called out to him, raising his hands and the crowbar over his head, 'it's only me, an amigo, do you mind?' He waved the crowbar at Hunahpu's rifle, its barrel pointing at his chest.

'So is this creeping up on people a habit of yours?' Hunahpu lowered his rifle.

'No more than your habit of hiding behind a mask.' Zeb moved closer to him and stared at his green eyes. He wanted to beat the life out of him there and then, yet he knew he had to be patient. 'Don't you think it is about time that, like men, we speak face to face? I mean, we are on the same side.'

'I am a Zapatista, not a terrorist, and my masked voice is my resistance. We neither need nor want your violence.'

'But you have, have you not, written the spy's confession? I've read it and, I hate to admit it, I couldn't have bettered your eloquent verdict of damnable guilt.' He smiled at the down-turned mouth in the mask. 'You really took a swipe at that pretty conservationist. The red ink in particular was a brilliant touch.'

Zeb held out his hand to shake. If he couldn't yet physically silence the man, he wanted to mentally do it.

'It was written for the benefit of the Commandante.' Hunahpu pushed Zeb's hand down with the barrel of his rifle. 'As for what it says, there is nothing new in it. We have released many reports against conservation groups and their corporate sponsors. The confession was lifted from my earlier work. It isn't even original. It's all over the Web.'

Zeb's grip on the crowbar tightened. The throbbing in his head was becoming incessant.

'And if you'd care to donate me a new pen,' Hunahpu continued, 'like most gringo tourists do to campesinos, who knows, I might branch out into different-coloured ink.'

'Let's leave the gift-giving till later,' Zeb said, imagining the satisfaction he would get from cracking open the man's skull, 'when we know each other better.' Zeb popped open a pouch on his black combat pants and pulled out a folded piece of paper. He dangled it as if it was a baited hook before the masked face. 'You are, though, too harsh on your own originality. You see, "señor who-poo", or whatever you like to call yourself, this confession, unlike the rest of your shoddy literature, will have a stamp of authority to it. It will have its very own signatory. Now that will make your silent war, the fight against injustice, audible to the world. Your mask, your resistance, needs a louder voice.'

Buoyed by the verbal beating he gave the arse in the mask, Zeb climbed back up the hill to do the easy bit: extract the confession out of the hostage. What he had not counted on, however, was the conservationist's steely resolve. The crowbar forced out of his hands by an increasingly concerned Stevo, who told him to pull himself together, Zeb failed to produce anything more than a *'Go stuff yourself, I'm not signing that bullshit.'* By the close of the session, the blank space at the bottom of the paper, above a line of red dots, remained just that. Then, as if to really piss him off, after he had hiked further up the hill and the midday heat had worked out an irritable sweat, his phone failed to pick up a signal. Unable to take the belligerent beeps and error messages any longer, the heat and the insects intolerable, he stumbled back down to the cave.

'How's Tammy doing?' Stevo asked Zeb, shaking small stones out of his dreadlocks. 'Is that Decker bloke fixing things up for her, now that we have the hostage in place?'

'Fuck off,' Zeb yelled, the crowbar arrayed over his shoulder.

Taken aback by Zeb's reaction, Stevo winced. His fingers wrapped a flesh and bone shield around his neck, while he slowly moved back along the stone platform, trying to get out of the range of the crowbar. Running out of ground on which to balance his boots on, he stopped and looked down the steep slope. Out of the corners of his boggled eyes he watched a few pinball pebbles pave the route down for him.

'Please,' Stevo pleaded on tipped toes, 'I'm really sorry about last night.'

'Come on mate,' Jamie said to Zeb, putting his hand on Zeb's shoulder and trying to calm him down, 'Stevo won't let you down again. We're here for you.' He gently lowered the crowbar in Zeb's hand. 'We're here for Tam, like you. I don't like seeing you like this.'

Zeb breathed in hard. He nodded at Jamie, then at a relieved-looking Stevo. They were the only people that he could genuinely trust out there, yet the heat was unbearable and he was growing more and more impatient. Thinking of the man in the mask, he turned round and stepped up to the cave's entrance.

'I suppose she hasn't signed it yet?' Zeb projected his voice into the cave. His head felt as if it was in a vice, his temples squeezed together.

'No,' Jamie said, still looking concerned because of Zeb's state of mind, 'we checked five minutes ago. She seems to be moving about a bit more, sitting up, crawling around, that sort of thing. We had to tie her up.'

'So she's starting to find her feet but not her conscience?' Zeb raised his voice so that it would carry through the cave's dark depths. Although it wasn't integral to the mission, the objectives set out by Decker, he wanted to give his Zapatista hosts something back in return for Hunahpu. The signed confession of a conservationist spy was the least he could do for them. 'What is it with this selfish lot?' he called out into the cave. 'Why do they have to be so damned inconsiderate?'

'Yeah,' Stevo said, cautiously joining in, 'she can wriggle, but she can't bloody write.'

'And I thought she was a bright and highly educated scientist.' Zeb put his head further into the cave. 'Stevo?'

'Yes, Zeb.'

'Would you like a go with the crowbar?' Zeb tapped the crowbar around the edge of the cave's entrance, his behaviour becoming more erratic. The ring of metal on stone reverberated through the cave. Suddenly a vast cloud of bats streamed out of the cave, their screams echoed by a human scream from a chamber deep inside the cliff. Zeb, Stevo and Jamie ducked down.

'It would be an honour,' Stevo shouted into the cave, when the flow of bats had ceased.

The three of them stepped back from the cave. Stevo sighed in relief when he realized that Zeb was not serious about using the crowbar on her.

Rachel sat still on her plastic mat. The candles had been blown out by the rush of the fleeing bats and she was left alone and in darkness. Cold and damp, she shivered as she faced the small split of daylight that shone through the slimy rocks. The fine shaft of light made her look even paler, while her dark hair was twisted and matted. Rope bound her hands behind her back and her feet together, and she had to flick her head back to remove a few wiry strands of hair from her eyes. She groaned at the piercing pain at the back of her neck, the rope burns on her wrists and ankles, the helplessness that she felt. The voices outside had gone and in the silence she could hear her deep breaths. Determined not to weep, the chill becoming unbearable, she crawled about on her knees to find the fleece that the man had given to her. When she had found it she picked it up with her teeth and spread it out over the tarpaulin, flicking away the bat pellets with her elbows. She lay down and tried to make herself comfortable. Her head went on its side and she faced the light in the crevice again. By her face was a piece of paper. She used what little light there was to examine its red-inked handwriting.

'Wakey wakey, Rachel,' a man said in English.

Three men manhandled her out of the cave. She grazed her elbows on jagged rock as they tugged on her sleeves, dragged and shoved her through the crevice. Outside she blinked at the blinding light. It was as if the sun was burning the back of her retinas, her bat eyes unaccustomed to the harshness of daylight. She tried to wriggle free from their grasp, but her feet were still tied together and she fell down onto a stone slab. One of the men heaved her up and she bit his hand. He slapped her across the face, pulling her arms right back so that she could feel her muscles almost tear off the bone.

'Careful, Stevo,' another man said, 'we need her in one piece.'

She tried to work out where she was, yet her eyes stung in the light and she had to keep closing them. With a man either side of her, lifted up by her bruised arms, they took her down a cliff of tundra and rocks. Too weak to resist, her pain turned to anger. She relaxed her arms and found the strength to bounce her bound legs off the ground, assisting them in taking her wherever it was. Her hopelessness made her feel reckless.

They arrived at a grassy clearing, her body in so much pain that she had become immune to it. Mules grazed around the clearing, while in the shade of a large tree she saw a circle of masked men, who sat down cross-legged on the ground. She assumed the men to be Mayan Zapatistas, and she watched them observe her through the slits in their black woolly knits. Identically dressed head to toe in black, their chests crisscrossed by cartridge belts, it was impossible for her to identify her visitor from the previous night. She was planted in the centre of the circle and forced to sit down on an upturned paint pot, from where she scanned the masked faces for his green eyes. Yet they all looked the same. She felt dizzy as she looked for him. Having been so cold in the cave she was now sweating uncontrollably.

The foreigners who dragged her there sat down and joined the circle. She watched everyone stare at her, in silence, like she was some freak or curio to be entertained by. Finally one of the Zapatistas stood up. He introduced himself as a Tzotzil Mayan, a commandante of the Zapatista patrol, as if she cared. Stressing that the Zapatistas were there as arbiters only, that her capture was denounced by his command, he tried to assure her that they wanted to mediate an immediate release. They were, he said, and she laughed, 'custodians of the Maya's ancestral forest and upholders of peaceful autonomy'. She was told that it was up to her to cooperate with her captors and earn her freedom.

Another man stood up. 'Did you sleep well?' he asked her in English. His accent confused her. She was too out of it, both then and the night before, to be able to pick up on the idiosyncrasies of the British voice. She was uncertain whether it really was him. 'Or did your guilt keep you awake? I do hope so, Rachel.' He sounded like a madman.

'How'd you know my name?' The man threw her wallet at her.

'And you can get your freedom back, too,' he said, the tone of his voice unlike the man who had given her his fleeced cloak. The man introduced himself as a 'doer', an activist who was not going to sit back and watch Montes Azules be destroyed by capitalist greed. He told her of his vow to prevent the eviction of the forest's legitimate inhabitants, to protect the forest from bio-pirates like her. His rant angered her and she momentarily forgot all about her pain, the rope around her wrists and legs, the masked faces that surrounded her. 'But you have a chance to repent, Rachel.' She found his first-name chumminess particularly nauseating. 'We are forgiving types.'

Another man, one of those who dragged her down the cliff, she recognized the dreadlocks sticking out from his mask, stood up from the circle and walked up to her. He flicked open a penknife, grinned at her through his mask and calmly went behind her. She tried desperately to wriggle out of the ties round her hands and legs. The rope cut into her skin and she twisted her stiff neck to see what he was doing. Her hands sprung apart after he had cut the rope.

'All you have to do is read, sign and go,' her interrogator said. He handed her a piece of paper and a red ballpoint pen. She noticed that he had brown and not green eyes.

She read the red handwriting on the piece of paper. Her hands shook as she took in the bullet points of her supposed confession. 'You've got to be kidding,' she said, finding the contents laughable. 'I'm not signing this crap.' She scrunched up the paper and threw it back at the man. The pen followed. 'It's a great bit of fiction, sure, but I think that, to be fair, the dick-of-an-author should sign it.' Her anger overrode her pain and terror. She couldn't believe that she had been knocked unconscious, holed up in a cave, treated as if she was an enemy of the very land that she wanted to protect. 'Let him take credit for its warped, badly researched, sanctimonious shit. It's certainly not having my name alongside it.' She didn't care what they did to her now.

The pen and paper was pushed back at her, a few times, with accompanying: 'So you deny that your work is a form of counterinsurgency?' He was, she could tell from his hurried voice and the incessant fidgeting of his hands, flustered by her resistance. 'Then why, might I ask, do you blame, on no supportive evidence, only Zapatista refugees for killing your bats? Have you ever visited an autonomous community?'

He circled her, his stare fixed on her as she sat shaking on her paint pot seat. She panicked when he stood behind her. Out of the corners of her eyes she tried to see what he was doing, her pupils darting from side to side, but she could only hear his breaths, the rustle of his clothes and his pacing boots on grass. She instead looked ahead of her, at the masked faces within the ring of Zapatistas, her terrified face pleading for mercy. All they did was stare back at her, impassive and unblinking.

'Have you ever seen for yourself,' the man said, reappearing and startling her, 'the respect these people show to their forefathers' lands?' His masked face was drawn right up to her face. He was so close that she could smell the coffee and cigarettes on his breath. She looked away from the accusative eyes in his mask. 'Did your science not tell you that it is the treacherous Lacandóns, the army and your American patrons, the scum in suits, who are robbing the forest of its biodiversity? Are you not, Rachel Rees, just helping them to murder the creatures that you wish to save?' He turned away from her and scratched the back of his head. She saw a Z-shaped tattoo on his neck.

Each time that she was bombarded with the accusations, the lies, she looked away over the forest, ignoring him. The man stormed up to the Zapatista Commandante in the circle of men. He whispered into his ear and she heard the Commandante reply in Spanish. 'No, we forbid it,' he said, as he put his boot on something lying on the ground. Craning her neck upwards, biting her lip, she saw that it was the crowbar. She scanned the masks around her, listened to their mutterings in Spanish, and tried desperately to identify the visitor to the cave. She was angry with herself that she had believed him, that she thought he was different from the others.

'We will meet again later,' her interrogator said, as he patted her on the shoulder. She recoiled from his touch. 'Then you will sign the confession.' He walked away, picked up the crowbar by the Commandante and disappeared into the trees.

The two men who had carried her to the clearing then picked her up. They dragged her kicking and screaming back to the cave, her resistant legs bashing against the roots and rocks on the way up to the cliff. The pen and the paper confession were thrown into the cave with her. She collapsed onto her tarpaulin bed, crying into the stranger's fleeced cloak.

Rachel opened her eyes and looked at the piece of paper by her face. The light from the crevice had grown weaker and soon it would be night. It had been a couple of hours since anyone had checked on her and the candles remained unlit. She knew that it wouldn't be long until she would be in total darkness. Squinting at the dim ray of light and the red ink on the paper, there was little doubt in her mind that the handwriting on the confession was the same as that on the warning note. She had tried earlier to retrieve the note from her pocket, to make a proper comparison. With her hands tied she had to use her mouth and elbows again, and she spat out the dried mud that caked her combat pants, that lined the flap to her pocket. A stinging pain from her neck stopped any further movement. She thudded down on her back.

She closed her eyes and imagined the man laughing at her gullibility. He had seemed so genuine, so apologetic, yet he had condemned her on paper and allowed her to be intimidated by the man with the 'Z' tattoo on his neck. Twisting and turning on his cloak, she thought of him sitting in the circle of men, hiding behind his wretched mask and doing nothing to help her. For all she knew he could have been one of the men who dragged her away to be interrogated, who tied her up and shouted out threats through the cave's entrance. Believing his words and deeds from the night before to be a charade, his water- and cloak-giving to be just an act, she could not discount the possibility that he was her interrogator. She couldn't be certain that he had green and not brown eyes.

The light in the crevice grew weaker and the cave went darker. Above her the bats started to wake up. They stirred on their stalactite perches and emitted high-pitched squeaks. Rachel looked up at the moving ceiling and smiled at her fluttering companions. She then thought of the confession again. It angered her that she was kidnapped because of her research.

'What do they know,' she said to the bats, as she closed her eyes, 'my little friends.' Her hunger made her stomach constrict.

A silhouette of a man appeared in the crevice. The bats screamed, jumped up and down, flapped wings and swooped over Rachel's closed eyes.

'Shush,' Rachel said, half opening her eyes and drifting in and out of consciousness, 'we'll be OK,' she slurred.

A kernel of maize hit her on the cheek. She looked up and saw the blurred outline of a man standing over her. He had what looked like a bag in his hand.

'Is that you?' she asked the man, seeing stars over his masked head. The thing in his hand moved closer to her.

The man dropped the mule's nosebag over her face. It silenced her scream.

Seventeen

It was night and heavy rain pierced sagging leaves and bowing branches. Water flooded bark flumes and evergreen dams, the roar of the deluge subsuming the screech of crickets and the howls of territorially possessive primates. In the swirl of the storm's black and blue eye, a whirlpool of swollen clouds, stars were swallowed up and a pale moon was dissolved into a fuzzy grey haze. The heavens darkened and lightning struck above the treetops, as if it was a wartime blitz.

Itzamna reared up at a nearby lightning bolt, a crack of wood. Hooves slipping in the slurry of a replenished stream-bed, the mule's silvery mane and two drenched passengers were lit up by the flash. Rachel held onto the mule's head so that she wouldn't fall out of the saddle. The masked man behind her had his arms around her waist. He pulled hard on the mule's reins and his chest pressed against her back. She could feel his breath on the back of her neck and she pushed him away with her elbow. The matter of the mask was also not helping her to trust him. They had been riding for over an hour and she still didn't even know his name.

In spite of the storm and the rising waters, they kept travelling down the stream, away from the cave, the Zapatistas and the anarchists. It was the fastest route to safety, Hunahpu had told her in the clearing where she had been interrogated, once he had removed the nosebag from her face and cut the rope around her wrists and ankles. Without the moon and the stars to light up the way, he used the lightning flashes to steer them down the gurgling gully. He slashed away the branches that overhung the stream with his machete, diverting Itzamna around the trunks and deadfall that were too mature for his blade. Surprised by her overall restraint, her silence, he regretted his earlier use of the nosebag. He had no idea how she would react on seeing him in the cave, thinking that she might confuse him with the foreigners, and he couldn't risk her screaming out. It was up to him to put an end to the mess that threatened the Zapatista patrol. Horatio had at last seen sense and he supported Hunahpu's plan to take her to Nuevo San Felipé.

Rachel watched the mule's legs wade through the water below them. The rain had died down a little and the lightning was now in the distance, the thunder a quieter rumble, insects noisier. Stars appeared in small patches of the sky, framed by the remaining clouds, and she watched their reflections on the stream's rippling surface. The man's arms were no longer tight around her waist and she wondered what sort of place it was that he was taking her to. Before he had lifted her onto the mule, he told her that he was taking her to a 'friendly village'. She had demanded to be taken straight back to the research station, but he refused, saying that it would be suicidal for him to go there. 'The army will be all over the place,' he had said, 'and they would just love to see me.' He said that she was free to go whenever she pleased, take her chances in the jungle, yet he could arrange safe transportation for her in Nuevo San Felipé. She had little choice in the matter. She was too weak to cross the jungle by herself. Somehow she also found herself believing him again.

He guided them round a sharp bend in the stream. Vines blocked their way and he drew his machete out of its leather scabbard. One hand on the reins and the other on his machete, he skilfully cut through the vines, created a clear passageway so that she didn't have to duck down. The noise of the rain was reduced to small splashes on the stream and the patter on leaves. He wanted to break the silence between them, say something to her, but he was lost for words. Noticing the bruise on the back of her neck, her black and red skin caught in starlight, he thought of asking about what they did to her. He had been impressed by the way she had handled her interrogation, deeming it unnecessary to intervene as he watched her from within the Zapatista circle, and he assumed that the bullies hadn't severely damaged her. It then dawned upon him that perhaps her scars were worse than he first thought, that they had interfered with her, given her every right to remain silent towards him. He berated himself for not releasing her sooner, for writing the confession and for keeping silent as they tormented her.

'How are you doing?' he asked her. It was the safest thing he could think of saying. She ignored him and he shook his head. His concern switched from her to the Zapatistas, his duty to his family and the Maya. If she was to report back to the authorities, tell them what had happened to her, he expected the police and the army to react ruthlessly. Zapatista villages would be burnt down, men rounded up and women widowed. Their only hope lay in the conservationist's visit to Nuevo San Felipé. If she learnt more about the Zapatista communities, succumbed to Maria Gomez's hospitality, she might change her position on his people and the evictions that she endorsed. Squeezing out the water from the hem of his ski mask, the rain picking up again and the stars disappearing, it was on his shoulders to stop the bloodshed that she could invoke. He kicked his heels into Itzamna's sides and speeded them up. Water splashed up from the mule's trotting legs.

Rachel was thinking of the note in her pocket and the confession left in the cave, his red handwriting, when he finally spoke. In the silence she had questioned his motives and imagined him taking her to some terrorist camp, where God-knows-what they were going to do to her. Large drops of rain pounded her forehead and she wiped the water away from her eyes. She scolded herself for so readily agreeing to go with him, a wanted man, a criminal, some weirdo who wore a mask and who was neither an Indian nor a westerner. She panicked as she looked at the dark and dense trees around her, the twinkling lights in the sky dimmed by large clouds. He had her to himself in the forest. Should he try anything, only the bugs and hidden creatures would be able to hear her screams. But so far he had done nothing to alarm her. Holding her gently on the saddle, he had not once threatened her. She wanted to know who the mysterious man was.

'The storm is returning,' he said, pointing at the clouds which jostled for space in the sky. She felt his bare arm touch hers. Hairs pricked up on her forearms and she unrolled her sleeves, covering herself up. 'We must find shelter.' He scythed back the thorns and weeds that spilled over the stream.

The thunder was booming again. Itzamna nervously twitched his head. Lightning lit up the forest and Hunahpu saw a large palm tree not far from the banks of the stream. The palm's wet and bushy branches flashed white under the electric sky. He jumped off Itzamna and his boots splashed down into the stream.

'Here,' he said to her, blinking away the rain and raising his hand up at her, 'let me give you a lift down.'

She dropped her arm down and tentatively took his hand.

Lightning struck again and in the starkness she saw his green eyes looking up at her. He quickly looked down at the stream that ran through his legs while he scooped her out of the saddle. Wrapping her arm over his shoulder, he was pleased that her stubbornness appeared to have abated.

He carried her to the palm tree and she felt the warmness of his skin through the wet wool of his mask, the sodden cotton of his shirt. Clinging onto him as he kicked his way through the bush, she wondered what had brought him to the Selva, where he originally hailed from and what had driven him to join the Mayan rebels. When they arrived at the palm tree he gently lowered her down at the driest spot, under the thickest of the branches, and he propped her up against the palm's soft and spongy bark. Through the water that dripped off her shelter and the sheets of rain that flashed with the lightning, she watched him run back to the mule. He pulled the mule out of the stream and tied its reins to the trunk of an old mahogany tree, its branches a barrier to the worst of the rain. She then watched him wipe the water off the mule's silvery face with his red bandana, saw him whisper into its ear as he patted a blanket over its back. A weirdo he might have been, but she nevertheless admired him for his gentleness towards his mule and his knowledge of the forest. Seeing him run back towards her, she bowed her head and rubbed the back of her neck.

The rain was relentless. Neither of them daring to speak, for fear of what the other might say, the minutes dragged on. Sitting in silence under the palm tree, they both stared ahead and watched a mini waterfall flow off the fronds above them. Lightning continued to strike around them, no pauses between flashes, thunder rolling continuously and the ballistics shimmering in the moist atmosphere. A couple of fireflies danced between the trees, their glowing thoraxes impervious to the rain, while a bright-green tree frog wallowed in a puddle by Hunahpu's boots. Rachel huddled her achy body under his woollen cloak, moving away from a leak in their palmed ceiling. She glanced at the masked man beside her and wondered if he was asleep. Hearing him sigh and seeing his fingers flex on his knees, she stared at the rain again.

Neither of them could sleep. Hunahpu bolted up at every noise he heard through the roar of rain and thunder, every crash of wood between the strikes of lightning. He was certain that the storm would have deterred the army and paramilitaries from venturing out, but he worried about the patrol. Horatio had assured him that he could deal with the anarchists, see to it that they returned to San Cristóbal and took the next flight back to England. Hunahpu, though, wasn't as confident as his brother. The man called Zeb troubled him. He couldn't see him giving up on his mission so easily. It was as if he had a personal vendetta against the conservationist, or even against him. He kept his machete close by his side.

The rain petered out, the thunder grew fainter and the lightning made way for a more constant moon. Insects resumed their hold over the forest, their uninterrupted screeching louder than before. In the distance, howler monkeys whooped and roared as if they were man-eating jaguars, their monstrous vocals carried over the trees, their blood-curdling noise belying their cuddly appearance. The stars restored to their rightful place next to the moon, the only water to fall to the ground was that which dropped off the leaves and into mud. Soon the sky was clear enough to see the Milky Way, the Wakah-Chan and the 'Raised up Sky' of Lucio's teachings. Hunahpu smiled at its restored brightness in the sky.

Rachel noticed him look upwards. She stopped thinking about her return to the US, the look on Erin's face when she would tell her about the anarchists, the weirdo who wouldn't take off his mask, and followed his upward gaze. The sparkling constellation in the sky kept them both still.

'Do you know as much about astronomy as you do terrorism?' she asked, snapping him out of his trance.

'It's the Wakah-Chan,' he whispered, blinking at the stars that sparkled in his eyes.

'What's that?' His calm response to her quip about terrorism took her by surprise, made her feel immature. She briefly glanced at him before she looked back up at the stars.

Hunahpu rubbed his eyes. He exhaled a cloud of mist and watched his breath float away, joining the steam that evaporated off the waterlogged soil. Lowering his head and closing his eyes, part in deference to the sky and part in annoyance at her, he stayed devout to the cosmic alignments and blank to her satire. He figured, from her unforgiving put-downs, her obvious hatred of him, it was pointless in even trying to enlighten and educate her. It was what he deserved, he thought to himself, and he believed that she would never listen to his side of the story. An introduction via Maya myths, he predicted, would only increase the put-downs. He therefore settled on a silent stalemate: fighting ignorance with ignorance and stubbornness with stubbornness.

'No, seriously, what is it?' she asked him, looking up at the Wakah-Chan. 'I'm interested.'

Hunahpu reopened his eyes. He tilted his mask heavenwards and puffed out another cloud under the palm tree. He pointed a finger at a triangular formation of three bright stars. To the right of the triangle's starry peak and arranged in a straight and horizontal line were two more stars. It was, to non-Maya astronomers, the belt of Orion.

'The Maya say,' he said, looking up at the stars, 'that the Maize God, their Creator, rose up from the three hearthstones on the broken shell of a turtle.' He illustrated the reptile by drawing an oval around the line of three burning dots. After he had rounded off his sketch with a fingernail, his hypnotic finger glided further up the sky, stopping over an abundance of glittery specks, stars and planets clustered into the form of a crucifix. Using the constellation as a luminous template, he crossed the air above him. 'The cross of the Milky Way, the Maize Tree, is the Wakah-Chan. When the Maize Lord rose up from the turtle's cracked carapace, he became the tree that connects man to the Otherworld.' He briefly faced her, saw that she was still looking up at the stars, and he continued. 'It is down the Maize Tree, along the 'Road of Awe,' the watery fall into the southern horizon, where we die and are reborn.'

His finger and her eyes remained fixed to the starred stairway. She waited for him to continue, but he remained silent.

'Tell me more,' she said, sounding, she realized and it annoying her, like her Lacandón student. 'What do you mean by reborn?'

He dropped his hand to his lap. The moonlight caught a jagged scar on his wrist. Pulling down the cuffs of his black shirt, he waited for the wisecrack. But she continued to stare at the twinkling representation of the beginnings of time. He presumed, from her prayerful head drawn to the sky and the frown set above her soulful eyes, that she was a good actress. She was pretty bait, he didn't doubt, for him to dig his own grave of humiliation.

'What would you care?' he asked her, looking down at the reflection of the stars in the puddle by his boots. 'You're a big-business scientist. To you, superstitious beliefs, sacred ties to land, are indices of failure – ideas belonging to those who are barely clinging on to the evolutionary ladder, a few stragglers on the rungs above the apes.' He flicked a moth of his leg. 'Why would you, a follower of rationality, want to know what the Maya believe in?' He waited for her composure to break, checking her dreamy eyes for flickers of a flare-up, science's comeback.

'Because I want to know,' she whispered to the Wakah-Chan, before she turned to face the faceless mystery who sat beside her, 'I'd like to know more about their Creation story. Tell me, please.' She couldn't believe that she gave him a 'please'. The spell of the stars, the return of the connection that she sensed under a sunset in the Yucatán all those years back, a sore neck replacing a hungover head, needed some sort of an explanation.

Embarrassed, he backed off from her puzzled stare and faced the map in the sky. Glimpsing her attention out of the corner of his mask's eyehole, he raised his arm again and pointed at the stars of Gemini, which sparkled in a north-easterly position above the Wakah-Chan.

'Those are . . .' he paused, 'the copulating peccaries of Gemini. When the Milky Way is flat on the horizon and the sky is black, the peccaries cavort over the portal to the Otherworld. The Maya call this dark entrance place the White-Bone-Snake, while the Maize Tree, the Milky Way, in its horizontal position, becomes the Cosmic Monster.' He checked to see if she was still listening, his mask dripping water onto his shoulders, the skin of his neck grazed by wet wool. Her position unchanged, the façade intact, he gave her the benefit of the doubt. 'It was via the canoe of the Cosmic Monster, a crocodilian lancha paddled by Stingray and Jaguar Paddler Gods, that the Maize God was taken away to be reborn. The Paddlers, with other ancestral beings, mainly of the half-man-half-beast school of deities, took him to the turtle and the three stones of Creation. It was there that he was reborn and he became . . .'

She looked at him as he paused. Though the mask made it difficult to tell, she detected what she thought was a smile. Before he caught her interest in him, she returned her attention to the far-off cross, looked beyond his finger and scarred wrist. She wondered if his face was also disfigured.

'He became the Wak-Chan-Ahaw. It was he, the resurrected Maize God, who made everything happen and created the new universe.'

235

'Wak-Chan-Ahaw?' she asked, trying to mimic his pronunciation.

They looked at each other: Rachel staying with his sparkling green eyes and Hunahpu smiling through his mask. He nodded.

'Yes. Wak-Chan-Ahaw. Quite a mouthful, eh?'

He could not make her out. The change in her attitude, the effect his story had on her, confused him. Her wide and inquisitive eyes, which now locked on to him, were as strong as the poisoned scowl that he was more accustomed to. Perhaps he was right about her. Perhaps, delving into the dregs of his optimism and recalling his own time of creation, remembering Lucio's lessons in the cave of the White-Bone-Snake, she really did want to listen and learn.

'What about the Big Dipper?' she asked, taking her turn to point a finger upwards. 'Does that have any role in Maya Creation?' She looked up at the inverted saucepan in the sky.

'You mean poor old Seven-Macaw?' He laughed and wagged his finger at the stars. She found herself smiling with him. 'Seven-Macaw was an incredibly vain bird with beautiful blue teeth and metallic eyes.' He flashed his teeth and eyes through his mask. His silly face made her smile even more. 'So self-obsessed was this bird, that he claimed to be the sun and demanded to be worshipped by everyone, even the gods. The Hero Twins,' he said, pausing to look at her again, 'who took offence at the nerve of Seven-Macaw's vanity, decided to teach him a lesson.' The stars above them were captured in his eyes. 'They lay in wait with their blowguns.'

Stopping for an interval on the cliff-hanger, a parrot about to bite the bullet, he opened his soaked leather bag and pulled out his water bottle. He unscrewed the cap and offered her the bottle. She thanked him, took a few sips and handed the bottle back.

'The Twins took aim and struck Seven-Macaw's beautiful teeth.' He took a swig of water. 'Thanks to the Twins, Seven-Macaw lost his greatness.'

They both smiled at the fable in the stars. The storm's leftovers, the tapping of draining vegetation and the exuberance of bathing insects, a drone of drips and inhuman delectation, filled the voiceless void. Steam off foliage and warmed ground thickened, the entire forest resembling one giant green Turkish bath. As dawn approached, the sky grew lighter, the thermal outflow increased and clouds screened the sky from their palm tree observatory.

236

Rachel watched the stars disappear behind the jungle smog. A drop of water fell off a palm leaf above her head. It splashed the side of her face and formed a streak down her grimy cheek. Hunahpu observed her in the blue light, while she dabbed her skin with the bandana that he gave to her in the cave. She caught him looking at her, her eyes interlocked to his letter-boxed gaze in the mask. Realizing the state that she must have been in, she dropped her head and hid her face from him. She ran her hand through her straggly hair, looked down at the ground and at a large leaf by her boots. Recently hatched flies skated on the water that the leaf had captured.

'You still haven't told me your name,' she said, keeping her face down, safely staring at the fledgling flies on the leaf.

'It's Hunahpu,' he replied, after a moment of hesitation. He followed her line of sight to the cycle of life that emerged out of rippled water. Nymphs spun in circles on the surface tension.

'I'm Rachel.' She wondered if he was still looking at her.

'I know.' He briefly glanced at her, thought of her lying semi-unconscious on the cave's floor, admired her for the way she had stood up to the psycho with the crowbar. He looked back down at the leaf, at the adult flies that ratcheted their wings on bandy legs. 'I'm sorry about earlier. I mean, at having a go at you about being a big-business scientist, giving you a hard time over your work. You've had you're fair share of crap and I don't want you to, I mean you shouldn't, see me like those that kidnapped you.'

They both kept their heads down while she thought of a reply.

'I should apologize, too,' she eventually said, 'I know that you're only trying to help.' They both looked up and at each other. 'The nosebag was unnecessary though.'

'I'm sorry.' He scratched his masked forehead.

'How did you get me past the others?' She tried to examine his eyes behind his fingers. In doing so his mask became all too apparent to her again. It was as if she had forgotten he was still wearing it, his mythical stories about the stars entrancing her, his unshakeable and gentle manner bewitching her. She reminded herself that she was with a Zapatista, a criminal who hid behind a mask. 'You didn't kill them, did you?'

'No,' he said, shaking his head and laughing at her ridiculous question. 'Although that's not to say that they didn't deserve to be snuffed out of their prejudicial misery. They have nothing to

237

do with Zapatismo and their presence here is just a minor cock-up.' He touched her on the arm.

'*Minor?*' she exclaimed, brushing his hand off her and pointing at her bruised neck. 'You call that "minor"? And you invited them, right?'

'I didn't invite them.' Her reaction took him by surprise. It reminded him how different she was from him, that she was a scientist employed to justify the evictions. 'The Commandante, my brother, assumed they were peace observers, and that they were here to stop our villages from being attacked. There are many foreigners in Chiapas.' He stared at her through his mask. 'Most of them, Rachel, do a great job. For peace and not money.'

Incensed by his final comment, she pulled the warning note out of her pocket. She threw the paper ball at his boots.

'What's this?' he asked, picking the paper out of the mud. He opened it out and read the warning that he had written for her, which he had left on her bat-catching path. His red-inked hand-writing was blotched by the damp. He folded it back up and looked out into the mist.

'You wrote it, didn't you?'

'Yes.' He handed the note back to her, shrugging. She snatched it out of his hands. 'I was worried about what they might do to you.' Sighing at the mist, he wished that he hadn't provoked her. She was almost as hotheaded as Maria.

'You also wrote that confession, right?' She scrunched up the note and threw it into the mist.

'I had no choice in the matter.' He wanted to take off his ski mask, be done with the secrecy, make her realize that he genuinely did care for her.

'Yeah, maybe so, but you wrote the lies about me. Do you honestly think that I condone the violence that is going on out here?' She wanted to pull off his ski mask and look at him right in the face, drum it home that it wasn't her who was in the wrong. It wasn't her who had anything to hide.

'I never said you did condone the violence. It's just that your evidence is all wrong.' He stood up, shaking his head as he moved out of the palm shelter, and brushed the dirt off his clothes. It was light enough for them to be moving on and he didn't want to waste time arguing with her.

'Like you're a qualified expert on deforestation,' she raised her voice up at him.

He turned his back on her, slung his leather bag over his shoulder and walked into the mist. His boots stepped on the warning note that she had thrown away.

'That's right,' she called out to him, 'just run away from the argument. You know I'm right.' She couldn't believe that he had just walked away from her like that.

'Keep the noise down,' he whispered to himself, smiling as he untied Itzamna's reins from the mahogany tree. He led the mule down to the stream.

Rachel tried to see him through the thickening mist, hear his movements through the gurgle of the stream and the screech of insects. He had been gone a few minutes and she hoped that she hadn't pushed him too far.

'Hunahpu?' she called out, poking her head out from under the palm tree, moving about on her hands and knees as she squinted at the mist. The birds were beginning to wake up and their songs added to the noise around her. It was as if the entire forest was ganging up against her, her former allies turning their backs on her and keeping her blind to what was around her. 'Hunahpu?' she shouted out louder.

There was still no sign of him and she started to panic. Unable to move her legs properly, stand up on her own two feet, she wrapped her arms round the palm's furry trunk. She slowly clawed her way up, her nails digging into the fibrous bark, and she wobbled about as she surveyed the mist from a higher position.

'You're getting better,' a voice called out from behind her. To her relief it was Hunahpu. She turned round and saw him with his water bottle in one hand, a bunch of bananas in the other. 'I thought you might like some breakfast before we get going.'

The chopper circled the trees for a second time. Rachel heard its blades buzz high over their heads as she sat in the saddle on Itzamna. Her hands shielding her eyes from the sun, she looked up at the bright sky through the gaps in the branches, the camouflage that Hunahpu had directed them under. She wondered if the chopper was Bruce's Huey, but she could barely see it, let alone make out the USAID markings on its doors. The glare of the sun made her eyes water and she wiped her eyes on her sleeve. It felt odd for her to be hiding from her rescue party, for her heart to be beating so fast, and yet she didn't want to put him in danger. Although she was not happy with the idea of going to the Zapatista village, she knew that he had risked much to free her from the cave, to escort her through the army-infested jungle. If he still felt it unsafe to reveal his identity to her, felt compelled to wear a woolly mask under the burning tropical sun, she imagined there to be one hell of a hefty price on his head. She looked down at him in the stream, as he guided them even further under the cover of weeping acacia, vines and buttress roots.

'Are you OK?' he asked her, noticing her watery eyes in a ray of sunlight, a beam that made her dazzle under the trees. To provide Itzamna with some respite he had opted to make the rest of the journey on foot, through the stream. The cold water numbed his feet and he could just about feel the blisters, the flaps of skin on his heels, that rubbed against his waterlogged boots. In contrast his head felt as if it was about to combust. Sweat dripped out of the bottom of his mask and the wet wool made his face itchy. He could feel the ticklish legs of tiny black salt bees on the back of his neck, a cluster of them lapping up the sweat under his collar. To stop himself from taking his mask off, having to explain to her who he really was, he had to frequently bob his head in the water to keep cool.

'Yes,' she replied, as she watched him sink his head into the stream again, his action like that of an ostrich burying its head into sand. She sniggered.

'This isn't funny,' he said, squeezing the water out of his mask. 'Do you realize how hot it is under this thing?'

'Well take it off.' She lashed out at the mosquitoes that floated above her wild hair. 'I really don't get it why you can't show me your face. It's not like it's going to make any difference if I know what you look like.'

'Not to you, perhaps.' He walked a little further out into the stream, ducking under a low branch to see if the helicopter had gone.

Of course he had considered the risks of her seeing his face, particularly now that the sun was out and he was cooking under black wool; Zapatistas didn't wear ski masks for prolonged periods of time. He knew that he could easily pass himself off as Latino, a Mexican, his mother providing him with Spanish blood, and he didn't expect her to doubt it. What stopped him was the questioning she would receive when she returned to the research station. All that Commandant Hernandez required was a simple description of him, a credible witness to link him to a missing foreigner, a rubberstamp to his suspicions. Marked as a mercenary, someone with no right to be in the Selva, the army and the Cardenistas would then use him to justify their attacks on the villages. He could never let that happen. As much as he wanted to show her who he was, tell her everything, it was his family who came first.

'I think it's safe to move on,' he said, letting go of the branch and allowing it to splash into the water. He returned to Rachel and Itzamna.

Rachel heard the sound of the chopper fade away. While he was spying on it she thought of the research station, of her colleagues and of Guillermo and Ofelia. She wondered how the little girl and her father were doing. Hunahpu had assured her that they had both escaped unharmed, yet she worried about how Ofelia was coping. Recalling the uncontrollable shakes that she had felt as she held the girl in her arms, the squeals of the bat blinded by torchlight, she hoped that the Lacandón girl would work with her again. She couldn't wait to see her, tell her how her teacher had seen off the bad Lokin and was perfectly well. She even thought of telling her about Hunahpu, her masked rescuer.

Hunahpu pulled on Itzamna's reins, guided the mule and Rachel towards the centre of the stream and out of their bushy hide. He carefully lifted the low branches over Rachel's ducking head, sweeping the vines to one side to ensure she wasn't hit in the face. She watched him as he laboured below her, fought resilient roots with his machete and struggled in the heat under his mask. It puzzled her as to why he was taking such great care of her, why he was risking capture to take her to this village of his. Although she couldn't see him harming her, she wondered how much control he had over the other Zapatistas, whether he would be able to protect her from the village's masked reception.

Her paranoia increased as they moved further down the stream. Every time she heard a rustle of leaves, the scamper of hidden creatures, her heart leapt and her lungs gasped. Between the trees, in the shades of blackness, she thought she could see the eyes of men, their stares through ski masks. She anxiously looked up at the sky and tried to listen out for the chopper.

'Tell me more about this village,' she finally asked him, as she watched him remove a fallen tree trunk that blocked their way.

'Are they squatters?' Her neck hurt because of all the looking around she had done.

Hunahpu threw the tree trunk onto the banks of the stream. The crash of wood caused a flock of parakeets to take off from the branches above them. He turned round to face her, his eyes glaring at her under the shrieks of the birds.

'Squatters?' he spat out the word. 'What do you mean by that?'

'I mean . . .' she hesitated, realizing that her choice of word was a mistake, 'do you think that I will be safe there?'

'These people are not terrorists, Rachel.' He took hold of Itzamna's reins and turned his back on her. 'Anyway, it's not them you should be worried about.' He moved them on again.

For the next hour or so they didn't speak. Neither of them felt comfortable enough to break the silence; both of them were now paranoid. Now that there had been a few hours of daylight, Hunahpu knew that the army and Commandant Hernandez's men would be spread out across the forest. The stream kept their escape route away from the old loggers' tracks, which the army used to drive their Humvees down, but he still froze at every crack of wood or sound of movement from within the trees. There was a danger, he realized, that the army had surrounded all of the Zapatista villages, set an ambush for them at any point. Pausing again to look ahead, to ensure that it was safe to go round another bend in the stream, he wondered whether the paramilitaries had already begun to storm the villages. If they hadn't, he couldn't envisage Commandant Hernandez holding off for much longer; the American woman's kidnap had provided the paramilitaries with the perfect excuse to attack. It made him question his idea of taking her to Nuevo San Felipé. His face sweating under his mask as they approached another bend, he hoped that what he was doing was right. Thinking back five years ago to his own moment of enlightenment, when his woodenness was washed away, he tried to remove his doubts about her. Once she had met his family and witnessed the reality of life in the Selva, she would no longer regard them as 'squatters'.

'What's that?' Rachel whispered to him. She pointed at a large black object ahead of them. It was waddling about on the banks of the stream.

In an instant Hunahpu quickly pushed Itzamna to the side of the stream, doing the best he could to hide them. He pulled his machete out of its leather scabbard and crouched down to see what it was, his knees underwater. Rachel identified it first, though.

'It's a tapir,' she whispered from behind his back.

'What?' He squinted through the glare of the sun on the water and confirmed that she was right. The half cow- and half boar-like animal pricked up its ears. Seeing the masked man rise out of the water it ran off into the forest, shaking bushes and branches as it fled from them. Hunahpu turned round and smiled at Rachel.

They decided to take a quick bathroom stop. Hunahpu lifted her out of the saddle and deposited her behind a tree away from the stream. He told her that he would wait for her until she called him. 'We can't stop for long, though,' he said, before he left her in privacy and went to check on the state of his numb feet.

A few minutes had passed and Rachel did up her belt. A column of mites ran up her boots and she used a sheet of spare tissue paper to flick them off. She was about to call out to him, when a tingling in her toes, a renewal of sensation, stopped her. Excited by the symptoms of her recovery, she used the trunk of the tree to pull herself up. Taking a deep breath she managed a few steps forward. She looked back at the few yards that she had covered, grinning at her achievement. 'Are you done, yet?' she heard him call out through the trees. It suddenly dawned on her that she should try to escape. There was no way that she was going to that village of his, risk her life at the hands of the Zapatistas again, be intimidated by men in masks. She reminded herself that she was with a wanted man. She couldn't take his word that she would be safe.

'Hang on,' she shouted back, while she looked for an exit route through the wall of intertwined trees and bushes, 'I need a few more minutes.' Her heart was beating fast and drops of sweat glistened on her nose and forehead. She spun around, the light of the sky flashing through palm leaves and spiky branches. Adrenalin pumped strength to her legs and, breathing in short and frantic bursts, she raised her foot. She couldn't hear or see him and so she stumbled forward another few yards, wrapping her arms round another tree. Trying to avoid the twigs on the ground, be as silent as she could, she moved from tree to tree, resting post to resting post, listening out for him while she caught her breath.

She had found her rhythm and she increased the number of strides between her rest breaks. She thought of what she might do when she was far enough from the stream, lost from the man in the mask, safe from the Zapatistas. A fire, a smoke signal, seemed like the best way to attract the chopper in the sky. The thought of the comfort of the research station made her move even faster. It was when she was thinking of one of Josita's deliciously spicy meals, a cold beer to down it with, that she forgot about her feet and her injury. One of her boots caught a noosed root and her weak ankle gave way. She tripped up and fell flat on her face. On her knees, cursing her carelessness and swearing at a fat maggot in the disturbed soil, she used her shirtsleeve to wipe the mud off her chin. The maggot rolled about, belly-up, as if her misfortune had it in fits of laughter.

'You're definitely getting better,' Hunahpu said, strolling up to her and checking her out in the dirt. 'Are you OK?'

She groaned at his voice and looked up at him.

'How long were you watching me?' she asked him, turning pink under her earthy make-up.

'A little while,' he said, before adding, 'but not when you were you know what.'

'I suppose that's something.' She winced at the pain in her ankle. 'So why didn't you stop me?'

'I'm not holding you hostage.' He handed her a tissue to clean her face with. 'I only followed you to make sure that you were OK.'

'Seeing that I can't move more than fifty yards without falling over and spraining my ankle, it's perhaps no bad thing that you did follow me. It was a silly thing for me to do.'

'A little silly,' he said, smiling as he offered her a hand-up. 'Although it's good to see you're on the mend.'

'Yeah,' she said, sort of smiling back. She took his hand and waist and hobbled upright. 'Although self-inflicted injuries are not exactly going to help me escape. Sometimes I can be my own worst enemy.'

He hooked her arm round his shoulder and pulled her body tight against his side. Gripping his black shirt and gun belt, hugging his chest, she felt even more stupid at trying to escape from him. Locked together, they shuffled over to Itzamna and the stream.

'How much further is it to this place that you're taking me to?' she whispered, drawn up close to him.

'About four hours,' he replied, trying to ignore the feeling her close proximity gave him, 'but we don't have to go, not if you don't want to. I mean, I could, if you feel up to it that is, take you to an old timber trail that leads to an army checkpoint. It's four hours in the other direction.'

'Four hours either way, then, I guess?'

'Yeah, for both journeys. It's your choice.'

She thought about it for a bit. The pain in her foot and the warmth of her prop led her in one direction.

'After my little mishap back there, I don't think that I have much of an option.' She saw his smile through his mask. 'I'll come to this village of yours. But you must promise me, and I mean promise me, that you won't allow the Zapatistas to lay a finger on me. And, as soon as we arrive, you'll make arrangements for someone to take me to back to the research station. Yes?'

'Yes. I promise,' he said, holding her a little closer to him.

Eighteen

'BIEN VENIDOS AL NUEVO SAN FELIPE', a sign greeted the three arrivals to the Zapatista village. Hunahpu walked Itzamna under the sign, while Rachel sat up in the saddle, snapping out of her slumber and now fully alert. The green words of welcome, which failed to reassure the wide-eyed conservationist, were written on a background of the Mexican flag, three revolutionary stars and a portrait of a Mayan man wearing a red bandana and brandishing a rifle. At the village's gate, a tree trunk painted with red and white stripes and rolled in barbed wire, a masked man appeared from an adjoining hut. The man stopped chewing tobacco and he and Hunahpu saluted each other. Staring up at the passenger on the mule, the man raised the gate. Hunahpu led Itzamna into the village compound.

Contrary to Rachel's expectations, the squatters' clearing was composed of a few clapboard shacks, with palm-thatched roofs and external stone-hearths, within a largely intact patch of forest. It was not the scorched wasteland that she had read about in the brief she had been given. As far as she could see there were no fields of cattle, stacks of timber or burning patches of forest. Between the basic homesteads and under uncut mahogany, ceiba and beech trees were orchards of banana, plantain, mango and papaya bushes. Each home had a small garden of herbs, vegetables and primary-coloured flowers, while chickens, pigs and dogs scratched and scampered on the leaf-swept high street. A group of Mayan children abandoned their games on the street as soon as they caught sight of the mule. Rachel watched them run towards their homes, spy on her from behind their mothers' embroidered dresses. As word of the new arrival, Hunahpu's foreign guest, filtered through the village, more and more onlookers emerged out of their homes and orchards. Soon both sides of the street were lined with the stares and chatter of 'the people of the bat'.

They continued down the increasingly crowded street. Hunahpu readjusted his ski mask and nodded at the cautious faces either side of them. A few of the men walked up to him, patted him on the back and pointed at his mask and then at the woman on Itzamna. They spoke in Tzotzil Mayan and Rachel couldn't understand what they were saying. He would occasionally look back up at her, smiling reassurance, but the attention that she was receiving made her feel uncomfortable. Her high-up position on the mule made her feel as if she was even more of a spectacle, and she wondered where he was taking her, whether he had his own hut. She looked past the mob and at a basketball court painted in a rectangle of compacted mud. Above the court a man on a ladder hung red, white and green flags from hoop-to-hoop, decorating the branches in between with the flapping flags. On the court itself women set up wobbly stands of tamales and tortillas, racks of fruit and maize snacks, unlit cooking grills and troughs of sugary soft drinks. Rachel searched the flags for a hangman's noose and the food-stalls for secret gallows.

They kept going down the street. Hunahpu patted Itzamna on the head and he looked up at her again. He asked her if she was OK and she just nodded. They passed a large shed of brightly coloured murals and he pointed at it. 'That's the village's assembly hall,' he said, noticing her observe the artwork on the shed's walls. She was entranced by the brilliant colours of the murals, bewildered by the blend of religious and revolutionary insignia. Rifles slung over their shoulders, masked Mayan men and women were painted alongside green maize shoots and golden cobs. On another wall she saw a portrait of Subcommandante Marcos, the masked and pipe-smoking leader of the Zapatistas, who shared space with the stern faces of Che Guevara and Emiliano Zapata. She felt the painted eyes of the revolutionaries follow her as she was guided past them. Their look added to the unease she felt.

Next door to the assembly hall she saw another decorated hut, a small church with a cross rising up from its slatted roof. The beams of the cross were festooned with red ribbons, while the church's roof and walls were painted in swirls of vibrant turquoise. On the church's front wall was a mural that depicted white doves flying above a field of maize. In the middle of the mural and painted on a large door she saw a Mayan woman wearing a ski mask. Dressed in white and holding up two maize cobs, the woman was framed by a border of red and black zigzags. Rachel observed the woman's calm and yet stoic expression, the eyes in the mask. It replaced the unease she felt with yet more bewilderment. The image of the angelic Zapatista remained with her as she was moved on.

Past the church and set slightly back from the dirt road was a wooden home. Its size and style were identical to the thatched huts that they had already passed. Outside an open front door was a cauldron steaming on a small fire. The cauldron spiced the air under a blossoming banana tree and Rachel felt her pangs of hunger return. Hunahpu let go of Itzamna's reins and walked over to the cauldron. He picked up a ladle and stirred the steaming broth. Lifting his mask up slightly, moving the wool away from his mouth, he slurped from the ladle.

'Get your filthy hands and greedy mouth out of it!' a woman shouted out in Spanish.

Rachel almost jumped out of the saddle.

Wearing a long black skirt and a stretched baby blue T-shirt, 'Miss Bossy' printed in italicized English across a large bosom, Maria Gomez charged out of the hut. Hunahpu dropped the ladle into the cauldron. Her face level to his chest, her brawn compensating for her shorter height, her biceps meatier than his thighs, she poked a finger into his stomach.

'That's for dinner and not for now,' Maria said to him, while he wiped the spilt broth off his chin, realigned his mask to his mouth. 'I don't care what you get up to when you are on patrol, but you eat at the table, with the rest of us, when you're at home.' She grinned and wrapped her big arms around him. 'It's good to see you Hunahpu.'

'And you, Maria,' he said, patting her on the back before freeing himself from her embrace. He breathed again.

'Now why are you wearing that mask? Aren't you hot in it?'

'I'll explain later. There's someone I'd like you to meet.'

They walked up to Itzamna and he helped Rachel down from the mule.

'Maria, meet Rachel Rees, a new friend of mine. Rachel, meet Maria Gomez, my mother of sorts and an excellent cook of chicken broth.' The two women smiled at each other and shook hands.

'You look sick, señorita,' Maria said, noticing Rachel wobble on her feet. 'Let's get you inside and fix you up.'

'Thank you, but I'm fine, really.' She tried to step back from Maria's open arms, but was too weak to fend them off. Her arms draped over the shoulders of both Hunahpu and Maria, her body lopsided by the difference in their heights, she hobbled into the hut.

They lay her down on a wooden-framed bed, cushioned her body with multicoloured blankets and padded her neck with a pillow stuffed with wild turkey feathers. She looked around her to find her bearings in the smoky interior. The bedroom was the kitchen and living room all in one: a bed at one end, four stools and a table in the middle, an indoor stove by the front door and a meshed window. Bunches of fresh herbs and long stems of red chillies hung from a beam on the ceiling, while igloo storage boxes, of the sort her mother used to pack for picnics on the beach, were placed on a dried mud-floor, pushed against the wall nearest to the stove. A steel griddle pan's oily black surface smoked over orange ash, the pan ready for the tortillas that were stacked up on a nearby work surface, a shelf of bundled poles wedged into a timber and mud-brick wall. Nailed above the bed and her head was a wooden cross painted gold.

Maria handed her a glass of water and two tablets. Rachel looked at Hunahpu for reassurance.

'It's only arnica,' he said. 'It should take away some of the pain.'

'And this?' She raised her glass.

'It's water. You drink it.' He took a sip and handed the glass back to her. Frowning up at him, she wiped the glass's rim on her sleeve and washed down the tablets.

Maria went on her toes and reached up for the herbs on the beam. She picked out four velvety leaves and, with a pair of tongs, held them over the fire to blister.

'Santa Maria,' she said, introducing her green namesakes, which were already curling up and beginning to smoke, 'to reduce the inflammation. This is . . .'

She was interrupted by Lucio, who skidded through the hut's doorway. He took a brief look at the stranger on the bed before he stepped up to Hunahpu.

'What happened?' he asked Hunahpu, gripping his black shirt and shaking him. 'This isn't her, is it? Where are the others? Where is my son? And why are you still wearing your mask?' He rested his hands on his knees to catch his breath.

'Sit down on your stool, Lucio,' Maria said to her husband, 'you can't go barging in on us like that. Can't you see that the young señorita is sick?'

'But . . .'

'How about we go outside?' Hunahpu said, leading Lucio by his backpack towards the doorway. He winked at a bemused Rachel. 'Let's leave the companeras alone. I'll fill you in on what has happened with the patrol.'

'That's a very good idea,' Maria answered on behalf of her husband.

Rachel's face begged him not to go, but the door closed behind him and she was left alone with Miss Bossy and her roasted leaves.

'That's better,' Maria said, when the men had gone and she could heal in peace. She removed the blistered leaves from the stove and dowsed them with water. Lifting Rachel's collar away from a large bruise, she applied the soggy Santa Maria and massaged them into her purple skin. A peppery smell of anise tickled Rachel's nose and she sneezed.

'You have a cold as well? I know a very good root for that.'

'No!' She was still jumpy. 'Sorry, no. I don't have a cold. Really, I'm fine. Thank you.' She tried to wipe her nose with Hunahpu's bandana, but it was snatched off her and replaced by a fresh red one.

'Who did this to you, child? Was it the Cardenistas? Was it the fat tapir?' She wrapped a leaf around Rachel's swollen ankle.

'I don't know who they were.' Rachel paused. 'Who are the Cardenistas? Who is the fat tapir?'

Maria pulled up a stool beside the bed. She stroked her patient's hair back, combing matted strands out with her fingers and nails, and they both closed their eyes. Rachel felt the pain eased out of her by the Santa Maria, the leaves and the palms of Miss Bossy on her neck. While she lay on her back she heard of life in Chenalho, the old San Felipé, where the women had tended to black sheep and wove textiles in the mountains, stocking the tourist markets in San Cristóbal de las Casas. It was, the story-teller's voice went quieter, five years ago that the Cardenistas came to San Felipé. She went on to describe the night of the full moon, Lucio's pilgrimage to First-True-Mountain, the murder of their youngest son by Commandant Hernandez, the 'fat tapir'. After they had buried their little boy, they packed what remained from their burned down home and escaped to Montes Azules.

'How long have you known Hunahpu?' Rachel asked, looking up at the cross on the wall. The afternoon sun shone through the mesh window and it caught the cross's flaky gilt.

251

'It was on the day that the trucks departed from Chenalho.' Maria took a breath. 'Lucio found him, and I, of course, was against it. I was never a true believer, not of the ancient stuff, especially not after the death of Urbano.' She blew her nose into her bandana.

'Where did you find him?' Rachel sat up on the bed.

'In the Pool of the Paddler Gods, at the bottom of First-True-Mountain and under that cross there.' She pointed at the cross above the bed, the icon brightening up the mud plaster of the walls. 'Lucio said that he was delivered by the gods, that the wooden man had, like the Hero Twins, escaped from the Death Lords in Xibalba, was delivered by the ancestors to help us. It rarely happens, trust me, but for once my husband was right and I was wrong. Now he is like a son to both of us.'

'Does Hunahpu keep in touch with his real, I mean his biological, family?'

'Biological? I do not understand. The only family that he has is the Gomez. His past, he says, is dead. He belongs in Chiapas now.'

'But he is Mexican?'

'For someone so sick, señorita, you ask many questions. It is wrong for me to say anything more. You should speak to him yourself.'

'I shall try to, if he'll allow me to that is.' She smiled at Maria. 'But can you tell me why he has to wear the mask all the time? He won't even show me his face.'

'Hunahpu has enemies who could use his identity against him. His reports tell the world about the bad government – he stops the army and the paramilitaries from attacking us and they would do anything to silence him. The mask is nothing against you. He just has to be careful.'

Rachel looked up at the cross again.

'You mean he doesn't trust me?'

'I'm sure that's not it.' She stroked back Rachel's black hair. 'Between you and me only, señorita, I think he is also a little shy.'

'Shy?' Rachel exclaimed.

'Yes. But he's not as wooden as when we found him.'

'He's not scarred as well is he?'

'Scarred?'

'His . . .'

'Enough now.' Maria stood up from her stool and pulled out a wooden chest from under the bed. 'Now let's find you a change of clothes and have you out of those stinky American things. I have a very pretty dress, in a gringo size, perfect for you. It's too good to go to a tourist.'

'Please. You don't have to.'

'I insist. You need to wear something smart to go to my birthday party. It's also the carnival of "Crazy Days", and you'll attract the wrong sort of attention if you go like that.' Rachel looked at her muddy khaki combat pants and her dusty shirt. 'But first we need to scrub you up.'

While Maria busied herself with her new toy, Hunahpu and Lucio retreated to the Gomez orchard. They swung on two hammocks and updated each other on events, their conversation hidden behind the cover of fruit-bearing banana trees. Lucio, to Hunahpu's surprise, as it was not in the shaman's character, was furious at him for bringing the kidnapped conservationist to Nuevo San Felipé. The navy, Lacandón lackeys, Paz y Justicia and the Cardenistas had all visited the village in the last two days. 'Half of the Mexican army and every pistolero available are hunting for her,' he despaired. If they were to return and find her, Lucio warned, shoving tobacco into his pipe and kicking out at a curious cockerel by his feet, they would burn down the village and imprison every one of its residents.

Hunahpu leant forward on his hammock. He told Lucio about the crowbar, the beating that she had received and the anarchists' plan to force her to sign the confession. If he hadn't taken her away, he argued, Horatio's patrol of Zapatistas would have had a potential murder on their hands. There was no alternative but to escape. 'If she is killed,' he said, taking a turn at kicking out at the cockerel, 'then every Zapatista-sympathizing community would be razed to the ground, not just San Felipé.' Because of her injuries, he thought of more excuses, it would have been wrong to have allowed her to walk home by herself. And, he paused, there were other things to consider, like her uses and his hunch. There was no disaster in the making. That he promised.

'So that's what it's all about,' Lucio said, as he shook his head. Pipe smoke passed through his grin. 'You brought her here because you like her!'

'Come on,' Hunahpu said, as he scratched his knitted scalp, 'I want her to experience life here, that's all, to learn what I learnt and witness the reality for herself. Let her see that we are not the ones cutting down the forest, that the evictions are based on politics, making money off ancestral land, and not for reasons of conservation.' He put his hand on Lucio's shoulder. 'If we give her a chance, Lucio, she might even become a well-placed ally of ours.'

'And what does she say about this enforced stay of hers? Or, like those English anarchists, did you not give her any choice?'

'I told her that she can go whenever she wants; that we would provide her with a guide and transportation to the road to San Quintín.' He paused. 'She seemed OK with it.'

'Well, she's here now, so, if we're going to convert her, we'd best make her stay a pleasant one. But she goes in two days' time, whether she is fully fit or not. It is too dangerous having her stay here.'

'We should also keep her true identity to ourselves. I know that no one in the village will harm her, but we can't risk word of her arrival leaking to the authorities. For that reason, I suggest we introduce her as a peace observer, one of my contacts in the international media. To everyone, including the council.'

'But . . .'

'No buts Lucio. I assure you it is safer for everyone if they don't know who she really is. And you must tell Maria to keep quiet as well.'

Lucio choked on his pipe.

'OK.' Hunahpu smiled. 'You'd better leave Maria to me.'

Laughing, one more than the other, the two men stood up from their hammocks and they left the orchard. The cockerel returned and ruffled its feathers. Outside the closed door to the Gomez home, Hunahpu's hand on a wood-carved latch, Lucio tugged on his son's shirt.

'What now?' Hunahpu asked.

'Don't you think it's about time that you took that revolting thing off?'

Hunahpu looked up at the mask above his eyes.

'Look,' Lucio continued, 'take it from a wise old shaman and freshen yourself up before you go inside. You might have a little more luck if you take that mask off.'

'Luck with what, old shaman?'

'You know what I mean, wooden man.'

The latch clicked and the door slowly opened. The women inside screamed.

'Get out!' Maria shouted at the opening door. 'Get out!' She cloaked a buttoning-up Rachel with her spanned girth, her apron raised up as if it was a magician's blanket. Lucio shut the door and backed off.

'OK,' she called out, a minute later, 'you can come on in now.'

His hand on the door latch, Hunahpu hesitated. Feeling naked without his mask, nervous about what she might say, he patted down his black hair with his other hand.

'What are you waiting for?' Lucio asked, standing behind him.

Hunahpu took a few breaths before he unlatched the door. Lucio pushed him forward and the door opened.

Maria stepped to one side. Hunahpu remained in the doorway, the orange glow of the early evening sun silhouetting him as he looked up from the ground. Lucio brushed past him and sat down at the end of the bed, beside an excited-looking Maria. In the warm light Hunahpu saw Rachel standing in the middle of the room. She wore a white cotton dress, its neckline embroidered with red and black animal motifs, and she dazzled in the sunlight. He bravely turned his attention to her head. His fingers twitching by his sides, he observed her platted hair, the Tzotzil Mayan tail that rested on her shoulders. Seeing her stare back at him, he looked back down at the floor. She did the same.

'Well?' Maria spoke first. 'Doesn't she look better without those dirty clothes? If she weren't so tall, she'd be a certain winner of the title of "Queen of San Felipé". Don't you think so? Hunahpu?'

He raised his look off the mud-floor to chance another glimpse of her. Stunned by her standing in the shaft of golden light, which tanned her fair skin bronze, she was incontestably beautiful. She was the most beautiful woman he had ever set eyes upon. He looked back down at the mud-floor.

'Yes,' he said to his polished boots, 'she looks beautiful.'

Rachel stood rigid as her eyes adjusted to the sunshine and the figure in the doorway. The halo of light enveloped him from head to toe, his cheekbones tinged with flashes of gold. Squinting at his shadowed face, she made out his nose and chin, the laughter lines to the sides of his mouth, the frown lines above his eyebrows. She then caught his more familiar green eyes. Seeing him look back at her, she looked to her side, at Maria and Lucio on the bed and under the cross. Her Mayan hosts smiled back at her and she nervously did the same. She risked another look at him. He moved further into the hut and she saw him in his civilian clothes, his black trousers and loose white shirt, his rolled-up sleeves revealing his tanned and muscular forearms. Her eyes drifted back up to his unmasked face. The dying sun picked out his wavy black hair, the soft wrinkles on his skin, the secret that he had wanted to keep from her. She looked into his eyes, her reflection sparkling in his pupils. 'No scars,' she thought to herself.

'It must feel good to have that mask off,' she said, not knowing what else to say. His height had always indicated to her that he wasn't indigenous, and yet that in itself wasn't a big deal to her when he was covered up. Now that he was stripped of his mask and black Zapatista uniform he looked almost other-worldly. The removal of the mask had increased rather than diminished his mystery. She wondered what in hell had brought him to the Selva, made him give up his life to be a Mayan Zapatista.

'Yes,' he replied, her Mayan makeover keeping him still. 'It's in the wash.' He felt so wooden, so lost for words, nervous even. Yet inside he was so alive. As he observed her in the darkened room of the hut, the sun beaming down on her, she seemed to control his rate of breathing. Having never experienced such feelings before, he looked anxiously at Lucio. His father nodded at him and he relaxed a little more. Facing her again, it was as if she was the final stage of his creation, his awakened sense of being ready for her. Not knowing quite what to do about it, it both excited and scared him. He desperately wanted to know what she was thinking, now that he was free of his mask.

'Oh,' she said, as she tried to put a meaning behind every flash of his eyes, twitch of his mouth and frown on his forehead. Touching the back of her neck, the pain removed by the Santa Maria, she felt her platted hair on the back of her hand. She then looked down at the dress that she wore. She began to think that he disapproved, that perhaps he felt she was intruding too much on his life there. 'Do you like?' she asked him, pointing at herself in Mayan clothes. She touched the pink ribbons tied to the end of her platted tail.

'Yes,' he said, watching her hands move through her hair, Maria's ribbons fall through her fingers, 'yes, I do.' He rubbed his chin, touched his skin free of wool and stubble. Feeling exposed again, he pointed a finger at his face. 'Do you like?'

'It's OK.' She bowed her head, hiding her smile.

256

Reading the situation, Maria stood up from her seat on the bed. She pulled Lucio up with her. 'We'll go ahead and help with the setting up of the party,' she said, squeezing herself and Lucio out of the doorway. Her beefy body eclipsed the sunlight that poured into the room.

'We'll come with you,' Hunahpu said, quickly turning around to look at Lucio and Maria. His face pleaded with them not to go.

'No, no,' Maria replied, shuffling her sandalled feet backwards, 'you two take your time. There's no need for all of us to go. We'll see you up there, when the party gets going.' She pushed her husband out of the door, grabbing him by his backpack. In Tzotzil she told him to 'leave them in peace'. Lucio took another look at the señorita before Maria closed the door to the hut.

With the door closed, the sunlight restricted to the hut's small windows, Hunahpu and Rachel were left in silence. They both looked around the hut, at the stove, the herbs hanging from the beams, the bed, the cross, anything and everything except each other. A few minutes of this had passed before Hunahpu finally said something.

'I hope . . .'

'Do you,' Rachel unintentionally interrupted him. 'I'm sorry. You go first.'

'It was nothing, really.' He looked out of the window, through the wire mesh nailed to a wooden frame. Outside Maria and Lucio disappeared round a bend in the dirt track. 'I hope Maria went easy on you,' he said, turning to look at her.

'What?' Now that he wasn't silhouetted she could see him far better. 'Oh yes,' she said, 'we had a good chat. She's quite a woman.' The setting sun in the window glinted in his eyes. 'She speaks very highly of you.'

There was another lengthy pause.

'You were going to say something,' he said. Her white dress was reddened by the sun. 'Do I what?'

'Oh,' she said, trying to remember what she was going to say. 'I just don't want to be in your way. I mean, perhaps, thinking about it, I shouldn't come along to this thing tonight.'

'What?'

She caught him frowning at her.

'I mean, it's not like I'll fit in,' she said, looking down at the embroidered creatures on the neckline of her dress.

'You'll be fine.' He held her bare arm while he looked into her

257

eyes. 'You have nothing to fear.' Under his fingertips he could feel her pulse rate quicken, it synchronized to his own pulse. He let go of her and stared out of the window at the fiery oranges and pinks in the sky outside. As he released her she watched his hand fall to his side. The dying sun splashed red onto the scar on his wrist. He turned his back on her and opened the door to the hut.

'Maria told me about their little boy,' she said to his back, the brilliance of the fiery sky entering the hut. He turned round.

'It was hard for them,' he said, his face in shadow again. 'It still is.'

Unable to see his face, attempt to read his thoughts, Rachel followed him out of the hut and onto the dirt road. The hut's door closed behind her and the latch clicked shut. Her limp was still there and he gave her his arm to hold. She subtly tried to look at his face, see him under the light of the sky, but he kept his face firmly fixed on the way ahead. They slowly walked up the dirt road and towards the music, the sound of trumpets and drums, which carried through the trees. Rachel looked around her as they passed the turquoise church, the simply constructed huts, the orchards and flowers under the trees. There was no one around and she assumed that the entire village was at the party. The music growing louder as they passed the Zapatista murals on the assembly hall, she grew increasingly anxious about the reception she would receive.

'What were they like to you,' she asked him, looking away from the painted faces that stared at her through ski masks, 'when you first met them?'

'What?' His face still stared ahead.

'The Zapatistas. Did they treat you well when . . .'

He stopped walking and faced her. His green eyes turned red under the sky. She loosened her grip on his arm.

'This war might be silent to the outside world,' he said, staring at her, 'denied by governments who are eager to steal the land from its people, but there are many more Marias and Lucios in Chiapas.' He briefly looked up at the sky, the moon appearing behind streaky red clouds, and took a breath before he faced her again. 'Did Maria tell you that, in the same year they left San Felipé for Montes Azules, twenty-one unarmed Tzotzil women, fifteen children and nine men were killed in the neighbouring village of Acteal?'

Rachel looked down at her feet and shook her head. The pain

in his voice stirred a mix of emotions within her. At one and the same time she felt ashamed, scared and upset. She had to swallow to stop herself from crying.

'No?' he continued, lowering his voice when he saw her lip trembling. 'Like the Gomez, they were abejas, peaceful people who refused to join the paramilitaries and fight civilian Zapatistas. They were praying for peace in a church when the paramilitaries arrived. They were shot in the back as they knelt before an altar.' He reached out for her arm. She wiped her eyes before she looked up at him. 'These people, these squatters as you call them, won't hurt you.'

'I'm sorry if I upset you,' she said, looking into his sad eyes. 'I didn't mean to insult them or doubt you.'

'Come on. We should be helping the others.'

She gripped his arm and they walked towards the party. Neither of them said anything else.

The forest in darkness, an orange glow hung over the bustle in the clearing of Nuevo San Felipé. Flaming torches were placed around the perimeter of the basketball court, while Maya marimba, pumping punta-rock and coupling Cumbia music blared out of an amp's speakers. Campesinos danced and mingled under the bunting that hung from the trees, the bongo drums, accordion, guitars and trumpets rocking the rainforest. Tables of food were arranged at one end of the court, cauldrons of stew and broth beside wicker baskets of barbecued maize, warmed tortillas, roast squashes and bowls of rice and beans. A crowd of smartly dressed Tzotziles tucked into the steaming spread. The women wore white sleeveless blouses, with red embroidery round their necks, while the men wore white smocks and trousers, the latter rolled up to their knees. Dogs, chickens and children darted through the dancers, chasing a football around the court and ignoring grown-up pleas to stop.

At the queue to the drinks' stand, a barrel and a ladle on an upturned igloo, Hunahpu passed plastic cups of fresh orange juice to Rachel, Maria and Lucio. When he had finished pouring a cup for himself, they guarded their drinks with their elbows, defended themselves against a rhythmic mass of japes and jumps, and moved into what little space there was. The whole village, all of twenty families, was out tonight. In addition to Maria Gomez's birthday, it was also the carnival of 'Crazy Days'. Maria explained to Rachel what the carnival meant. 'Men and women may couple with whomever they wish,' she said, unsubtly glancing at Hunahpu, 'without fear of reprisal or punishment.'

Feeling awkward and totally out of place, Rachel took a sip of her juice and hid behind her cup.

'Do they not drink alcohol here?' she whispered in English to Hunahpu.

'Not any more,' he whispered back in Spanish, 'it's forbidden.' He pointed at a sign behind the barrel of orange juice, a laminated piece of card nailed to a tree and above separate bins for organic and inorganic trash:

NUEVO SAN FELIPÉ, ZAPATISTA COMMUNITY:
INTRODUCTION OF ALCOHOLIC BEVERAGES, DRUGS,
AND OTHER ILLICIT ITEMS PROHIBITED.

'Is that a religious thing?' she asked in Spanish, following his lead.

'No. The women had enough of their husbands crawling back home drunk and being asses. It was outlawed.'

'Really?' She smiled at him. 'Female empowerment, I like.'

'The women are very active in Zapatismo. There are many commandantas.'

'Yeah? They do say that women are the stronger sex.'

'Maybe they say that in your science. Remember that I don't see things quite as clear-cut as you.'

'A tipple of posh is allowed,' Maria said, struggling to eavesdrop on their quick-fire Spanish and a few sentences behind. 'There's no harm in moderation. Especially not with posh. Would you like to try some, señorita?' Out of the folds of her blouse Maria revealed a Thermos flask.

'Thank you,' Rachel said, watching Maria fill her cup with a cloudy liquid. Hunahpu finished his juice and passed Maria his cup. Lucio did the same.

'To Maria,' Hunahpu said, putting his arm round her broad shoulders, 'happy birthday.' They chinked their flimsy plastic cups and drank to the evening's celebration.

'To the carnival of the Crazy Day,' Maria said, grinning at Rachel, 'when anything can happen.'

'To a Crazy Day,' Hunahpu added. He glanced at Rachel.

They finished their portions of posh. Maria took Rachel's hand and led her to the dancing, splitting them up from the men. Rachel's protest, her bruised ankle, was not good enough for her Tzotzil dance coach. She could, 'by Xibalba', Maria insisted, at least clap her hands and wiggle her hips. Rachel looked for assistance from Hunahpu, but he was already busy chatting to a crowd of men and women. They were laughing and she wondered if she was the source of their jokes.

'My husband tells me that you save bats.' Maria raised her voice above the grind of an accordion, live music having replaced the amp and speakers. In synch with the other women and to the beat of a bongo drum, they clapped their hands together.

'Yes,' Rachel said, nervously looking around her, watching the men and women kicking up their legs and flicking belts into the air. It surprised her that she was receiving such little attention from the other villagers. Only on the odd occasion did she catch someone staring at her. 'It has been an obsession of mine since I was a child. They are the most misunderstood of all animals.'

Maria pointed at the motifs around her blouse's brocaded neckline. Woven into squares and crisscrossed by red, black and gold thread, was a series of flying and swimming creatures.

'You see what this is?' She pointed at one of the winged animals under her chin. Rachel had to bend down to take a closer look.

'Is that a bat?' Rachel asked. Her face lit up as she studied the images on Maria's blouse.

'Yes, my dear.' Maria nodded. 'The bat is very important to the Tzotziles. The word Tzotzil itself means "place of the bat", and our home is a Tzotzilha, a bat house.' She pointed at the mud-brick homes opposite the basketball court. 'The bat, señorita, protects our people.'

Rachel smiled, little by little relaxing into the place.

'The Spanish tried to steal the bat from us. They say that the conquistadors destroyed a large stone bat in the village of Zinacantún. Now, today, the men of bad government, the Cardenistas and the army, attack our culture and our beliefs.'

'What are these?' Rachel pointed at one of the motifs on her own dress's neckline. The creature had long limbs and a curvy tail.

'That is the monkey. He was created in the second phase of Creation.' Maria paused. She looked in the direction of Hunahpu and Lucio, the crowd of villagers circling them. 'When the men of wood were washed away by a great flood, they were transformed into monkeys and outsiders. The monkey represents death.'

'You mean the bat is good and the monkey is bad?' Rachel was confused.

'No, no.' Maria smiled and shook her head. Her platted hair and ribbons swished from side to side. 'Death for us is both good and bad. As the home of our ancestors, death is the sacred place that contains ancient knowledge. It thus ensures the survival of our people.' She gripped Rachel's arm. 'But the monkey also represents those who attack our communities.' With her other hand she touched her collar again. 'The bats, however, can also symbolize death. Your bats can both give and take away life.'

Rachel looked down at the callused hands on her arms. She thought of the woman's murdered little boy, and what Hunahpu had said to her on the walk to the carnival.

'Your world is difficult for me to understand,' Rachel said, feeling Maria's grip on her arm tightening, 'where I come from we see things in opposites: humans and nature, man and woman, black and white, good and evil.' She looked out over the dancing, through the crowd clapping their hands, and saw Hunahpu watching her. He turned away when he saw that she had spotted him, resuming his conversation with Lucio. She faced Maria again. 'We like to classify things into groups.' She paused as she thought about what had brought him there. 'Hence there is always conflict.'

'Our worlds are one and the same.' Maria moved her grip from Rachel's arms to her hands. 'We share the same air, mountains, forests and seas. You still have much to learn here, señorita.'

Their hands clasped together, the dancing around them wound down. The accordionist, an elderly man hidden beneath a frayed hat and a curly moustache, stopped for a rest and refreshment. Maria and Rachel joined Hunahpu and Lucio by the buffet at the end of the basketball court.

'Hi,' Rachel said to Hunahpu, watching him finish off a bowl of stew.

'Hi,' he replied, briefly looking up from his food. While he had watched her with Maria, gazed at her in her white dress, a part of him had wanted to join them. As much as it pleased him to have her there, it also felt strange to him. Lucio had told him to not be so uptight, that he should just go ahead and ask her for a dance, and yet her foreignness confused him. The other villagers had laughed at him when he told them about his concerns, the fact that she was alien to him. It was a reaction that disorientated him further, for it made him question his own identity. Beyond the colour of her skin, however, he undoubtedly recalled something of himself in her. He helped himself to another tortilla and wondered how she felt.

Rachel looked at the cauldrons and the wicker baskets, not knowing if she should help herself. Hunahpu looked up from his bowl and suddenly remembered his manners. He grabbed a bowl for her and recommended the beef.

'I'm so sorry,' he said, while he poured out the stew, 'I was just . . .'

'Don't worry,' she said, smiling. She looked at him, examined his face once again, and found it endearing that he seemed to be less relaxed than she was.

'You must be tired,' he said, as he looked at her in the light of the torches. The flames that surrounded them tinted her black hair orange. 'If you'd like, I can walk you back to Lucio and Maria's. They have kindly given you their bed for a couple of nights. Your transportation back to the research station is all arranged.'

'In two days' time?' She sounded disappointed.

'I tried for tomorrow, but I couldn't find anyone to take you.' He was disappointed by the tone of her voice, her apparent keenness on leaving the village. 'If you go on Sunday, market day, you can catch a lift all the way to Comitán. Maria will go with you. You'll be fine.'

'Thanks.' She was surprised by his indifferent attitude to her leaving. 'But you don't have to make any special arrangements for me. And I can't possibly kick Maria and Lucio out of their home.'

'Really, it's no problem.' Hunahpu turned to look at the two Gomez, who were squashed in the crowd and queuing for food. Maria talked to a small girl with red ribbons in her hair and Lucio sipped his juice. He faced Rachel and smiled. 'But, if it's OK with you, I should like to tell them what you said. About not kicking them out of their home.'

Her eyes panned the party under the palm and ceiba trees, the kids dancing.

'Yes,' she said, looking at him and also smiling, 'I should like you to tell them.'

They took their time as they looked into each other's eyes. He took her hand, using her sprained ankle as an excuse, and they walked towards Lucio and Maria to say their goodnights. Her fingers touched the scar on his wrist, a story that she had yet to be told. Burning up with curiosity about him, she held on to him more than was necessary, her sprained ankle not that bad, while he held her closer than village rules would normally permit. It was a 'Crazy Day', he excused them both in his mind.

Despite Maria's insistence that they stay a little while longer, to dance, Hunahpu walked Rachel back to the Gomez's home. They said nothing as they trudged and limped down the dirt road. Their thoughts were busy, while the stars and their associated stories, in the clear sky above them, too vivid and too vocal for mere mortal's speech. Once inside the hut, he lit a candle and a pungent mosquito coil, gave her a fresh cotton sheet and checked that her water bottle was full. If she needed him, he said, tucking the sheet into the mattress of blankets and passing her some more arnica tablets, he would be just outside, in one of the hammocks in the orchard. She just had to shout and he would be there for her.

He was about to leave, his fingers already on the door latch, when she asked if he had picked up her rucksack from the cave. It was under the bed, he pointed to the straps that stuck out from under the wooden slats. She thanked him for his thoughtfulness.

'Don't be late,' he said, as he watched her lean over and reach out for her belongings, her hand dropping down to the mud-floor, 'we have an early start tomorrow. There are errands for us to run.'

'I won't,' she said, waiting for him to go before she opened the rucksack. 'Goodnight.'

He waited for a moment in the open doorway. Both of them wanted to say something. Instead there was silence, as they tried to think of what the other was feeling.

'Goodnight,' he said. He smiled, nodded and walked outside. He missed her smile back.

The latch clicked and his footsteps disappeared around the back of the hut. When she could hear only the crickets, the Cumbia music and the laughter in the distance, the party up the dirt road, she opened her rucksack and rummaged through its contents. She arranged her sketchbook and pencil on a pillow and blew out the candle. Using her torch under the cover of the blanket, she set to work, listening out for eavesdroppers as her pencil scribbled on paper.

Nineteen

Ofelia crawled along the forest floor. Her white smock was muddied and the sun beat down on her through the branches. Sweat trickled down her forehead as she searched the ground for footprints, hoof prints and any other signs left by the señorita and the evil Lokin. Sifting through dead leaves, moss and twigs, soldier ants had bitten her hands and thorns had cut her skin. She winced at the pain as she wiped the sweat away from her eyes.

Commandant Hernandez watched the Lacandón girl from the banks of the stream. The butt of his rifle was tucked into his shoulder and its barrel rested on his protruding belly. He spat into the stream and shook his head at her. They had lost the trail of hoof prints and he was growing increasingly impatient. Knowing where Hunahpu had gone, that the criminal would obviously run to the shaman, he wanted to strike now. Lighting up a cigarette, he couldn't see there being a problem if they were wrong, if they burnt down an illegal squat and rounded up the terrorists within.

Decker and six Cardenista paramilitaries were a little further up the stream. The American agent had taken off his beige suit and changed into black combat pants and a black T-shirt, the same uniform as the others. He ordered the Cardenistas to move back from the stream, to make sure that the hostage taker hadn't changed tack and taken one of the overgrown logger's tracks. After the rains of two days ago the stream was full. It seemed implausible to him that Hunahpu would have done the entire journey in water. He walked over to Commandant Hernandez and past an anxious looking Guillermo, who was taking a quick break from his machete duties and peeling a hard-shelled fruit.

Moving towards a large palm tree, Ofelia spotted a small white triangle sticking out of the moist leaves. She scurried over to it and pulled a piece of paper out of the mud. The red-inked handwriting was badly smudged, the English words almost illegible, and yet she recognized that it was the same note that they had found by the bat nets. Her heart beating hard, she waved the paper above her head and cried out for her father. Guillermo dropped his machete and ran towards her. Commandant Hernandez and Decker quickly followed, the former bounding his weight through the bush.

Commandant Hernandez snatched the note out of Guillermo's hands. The wet paper almost tore in half. He couldn't read English and so he reluctantly passed it to Decker, handing it over to him as if it was worthless. Ofelia hid her face behind her father's legs, peering out over his machete's leather scabbard. She stared up at the rotund paramilitary.

'It's the note we found,' Guillermo said to Decker, while he reassuringly patted his daughter's head. 'It was pinned to the palm tree, where we caught the bats that night. The señorita had put it in her pocket.'

Decker brushed the dirt off the paper and read what he could of the warning note. 'The poor girl,' he said, folding up the paper and handing it back to Commandant Hernandez. He nodded and Commandant Hernandez grinned back. Decker turned away from him and yearned for professionals, a straightforward mission with straightforward personnel. The Cardenistas, or more particularly their overweight leader, didn't seem to care much for Rachel Rees' welfare. Sebastian Townsend, the calm and intelligent recruit he had signed up in London, was also concerning him. In their last phone call the anarchist had said something about a crowbar and a confession; the man even spoke of the insects, as if they were colluding against him. He walked back to the stream, pushing back the branches in the way with more force than was necessary.

'Get back to work,' Commandant Hernandez shouted at Ofelia, putting the note in his pocket. He shoved Guillermo back towards the trees. 'Find out which direction the son of a bitch was taking her.' He followed Decker and walked back to the stream's banks.

Guillermo stared at the man's large back, cursing him under his breath as he wiped the sweat off his face with his bandana. Ofelia ran back up to her father and hugged him round his waist. Tears ran down her cheeks. In the language of the Lacandón Maya, their words secure from the others, he told her it would be all right.

'Maybe she left that note,' Decker said to Commandant Hernandez, his face looking concerned as he surveyed the stream, 'to help us find her.' Despite his experience, the horrors he had

266

witnessed, the butchers he had to deal with in places like Guatemala, their bait in this instance was a young American woman. Things were spiralling out of control and he was beginning to feel sick at having a hand in it. If anything was to happen to her, he alone would take the rap; the order for Sebastian Townsend to capture the conservationist came from him. His buddies in Langley would hang him out to dry, deny that he worked for the CIA and send him down for a few years to shut him up. While he thought of the consequences of failure, an injured or dead hostage, the sound of machetes cutting and smashing through bush resumed. He looked over his shoulder and watched the six Cardenistas and two Lacandóns scour the forest for more signs. It would be the last time he accepted one of these missions.

'Smart for a woman, eh?' Commandant Hernandez snorted. It frustrated him that Decker seemed overly concerned with the conservationist. He felt patronized by the American, as if the safety of a white woman was taking precedence over him and his compatriots. For years he had to put up with Hunahpu's interference, his peace observers and reports to the media, the whingeing that he would do on behalf of his Indian friends. The foreigner had humiliated him, made him look weak and treated him like a fool in front of his men. Decker's evidence-gathering, the set-up with the conservationist and the three English anarchists, was now beginning to seem like a waste of time. He spat onto the barrel of his rifle and polished the metal with the folds of his T-shirt.

They found no more signs where the note had been left. The heat, bugs and Commandant Hernandez's impatience were wearing Decker down. He sent the patrol down the stream on a south-easterly course, the route having the advantage of taking them nearer to the squatters, their likely destination. Wading in water, the day growing hotter and him more irritable, he once again thought of the other set of amateurs he had to deal with, the anarchists he had recruited in a dingy London squat. Vengeance was a weakness that he could easily exploit, especially if it involved a loved one paralysed from head to toe, and yet Sebastian Townsend's condition continued to worry him.

They had not gone more than a mile, when Ofelia, who was rummaging about amongst the bushes on the banks, called out.

'More paper,' Ofelia shouted out into the trees that surrounded her. 'More paper.' She picked up a piece of tissue by her plastic boots.

Decker, Commandant Hernandez and the six Cardenistas ran towards the girl. Leaves rustled and branches moved about, as if the forest was aggrieved and was trying to hinder their passage towards the young girl's screams.

Guillermo was already beside his daughter when they arrived. The smile of a proud father disappeared as soon as he saw Commandant Hernandez's face, the look of disdain that he showed towards his hard working and scared daughter. Ofelia held onto his leg as her other hand dangled the tissue at Decker.

'There's no writing on it,' Decker said, turning over the tissue to check its other side. 'It isn't necessarily a sign. It could belong to anyone.' He looked forlornly upwards at the patches of blue sky between spiky branches, his concern for Rachel now a priority. 'We must assume that he has taken her to Nuevo San Felipé.' He looked at his watch to see how many more hours of daylight they had. The sun would be gone in a few hours. 'We should head back to San Quintín and gather some more men. I'll call the others and let them know what we are doing.'

Commandant Hernandez's broad smile revealed his tobacco-stained teeth. They were the words that he had eagerly been waiting for. As he watched Decker amble off, hack his way back to the stream, he caught Guillermo staring at him.

'What are you looking at, Indian?' Commandant Hernandez asked the Lacandón man.

Guillermo ignored him and whispered into his daughter's ear. Ofelia let go of his leg and ran off into the trees. Before she disappeared she looked back towards her father and the Commandant. Her face was riddled with fear. Guillermo nodded and smiled at her. She was then lost behind vines, leaves and twisted tree trunks.

'I said, Indian, what are you looking at?' Commandant Hernandez repeated, with even more contempt. He squinted at Guillermo and raised his rifle further into his sweaty shoulder.

Guillermo turned away from the spot where Ofelia had gone. His smile had dropped and his dark brown eyes stared at the Commandant of the Cardenistas. He placed his hand near the handle of his machete, which was in its leather scabbard, while he looked at the man before him. Examining his pot belly, hoggish face and shaved head, the pricks of bristly hair that ran all the way down to the man's back, he tried to hide the fear that made his body stiff.

'You tell me,' Guillermo said, standing his ground. 'What indigenous ancestry do you have? Is it Mayan?'

'How dare you.' The Commandant's rifle shook in his hands.

'Was it your mother or father? Or is the Indian blood in you much older, Commandant Hernandez?'

The butt of Commandant Hernandez's rifle sent Guillermo flying to the ground. Blood trickled out of his mouth as he watched the paramilitary storm away from him. He wiped away the blood with his hand and smiled.

Back at the stream, Decker was finding it difficult to receive a signal for his mobile phone. Forced to wade out into the middle of the stream, to move away from the obstructive trees, he was finally able to call Bruce. He instructed him to fly the chopper slightly to the south of them, to observe what was happening in the squatter communities.

'I want you to look out for Zapatista troops,' he instructed the pilot. Bruce sounded panicky and Decker had to calm him down, reassure him that the Zapatistas wouldn't try to take a pot shot at him. He then made another call.

'Your job's done,' he said to Sebastian Townsend, 'he's taking her to where we want him.' There was shouting down the other end of the phone. 'Calm down, pull yourself together, Callaghan will be brought to justice. You have my word on that.' The shouting was becoming more hysterical. 'For Christ's sake,' Decker raised his voice, 'sort yourself out, go home and look after that girl of yours. The money will be with you when you get back to the UK.' He ended the call, shook his head and used a vine to climb out of the stream.

Although Maria's medication had alleviated the pain in both her ankle and her neck, Rachel declined the invitation to join Hunahpu for a cool swim in the jade-green pool. Their chore of the day, he had told her over a breakfast of refried beans, tortillas and scrambled eggs, was to collect drinking water from the falls to the north of the village, a task that would take up the best part of the day. Itzamna was saddled and two large empty containers, former gasoline carriers, were tied together by vine-rope and fastened to the mule's haunches. With Rachel clinging on to Hunahpu's back, they trotted through a dawn rush hour of Tzotzil women, men and children. The bat people's faces peered up at them from beneath bulging maize sacks, boxes of fruit and floppy straw hats. Apart from the bunting, which hung in the morning mist that vaporized off the trees, there was no trace of the 'Crazy Day' party in the basketball court. The overnight clean-up had been meticulous. At the village gates the masked guardsman saluted them both and raised the barbed barrier. They passed underneath the rebel's welcome sign and went down a path cut into the forest. It took them over three hours to reach the falls, the temperature rising with the sun, and low branches and vines whipped the flies off their faces.

'Come on in,' Hunahpu called out to her from the middle of the pool. His voice was drowned out by the falls behind him, the water which cascaded down a small cliff face of volcanic boulders and twinkling green moss.

On the bank of the pool, sharing a palm tree's shade with Itzamna and too far away to hear him, Rachel waved at him and returned to the work in her sketchbook.

The plastic containers were positioned under the fall to fill up with water. It was, he had explained to her, the water washing over his scarred wrists, less polluted than the pool. 'You don't know what you might be drinking from down there,' he had said, pointing at a line of bubbles on the pool's surface, the trapped air strung together as if it was a string of pearls. He unbuttoned his shirt, removed his boots and placed his watch in his tatty leather bag. She flinched at the splash created by his diving, half-naked body. Rather than risk the effects of water on white cotton, and in spite of a longing to cool down, she chose to watch him from the safety of the bank.

Keeping an eye on her under the palm tree, Hunahpu swam to the pool's edge. He pushed the palms of his hands down on a ledge of rock, sprung out of the water and walked up to her and Itzamna. Sitting cross-legged and on a red and black zigzagged blanket, engrossed in her sketchbook and deafened by the noise of the falls, she neither saw nor heard his approach.

'Hey,' he said, ten yards from her, his bare feet undisturbed by the sharp and biting objects on the forest floor, 'what are you doing?'

Dropping her pencil into her lap, losing it to the folds of her white dress, she threw the sketchbook on her rucksack and moved her belongings closer to her.

'Not much.' She picked up the pencil. Her blush deepened as she looked up at the man dripping in front of her. 'Just trying to keep cool in the shade.' She fanned her face with her hand and, moving up from his wet chest, she saw those accusative eyes of his, the look that he had given her when he had worn the mask. 'What's up?'

'What's in your notebook?' He pointed at the sketchbook on the rucksack.

'None of your business.' She reached for the sketchbook and held it guiltily to her chest.

'And I suppose that what you were doing last night was also not my business?'

'What are you talking about? Have you been spying on me?' She stood up, her fragile ankle making her wobble in her ascent. Her hands veered dangerously close to his firm and yet slippery chest. She resisted grabbing on to him.

'You haven't exactly been subtle.' His green eyes were piercing. 'I don't know what you are writing, but hiding under the bedcovers and scribbling secret notes till late in the night isn't helping me to trust you. What is it? Is it a diary of how badly we are treating you?'

'You're crazy.'

'I thought you had changed.' He looked away from her, towards the falls, his mind at odds with his heart. He began to question everything. It was like she had healed old wounds only to create new ones.

'Change? I haven't changed.' It hurt her to see him like this. She wanted to know what had happened to him, what it was that made him so doubting, so untrusting.

'Did you learn nothing yesterday? Was it all an act? If anything happens to my family . . .'

'What are you on?'

He snatched the sketchbook out of her hands and, stepping back, dodged her slap. The book fell open in his hands and two loose pages glided to the ground, landing by the pool's edge. He picked them up, his legs faster than hers, and studied the drawings. One of the drawings was of the Gomez home, with Lucio and Maria in the foreground, and the other of him swimming at the bottom of the falls. He wiped away a drop of water off one of his eyebrows. Written in thick pencil and tucked into the bottom right corner of his portrait, he read:

> *H taking a swim during water duties. Not sure what to make of him: he either likes me a little or hates me a lot. I'll miss him when I go.*

'Incriminating enough for you?' She snatched back the sketchbook and drawings off him. 'They might look like crap to you, but the first was done from memory and, an uptight subject not the easiest of things to draw, the second was done in a rush.'

'I never said they were crap. I thought . . .'

'I know what you thought. You thought that I was trying to set you up.' She paused and toed the grass with her boots as if she was about to charge, her platted tail of hair and pink ribbons swinging over her shoulders. 'Sorry to disappoint you and your ego, but I have absolutely no interest whatsoever in you. And I certainly shan't be wanting this anymore.' She scrunched up the sketch of him and threw the paper ball at the pool.

He caught the paper in time and she turned her back on him. Straightening out the drawing and flattening out the creases, he reread, to himself, the bit that she would miss him.

'I'm sorry,' he said to her Tzotzil tail and ribbons. 'You trusted me and I should've trusted you.'

'Too right I trusted you.' She turned round and saw his eyes soften. 'Sometimes you behave just like that moron with the 'Z' tattooed on his neck – a real jerk.'

'I'm sorry. What more can I say?'

There was a pause as they looked at each other.

'I don't even know who you are,' she said, looking into his eyes and then looking away. 'In fact, I don't even know what I'm doing here.' She buried her face in her hands.

He reached out to her, unfurled her clenched fingers and looked at her straight on.

'Do you remember the story about vain old Seven-Macaw,' he asked her, lowering his voice, 'and his defeat by the Hero Twins? When the Big Dipper dips out of the night sky?'

'Yes,' she faltered, hating to have let herself go. A florescent blue dragonfly hovered above her head. She batted the bug away with her sketchbook.

'One of the Hero Twins was called Hunahpu.' He pointed at the zigzagged blanket on the ground and they sat down. 'In the Third Creation,' he continued, looking at the falls, 'after the Creator Couple had washed away the wooden people in a great flood, Hunahpu and his twin, Xbalanke, were summoned to Xibalba by the Lords of Death.'

She studied him while he breathed in hard. There were goose pimples on his wet arms and he was nervously rubbing his wrists.

'The Lords of Death planned to kill the Hero Twins,' he said, feeling his heart beating fast, 'but they underestimated them. Knowing that they were going to die, the Twins prepared for their resurrection in advance and, colluding with two diviners, were burnt to death in the inferno of an oven.'

The dragonfly reappeared, only for it to speed off again and vanish in the direction of the falls. She watched it disappear into a rainbow in the spray.

'Their bones were crushed and the diviners saw to it that the powder was cast into a nearby river. Five days passed and, just as the holy men had predicted, the Twins rose from the waters as fish men.'

Picking the pages of her sketchbook, she looked down at his hands, the scars on his wrists and the sketch of him in the pool. He put her hands in his.

'Dressed as vagabonds,' he whispered, watching her every reaction, 'and blessed with the power to bring people and animals back from the dead, they tricked the Lords of Xibalba into sacrificing themselves, failing to revive them once they were dead. Thus, the Popol Vuh says, the Hero Twins banished the Xibalbans from the Maya world. The stage was set for the Fourth Creation.'

'I'm not following you,' she said. 'You're a frogman hero?'

He turned his face from the falls and smiled at her.

'No.' He shook his head. 'I'm not a hero. I'm one of those wooden idiots, one of those unfeeling monkeys that the Creator Couple flushed away with a great flood. The only thing that I have in common with the Hunahpu of legend, is that I came back from death, was plucked out of a river by a diviner and given a second chance.'

'So you lied to me when you said that you were Mexican. You're a Lokin, like me.'

'Yes,' he paused, 'I'm a foreigner here, like you. I never studied in London – I lived and worked there. I'm English – well, half, my mother was Spanish.'

'What happened to you? What brought you here? And what, for Christ's sake, were you doing in a river?'

'I was trying to run away from my life. After my mother died, there was nothing but loneliness left there. Of all the things to drive me off the edge, it was a stupid business trip, to a Mexican sweatshop, that gave me my chance to escape.' He put down the drawing, leaving the picture of him swimming face-up on the woven lightning bolts, and showed her the faint scar lines on his wrists. 'Lucio found me in one of his sacred pools, its pure water dirtied by my blood, my unconscious body floating amongst his candles, gold cross and husks of incense. He said that it was a miracle that I survived the fall and missed the rocks; that I was delivered to him by the ancestral gods in First-True-Mountain. Maria nursed me back to health and, in the highlands of Chiapas, a place of which I knew nothing about, taken there by fate, I found myself a new family and a new life. I became Hunahpu.'

'You became a Zapatista.' She re-examined the scars on his wrists.

'Although I told Lucio that our meeting was a coincidence, not a miracle of the ancestors, that I was definitely not their reborn hero, I was indebted to him for not only saving my life, but also changing it. I promised them that I would do all I could to help his people. The reports from the frontline that I send to the outside world, distribute to the human rights agencies in San Cristóbal, are my contribution to the resistance.' He thought that he could detect sympathy in her face. 'I was, at least for a bit, paranoid that you might have been writing notes for the other side. I don't want to be responsible for bringing danger to San Felipé. Especially not to Lucio and Maria.'

She moved closer to him, still holding his wrists.

'Do you miss your home back in London?' she asked, her fingers enmeshed with his.

'No, there was nothing left for me there. Here, as part of a community, with my family and friends, is where I now belong.'

'If it's any consolation to you,' she said, smiling, 'I have no wish to cross pencils and pens with either you or your community. Although an idealistic teenager once fancied herself as a female James Bond, she ended up growing into a boring biologist, a geek who specializes in collecting bat poop for a living. No disrespect to the bat, the Tzotzil Earth Lord, but I'm not the CIA.' She winked at him and, their hands still clasped together, he smiled.

274

'And I'm also not much of an artist.' She focused, for a brief moment, on the drawing of him, which was in his other hand, and then returned her gaze to the real him.

'You shouldn't be so critical of your work,' he said, feeling her warmth as his fingers traced a small circle in her palm. 'There was really no need for you to draw in secret from me, especially by hiding under the bedcovers. You have quite a talent, a gift that you should show more of. It sure as hell beats my stab at writing.'

'And like that is something to be proud of.' She grinned, overcame her weak muscles and squeezed his hand. 'I mean, from that corker of a confession, don't you think that you should stick to fiction? Facts are hardly your speciality, are they?'

'Do we really have to go over all that again?' His face pleaded and grimaced, his now visible eyebrows and soft wrinkles doing the talking. 'I wrote nothing but the truth. The only error was in the name of the signatory. In hindsight, Rachel Rees just doesn't sound like your average agent of counterinsurgency. It was a literary mistake of mine. I'm sorry yet again.'

'OK, let's call it quits. We both screwed up. I was also wrong: you are not a fanatical terrorist bent on death and destruction, motivated by decidedly shaky morals.' To change the subject, she flipped open the sketchbook and removed the picture of the Gomez home. She placed the sketch on the rug and lined it up next to the drawing of him. 'Do you think Maria will like it? It's a sort of belated birthday present, a little token for her to remember me by when I leave.'

'She'll love it,' he said, briefly looking at his bare feet, an ant scaling his big toe, 'it's very kind of you. I know that she, all of us, will be sorry to see you go.' The talk of her going made him hesitate. He pointed at the creased drawing of the falls, the picture of him. 'What were you going to do with this one? I mean, before you decided to throw me back into the river?'

'I don't know.' She let go of his hands.

Nothing to say, they looked up at each other, the thunder of the waterfall behind them.

Hunahpu heard the chopper first. The noise reverberated over the trees, the sound of crashing water replaced by the whirring of rotor-blades, the squawks of parrots and the rustle of windblown foliage. He jumped up and helped Rachel to her feet. They picked up the drawings, the rug and their bags, and he pushed them up against Itzamna under the cover of the palm tree's branches.

Looking up through the fronds, their hearts beating together, her head tucked underneath his chin, they saw nothing but a cloudless and chopper-less sky.

'Can you see it?' she asked, pressed up against his chest and with his arms wrapped around her waist.

'No.' He pulled her closer to him.

They waited in silence for the chopper to pass, her breath tickling his neck and his grip warming her hips. The unseen danger, the hidden Huey, kept them like that for a few minutes.

'Did you have a name in your previous life?' she whispered, the sound of rotor-blades disappearing. 'Before you became Hunahpu.'

He looked down from the blue sky and at the woman who held on to him.

'I was called Justin,' he said, his fingers combing her hair back, their noses nearly touching and them breathing the same air, 'my name was Justin Callaghan.'

Twenty

A moonless night blackened out the clustered huts of Nuevo San Felipé. With the exception of a pack of dogs, which explored smoking hearths for charred maize cobs and boiled chicken bones, and a few people dispersing from the assembly hall, the village's high street was deserted. Inside the huts that lined the dark and empty thoroughfare, Tzotzil conversations filtered through mud-brick walls. The banter before bedtime was rendered inaudible by external and more boisterous forest sounds: the buzz of bugs, the movement of leaves and the scampers of rodents and reptiles. Successive days of sun, a prolongation of the dry season, a Mayan ill omen, had turned mud into dust and two cloudy slipstreams followed the footsteps of two men.

Hunahpu and Lucio scuffed their feet on the scorched earth. They stopped outside the turquoise church, their white and dark faces illuminated by a cemetery full of candles, flames flickering in glass pitchers that were stained with colourful portraits of Catholic saints. Ahead of them and neighbouring the church and its candlelit crosses, splinters of amber light pierced the gaps in the walls of the Gomez home. The sound of women's laughter came from inside.

'It's very unlike Horatio to miss a meeting of the council,' Lucio said, patting the head of a dog. 'He has his faults, his crazy ideas, but he always reports to the community council. I don't understand it.' The mongrel licked salt off his wrinkled hand. 'Do you think that the English have something to do with it? Do you think that the patrol is OK?'

'Horatio can look after himself,' Hunahpu said, stroking what hair there was on the dog's bony back. 'Your son is strong. You should have faith in him and trust him more. He knows that he did wrong.'

Lucio sighed and pulled a pouch of folded newspaper and tobacco out of his pocket. Having packed his pipe, he struck

277

a match above its overflowing bowl. A large flame lit up his face and he sucked hard. The smoke went down the wrong way and he coughed, causing the dog to limp away into the shadows. Drawing on the pipe again, Lucio rapidly inhaled and exhaled.

'I have faith in him,' Lucio said, blowing smoke up at the stars, 'I know that he only wants to bring his brother's murderers to justice.' He hesitated slightly, the pain of his loss still strong. 'But it was his fault that we ended up in this mess. If it wasn't for . . .'

'Me?' Hunahpu interrupted, his raised eyebrow caught in the starry twilight of the candlelit cemetery. 'I mean it was probably one of my reports that gave the English the idea to come here. I even provided them with details on the whereabouts of Rachel, where she was catching bats.'

'You can't blame yourself. We mustn't let it stop the publicity over the expulsions. Horatio should never have invited them.' He looked at Hunahpu. 'Still, it's not like I can criticize him for welcoming foreigners.'

'Thanks Lucio. It's nice of you to categorize me with those psychos.' He faced the glinting mud-brick hut.

'You know what I mean.' Lucio sucked on his pipe, thinking about Horatio's absence again. 'We should have heard something from the patrol by now.'

'Look,' Hunahpu said, smiling reassurance to his father, 'the patrol will be fine. I expect Horatio is keeping his distance from us until he is certain that the foreigners have gone, that they're on a plane back to London.'

'Hmm.' Lucio scratched the start of a beard. 'I hope you're right. More importantly, for all of our sakes, let's hope you're right about the conservationist. I still think it was wrong to bring her to San Felipé. We can't be sure that she has switched sides.'

'I trust her.' Hunahpu nodded to himself while he thought of her by the pool, the sketch she had done of him and the way she held onto him. 'I've seen the change that she has undergone. It's not like . . .' he paused, grinning, 'she's the enemy's wooden horse.'

'What?'

'The Greek army used a wooden horse to enter the city of Troy. It's ancient Greek mythology.'

'A wooden horse?' Lucio looked at him as if he was crazy.

'Yes, a wooden horse,' Hunahpu said, enjoying his moment of

teaching his teacher a new myth. 'The Trojans thought it was a gift from the gods and they let it into their walled city, not realizing that their enemies, the Greeks, were inside.' Hunahpu shook his head and smiled. 'But she's a wooden woman, not a wooden horse.'

'Hmm.'

Lucio shaking his head and Hunahpu with a spring in his step, they resumed their walk down the dirt road. The door of the Gomez home sprung open and Maria, who was silhouetted by the orange candlelight in the hut's interior, stepped outside. She marched up to them, the dry ground quaking under her bare feet.

'About time,' she said, looking up at her adopted son and down at her husband, 'you've been gone for a good three hours. I was going to check on you, drag you out of the assembly hall and kick you back home.' Her two targets remained speechless. 'It is, in case you'd forgotten, Rachel's last night. It's not the sort of manners I expect, from either of you.'

'There was much to be discussed,' Lucio struggled to respond, his body crushed by a hug.

'Excuses, excuses,' she said, grabbing Hunahpu by his hands, 'and what about you?' She had to stand on her toes to reach his ears. 'I thought, out of all of us, you liked her the most. You certainly took your time at the waterfall today.'

'Please, Maria,' Hunahpu replied, as he took the strain of her tug, his feet dragged towards the hut's entrance, 'it sounded, from outside anyway, like you were getting on fine without us.'

'We shared a few laughs.'

'I dread to think what about,' Lucio said under his smoky breath.

'What was that Lucio? You can speak up if you have something worthwhile to say.'

'Nothing,' Lucio replied, sucking on his pipe again.

'Well, if it's nothing, my dear husband, I think it's perhaps time we got ourselves ready for bed and left the youngsters to say their goodnights. Don't you?'

With her arms spread apart, she pushed Hunahpu in one direction, into the hut, and her husband in another direction, into the banana tree orchard. Steered by her palm pressed against his back, Lucio was herded round the rear of the building and towards separate hammocks, his bumbling goodnights lost to the night and the cackling crickets.

279

'Goodnight,' Hunahpu and Rachel called out from inside the hut. The door latch clicked shut.

'How . . .' Hunahpu paused as he moved away from the door. The sight in front of him, beyond two altar candles on the floor and under the gold-painted cross on the wall, caught his tongue.

Rachel was perched on the edge of the slatted bed. Her legs were crossed casually and she was in a new white dress, embroidered bats going round the dress's red and black neckline. Yet it was her face, the ski mask that she wore, that kept him still and silent. Her brown eyes, which were seen and seeing through the letterbox-shaped slit, flashed and flickered with the flames of the candles. She smiled at him through the mask's mouth hole. He just stared back at her.

'I hope you don't mind,' she said, feeling uneasy by the way he looked at her. Her smile rapidly disappeared. It concerned her that she may have offended him by trying on his mask. It was not as if it was even her suggestion. 'Maria told me to try it on,' she blustered. 'We were just playing around.' Her fingers stroked her covered cheeks.

'What?' he asked, her appearance keeping him in shock. Her windowed eyes, the snippets of her covered charms, stayed with him as he blinked in the candlelight. He didn't know how to react towards this difference in her. Combined with the Tzotzil dress and her plaited tail of hair and ribbons, the mask had changed her, or rather it had changed his perception of her. It was only her eyes, those mahogany-coloured irises of hers, the spirit of her accentuated by the mask, which gave her away. He continued to stare at the masked angel who sat on the bed, on the zigzagged blanket and under the gold-painted cross nailed to the wall.

Rachel took off the mask, regretting that she had ever put it on. She placed it on the bed and shook her freed hair.

'Definitely better with it off,' he said, trying to make light of his reaction towards her, not wanting to make a big deal out of it. He was saddened by the thought of her leaving.

'Sure.' It irked her that she had felt guilty for trying the mask on.

The sound of dogs barking outside filled up the silence between them. They blocked out the noise, looking at one another.

'It's good to see you fitting in here,' he said, the dogs going quiet. 'You've done well.'

'What?' she replied, slightly annoyed that he was treating her stay as some sort of test.

'I mean . . .' he paused, smiling at her, 'I'm pleased that you now realize you were wrong about the villagers and the Zapatistas. It's good to see this change in you.'

'I was never wrong,' she said, standing up from the bed, now actually angry with him, 'I haven't changed.' Her reaction made him take a step back. Gathering up her long dress, to keep it clear from the candles on the floor, she hobbled up to him. 'I never accused anyone of doing anything. I was just gathering the facts, until I was kidnapped by those guests of yours.'

'I didn't mean it like that.' He looked into her wide eyes, then watched her grab the collar of his black shirt as she squared up to him.

Misjudging the rate of her recovery, her ankle pricking her with pain and her feet giving way as a result, she fell onto his chest. Her arms automatically wrapped around his back. Feeling his cool breath on her healed neck, she pushed herself off him and grabbed the low ceiling beam for support. The leaves of Santa Maria shook on a hook and dust, which fell from the palm-thatched ceiling, fizzled on the candles below. She felt his hands and arms wrap around her waist. They both held each other tight.

'It's a little temperamental,' he whispered into her hair, their cheeks touching.

'What?' she whispered back.

'The beam. It needs fixing. Sorry, I should've warned you.'

'Oh, right.'

'I was supposed to help Lucio to mend it. Should've done it this afternoon.'

'Yeah?'

'It's dangerous like that. It just needs a good . . .'

She kissed him quiet.

'Binding or something.' He touched his lip and, her heart beating in time and next to his, he kissed her back.

'I lied,' she said, their lips eventually parting, 'I have changed.'

He read her eyes and, seeing the same face that he saw under the stars of the Wakah-Chan, saw no contradiction to what she said.

'And we, I, in particular, won't be the better for when you're gone. Actually, it couldn't be further from the truth.'

'You seem, so far, to have coped pretty well without me.' She held him tighter, not wanting to let go of him. 'Why would it be any different now? It's not like I've done much. I mean, if anything, I must've been a burden to you, what with me and my injuries.' She pointed to the bruise beneath her pony-tail, and swivelled her lame and bare foot towards his dusty combat boots. He gently stroked the back of her neck.

'Perhaps I've also changed.'

'How do you mean?'

'I don't know.' He looked at the cross on the wall and then at the candles on the floor. 'I guess I thought I had everything here.' He returned to face her. 'Without taking anything away from Lucio, Maria, the village and the Zapatistas, who have given me a purpose to my life, I now realize that there was something missing. It's either that or I've got malaria.' He smiled.

'That's a more likely reason,' she said, as she straightened the red bandana under his chin, 'it's not, after all, like wood to have those sorts of feelings.'

'No. Probably not. But I think you washed the last of the wooden stuff away.'

A dog barked outside and, she kissing him again and him running his hand through her hair, they ignored it. Through the gaps in the timber and mud-brick walls, a breeze sneaked into the hut. The candles on the floor flickered.

'Did you hear something?' he said, looking behind her and checking the closed door.

'It's only a dog. Ignore it.' She pulled his face back to hers and he did as she said. They neither saw nor heard the door latch unclick.

'Get your hands off me,' Rachel screamed at the two masked men. Her hands were whipped behind her back and her wrists were cuffed by wire.

'Leave her alone,' Justin groaned on the dirt floor. The candles were knocked over and extinguished. Pools of wax hardened around his felled body and a torch shone down on his bloody face. On the bed above his head, shaken off its nail on the wall and beside his ski mask, the gold cross sparkled on the zigzagged blanket. His ribs cracked on the impact of another steel-capped kick.

'No,' Rachel shouted, on seeing what they were doing to Justin.

The masked men pulled her back and pushed her towards the hut's doorway.

'Would you shut her up?' Zeb said, cleaning his boot on the back of his black combat pants and flashing the torch from Justin to Rachel. The crowbar swung in his other hand. 'She'll wake the whole fucking village up. This is all about Mr Callaghan here. I don't want to have to hurt anyone else.' Using the tip of the crowbar, he etched a semicircular line into the mud-floor. The curve stopped at Justin's neck.

'Sure Zeb,' Stevo said, taking off his black bandana. With Jamie's help he used the bandana to gag Rachel. He pulled down her Tzotzil tail, the ribbon falling to the floor, and knotted the bandana at the back of her head, over the bruise on her neck. She shook her head from side to side, tried to bite her way free, but they were too strong for her. Looking up at her from the floor, his eyes swollen from the kicks to the head, Justin groaned again.

'Take her back to the Humvee,' Zeb said, looking down at Justin, 'I'm just going to have a chat with this piece of shit.'

Stevo and Jamie dragged her towards the open door. They stepped on the ribbon and kicked a candle out of the way.

'Come on, you,' Stevo said, as he pushed her out of the hut, 'this has nothing to do with you. I don't want to have to hurt you.'

'Take off the gag and cuffs as soon as you can,' Zeb said, still staring at the unmasked Justin, using the torch to examine his bruised features, 'she's been through enough as it is and you can let Decker do the explaining to her. I don't want him to think that we've treated her badly. It might jeopardize things with Tam.'

'Sure Zeb,' Stevo said, while Rachel's bare feet kicked out at his shins. Undisturbed by her floppy kicks, they dragged her up the road, her feet pedalling clouds of dust.

Justin managed to roll his head to face the doorway. He watched her disappear from him.

'What are you going to do with her?' he asked the man who stood above him; the torch continued to blind his eyes. He tried to raise his head off the dirt floor, but his stinging neck kept him down. 'Are there to be more confessions?'

'Very perceptive, Callaghan.' Zeb smiled. 'Right first time. Only I don't give a shit what the conservationist had to say. It's your turn to do the confessing. I want to hear what you have to say.'

'What are you talking about?' Blood trickled out of the corner of his mouth. Dragging his arm off the floor, he mopped his lips on his sleeve. 'And why do you call me Callaghan? My name is Hunahpu.'

'So the fall gave you amnesia, to go neatly with your new identity, did it? Don't bullshit me Callaghan. The Bishopsgate riots of '97 – does that ring any banker bells?'

'What?'

The courier's boot cracked more ribs. Justin clutched his chest and cried out. A scream, a revving engine and panicked shouts, the village waking up to danger, could be heard from outside. Flashlights scanned the hut and, entering through the gaps and cracks in the walls, beams of light striped the black shirts and combat pants of the men inside. Apart from Zeb's ski mask, they were identically dressed.

'How did it feel to hit her? Did it feel good?' Zeb crouched down to take a closer look at him. 'I bet you impressed your mates in the office with that one. A direct hit on a pikey, commie woman. Now that's got to be worth a few bottles of Cristal down at the Club.'

'Hit who? I never hit anyone.' Forced to squint through his bruised eyes, the anarchist's torch shining directly at his black, blue and red face, he saw the crowbar plough the mud-floor by his neck.

'Permanent paralysis in one swipe is quite an achievement.' Zeb stood up and looked away from him. His jaw was tensed and there were tears in his eyes. 'You took her from me in one go.'

'I said that I've never hit anyone. All I remember of the riot is seeing some girl on the road.' Justin paused and gasped for air. While his broken chest stabbed him in the lungs, squeezed his heart, his mind raced through his past, the memories he had tried to forget. 'She was bleeding from the head,' he said to the blurred outline of the anarchist, 'I think it was the police who did it. She looked pretty bad and I was worried about her getting crushed.' He gasped again as he thought back to that time in his life, when he fielded the call from the police in the supermarket, when he was informed of his mother's death. 'I tried to help, but I was pushed away.' He coughed and his body flinched at the resulting pain.

'Don't go fucking me around.' Zeb flicked up the crowbar, his weapon shaking in his hand, his body almost convulsing. 'I know that it was you. I've been told, by good sources, it was you. It all makes perfect sense: when you think the pigs are on to you, you conveniently go missing. You vanished without a trace, fucking disappeared off the face of the earth.' He paused to wipe the tears away from his eyes. The crowbar was now shaking violently in his hand. 'What was the matter? Were you too much of a coward to take responsibility for what you did? Is that what happened? You just pussyfooted it to Mexico to escape from it all?' This time he kicked one of Justin's thighs. 'Was it?' he shouted.

'No.' Justin rocked his head from side to side, his blood-drenched hair painting the floor a glossy red. 'I ran because . . .'

'You ran to evade justice.' The crowbar twitched in Zeb's hand. 'But it's finally caught up with you. I've finally found the cunt who stole her from me.'

'You're wrong.'

'They say that they want you alive, so that they can interrogate you about the Zapatistas. But why should I sell out these good people? I've gone against too many of my principles to catch you. I'll ensure that you go silently to the authorities. It's the least you can do for these people.'

'Please, listen to me.'

'You haven't defended the Maya.' The crowbar slammed down again. Justin winced at the near miss. 'No, you've just given the paramilitaries more reasons to attack them. You've been selfish to the last.'

'You're the one who has endangered them, not me.' Zeb's words hurt him more than his kicks. 'Why would I want to bring danger to my home?'

'You just don't think, do you? I think it's time for you to shut up. I've had it with you and your pathetic, whining lies. You are, if anything, a disappointment. You are a fucking embarrassment: a sad, lonely fugitive, who has sponged a living off these poor people. By taking out their white trash, I'll be doing them a favour.'

The leaves of Santa Maria swayed above Zeb's masked head. Specks of dust fell off the beam and landed on his black lapels. Justin watched the crowbar take off from the ground, feeling the rush of air on his face as it swept upwards. His eyes were shut when metal struck wood.

The dust settled in the hut. Coated in powdery, crushed palm, Justin opened his eyes and blinked away the dirt. Through the hole in the thatched roof he saw the Wakah-Chan sparkle in the sky. He searched for the Big Dipper, Seven-Macaw, but the hole wasn't big enough. With his legs trapped under Zeb and the beam, he was unable to check the stars on the horizon. Extending out his arm and gripping a leg of the bed, the cross and the mask on the slats and blanket above him, he tried to pull himself free. The weight of the body and the beam, the biggest casualties of the crowbar's back swing, was too much for him and he gave up. Oblivious to the screaming and shouting that surrounded him, the sound of liquid splashing on walls and the fumes of gasoline on his nose, he looked up at the stars again, as if they had somehow protected him. The anarchist's revenge had raised as many questions as it had answered. Suspicion gnawed at reason and there was only one thing that he was in no doubt about. He, as an outsider, a wooden foreigner, had brought danger to Lucio, Maria and the other villagers. His would-be assailant, who lay unconscious at his feet, the wrong head taking the blow, had been right in that respect.

The collapsed ceiling, mainly dried fronds and stems, crunched beneath two black boots. Something wet hit Justin's face. Wiping the foamy substance off his forehead, he looked up and into a rifle's barrel. Although the bruises blurred his vision, he could make out a wide grin from behind the rifle's telescopic sights.

'Is he dead?' Commandant Hernandez asked him, licking the drool off his lower lip and wiping off the spittle on his double chin.

'I don't know,' Justin croaked, coughing up an earthy mixture of dust and blood. Commandant Hernandez eclipsed his view of the stars. He could no longer see the Milky Way, the 'Road of Awe'. 'Why don't you check on him yourself? He's your man, isn't he?'

Commandant Hernandez laughed like a howler monkey. He swung the rifle on his back and stooped down. His finger under Zeb's mask, placed on the 'Z' neck tattoo, he checked for a pulse.

'He's alive,' Commandant Hernandez sneered, standing up again and returning his finger to the trigger of his rifle. He pointed the weapon at the bodies on the floor. 'Not that I care. His death would mean one less tongue to speak to the media, one less interfering gringo to deal with.'

Justin looked up at the blurred paramilitary. He had only met him once before, many years ago and when he was a different man, on the journey to the falls in Chenalho, and yet his hatred of him was all-consuming. He had seen the pain that Commandant Hernandez had brought about, his family's tears for their little boy.

'Murder, you see, Justin Callaghan, can easily be added to your list of offences.' Commandant Hernandez fired the rifle directly into Zeb's back.

The crack of gunfire made the screams outside grow louder. The village had erupted into chaos. Torches and the headlights of trucks flashed through the forest clearing. A patrol of ski-masked Cardenistas began to round up the men, women and children, beating those who resisted with the stocks of their rifles and large wooden staffs.

Justin felt Zeb's dying body twitch on his knees. The anarchist's warm blood seeped into his combat pants and wetted his skin underneath. He turned his head towards the doorway, in the direction of the screams, more anxious of what was happening outside than for his own predicament. Desperately wanting to stand up and help the villagers, he tried again to move his trapped legs.

Commandant Hernandez pointed the smoking rifle into Justin's face. He used the pale and blue light of the starry sky to examine his new target.

'So you are the great Hunahpu.' He placed the end of the rifle's hot barrel under Justin's chin, tilting his head back to look at him in the eyes. 'You're just a stupid fucking gringo tourist.'

'It beats being a fat, psychotic tapir.' The barrel burnt his chin and he clenched his teeth. 'Your mercenary on my legs said you wanted to have a chat with me.' He spied a shooting star in the distance, in the gap in the roof, and watched it speed like a bullet into the Commandant's head. 'I hope, for your sake, that your torture, your ability to extract information, is better than your counterinsurgency tactics.'

'Who says I want information?' Moving the rifle away from Justin's face, Commandant Hernandez prodded him in the stomach. 'I just want you silenced. You and your reports are a fucking pain. Bad press means bad business, no land sales, no money. Fuck what the Americans say. I want you dead.'

'What do you mean by Americans?' Justin felt his heart skip a beat. The pain in his broken chest returned, making it difficult for him to breathe. He gagged on the now overpowering smell of gasoline. It was like five years ago, when he released the contents of his stomach after his mother's cremation, before he bagged up his belongings and fed his trashed life to an unappreciative tramp.

Commandant Hernandez pulled a piece of paper out of his pocket. As if it was a dead butterfly, the crumpled warning note and its red handwriting fluttered down. It landed on Justin's fractured chest.

'You took the perfumed bait,' Commandant Hernandez said, grinning as he watched Justin pick up the note. 'You brought an American hostage into the heart of a filthy squatter's community. You fucked your tiny Mayan friends over. Now we can round them all up, like the terrorists that they are.' He laughed, wheezing, and then spat.

Justin looked at the dissolved words on the warning note. The paper absorbed the blood on his fingers. Crushing it in the palm of his hand, he dropped it to his side and watched it hit the dusty floor. The numbness, the quickening of his pulse, the feeling of desolation, passed through his entire body. It was as if he had died again.

'Maybe she even left a trail for us,' the Commandant continued, seeing the effect that the note had on Justin, stabbing him further in the heart.

'No.' Justin looked up at the stars, frowning beneath his bruises. There was still the sound of screaming and shouting outside the hut. He closed his bloodshot eyes and shook his head. 'No.'

'Don't be too hard on yourself. You can't expect to manipulate everyone.'

'What about him?' Justin pointed at the body on his knees. 'Where does he fit in?'

Commandant Hernandez's grin went wider.

'It was the price on your head that did it for him.' Breathing in to suck in his belly, he crouched down and retrieved a wallet, a mobile phone and a passport from the pockets of Zeb's combat pants. He transferred a wad of pesos and the phone into his own pocket, dropping the empty wallet and the passport to the ground, by Justin's head.

'Money?'

'It was for an operation on some woman of his. He was also very keen on meeting you.' Commandant Hernandez paused to look at his watch. He glanced over his shoulder and looked out of the hut's doorway. His men had formed a barricade around the hut, keeping back the villagers with their staffs and guns. 'The Americans found him,' he continued, smiling at the mayhem outside and then at Justin. 'As an anarchist, a foreign peace observer, he was perfect to get into the Zapatista patrol.'

Justin tried again to kick the body and the beam off his legs. Again, it was no use. More footsteps entered the room and he looked up through his swollen eyes. His heart beating fast, in his blurred vision he saw two masked men standing either side of Commandant Hernandez. The absence of red bandanas, he noticed, marked them out as Cardenista paramilitaries. One carried a red fuel canister and the other a rifle.

'You took your time,' Commandant Hernandez said, to the man with the fuel canister. 'Are we ready?'

'Yes,' the man replied, his masked face staring at the crossed layout of bodies on the floor. He looked at Justin's bruised face.

'Well? What are you waiting for? Get the anarchist's body out of here and we can start ourselves a fire. It will be something else to pin on these fucking squatters.' Commandant Hernandez turned on his heels and walked towards the door, stepping on the leaves of Santa Maria as he left.

'Burning me to death won't save your fat arse,' Justin shouted out, lifting up his neck an inch or two, the only movement that he could manage. The masked men lifted the corpse off his legs. Zeb's blood had saturated his combat pants.

'Perhaps not,' Commandant Hernandez said, stopping in the doorway and speaking through the mess of the collapsed roof, 'but it amuses me. You, who are named after one of the Hero Twins, burnt to ash in a peasant's home. I know what these halfwit Maya believe in.' He stepped out of the hut and called back to his men. 'Get a move on, you two, unless you want a roasting as well.'

Maria broke free from the line of people that had encircled her home. She charged forward, palming off the men with the machine guns and wooden staffs, and used her weight to skittle down a few of the Cardenistas. The butt of Commandant Hernandez's rifle struck her in the face before she could land her punch. She fell to the road, her white blouse ripping on rocks, her nosebleed dyeing her embroidered neckline a darker red. Not down long, she jumped up and confronted Commandant Hernandez. The circle of spectators, the ones without the guns and masks, predominantly women and children, cheered her on.

'Señora Gomez,' Commandant Hernandez said, raising his voice above the jeers and screams of the villagers. Maria's muscular arm batted his rifle away from her face. The rifle's barrel slapped against his belly. 'To lose one home and son is careless.' He rubbed his stomach and returned his rifle to his shoulder. 'To lose two, though, is fucking stupid.'

'What have you done with him?' she shouted at his grinning face.

'Who? Hunahpu? Nothing. He's taking a siesta. He needs a rest.'

Three masked men, the two Cardenistas and a corpse, emerged from the hut. Dragged past the Commandant and Maria, the corpse left a bloody trail in crumbly soil.

'Hunahpu,' Maria said, when she saw the lifeless body. 'Hunahpu,' she wailed out loud. The Cardenistas stopped her from nearing the corpse, beating her back with their rifles and staffs.

'That's not Hunahpu,' Commandant Hernandez said, wiping the sweat off his forehead, 'we've something more exciting for him.' He stepped onto the shiny red carpet and looked towards the two men and their human paintbrush. When the men had reached a wall of guns and staffs, he ordered them to stop. Something gold, which shone out of the back pocket of one of his men, caught his eye. 'You,' he said to the man, 'what have you got there?'

'What?' the man asked, letting go of the corpse's arm.

'In your pocket, what is it?'

'This?' The man put his hand round his back and pulled out the gold-painted cross.

'You know the rules. All trophies must go through me. It's why I pay you. It's how I fucking pay you.'

'Yes, Commandant.'

'I'll collect it off you later. *Understand?*'

'Yes, Commandant.' His masked head nodding, the man returned the cross to his back pocket and picked up the corpse's floppy arm again. The two Cardenistas continued to drag the corpse up the crowded high street.

'And tell Decker that it was Hunahpu who shot his man in cold blood,' Commandant Hernandez called out to the painted trail, the red line disappearing into the crowd, 'Tell him that we lost the murderer in a fire.'

'Liar,' Maria shouted at him, slapping his fat and sweaty cheek. He caught her hand and threw her back to the ground. This time she stayed down. The onlookers wailed with her.

'That's right, Mayan bitch, keep grovelling.' He spat on her by his feet. 'You're like your husband, a coward. If I remember rightly, he also wasn't there for you when you lost your first son. Your youngest, wasn't it? It was a good shot, I recall.'

Her grazed arms lashed out at his boots. He kicked dust into her face. The dust stuck to the tears that ran down her cheeks.

'It looks like your old man's abandoned you again.' He spat at her again and wiped his sleeve over his lips. 'No matter. We'll find him eventually. Dead or alive, we'll bring him in, punish him for terrorism against the state, for harbouring a wanted criminal.'

He clicked his fingers at a group of Cardenistas. Although they outnumbered her, four of them to one of her, they struggled to return her to the other villagers. In the end, several kicks to several groins later, their masks whipped off and their faces scratched by her fingernails, they had to use a staff in the stomach to stop her from fighting back.

Maria rolled about on the ground. She used her hands to protect her blood-, tear- and dirt-streaked face from the boots of the Cardenistas. When they stopped kicking her she was able to see Commandant Hernandez walk back to her home. She watched him go down the trail of blood left by the dragged corpse. A few yards from the hut's open doorway, he stopped and picked up the fuel canister left by one of his men. He stuffed a red bandana into the canister's opened lid and struck a match.

'No,' Maria screamed, raising her arm in his direction.

'Goodbye, Hunahpu,' he called out towards the hut, lighting the bandana. He swung back the canister.

A bright yellow flash captured Maria's horrified face. The explosion clapped like thunder.

The branches above a parked Humvee shook about. Woken by the explosion, followed by the crackling of fire and suffocating smoke, screeching birds took flight from a prickly ceiba tree. Rachel hung her head out of the vehicle's passenger window. She soaked up her endless tears with a red bandana, frantically looking down the dirt road high street, past the basketball court and the Che Guevara mural, which rippled in the animated shadows that fell on the clapboard assembly hall. Beyond the bunting left over from the carnival, she saw huge flames rise to the tops of trees, heard the wood spit and branches crash. The fire appeared to be spreading. Burning leaves shot upwards, embers twinkling as if they were stars, and they shared the sky with fleeing birds and bats. Pushing herself further out of the window, shaking her head as she wept, she realized that the fire was coming from the direction of the Gomez's hut. A hand pulled on her white dress. She fell back into her seat.

'Please, Rachel,' Decker said, one hand on the steering wheel and the other on his passenger's collar of bats, 'keep your head inside the vehicle. There's at least a dozen M16s out there, not to mention some pretty pissed-off insurgents.'

'What have you done?' she asked him, pushing his hand off her like he was diseased. 'Who the hell are you?' she shouted at his face.

'We're here to rescue you.' Decker sighed. 'That's all you need to know. I'm sorry you got caught up in this.'

Rachel slapped him.

'I didn't need rescuing,' she said, crying into her hands, 'I didn't need rescuing,' she kept repeating to herself, her body shaking in her white dress. The embroidered bats around her neck caught her tears.

Watching her, Decker awkwardly drummed his fingers on the steering wheel. He then checked his side mirrors and his watch.

Somebody moved about on the backseats of the Humvee.

'Is Zeb coming with us?' Stevo asked, leaning forward, nervously playing with his ski mask in his hands. He was sitting next to Jamie, who was staring at the fire through the windows. Both of them looked concerned.

Decker didn't reply. Instead he turned the ignition key. The Humvee's engine roared into life.

'What's that fat shit up to now?' Decker said, observing the flames in his rear-view mirror. 'We're going to get into some serious shit for this. I told him to bring in Callaghan in one piece.'

'What are you trying to achieve?' Rachel asked him, removing her hands from her face. Her eyes and skin were red from all her crying. 'What had they done wrong?' She slapped him again. 'Why are you doing this?' She raised her hand to hit him harder, but this time he managed to restrain her, gripping her tense wrists. 'Let me go!'

'Calm down, Rachel,' he said, moving away her hand, his voice sympathetic, 'take a deep breath. Nothing bad is happening. No one is going to get hurt. OK?'

Rachel hid her face from him, her fingers rubbing and digging into her sore skin.

'Fuck it,' Decker said to himself, slamming his hands down on the dashboard. He released the handbrake and shifted the Humvee into gear.

'What about Zeb?' Stevo spoke out from behind Decker.

'Zeb can catch a lift with Commandant Hernandez.' Decker looked across at Rachel, who was still buried in her hands and shaking. 'We need to get Rachel out of here. I'm not waiting any longer.' He checked his mirrors again. 'The Zapatista patrol could be just around the corner.'

Slumped forward in her seat, Rachel removed her fingers from her face and watched the fire's reflection on the windscreen.

Decker floored the accelerator. The Humvee spun sideways before it jerked forward. Skidding tyres kicked dust up into the air.

Rachel jumped out of her seat and stuck her head out of the window.

'Hunahpu,' she shouted out into the dust and smoke, towards the flames which flashed through the trees. Her plaited hair, her Tzotzil tail, blew into her face as they sped away from the village. 'Justin,' she cried out, trying to be heard above the engine, screaming villagers and raging fire. '*Justin*,' she screamed as loud as she could, the back of her throat stinging because of the smoke. As the Humvee passed under the village's welcome sign, the barbed barrier raised up, the fire turned into a small glow tucked behind dark trees. The fire's reflection eventually disappeared from her streaming eyes.

Twenty-One

A clock ticked away the seconds in the hospital's starkly lit waiting room. Apart from an occasional cough, a blown nose and a distorted voice on a hissing speaker, the ticking hand was the only noise in the near empty room. Beside the clock and hanging on the wall above a pair of swing doors, a black box scrolled digital information from the 'staff and management of Homerton Hospital'.

Justin flicked through an old magazine. He shook his head at the glossy pictures of celebrities, closed the magazine and returned it to the table. Beth had spent the entire summer helping him to readjust, providing him with a bed in return for him babysitting her three-year-old son. Eight months on, though, and he still felt like a foreigner in his former homeland. It was why he came here, to a hospital in east London, where he hoped to find an address to take him to a paralysed woman called Tam.

He retrieved Zeb's leather wallet from the inside pocket of his coat, which was lent to him by Jeremy, Beth's husband of four years. Flicking through old receipts and library, Socialist Worker's Party and Amnesty International membership cards, he took out a hospital appointment card. Written on the back of the scrappy bit of paper was the name Mary. After visiting the emergency contact address in Sebastian Anthony Townsend's passport, a luxury warehouse conversion at the end of Ridley Road Market, a site foreman had informed him that the squatters had been moved on. The appointment card, the hospital and the name Mary, were now his only means of tracking Tam down.

Returning the card to the wallet and then the wallet to his coat pocket, he stood up and walked to the barred window at the end of the room. In the car park outside and behind a windscreen mirroring a winter's sun, the glass dazzling his eyes, he watched Beth read a newspaper at the steering wheel. Hospitals, she had told him, as she parked the car, a Volvo estate which was littered with toys and rolls of architectural drawings, were not really her 'cup of tea'. He didn't blame her. The memory of the morgue in Kent had returned as soon as he was hit by that sickly, antiseptic smell. He had no wish to stick around for longer than necessary.

There was another, altogether more important reason for him wanting to leave on time. Jeremy, who was waiting back at home with the baby, had planned a weekend away, alone with his wife, to the Lake District. Feeling responsible for disrupting their lives and only recently able to afford his own place, his new job as a media activist providing him with a small income, Justin had more than encouraged them to go. He had volunteered to look after baby Justin while they were away. For since he made the call to Beth from San Cristóbal de las Casas, tracked her down via the bank's switchboard, accepted the loan for his flight and then lived in their spare room for the best part of the year, he could sense the tension of his presence.

'Mr Jafari to room four,' the intercom hissed. Snorting and coughing, restored to life by the cockney summons, an old man wobbled up from his seat and disappeared through the swing doors. A stuffy whiff of age and poverty followed him out of the room.

Remaining at the window and still looking out at Beth, the reflected sun brighter than before, Justin thought back to the moment when Beth had greeted him at the airport. Although the real shock was the phone call from Mexico, nothing had prepared her for the ghost who limped out of Gatwick's customs. Dropping his battered leather bag by his feet, his only piece of luggage, they shook hands and then, before the tears and the hug, she shouted at him. *'How could you? I thought you had died.'* On the drive into London, the Volvo crawling in traffic, he tried as best he could to answer her flurry of questions. He described, in between her interruptions, the attempted suicide on the misty falls, the loneliness that he had kept from her, the betrayal of his mother, and the second chance that he was given by Lucio. It was Lucio, he said, peering out of the car windows and looking at the greenery of an English springtime, pink and white blossom in the trees, who had found him in the Pool of the Paddler Gods. It was there, in the wash of a sacred mountain, that he was given a new beginning, a new family and a new life. He then told her about the masked Zapatistas, the silent war in the mountains and jungles of Chiapas, the violence of the army and paramilitaries, the land-grabbing multinationals and the resistance of the Maya people. He told Beth of his vow to the people who had saved him and how, as a foreigner on the frontline, he increased awareness of their plight through his anonymous reports.

Stopping at a red light, she turned to look at the pale, scarred and long-haired stranger next to her. She asked what it was that made him return to London. As they drove through the industrial wasteland behind King's Cross Station, past the tramps who hung out outside McDonald's, he told her about the anarchists, the smear on his name, and the woman.

'A woman?' Beth asked, losing her concentration at the wheel. The tailgate of the car scraped a speed bump which she had failed to spot. 'What woman?'

They pulled over, parked the car and Beth bought them both a couple of pints in the Green Man, their Islington drinking den of five years ago. The pub's plush interior and organic menu came as a shock to him. Gentrification had transformed his dingy local into a trendy gastropub. Carpet walls had been replaced by abstract art, flat-capped boozers by black polo-necked media types, who slurped Chilean Chardonnay rather than belched Bass. Putting down his pint glass and pulling out a chair for her, he explained how Rachel might have deceived him, used him to get at the village and betrayed them all. He admitted that he was not sure.

'The paramilitaries,' he said, stopping to gulp his pint of St Peter's bitter, 'arrived the night before she was to leave. They came with the anarchists. If it was not for Lucio and Horatio,' he paused to finish his drink, pushing a beer mat across the table and playing with his matted hair, 'the switching of the masks, Zeb's body taking my place, I would have been burnt alive.' He paused while she watched him. 'They never left me, in spite of what I had done to them. It was because I . . .' He paused again, tilted the pint glass on its base and made circles out of spilled St Peter's on the wooden table. 'It was right that I left. They are safer without me.'

'You still should've contacted us,' she said, screwing up an empty packet of ready-salted crisps, 'I mean, damn it, you led us to believe that you had died.'

'I'm sorry, Beth. But in many ways I had died. I was a new person out there.'

'Even so, you would've saved me a small fortune on your memorial service.' She smiled at him, examining his tired and rugged face.

'You held a service for me?' He stopped playing with his glass and looked up at her.

'Yes.' She shook her head while she smiled. 'Dan was blubbing like a baby, until he passed out in the loos of the Sky Bar. He's missed you almost as much as I have.'

'You had the service in the Sky Bar?'

'Sorry about that. I knew how much you hated it there, but that waitress Stephanie, who always had a crush on you, I don't know if you remember her, is managing the place now and she insisted on it. At least it saved me some money for the food and drink.'

'Who else went?'

'God, I can't remember. It was a few years ago now, when we finally gave up waiting for you to stroll into work with a Mexican tan and apologize for being late. But Martin showed up with some of your Edinburgh drinking mates and there were a few from the bank, mainly the secretaries and facilities workers who you used to smoke with. Damn, even that woman who worked in HR, who you used to loathe, came along. In the end, we easily had enough to fill the VIP room.'

'That's pretty big, isn't it?'

'Yeah, alright, don't get a big head over it.' She smiled again and he looked down at the liquid circles on the table. A barman picked up their empty glasses and Beth handed over the scrunched-up crisp packet. 'And it wasn't like you made it easy for us. I searched your flat from top to bottom and found nothing more personal than a broken alarm clock, an instruction manual for your TV and a chewed pen.' She paused for a moment. 'Why, Justin?'

He said nothing. His face still looking down, he drew a picture of the sun out of the spilt beer, flicking rays out of a solitary circle with his finger.

'I'm sorry,' she said, touching his hand and stopping his fidgety art. 'Though you should know that it was bloody hard trying to track down your family in Spain.'

Justin looked up, astonished by what she had just said.

Mary no longer worked at the hospital. She had died two years ago, a kind woman at the desk had told him. Luckily the woman knew of Tam and she believed his story of being an old friend of Zeb's. Fortunately she had also planned a holiday to Mexico. With a little charm, some suggestions on where to go off the tourist trail, he persuaded her to write down an address of where to find Tam. Back in the car, he consulted a map and directed Beth to drive them south. The sun appearing and then disappearing behind gleaming tower blocks, they went past Turkish kebab houses in Stoke Newington, Afro-Caribbean 'New York Nail Centres' in Dalston, and Vietnamese minimarkets on the Kingsland Road. Putting down the map to look out for street signs and determine their exact position, Justin observed the graffiti sprayed on dilapidated and out-of-business shopfronts. On an old shoe factory was the simple 'War is so last century,' while a former strip bar was decorated with a stencilled rat with a tommy-gun. They drove over the Grand Union Canal and, painted in white on a footbridge, he spied his favourite slogan: 'PLEASE DRIVE-BY CAREFULLY IN OUR VILLAGE.'

'What are you smiling about?' Beth asked, smiling herself as she looked across at her passenger, whose breath was misting up the cold car windows. She stopped the car at a junction and waited for a gap in the traffic.

'Nothing much,' he replied, facing her, 'I forgot what it was like round here. Only I never really used to look at things properly then. To be honest, I was a bit blind to what was around me.'

'Telling me,' she said, laughing. Thinking that it was probably wrong to laugh, she quickly shut up.

'I was pretty bad, wasn't I?'

'You were just a bit stubborn, bottled things up too much.' She was relieved that he didn't seem offended by her laugh. 'I mean, I've always been your friend and you could have talked to me about things. Especially about your mum.'

'I know that now.'

A horn beeped from behind them. Beth raised an apologetic hand off the steering wheel and lifted her foot off the clutch. Justin gestured to her that she should take a right turn.

'Anyway,' she said, putting the car into third gear and taking them down a clear Great Eastern Street, 'that was all in the past. It's good to see that bloody smile of yours returning to your face. I've missed it, you know.'

Nodding at her, showing off his 'bloody smile', he felt the rusty-red pottery shard touch his neck. His necklace reminded him of the family and life that he had left behind in Chiapas. While they drove in silence, the sun and buildings casting the car in light and then shadow, he remembered clearly the day he departed from Nuevo San Felipé. The dawn mist which had evaporated off the ceiba and palm trees was particularly thick. Villagers stood in silence outside their mud-brick homes as he walked past them. Children threw red and white petals of frangipani, the symbols of the sun and the moon, at his feet. At the entrance to the village were Lucio, Maria and Horatio. His eyes welling up, he hugged his family, swung his bag over his shoulder and climbed on Itzamna. From the height of the saddle, he looked down at the crowd below, the straw hats and the ribbons on plaited tails.

Lucio removed something from around his neck. He stepped forward and stroked Itzamna's head. He then raised his arm up towards Justin. His hand opened up to reveal his necklace, the pottery shard of the spider monkey in his palm.

'Please,' Lucio said, his speech broken, 'I want you to have this.'

'I can't,' Justin faltered, 'that was Urbano's.'

'It belongs to you now. Please, take it Hunahpu. Maybe one day you can return it to me.'

Justin leant over from the mule and lowered his head. Lucio reached up and put the necklace on him. They exchanged sad smiles while Justin touched the ancient Mayan pottery. Opening his leather bag, he took out his ski mask.

'You'd better have this,' he said, handing the mask to Lucio. 'Make sure that it goes to someone worthy of wearing the Zapatista uniform, someone whom you can trust.'

'I promise.' Lucio passed the mask to Horatio, who had his arm round his weeping mother.

The shaman and the wooden man smiled. One reaching up and one reaching down, they shook hands. Wiping his eyes on his shirt, waving to the crowd and nodding at his family, Justin tapped his heels into Itzamna's sides. As he rode out of the village, disappeared down an old logger's track, he heard the people of the bat call out after him, their Zapatista songs ringing out through the trees. He kept going, a canter turning into a gallop, until their songs and shouts were lost to their ancestral forest. For the rest of the journey, at least as far as Comitán, where he was to take a truck, the sounds that gave him company were

Itzamna's hooves splashing on mud, crickets, squawking parrots and the distant rumblings of thunder. The rainy season was well under way. He had left Chiapas in the season of rebirth and renewal.

'You want to take the next left,' Justin said to Beth, his finger on the map and checking the address that the woman at the hospital had written down. 'There it is. Radnor Street. Kempson House must be one of these council blocks. It's probably that one at the end.'

Flicking the indicator, Beth turned the Volvo left and they drove into the shadow of two tall concrete buildings. She parked the car opposite a red anarchy sign, which was spray-painted on a cracked glass door. Nervously looking around her, her eyes wandered up the grey tower that rose up into the blue sky. She put her car keys in her handbag and her handbag under her seat.

'Are you sure that you don't want me to go with you?' she asked him, frowning at a plastic bag which sailed past the windscreen, observing a group of kids who hid their faces under black hooded tracksuits. 'I know that you've cleared your name with the police, but we don't know that you're clear with these,' she hesitated, watching the kids kick an empty beer can against a wall. 'They might still think that you're responsible for what happened to that poor girl.'

'It's a risk that I'm prepared to take.' Justin unfastened his seatbelt. 'I want to be honest with them.' He opened the car door and climbed out. 'I shan't be long. I've got my mobile with me if you need me.' He closed the door. Beth leant over the empty passenger's seat and locked herself in.

Crossing the road, stepping over the litter that blew in the wind, he walked up to the cracked glass door, the red-painted anarchy symbol, and put a hand in his coat pocket. 'Flat 17D, Kempson House,' he read to himself the address he had been given. He pressed the buttons of a dented intercom.

'Who is it?' a voice blared out of a crackly speaker. He composed himself before he answered.

'Someone who knows what happened to Zeb.'

There was a slight pause before the speaker crackled again.

'You a cop?'

'No, I'm not a cop.' Justin looked over his shoulder. He watched the hooded kids kick the beer can at a mangy looking squirrel. 'I was in Mexico with him.'

After a lengthier pause he was buzzed through. He pushed open the door and entered a dark and dank hallway. The lift, a metal box of expletives and espousals of love, from *'Ravi 4 Sexy Debs'* to a less personal *'fuck you'*, shook as it carried him up to the seventeenth floor. Walking down an open balcony, with views of St Paul's and the London Eye in the smog to his left, he found the door to Flat 17D. He stopped, looked at a hanging basket of dead geraniums and desiccated ivy, and then knocked on the door. A chain rattled on the other side of the door and he was let in.

'Hi,' he said, to a face full of freckles and dyed pink dreadlocks, 'I'm Justin.' The woman refused to shake his hand. Instead she pushed him forward, towards a smoky room at the back of the flat.

'I'm Jules,' she said to his back. 'What do you want?'

The smell of stale cigarettes and damp rot left a sour taste in his mouth. On the walls of an unlit corridor and sticking down curled-up floral wallpaper, which peeled off discoloured concrete, was a collage of anti-war and anti-globalization posters. Feeling her hand prod his back, given no time to read the slogans on the walls, he walked into the source of the smoke.

Harsh sunlight streamed through the grimy windows at the end of the room. The beams of light caught the smoke, which spiralled up from a cigarette in an overflowing ashtray, while the floor was covered in blankets, empty beer cans and old newspapers. In the yellow haze, the smoke stinging his eyes, he saw a young woman propped up against a wall. Her red and curly hair buttressed a window sill of cracked white paint and black mould. Above her, a wooden wind chime hung outside the window. The wind made the wood tap against the glass.

'Hi,' he said to the woman, to the pale face that stared straight through him.

'Don't waste your breath,' Jules said, crawling through the refuse on the floor to reach her cigarette. 'That's Tam. She can't say a word. But she can still hear you, so mind what you fucking say.' She sat down beside Tam and leant against the wall.

He looked for somewhere to sit down. The lifeless Tam continued to stare through him, unnerving him. Jules threw a dirty sleeping bag at his feet and he sat down.

'If you're not a copper, then who are you? You look familiar. Do I know you?' She exhaled smoke in his direction.

'I was a Zapatista,' he said, looking at the two women, 'I was in the patrol that Zeb came to visit.'

'Fuck off,' Jules snorted, coughing on her own smoke. 'The Zapatistas are Indian.'

He waited for her to stop laughing before he continued.

'Most of them are Mayan, true, but there are a few of us white people who, for some reason or whatever, joined their struggle and became their friends.'

Jules looked him up and down through the smoke. She then looked at Tam. Her face had turned serious when she faced him again.

'So was it your Mayan friends who fucked over Zeb, stole Tam's treatment money and left us to rot in this high-rise hell?'

'No. The Zapatistas never betrayed anyone.'

'Well, where are my mates now?' She stubbed out her cigarette, using the floor rather than the ashtray, and disposed of the butt in an empty beer can. Tam kept staring ahead. The wooden wind chimes banged loudly against the window.

'Zeb is dead.' He looked down at the mess on the floor. 'I'm so very sorry.'

Jules squeezed Tam's limp hand while Justin told them everything, or at least all that he knew. He told them how Zeb had been given false information about him, that he never hit Tam and that the anarchist was murdered by a paramilitary, a man called Commandant Hernandez. Admitting that he was uncertain as to who masterminded the operation, he told them that the Commandant had said something about American involvement. 'The CIA,' he said, 'have, we know from witnesses, been assisting the Mexican army. They say that they're there to stop drug trafficking. In reality, though, they seem to be more interested in the land that the Maya are sitting on.' He thought carefully of what next to say, not wanting to besmirch the deceased anarchist in front of the paralysed woman. 'They must have paid Zeb to take the hostage.'

There was silence while Jules took in what he had said. The wind chime banged on the window and the beams of sunshine continued to intersect the smoky air.

'Zeb would never sell out like that,' Jules eventually said, stroking back Tam's hair, trying to soothe her friend. 'There's no way he would allow himself to be responsible for an attack on the Zapatistas.'

'I didn't say that he did.' Again he had to think carefully of what to say. 'They lied to him about me, so they must also have lied to him about the reasons for taking the hostage. Perhaps he didn't know about the plan to attack Nuevo San Felipé. I'm sure that he was there just to get at me.' He paused while he thought of Rachel. 'Forgetting about the politics and principles for once, perhaps there was just one thing that he cared for, one reason why he risked his life.'

He faced Tam. But for the twitching of her fair eyelashes, she remained motionless.

'He never betrayed you,' he said to her expressionless face. 'I came here to assure you of that.'

'You came here just to tell Tam that?' Jules watched the sun shining on his face.

'I didn't want her to think that Zeb had run off, taken the money or something. I mean . . .' he paused, thinking of Rachel again, 'I feel better that she knows.' He ran his hand through his hair and squinted at the bright windows. The pain of not knowing the truth was still strong.

Jules wiped a tear off Tam's pale and freckly cheek. She started to roll another cigarette.

'What happened to the Commandant,' she asked him, striking a match and lighting the cigarette, 'the bastard that killed him?'

He looked away from the window and faced them.

'Fate caught up with him. He had an accident with a petrol can and a match.'

In response to further questioning, he told them about the switching of bodies, the exploding Commandant, Stevo and Jamie going off with the conservationist. He asked Jules whether she had heard anything from Zeb's accomplices, explaining that he had found no trace of them in his research, either online or via his contacts in Montes Azules and San Cristóbal.

Jules stood up and walked to the corner of the room. In the haze of the sun on smoke, he saw her rummage through a cardboard box, flick her tobacco-stained fingers through a stack of papers and anti-war flyers. She returned to the floor with two sheets of paper.

'I printed these out yesterday,' she said, waving the paper about. 'It's an article that I found on the Internet. You see,

Justin, I've done a little research myself.' She looked at his green eyes, which had widened. 'And I believe what you've been saying.'

'Really?' he asked, sitting up straight on the sleeping bag and trying to see what was on the paper. 'You're sure that it's not something that I've written?'

Jules laughed as she held the article up to her face.

'No,' she said, lowering her paper mask, 'it's definitely not you.'

'It's not signed by Hunahpu?'

'Who the hell is that?'

'May I?' He pointed at the paper in her hand.

She passed the article to him and he skim read the first page:

'LACANDÓN AND TZOTZIL WOMEN UNITE AFTER PARAMILITARY RAIDS IN MONTES AZULES ... After the discovery of two skeletons, the remains of which were discovered in a ditch outside the village of Nuevo San Felipé, the mystery of the two missing British tourists appears to be solved ... Despite the denials of CONAFOR, the Mexican Forestry Commission, and the offices of the Governor of Chiapas, there is evidence to suggest that the Cardenista raid on Nuevo San Felipé in March was indeed sanctioned by officials in State and Federal Government Departments ... The US Embassy in Mexico City, meanwhile, still refuses to comment on eyewitness accounts of a US military advisor being present at the time of the killings. A spokesman from the Embassy would only say that the attacks were: "a classic example of tribal differences boiling over between rival, indigenous groups – a regrettable, yet sadly typical episode of ethnic tension in the region" ... Refuting this assertion of disunity, last week Tzotzil and Lacandón women held a meeting of Indigenous Solidarity and Resistance in the clapboard Assembly Hall of Nuevo San Felipé ... The creation of the new alliance was rounded off by marimba and masks in a flagged basketball court. Your obedient, gringo observer joined the "Intergalactic Celebrations," trying to wash away her wooden dancing with cup after cup of very potent posh. As a finale, with everyone on the muddy dance-floor and looking upwards, fire-works exploded above the jungle and sparkled with the stars in the clear sky. That night, the Milky Way, the cosmic umbilical cord that links the Maya to their ancestral gods, burned brighter than before. It was an honour for me to have been there. X.'

He was about to turn the page, view the photograph on the other sheet, when he felt a hand on his shoulder.

'Do you know her?' Jules asked, leaning over his shoulder. 'Do you know who 'X' is?'

'I don't . . .'

He quickly turned the sheet over and looked at the black and white photograph on the other page. Standing in front of the murals of Emiliano Zapata, Subcommandante Marcos and Che Guevara, the portraits painted on the village assembly hall, were four masked women. Two of them, a woman and a girl, were dressed as Lacandóns, their long black hair sticking out of their ski masks and their bare feet peeking out from under white smocks. He recognized neither of them. Another woman, who wore a Tzotzil blouse and had a plaited pony-tail with ribbons tied to it, he did. Her biceps and broad shoulders were unmistakably Maria's. He smiled as his finger touched the image of her.

In the middle of the photograph, standing between Maria and the Lacandóns, was, he assumed, 'X', the author of the article. Taller than the others, she was wearing a white dress with bats embroidered round its neckline. He examined her eyes in the ski mask.

'Well?' Jules asked. 'Do you recognize any of them?'

Justin lowered the sheet of paper, his face reappearing through the smoke and sunshine. He looked at Jules and Tam under the blinding window.

'Yes,' he whispered to them, 'I do.'

'Who is 'X'?'

He looked at the picture on his lap again, at the woman dressed in white, just as she was when he last saw her.

'Xbalanke,' he said, nodding to himself. 'I know,' he continued, his smile turning into a grin. 'But it's not like she had a choice of names to use. Hunahpu, the other Hero Twin, belongs to another Lokin.'

'What?'

Justin studied the masked eyes again. He returned the article and photograph to Jules and, as he stood up, felt his heart beating fast. From high up, looking out across the smog and viewing the miniaturized city through the grimy window, he no longer felt blind.

'I must be going,' he said, addressing them as they sat under the window sill, 'I have a friend waiting for me outside.'

306

He wrote down his contact details on the back of an anti-war flyer, telling them that he would try to help with Tam's treatment, and saw himself out. Breathing in the fresh air on the balcony, he waited for the lift. While he gazed southwards, looked beyond the London Eye and the jungle of concrete, he wondered if his Spanish relatives would prefer tapas and sangria to cucumber sandwiches and sweet sherry. For as well as planning his mother's memorial service, there was much to do in so little time. As the lift's door opened and he was confronted by scribbled and spray-painted words of love and hate, he thought it was time he took a holiday. Smiling, he thought of Mexico.

Glossary

The Abejas	A civilian and predominantly Catholic group of Mayan Indians who live in the Chenalho region of Chiapas. They are called abejas because they are like the 'bees:' they are organized and they will sting until they achieve peace, justice, freedom and democracy. They share the same sentiments as the Zapatistas.
Campesino	A farm worker who aims to survive rather than generate profit.
The Cardenistas	A paramilitary group affiliated to the PRI political party of Mexico. They are against furthering the rights of Zapatista communities.
Chenalho	A highland region in Chiapas and the focus of paramilitary attacks against Mayan Indians and Zapatista support bases.
CONPAZ	The Coordination of Non Governmental Organizations for Peace (CONPAZ) is a group of Non Governmental Organizations (NGOs) who have provided humanitarian relief to Mayan communities affected by paramilitary and Mexican federal army attacks.
EZLN	The Zapatista Army of National Liberation (Ejército Zapatista de Liberación Nacional) is the armed unit of the Zapatistas.
Hunahpu	One of the Hero Twins in the Popol Vuh. Together with his twin, Xbalanke, Hunahpu defeated the Lords of Death in Xibalba, the underworld. Although the Hero Twins were not gods, the ancient Maya revered their

cleverness and they credited them for banishing evil from their world.

The Lacandón	The Lacandón Maya live in the jungle of the Selva Lacandón, in southern Chiapas. They were controversially given land by the Mexican government in the 1970s, and many other Mayan groups view them with distrust.
Lokin	A sasquatch-like being from Mayan mythology. Some say that the wooden people in the Mayan creation story became Lokin, and that they are responsible for lost travellers in the forest.
Mestizo	People of mixed European and indigenous descent in Mexico.
Paz y Justicia	A paramilitary group affiliated to the PRI party.
The Popul Vuh	Written around 1550, the Popol Vuh is a sacred book recounting the creation story of the Maya in Central America. It is often considered to be the most important literary piece of work to have survived from the ancient Americas.
PRI	A political party that wielded power in Mexico for more than 70 years. Their supporters are generally against the demands of the Zapatistas.
Tzotzil	The Tzotziles, the Maya people of the bat, mainly live in the highlands of Chiapas. Displaced from their communities by government-backed paramilitaries, many Tzotziles joined the Zapatista Army of National Liberation (the EZLN).
USAID	The United States Agency for International Development (USAID) is an independent federal US agency responsible for non-military foreign aid.
Wakah-Chan	The Raised-up-Sky or World Tree is considered to be the centre of the Maya cosmos. Taking

the form of the Christian cross for contemporary Maya, the Wakah-Chan is depicted in the art of the ancient Maya as a foliated tree and it is also symbolized by the Milky Way. It is considered to be the source of life for the Maya.

Xbalanke	See Hunahpu.
Xibalba	The subterranean and watery underworld of the Maya is recounted in the Popol Vuh. It is here that the Hero Twins, Hunahpu and Xbalanke, defeated the Lords of Death.
Zapatistas	The Zapatistas are an armed, revolutionary group of guerrillas in Chiapas. Championed by the international anti-globalization movement, the Zapatistas' primary aim is to secure autonomy for indigenous Maya Indians in southern Mexico. They have not used weapons since their largely peaceful uprising in January 1994, and their spokesperson, Subcomandante Marcos, is renowned for his romantic and ironic style of writing. There are also many Mayan Indians who consider themselves civilian Zapatistas.

Muchas Gracias

To Claire, my editor, who picked up my manuscript and ironed out the creases. Without your guidance and encouragement this book would have become an archaeological deposit in a bottom drawer, lost with the broken pen and the old VCR instruction manual.

To Peter Ford and Professor Ian Hodder for making sense of the world.

To Professors Norman Hammond and Patricia McAnany for introducing me to the land of the Maya. I am also incredibly grateful for the welcome all the Boston University students gave to a wide-eyed Brit – the gin, jungle and beef worm wouldn't have been the same without you. I miss you all.

To the Mexico Solidarity Network, the London Zapatistas and Erin Slinker, for the doors they opened for me, both physically and mentally. Ya Basta!

To the East Eighters who bought me pints in the Prince George and who put up with my Mexican rants. Ruth, Frode, James, Rob and Georgie you are my true amigos.

To the team who literally made this book: Barcheston, Sue at Word4Word, David and Kirsty at Creative Thing, Charlotte and her camera, my best friend and brother Toby, and the amazingly talented Antonia.

For the incredible support given to me by Nick. I so want to use an adverb or a metaphor to express my gratitude, but I now know to keep it simple. Thank you.

I reserve my special thanks to mum and dad. Nothing would have been possible without you. I love you both dearly and I shall forever be indebted to you. This book is for you.

Finally, to the Maya of Mexico and Central America. Your true story has been suppressed for too long and we gringos have so much to learn from you. Please forgive me if I have not shouted loud enough.